LIVING LIKE
THE SAINTS

Liston Pope Jr

LIVING LIKE THE SAINTS

A Novel of Nicaragua

N.A. GILBERT & SONS
NEW YORK
1996

Library of Congress Cataloging in Publication Data:

Pope, Liston Jr.   1943–
Living Like the Saints: A Novel of Nicaragua
I.   Nicaraguan Conflict   Fiction
      FSLN (Frente Sandinista de Liberación Nacional),
      Somoza dictatorship, U.S.-Latin America relations,
      Revolution in Latin America,
      Third World liberation movements   I.   Title

95-80678

ISBN 0-9638900-1-8

Distributed to the trade in the United States and Canada
by N.A. Gilbert and Sons, 126 West 73rd Street, Suite 11A,
New York, N.Y. 10023-3031
FIRST EDITION

In Memory of Nora Astorga

PART ONE

I

A few days before Christmas, 1978, the poet Miguel Giner was ushered from his prison cell, in solitary confinement, to a crowded visiting room. He went along in a sullen trance, the light murdering his eyes, the smell of his sweat as pungent as sour tamarind. He looked like a man with reason to be afraid, flinching from the daylight, struggling to keep his head up. While he went along the cell block other prisoners called out his name.

Then, some thirty stood on this side of a double grating, with frantic wives and mothers two, three deep on the far side. They called through the screen and competed in an uproar. Their attempts to settle this or that family matter had an opposite effect in the noise and confusion. Women broke down; they burst in tears. A prison guard assigned to watch the grating saw only fingers that grasped at a void.

Miguel took a seat at one end: as a political prisoner he was separated from the others; and, squinting after weeks of darkness and seclusion, his first instinct was to glimpse, here and there, for a hidden microphone. The excitement began to enliven him. His hands, trembling with expectation, went on the grating as he tried to make out his wife's beloved features. Who but she would dare visit him after the publicity, the vilification in *Novedades* at the time of his arrest?

If the warden did permit him a visitor, it wouldn't be without payment in kind.

II

The ray of hope faded from his features and gave way to a kind of pity. There, staring woefully across at him, her cheeks shiny with tears that glistened on her large red birthmark, stood his foster mother, Doñita Reyes. It didn't take her long to blurt out the bitter words: the reproaches stored up in her soul, over weeks and months.

—Ay! Look at you now. Cooped up in here like a jailbird!

Doñita looked stooped, older; and, miracle of miracles, not quite so fat. The light seared Miguel's eyes; he felt vulnerable: yearned to put his head on the big woman's shoulder and forget his pain. But he tried not to look down since she would take it for a sign of guilt. Doñita Reyes, slobbery, self-righteous, willful, limited. And she looked panicked now, ready to clutch at any straw.

She went on with a sniffle:

—Your mother, pour soul . . . By God's mercy she never lived to see this.

—I'm glad you came here, Doñita. How did you get inside?

—I was out there with the women.

—Really?

He stared at her. Since Purisima the women had picketed outside the prison gate. Long lines of solemn angry women filed back and forth; they shouted their slogans against Somoza, hunger and sick children, the unlivable conditions in the country. Some had men inside. All day and through the night he listened for Josefa's voice, chanting along with them, fighting for her man. Across Nicaragua, in those days, there were demonstrations against the dictatorship which had devalued the cordoba and enfeebled it further, in return for an international loan.

Miguel smiled. On his bearded face, granulated with sweat and grime, the sun seemed to come out. The idea of Doñita Reyes marching was just too picturesque: such an ungainly woman, a hopeless hypochondriac, always sending Almita to Chepe's store for aspirin on her better days.

III

—I got here yesterday. I left Alma with Padre Velasquez.

She bowed her head and, giving way to the tears, glanced up timidly at her foster son.

—Ah.— He chuckled, low. That was like him, to laugh at such a moment.— How is she?

The big birthmark on Doñita's cheek, like the map of a continent, seemed to drain of color. It hardly surprised him when she wept for no reason, blustery as an afternoon in rainy season. She would use any tactic to impress him with his waywardness, his failure in her eyes, and those of his dead mother.

—Poor little thing.

But now she frowned. Her upper lip trembled. What surprised him was the way, suddenly, she fought back her weakness and tried to hide her emotion. Had something happened?

—She'll be alright, he said, and frowned in turn.

Alma had been present at his arrest: a scene, a shock too much for most adults, let alone a child.

He tried to locate the nearest guard in the corner of his eye, as Doñita Reyes wept softly, with a glance of wonderment through the grating, at the state he was in. Always, she had wanted him to treat her like his real mother and call her Mama. Always, they both knew and felt that Juana was his mother: a specter there between them to complicate the simplest things.

Doñita raised her head. She gave a sort of defiant hiss and said:

—Some of those women, outside, are *comunistas*.

IV

—Listen . . . you listen to me. —She tried to pull herself together. —Here's what we decided, and what you have to do.

—Who is we?

—Padre Velasquez and . . . all of us. Her voice fell.

So she had come to Tipitapa with some sort of scheme. Like the other women she would petition for her boy's release in any way she could.

A few years before, as a teenager, he had written a play called *Fiesta of Saints and Devils* with a concern for religious themes. At the time Padre Velasquez was amused by the immature production and urged his prize student to study the great Calderón. Now one of the Catholic bishops had shown an interest in the plight of poet Miguel Giner, based on the mysticism and literary promise of the play.

In a hesitant tone Doñita laid out the details. The visiting room had become a meatgrinder of emotions—men and women shouted and churned out the minutes in a long crescendo. A few wept. Others laughed. He felt sick physically: the day to day struggle for existence left him weak, in morbid exhaustion; now it cost him an effort to follow Doñita's idea, her plan, and think how best to respond. Apart

from the monitoring system, the warden tuned in to their conversation word for word,—his enthusiasm at her visit had begun to fade.

—Forget about it, he said. There are many of us in here. A man
like him: do you think he would work to get us all released?

How often, in the past, the poet's own words had astounded him.
They flew out like blue heron soaring at noon over the swell of waves
on Lake Cocibolca. And then, in the February uprising, he made a
speech that came from some unknown place in him, out of character.

Now he stared at Doñita, for a moment, in a way she took for encouragement. Stern look, harsh reply; yet he wanted nothing more
on earth than the help of that man, the church dignitary, with whom
he disagreed. In his deepest soul he had learned to hate politics, the
nastiness of prison, torture, pain, sickness. He yearned to see his wife:
hold her in his arms.

—Child, look at you. Look what you've done to yourself. It's a shame.

He frowned. A shame: she had that right at least. What else could
you call a literary vocation going to waste, years of growth and experience, love for Josefa, children, wildflowers, sunlight, the sky,—all
wasted, lost to him, a shame. Suddenly tears welled up in his eyes.
The hand of his destiny had him by the throat, but he said to her:

—Never mind that. I'm not important.

His words were lost. A wave of voices crashed like a surf along the
double grating.

—Juana's son, she grumbled, and a criminal.

The joy had ebbed from their first visit together in ten long months.

V

—Selfish! she muttered. Beneath the boasting and big macho
words, you're selfish. Would you ever think about me for a moment,
or little Alma?

—You'll be alright.

Doñita Reyes' face with the birthmark looked on the verge of
combustion.

—Listen, there are mothers who come here day after day, pining
for a visit with their husbands. Do you know how long that line is?

—How did you get in?

—Padre Velasquez—

He nodded.

—That's what I thought.

—The picket extends around the prison, you can't see the end. And they give us forms to fill out, and get up our hopes. But some can't read. Yesterday a woman learned her son was dead: committed suicide in his cell. More selfish than all the rest!

For a moment Miguel seemed distracted; he glanced at the guard named Robles and feared some further indiscretion on Doñita's part. He shook his head at her lack of tact, her emotionalism.

But now he started forward. His forehead touched the grating and he fairly snarled:

—First, you get back out there, and tell that woman her son was no suicide. Do you understand? And tell her, tell all of them not to come here anymore if the idea is to see their menfolk.

—You're hard.

—No, you are. What do you think, those forms are a technicality? They are used to gather information, and because of them you'll see a lot more mothers crying. No more forms! And even if it means no visits, do you hear? The warden likes to play on your maternal instincts. Somoza has the mothers of Nicaragua acting as spies. Either learn the rules, or go away till this is over.

—And when do you suppose it will be over? she said, wide-eyed. By that time we'll all be dead, if not gone crazy like Alma.

—What?

He bolted upright in his chair. The guard assigned to stand between the double grating saw another set of fingers move, like tentacles, in a void.

—She thinks it's her fault you were arrested. She won't talk to me or anybody else.

—Then tell her I said don't give up. Tell her start helping Chon, she's old enough to run errands.

—She can't help anyone right now, even herself. She sits in her room and mumbles strange things, scratches her head. I can't make any sense of it. Thank God, the person I told you about is helping us through Padre Velasquez.

For the first time in the interview Miguel's eyes dropped. His brow had the kind of contraction she used to see when, as a boy, he was on the verge of a tantrum. He looked up and said, in a tone which drew a look from the guard Robles:

—She owes that man nothing. I'm warning you, Doñita, stay away from him; or there will be a prisoner who commits suicide in his cell!

—Always the selfish child, she said, shaking with anger. All your years in my house, I had to put up with it . . . But I did so for la Juana, and because your father asked me. Oh! the bunch of you, big brave men, and meanwhile hundreds of innocent people are killed.

—We're not the cause.

—Oh, no? So many campesinos, peasants, everyday more of them, in the North . . . —Now she had reached the end of her patience. She always avoided arguments and felt afraid of the passions they stirred. But this was too much. She paused an instant to get her breath, and then said: —Juan Ramón is dead, too.

—What?

—Sí, señor. Poor Juan Ramón: he was good.

She blurted it in a hurtful tone. All her long life of frustration was contained in the words, in the overtones of blame.

At the far end of the room a woman handed tortillas to a guard.

VI

As with little Alma, so with Juan Ramón who was their next door neighbor: Miguel hadn't heard the news. Juan Ramón was like a father to him at one remove: in the absence of Iván Giner who went up into the northern mountains and joined the guerrilla. And now, just as when a boy worn out by his day trapsing and fishing down by Masaya Lagoon, and he dragged back a slimy yellow carp which died of old age, and it cut him, with its fin, when he pounded it in the dust of Calle Calvario and had one of his tantrums right in front of Doñita: now he gave her a look of pent-up rage mingled with pleading.

He lowered his head to the grating and groaned.

When his eyes ventured up again, they glowed with grief and seemed to gaze on defeat.

—No, he said, quietly.

Doñita Reyes waited in silence, thinking she had just done a terrible thing. She expected him to get up and leave her alone: the way he always had in the past. Yes, he was stubborn, wayward. He went away in the first place because he never really cared about her. He only used her like an old worn-out shoe he could knock around when he felt bored. But the one he really loved, and as a boy hopelessly needed, was Juana. Of course, everything was all Doñita's fault back then, and it was still her fault to this day. If only she had been his real

mother then their lives would be different. She would have the right
to scold him, caress him when he fell, love him, be obeyed. But Juana
was his true mother: Juana who died in childbirth, twenty-four years
ago, and then Iván went up into the mountains.

She had said the awful words and wanted to hurt him as deeply as
she could. Alma, gone mad: that was for all the times he had hurt her.
Juan Ramón, gone forever: that was for bullying her with laughter,
supposing she was some old *estúpida* who never managed to get herself married. She had said the worst and now waited for God to punish her. In a moment Miguel would stand up, nod to the prison
guard, and leave her alone. Even though she had brought him up
from a child. Even though she loved him with all her heart and soul
but had no right to do so or even expect to be loved in return.

Doñita felt on the verge of something too sad to endure, with her
other child, Almita, no longer of this world. If only there was no grating: so she could pound his face with her two fists. She would beat
on him with all her might and then hug him to her, a long time, like
the mischievous boy he still was, running wild through the streets of
Masaya with his friend Chon Muñoz.

She waited there, head bowed, for the hard blow to fall.

PART TWO

I

How was he arrested? Had the girl been to blame? Or was it . . .
«the eagle's claws»?

He lay on his prison bunk and sifted the details: the February uprising, the turbulent days. Word came in the underground network
that Alma's state had worsened: a child recluse who stared at the wall
and mumbled a few bizarre words if she spoke at all. People in the
barrio thought she was possessed by a devil. And then, as a kid skipping to and from the Colegio she had never been quite like the others. Padre Velasquez could do nothing with her. Twelve years old,
said Doñita, with a look of despair, and now look at her life.

Miguel lay on his bunk. He daydreamed, remembered . . .

—Iván?

He heard his foster mother's voice: the catch in her throat the moment she saw him.

—Not Iván, Mamita, not yet!

He stood on her low threshold in the sunlight, grinning at Doñita
who blew and sighed because she knew trouble was surely in store.
Sí, señor! She knew by the sight of him as he stood there like a prince
from the Thousand and One Nights, long black hair atangle, even
teeth glinting as if Miguelito carried the sun around inside his mouth.
And then nobody on earth could say what he was liable to do next,
or whether he was joking.

—Hola, said Alma, birdlike, and squinted in the noontime glare.

—Hola, compañeros! he said, deep-voiced, advancing on Doñita to sweep her off her feet.

This wasn't easy since she had grown monstrously fat in those days: a stay-at-home who sat in her rocker on the porch from dawn until dusk. And the squeaky wicker chair mingled with her breathing, her half-audible thoughts.

—He's going to kill her. —Alma half-shut her eyes. The freckles jumped about in her excitement, on the bridge of her nose. —If the macaw doesn't screech at him with its harsh voice from the tigüilote tree: if it doesn't say a curse word then this is serious, I'll start running to Chepito's store for an aspirin.

Now Doñita Reyes put up her dimpled hand and backed away. But he was on her in a flash and lifted her up in a bear hug. Her swollen ankles kicked furiously. Almita watched closely, humble girl who knew she was next and felt a tingle. Her sticklike body was all expectation of a tickling; no doubt she would pee her pants like sometimes before he went away.

—Let me down. Owww!

That was how he said hello after so long. He couldn't bear the sight of women cooped up all day.

II

It was nearly two years since he left Masaya to go seek his fortunes in the capital. He sent a card upon leaving Managua to join a circus called the Americano Infantíl. And then, weeks later, Padre Velasquez brought by a page from La Prensa Literaria with three of Miguel's early poems. In June of '77 he brought them his teenage wife, Josefa, for a look; she was a dancer in the Americano.

—What are you doing here? said Doñita, in her tone of ruffled dignity.

He smiled at her:

—Just came to see you.

But she knew. Even Almita knew, almost, he was there because of the strange events: voices at night along the Calvario, shots from off toward San Sebastien. Alma thought there must be a panther loose in Masaya, and the men hunted at night and that was why Doñita went under the bed sometimes and she made a little game out of finding her. But only the cockroaches, scaly ones that could fly: only they could persuade Doñita to reemerge when they got in her hair.

In following days they heard rumors not of a panther but of men converged on the barrios: muchachos down from the mountains who hid in safe houses where they spoke in whispers and plotted an insurrection. Was Iván, their own father, among them? And then you could smell the bonfires, see the smoke rise up in the mauve dusk of Masaya. And the volcano outside town spoke angrily and spewed its ash, embittered the twilight. Beneath a crescent moon, like a peasant's machete wielded by the great dark hand of God, the people of Monimbó and Magdalena and Santa Rosa barrios held their meetings. Alma asked her brother who the strange men were: gauchos?

—That's what I was going to ask you.

Alma wrinkled her nose.

—Well, she said, they're . . . —He stared at her, as if her opinion were the one that counted. His dark eyes sparkled. —They're cowboys?

—Ha, he said. Do they catch Indians?

—Maybe.

—Are you an Indian?

—Yes, said Alma, looking down.

—Will they catch you?

—N-no, she said, very low.

—What do they do?

—Bueno . . . they drive up in their van,—she explained in a low voice so Doñita wouldn't hear,—and shoot it out in Parque Central.

She knew about an assault the previous October on the Guardia garrison.

—Why? Do they like doing that?

—I think . . . no, some die, some run away.

—Would you like to be one?

—Dios primero! What would Doñita say?

Miguel laughed. He went outside to read or hold a conversation with the long-tailed macaw perched in the tigüilote tree. Almita followed him, but she kept to one side and stared at this brother she hadn't seen for two years.

—Jesucristo! said the screechy voice, cracking a nut.

Doñita was jealous because she usually talked a blue streak to that parrot, just like she did to her teapot and the *comal* where she cooked tortilla.

—Somoza puta! said the gaudy macaw, and chewed with its hooked bill like a coy snail, Alma thought, that got in the corn. It dropped shells on her brother's curly hair where he let them stay, so deep in his reading.

On the porch Doñita looked scandalized. Her rocker squeaked with an energy, like you heard some nights across the way, at Juan Ramón and Faustina's. And Alma associated those secretive sounds with the panther that prowled.

—Don't teach it subversive slogans, said Doñita. You'll get us arrested.

—Down 'with Somoza!

And if a Guardia patrol came by and heard those words? They would think Doñita's place a safe house of comunistas!

Alma, humble, timid, hung by Doñita's side since at any moment Miguel could tickle. For a full year before he went away she had dropped in her tracks on sight of him and given a sort of whimper. Now maybe she wanted to be badgered some more. She did and she didn't.

III

Doña Faustina was outside hanging her laundry. From in back came Juan Ramón's carpentry sounds.

—Can't talk now, Doña!

Miguel strode by with a glimpse of her forestial charms, her figure, the glint in her eye. Since a boy she had stared at him that way. She loved what Doñita Reyes hated: his wildness. And she hinted sometimes, sensuous challenges that would never be taken up.

Speckled with morning sun he made his way down the deep-rutted Calvario. It was more a shallow ravine in the woods than a proper road, but the mules didn't complain; they bumped along and lugged supplies to and from Pacayo. Doñita Reyes' house stood on the edge of Monimbó, set back among the trees. During rainy season the Calvario became a brook which shimmered with little fish, but now in dry weather it lay dusty. Each day the sun rose high toward a scorched noon. And the barrio dwellers trod this road in the intimacy of their pores, in the sandpaper taste of their saliva.

Miguel broke into a jog, mulling over what he was about to do. Behind him Juan Ramón's scraping sounds faded. A cock gave its hoarse crow halted by a firecracker. Up ahead a few more detonations rang out from direction of San Sebastien where the people had already gathered.

Sunlight dripped like dew from dense vines and patches of plantain, tall coconut palms on either side. Cicadas gave their rhythmic screech from the treetops; a guinea pig pecked at grains down a side path. In the February air there was a scent of tobacco harvest in the fields around Masaya, out toward Nindiri and the volcano. —Pum, pum, he knew Doñita wondered, with a shudder, if he was one of them. Pum, pum: what was a guerrilla, Alma asked, her brow knit; was their father, Iván, really one? Oh, they must be pretty bad the way Doñita went around cursing them out to herself, because each time she bumped into something or stubbed her toe or got a splinter it was all their fault. So they must be invisible beings who made awful things happen the minute God took a siesta. Pum, he moved along. What was he going to do?

He spotted two men up ahead. They had a look of Guardia, big, with the watchful air of soldiers. He stepped to one side of the road and moved nimbly among the treetrunks.

A little further on stood the church called Calvarito with its cross of iron, rusted and warped, above the crooked entry. It sat on a mound of dark earth like the breast of an Indian woman suckling her child. Now he breathed in the moldy coolness before entering: so often he came here with Doñita as a boy, for a prayer at midday. He hugged the shadow of the Calvarito and tried to slip inside without being seen.

Click-click went their intricate gear. They had fine boots, walkie-talkies, a stern look because they didn't want to hear anything from the barrio. The voice of one, amid static, lent a hesitant note to the chirping birds. Were they coming in for a muchacho holed up along the Calvario? As Miguel's eyes adjusted to the darkness he saw an old woman in a black shawl who knelt from one of the simple pews. Her prayers made a tinny sound in the silence. A candle dripped wax like the pathetic tears of Chuno (Jesus) where he stood among the saints carved in oak by Monimbó artisans.

—Hombre, said the old woman, her voice roughhewn, like the saints.

Miguel slid beside her on the pew. Outside, the splutter of the Guardia two-way; in here, the murmur of the old woman. Along with statues of the Savior, hammocks, embroidered blouses, the adults made pyrotechnics for the festivals like San Jerónimo.

—Give me your shawl.

—In trouble again?

The radio buzzed like a hornet outside the door. In the distance, fireworks. He took her bonnet and stuck it on his curly head, saying his rosary. Carlita Garcia was almost bald, with blue veins, a sampler of moles on her skull. Her eyes were like an eaglet's, while outside the leather boots crunched pebbles and dust. Here they came, and they would shoot: Miguel heard their voices, but Carlita wanted to gossip more than say her prayers. Up front the statues might have been barrio folk who died many, many years ago, and found their way here: their petrified forms, too heavy for entry into heaven, grimaced at eternity from the crevices.

IV

Light poured over the primitive pews, as the two Guardia paused in the sunlit entry. A bat flapped over the altar amid the roofbeams. The bulky figures looked restless with their submachineguns, starched uniforms, dark helmets in the growing heat.

—Vamonos. Old biddies.

Carlita tugged Miguelito's sleeve, but it was not time for chatter. Had they come for him? a pair of Guardia meant to snatch him away and put him in jail? But how would they know what he was about to do unless from Padre whom he had visited the day before at the Colegio, and the priest said he would also speak a few words at the rally?

On the threshold he saw their broad olive drab backs streaked with sweat, gorillas on tiptoes. Then he went skipping over ruts and runnels along the Calvario. A tree lizard, pisoti, darted down lianas on a wild fig as Miguel left the dirt road behind, and plank huts became walls of adobe with weedy tufts in the cornices. A group of kids watched him sprint past with Carlita's flowered bonnet on his head and then trotted after, like a boat making wake.

—Where to, papá?

Would he be late? The facade of San Sebastien hopped up and down as he ran along. Bits of glass crunched beneath his sandals, where the people smashed bottles in the rear of marches to hinder

Guardia jeeps. The air hung smoky with bonfires from the night before, burning tires, political meetings at the street corners. Words of
anger spewed like cinder and sparks from Nindiri Volcano.

V

Some men stood at the entry of the church and among them
Choncito Muñoz. Chon was Miguel's best friend from when they
were boys. If Miguel was an Arabian prince with a smile like a great
exploit, or a prank, then Chon Muñoz was a caliph. Stockier, after
three years of marriage, though with a touch of softness, also a stubborn seriousness, he spoke calmly and to the point. Chon was a
teacher at the Colegio with Padre Velasquez as his superior. He made
things clear, one and then the next, the best way for Alma and the
children and barrio folk as well; whereas Miguel talked a blue streak
and said obscure, mystifying words, like a poet. He joked; he grew
excited; he rhapsodized.
—Should I go inside?
Chon said hello with his eyes. They embraced. It was two years
since their last meeting; and the experience of becoming men, marriage to the women they loved, the adult world, had intervened. One
stayed at home, one went away; each in his own manner responded
to the political situation. But beneath this, even deeper, in the sub-
stratum of their lives, there was something else between them. Like
a stream with its source in childhood that coursed through adoles-
cence and broadened into manhood;—it would flow in the sunlight,
as Miguel now understood, gazing at his friend, beside their graves.
—Sí, hombre.
Chon's eyes shone for a moment with a sort of admiration.
Miguel brushed past him but asked over his shoulder:
—Where is Padre?
—Speaking.
The square in front of San Sebastien pulsated with morning light.
The yellow dust seemed to evaporate.
—Marriage changed you? said Miguel.
—Could be. Are you going to keep that bonnet on?
Miguel took Carlita's sleeping cap from his curly hair and put it on
the schoolteacher's.

VI

In the mid-'Fifties there was a period of trouble between the seasonal workers and the plantation owners near Rivas in the South. Winds of rebellion swept through the villages and the situation was not far from coming to a test of force. There were agitators on hand, men from the Conservative opposition to the old Somoza's National Liberals; and they spoke in open defiance of El Hombre, telling the workers of their country's great natural resources. Of mineral rich mines, gold in Puerto Cabezas on the Atlantic Coast; of fisheries owned mostly by Somoza Garcia in abundant waters off the Pacific beaches: palmy strands so beautiful, like emerald on beige satin, that a famous singer in the States wanted to open casinos from Rivas to Corinto. The agricultural production was lush and generous: hadn't God created Nicaragua because He wanted Nicaragua for His holidays? In May the plantains ripened, while pithy yucca absorbed the sunlight and minerals from the fertile soil. In August the tender maize grew heavy along furrows extending to the horizon: golden maize used a hundred ways. By then the fields were covered deep green and swayed to a sea breeze. The rains came daily from dramatic clouds, but in November they subsided, and the coffee grew ready for harvest. And, as the year turned, there were basic grains, sugar cane, beef, cotton. From Carazo's verdant hills to the long coastal plains a rich scent of tobacco hovered in the air.

Among the droves of seasonal workers who packed their few possessions in a knapsack and moved about the country harvesting was Iván Giner. He worked all day and into the evening for a few cordobas. At night he drank rum or the more potent guaro in a stupor of sunstroke and hunger. The owners had sets of hard wooden drawers for the field workers to sleep on. Iván, eaten alive by mosquitoes, his body reeling from the preceding day's abuse, rose in the predawn light to the shrill whistle of the capataz. From Masaya, Estelí, or some village in the North, a worker got word his child had died of tuberculosis, the bleeding measles.

That year, during the disturbances, Iván Giner fell in love with Juana, the oldest daughter of Cornelio Ferrán's plantation manager in a village called Las Salinas near Rivas City. One night they eloped. There are people down there who still remember the story, the attractive girl, the father's wrath. Over and over Doñita told little Alma that old tale of heartbreak, when Miguel and Chon had gone off to the Lagoon fishing. She told her because it stirred up the past, and then the poor woman's solitary life seemed to take on meaning.

—They came here, said Doñita, the two young people looking for a priest. You see Juana's father, Don Justo, would never give them his blessing. No, señor.

Cornelio Ferrán was a friend of the Man himself, old Somoza, who had the guerrillero, Sandino, put to death. And Don Justo's wife, who went away for the sake of high life, fancy dress affairs with the President's clique in Managua: she had her own influential friends. So for the young lovers, Iván and Juana, it seemed even the government must be against them.

One April evening they were married by Padre's predecessor at the Colegio Salesiano. A few days later they crossed the wide lake, with its rolling waves, from Granada to San Carlos where Iván found a job hauling boats on the Río San Juan. Life was hard: by day he labored up to his neck in a river filled with leeches, while the white-faced monkeys cried in the treetops and the great birds, toucan, sisitoté and egret, gave quizzical looks from the Costa Rican side.

He began to argue with his foreman and one day had a fistfight; the two men floundered in the muddy shallows. He lost his work, while Juana, who seemed on the verge of a nervous breakdown, sided that night with his boss. She was pregnant with Miguel by then, underfed for the first time in her life, in muddy San Carlos with its waterside structures and torrential rains that alternated, daily, with a vertical sun. Raised at Don Justo's like a daughter of aristocrats, now she fell into a depression. Two passionate people: they had bad quarrels; and Iván stormed out to a bar on the dock where he spent their last few cordobas. At midnight he came back, and they faced the dawn in one another's arms. One night he lost control of himself, and hit her—slapped Juana so hard she fell and knocked over a candle which went out on the earthen floor. After that she grew afraid to provoke him. But her moods flew from morbid to nearly hysterical, and Iván Giner thought his wife might go insane. And so he relented and brought her back to Las Salinas; though he knew it could cost him his life to return there: a man who ran off with the plantation manager's daughter.

Don Justo shut them both out completely. He didn't interfere, but he cut his pregnant daughter off without a peso.

Don Cornelio Ferrán, the master, only smiled when he heard the story and called it too typical of the campesinado, peasants. By then Iván had started to take risks; he fished illegally in offshore waters beyond the estuary controlled by Somoza's consortium. Juana's condition, malnourished, in a shack near the seaside plantation, had gone from bad to worse. Late one night she gave birth to a pink shrivelled parcel of humanity, a poet, and then died in misery the following day.

Iván was beside himself with grief, rage, remorse. He walked out wild-eyed, machete in hand, intending to kill Don Justo who had refused to let the local veterinarian see to his daughter until a certain mare foaled. Fortunately the plantation manager had left his house an hour earlier to drive into Rivas. Eyes bloodshot, his mind ablaze, Iván continued up to Ferrán's manor house; but Don Cornelio was spending the month in Miami with his wife.

That afternoon Iván Giner took Juana into the fields and buried her in the shade of a ceiba tree, on the western edge of the plantation. From the summit of that ceiba a boy who climbed it could see the Pacific Ocean.

Then he punched two holes in an old saddlebag for the infant's stumpy legs and set off to trek up the Pan American Highway: the same route they had taken the year before when they eloped.

He brought the baby to Doñita Reyes in Masaya.

—This is Juana's. Love him, and bring him up well.

—What about you?

Doñita stared at him with pity.

—I'll go out to the Atlantic Coast and find work in the mines.

From year to year Iván reappeared in all his hairy-chested bulk among the palm trees and quequisques of the Calle Calvario. He made his way followed by a bunch of barrio kids up to the house where his son lived. There he stood, dwarfing Doñita's gray porch, and asked to see the boy. He had been down in Costa Rica working for United Fruit as a packer. He had spent six months in the jungle along Río Escondido, hunting spider-monkeys since some U.S. entrepreneur paid a dollar apiece for them if delivered caged and healthy to Bluefields.

And then, one springtime, Iván Giner met Doñita on her threshold:

—Hola.

—Hola, she said, and sniffed the air.

—Where is he? said Iván like a big chunk of jungle, of sweaty monkey, making her porch sag.

This time there was something different about him. He spoke in a low, serious voice and went about his affairs, during the few days he stayed with them, mostly after dark.

Then, toward noontime, he went to the Salesiano and saluted Miguel's classmates where they played their first games of *futbol* on the wide school grounds.

—Hola, compañeritos!

From his second floor office Padre Velasquez stared down at the strange visitor and frowned. He went out and met this man he had heard about. Doñita Reyes was right: Miguel's father had an odor of monkey and the fungus-ridden jungles of Zelaya North. Virile, untutored, he looked like a creature of legend.

By midday, siesta at the Colegio, he had said goodbye to his son with a handshake and a hug. He turned his ruguous face, dyed indigo by the tropical sun, out toward the highway but gave no indication where he was headed.

Time and again, during his boyhood, Miguel heard the story from Doñita Reyes whose family had been friendly with Iván's, long ago, in a small village on the windswept hills of Carazo, midway between Managua and the sea. But it was only today, as he moved through the packed crowd inside San Sebastien, that he seemed to understand, and hear echoes of destiny in the footsteps of his father.

VII

The fine florid words of Padre Antonio Velasquez seemed to waft like butterflies along the cool San Sebastien nave. He spoke in the accents of his adored Calderón, telling the Masayans of God's will, of Christian duty and the sin of violence. Padre exhorted them to have patience and show faith in the divine will. But a high voice shook off its timidity, cried out:

—Centuries of patience!

And another:

—How long, father?

A third, Presencio, the artisan:

—Diriangén committed suicide, he was so patient!

—Silencio, said Padre, and held up a hand.

Miguel, standing alongside the altar, heard a flap of wings beneath the vaulting. A pigeon veered over the large crowd intent on each word. Bright sunlight pierced the jagged stained glass and cast flecks of red and blue on the poet's hair and shoulders.

With a glance over the scene he had a surprise. Was that Alma creeping in toward the back, beside a pillar? A flit of cute girlish face, white blouse. He couldn't believe Doñita, afraid of her own shadow as she might well be, it was so big, would send out the overprotected girl on this of all days. What was going on? Did she have a message?

The old church appeared to bestir itself as Padre Velasquez gave the last of his sermon on non-violence: words filled with the authority of his position. He stepped to one side with a peeved look, irritated by the need to speak. Noon burst like an angel's wing through the cracked stained glass.

There were rumors of revolutionaries in the city; though so far the people headed by Chon Muñoz, the Monges, Elias Rodriguez had done everything on their own. The day before, after a mass marking forty days since the death of dissident journalist Pedro Joaquín Chamorro, assassinated by the dictator, marchers were attacked with teargas and grapeshot by a detachment of Guardia. Beneath an impassioned moon the first homemade bombs began to blast in the streets of Masaya.

—Free homeland! cried Miguel at the crowd, and he thought: caramba, that's Alma; her hair lighter, a blondish tress over the Indian ingredients of her features.

—Or death! cried the Masayans, enraptured to hear the poet they had known as a boy.

Then the words came more quietly than Padre's. His circus experience, his time with the Americano Infantíl had taught him the art.

—I'm going to tell you, compañeros, of the day Sandino died.

Bolt of wings: two pigeons shot from the clerestory, soaring up on distended wings.

—Forty-four years ago, on this day . . . —But he thought in midsentence: Almita dressed in her faded blue skirt with plaits and white blouse, her Colegio uniform. —Sandino had come down from the Segovias wanting peace with all his heart. And the people turned out to greet him as he entered Managua . . . that day. —So painfully shy, as zany in her way as the chattery macaw on its limb; now she bit her lip, affected by waves of emotion his words stirred in the crowd. — And the old Somoza, the man who had danced so charmingly with the U.S. Ambassador's wife, invited the General of Free Men to a friendly dinner.

Miguel's voice seemed to summon the two white birds to flight. But now he became aware of another sound, as if the ancient stones of the church had begun to grumble.

—The guerrillero was tired of the long war, and the Marines were gone home, defeated. So he came down from the mountains, into the city.

Alma stood blocked about halfway up the right aisle, squeezed against a pillar. Yes, she had some sort of message.

But a high voice rang out, interrupting Miguel at the altar. The sharp cry of Chon Muñoz called their attention to the rotors of an approaching helicopter. Suddenly, they all flowed back in a mass; and Alma was borne with the undertow through the wide front entry into the square when Chon waved his arms and cavorted the way he did at the yearly fiesta.

With one voice they shouted slogans against Somoza. Above the patios and courtyards the feathery palms stood still in the azure of noon. The long green fronds looked like arms urging calm on the dangerous scene below. But then the helicopter angled over the barrio, agitating the palm trees, stirring the cauldron heat. In high-pitched voices the hundreds of Masaya Indians cried out against the dictator, and his father who had sold used cars in Philadelphia before coming home to put his country on sale. From the moment he had Sandino shot until this day, all Nicaragua had been his family hacienda. And now his son Tacho, with La Dinorah by his side, shapely witch. While for years, decades the masses went half clad, shoeless kids, hard protruding bellies, illiterate workers and peasants, artisans without materials, men and women without dignity, towns with no public services, a nation orphaned by greed. And now they walked arm in arm shouting in anger. Alma bobbed in their midst, her scrawny breast heaved with excitement beneath the frayed white blouse she wore weekdays to the Colegio. And Chon Muñoz, and Juan Ramón, and Lorenzo the young poet from Pochotillo barrio: those three leapt in front of the crowd which rippled with banners and fists as far as the eye could see. Choncito liked to dress up in a toga costume each year, during San Jerónimo, when the streets of Masaya became a furious dance. Alma liked him a lot when he did that; and she liked the way he treated her and Doñita whenever he came to visit.

VIII

They drew her further away from her brother. She emerged unable to look up at a helicopter which roared and sounded huger than the church organ. Above all she wanted to run to Chon Muñoz and tell him what happened because he had been her teacher at the Colegio and she trusted him.

At mid-morning, after Miguel went out, a muchacho approached their house from the back, among the snakewood and guanacaste trees. She stayed in her little room, but lurked: so she saw him smile when Doñita lifted herself from the outsized wicker rocker Juan Ramón had made her, saying an elephant could take a nap in it. Gracias! said Doñita to Juan Ramón.

Almita ducked: her plaited skirt billowed, the brushwood bent and swayed with the gale from the copter's helyx. Now another appeared swooshing, bending palm trees, plantain patches this side of Coyotepe Fortress on its hill above the city. Juan Ramón had a sow that liked to chew nettles: Alma thought of Juan Ramón's sow and the way it looked around, deep in thought with a mouthful of prickles. Could it really see the wind, as Juan Ramón said?

—Here comes Macho Pedro!

—Ay! The beast.

Across the square a row of jeeps and armored personnel carriers seemed to catch fire in the glare. Macho Pedro's troops wore bulky uniforms, boots and helmets. They had a stubborn air; all with bandoleros, grenades, teargas canisters, handcuffs, more decorated than a Christmas tree.

—See that one? a woman pointed. His mama had him for the pleasure!

Alma wondered why she had him for the pleasure. Was it because he dressed up that way, like a lumpy toad? She felt sorry for him: in the sunlight he must feel hot, pasted together, plus the thing about his mother. But the muchacho who came to their house that morning was missing a tooth; he spoke in whispers, respectful, because sounds travelled along Calle Calvario, and he told Doñita a secret. You could hear the pitterpatter of kids coming home from the Colegio, a long way off, when Doñita made her stay home all day. Why did Doñita make her stay home?

Now she saw Choncito turn and glance at the line of jeeps. A Guardia broke his rigid pose; his arm windmilled, something spun through the air. It landed hissing in the dust and spewed smoke. Oh! Lorenzo leapt forward and grabbed it with a handkerchief, he lobbed it back across. Suddenly Alma had a bad feeling. She could faint. She felt giddy like the time she got lost on her way to Chepito's store when Doñita had her toothache and wrapped her jaw in a sling and moaned. A second smoke bomb was snatched up by a woman who ran toward the fountain in the middle of the square.

The crowd gave a yell. Children screamed. Grown men leapt about and gestured.

But Alma stood still and wondered: was this why the muchacho came to them? because something terrible was going to happen? And the Doñita grabbed her by the shoulder and shook her, fear in her eyes like the flying cockroaches:

—You have to go to San Sebastien. Look for Padre Velasquez, only him. Tell Padre to tell Miguel—ay Maria!

—Tell him ay Maria?

Doñita leaned down and whispered, in Almita's ear, like a message straight from hell and everlasting death:

—The eagle's claws.

—The eagle's claws? she repeated, out loud.

She stared at Doñita. Nothing like this ever happened before.

—First get on your school clothes. I won't have them thinking we're dirt poor, *pobretería!*

IX

In the broken ranks of the march she saw someone fall to the ground. It was Lorenzo, the young poet a few grades ahead of her at the Colegio. He liked to poke her in the hallway between classes; and he shook his head staring at her, and said: —So humble! . . . She had a kind of tender feeling and talked about him to her doll, Consuelo, who was a shred of cloth pinned to a stick. Why did he poke her? Padre had trouble with Lorenzo who was rebellious and came into Monimbó one night with his friends to talk about Macho Pedro, calling him a maricón. Doñita grew angry at that and said: —Guardia captains are not maricones.

Alma saw Lorenzo squirm like a wounded animal by the church entrance. She wanted to brush the dust off his hair and face. She felt a wave of pity and started to run across the square.

What she saw next caused a spasm of nausea. Oh! oh! He lay wounded in the stomach, badly, and a slimy mass oozed on the ground. Like tripes the women sold in Masaya market; and his hand was bloody and shook as he tried to push them back. In the haze of a dream she saw people scamper for the maze of back paths and alleys through the barrio. Alma heard the ranting clatter of submachinegun fire and pop, pop of more teargas. She saw, in a blur of smoke and sunlight, men sprint with guns and two-way radios amid the adobe dwellings where they took up positions. Then Chon Muñoz was by her side: he leaned over the wounded boy on the stone steps. She glanced up and saw people hurl rocks to cover their retreat.

She heard screams. Nausea swept over her.

—Don't do that! Please!

Was it her own voice—shrill enough to tear anyone's hope to bits? Now her only white blouse for school was blotched with Lorenzo's blood and torn at the armpit. What would Doñita say? She wouldn't let her go out and play for a month.

Suddenly she seemed to see the cock tied up by Juan Ramón's woodpile. The men used it for fights. They goaded the poor thing with no mercy until it became all mean and macho like themselves. Was Iván like that, her father? Would she ever see him again, and smile in his bearded face, and give him a kiss?

Then, for an instant, Alma thought of animals: the pacas and coatis that scurried along Calle Calvario late at night, looking for food.

She went to her knees. She fell with a groan on one shoulder.

—Ay!

Her voice sounded so alone. She lay helpless in the dust, unable to move. Was she wounded like Lorenzo? She glimpsed the irate eyeball of the cock: Macho Pedro! And that was all she knew.

X

Above the dark eaves of the Colegio stars twinkled in a clear night sky. The Milky Way was a luminescent smear across endless blue depths, while the low dwellings glimmered, huddling together. Cicadas hissed. A breeze off the wide lake stirred almond trees in blossom, madroño and delicate mimosa and maidenhair fern. Acacia glinted silvery amid the motes of celestial light.

In the barrio there was a smell of wood burning, and garbage fumed in the ravines. At the far end of Calle Calvario a few pigs snorted among the cornshucks, old containers, weeds. A herd lowed its way toward evening fodder, raising a dust cloud, mulling over ruts for a spear of grass. A dog gave its naked bark, and two more joined in from the undergrowth behind Doña Faustina's; and then a fourth, ornery hound Lazaro kept in his pyrotechnics workshop to warn off thieves.

High above the stars twinkled. Down below the barrio smoked. On someone's porch a mandolin played a folksong, sad, like an elegy for Lorenzo whose guts spilled in the dust in full view. The flocculent stars, the sweet breeze mingled with burning odors. A mandolin strumming for the young poet. Monimbó filled with whispers.

Inside the Colegio Padre Velasquez applied compresses to Alma's forehead. She had a high fever after being carried from the square by Chon Muñoz. Padre put on the cold compresses which she shook off, murmuring something about her brother and an eagle.

Velasquez was in his mid-fifties. He wore glasses, and his hair had grayed at the temples. Though not a big man he had a bull neck beneath his clerical collar, and seemed to go about yoked firmly to an ecclesiastical will. His body, beneath the black robe he removed only to sleep, was not stocky or muscular like Chon; rather, his neck resembled the sturdy stipe of a lifelong vocation.

There was a knock on the door downstairs. The barrio lay under siege, with outsiders arriving quietly from Managua, Granada, Boaco. He knew they would gather in safe houses up in the Rinconadas, where they hid out to plan a guerrilla campaign: so he thought. Meanwhile there was a delirious girl on his hands, probably in shock, as the knock-knock went on insolently. Must be urgent, he thought, and rose from Alma's bedside; but then recalled the expected visit of Morell, from Rivas, and an important message.

Padre took the stairs, surprisingly nimble, and found himself face to face with Morell, the Somocista spy.

—Buenas noches.

—Buenas.

Morell was a creature of bureaucracy, of staid everyday usage. Thus a vulgar soul but not without his poetry, since charged with many a critical mission. He carried messages for the chain of command, from Don Cornelio Ferrán on down to the valiant Macho Pedro, a heathen if there ever was one, a torturer by propensity, up on Coyotepe. Morell had spent a season as an infiltrator, Padre knew, for the warden of the Tipitapa prison. All in all, the sort of snake that could blend in anywhere and never betray himself with a false move. Perfect courier, political detective, operative, informer. In the front entry he looked out of breath. The sweat ran on Morell's face, his eyes aglow with the light of bonfires deeper in the barrio.

—You have a letter? said Padre.

They went upstairs where Alma lay on her cot mumbling something. Padre Velasquez wiped his kindly forehead with a handkerchief and went to the secretary where he kept Colegio accounts. He began a letter in response to Ferrán while the spy recounted an adventure.

—They had them at Los Coquitos, dammit! Four leaders with Camilo Ortega: what a jolt when I spotted him. And carrying thousands of cordobas and a Garand. The mob thought they were mercenaries, but the four insisted they were Frente. I suggested execution. People's justice! But we're innocent, says Ortega. FSLN, says an Indian they call Claudio. How long have you been here? Three days. Where are you staying? Doña Faustina's, on the Calvario.

Morell paused. The story made him breathless: how he almost got a mob to execute four leaders, and Ortega, member of the Frente directorate.

—So I said, you're lying. And the thing was an inch from decided. But along comes the meddling schoolteacher, Muñoz, and recognizes one of them. Bueno, you wait. Now we know where you're holed up.

Padre Velasquez moved his pen across the white page. Impatient with the coarse Morell, he felt little interest in the man's thoughts.

"Masaya, Nicaragua
21 February 1978

Don Cornelio Ferrán
Ferrán Plantation
Las Salinas

Dear Don Cornelio:

Grateful for yours of the 20th. Information rec'd and shall be transmitted.

I must tell you word has reached us of an unfortunate occurrence. Certain of the more virulent elements have led rioters from La Reforma, Monimbó and elsewhere in a shameful attack against the municipality. The grievous report being, according to sources which I consider reliable, that the house of your secretary here, Señora Velia Suazo, was burnt to the ground.

As this indicates, the situation is very serious. The delinquent segment has armed itself with sticks, machetes, and a homemade explosive they've invented calling it the *bomba de contacto*. We, as prominent citizens, view such factors with the utmost gravity and await necessary measures on the part of President Somoza in conjunction with trusted national leaders like yourself.

Today, the people of Monimbó were stirred up by the asphyxiation of a number of children during a helicopter operation. Such excesses are hard to avoid, of course, when barrio residents comport themselves as common felons. But we were better off, I think, not provoking them.

Most regrettably I must tell you so that you in turn can notify the proper authorities, in State Security, that one of my teachers at the Colegio, Asunción Muñoz, called Chon, has emerged as a ringleader and should be dealt with firmly. Even more painful to myself is the role played by the most promising student ever to grace these Salesiano halls: I refer to the poet Miguel Giner of whom you, and our nation as well, are familiar.

A teenager named Lorenzo Lopez has been badly wounded in the mêlée. If he dies, and rumors have him on the verge, there will no doubt be a funeral procession. It may become political since even the dead are exploited by godless causes. Miguel Giner will be on hand, giving an oration: he has revealed himself as a first-rate demagogue. To think Nicaragua might have had its Virgil, first in poetics, oratory, theology, philosophy. He was my student, but beyond this I sensed a soaring talent in him.

Chon Muñoz should be there as well. A helicopter operation from Coyotepe might pluck such so-called leaders in media res before anyone knew what was happening. That alone would make things easier. The people respect them, having known them as children.

Word reaches us, lastly, of the presence here in Masaya of longterm subversives such as Camilo Ortega, staying with three of his kind up on the far end of the Calle Calvario, at Doña Faustina's.

Don Cornelio, I confide this into the careful hands of Morell, and submit it for your prompt consideration. I assume, moreover, the destiny of our country to be under good auspices: namely those of statesmen like yourself whose wisdom is commensurate with a great and equitable influence.

Yours in Christ,

Padre Antonio Velasquez."

XI

—Padre, said Miguel, in the Colegio entry an hour later, Lorenzo Lopez is dying. He was hit in the stomach but managed to staunch the blood with a piece of wood. He dragged himself to La Calzada Bakery, and the Red Cross came for him. But the ambulance was stopped by Guardia with Lorenzo's intestines hanging out. They questioned him while he bled.

The Padre shook his head. From upstairs came a childish voice calling someone's name. Alma sounded pitiful in the silence. Padre knew
what Miguel and the others wanted: it was a serious step whether he
accepted or refused. The Colegio was centrally located, so they intended to use it for defense of the barrio.

—People are stirred up, said the poet. Lazaro is busy making contact bombs in his workshop. Fight or die, and that's it.

—I see.

—How is Alma?

Padre gave a nod.

—As usual the children suffer.

—Let us deploy here, said Miguel. The Guardia will attack tonight,
and if they overrun us, many will die.

—And your sister? I don't suppose you've thought about her.

—We'll move her, somewhere safe.

—In any case this is a religious building. I can't let you.

—What is religion? A house made of stones, or people's lives?

Antonio Velasquez met his former student's gaze.

—You say you want a better life for all. You will end up bringing death.

—Then it won't be on our knees. Those who oppress us, let them
oppress. But if they tell us don't fight back, it's a sin, then who is
the sinner?

Padre shook his head:

—You should be studying, writing, far from this business. What
about your wife?

—Josefa is safe.

—Where is she?

Intent on the Padre's stare he seemed to glimpse, for an instant,
past the clerical mask.

Velasquez glanced back over his shoulder. Upstairs, the girl raised
her voice, plaintive, the words jumbled.

—What is she saying?

—Nothing.

Thoughtful, Miguel nodded a moment to the rhythm of events.
His task was to get Padre's consent before fighters took positions
along the eaves with their .22 rifles and contact bombs. Now his fate
was bound up with that of the barrio. This wasn't the excitement of
sitting down to write and realize an idea; or the exuberance of center ring in the Americano Infantíl, the circus. Masaya, struggle, life
and death: such things rode on his own activity.

—This building is a key position.

—I cannot sanction violence.

—With us, said Christ, or against us.

—Us? Padre smiled.

—If you close your doors . . .

—Ah, not on my own authority.

—Then whose?

—A somewhat higher one.

—Just following orders?

The priest flushed, turned away suddenly.

—Listen, boy, don't blaspheme. I can't endorse it.

—Well, it's coming, said Miguel, endorsed or not.

XII

At dawn, and through the daylight hours, the barrio lay quiet with few venturing out. A lone figure, was it Fasael the mechanic? trailed his shadow over the scorched dust, and the most casual movement seemed to prepare for attack. Then the second night fell; the brief blazed sunset of the tropics glared chartreuse and crimson beyond the African palms. Night closed over the Calle Calvario with its spidery foliage. Soon there were bonfires that crackled in front of the Magdalena, and up on the Lomas, and deep in the Rinconadas. The stars gathered like spectators above the sprawl of dwellings.

It was past ten p.m. when a voice cried in the square, beneath the Salesiano windows:

—They're coming!

Padre Velasquez clasped his hands in prayer.

—What direction? said another.

—Cuatro Esquinas!

The first shots rang out across the city. The night jumped alive outside the windows of the Colegio. Women beat on their pots and pans. A motor raced. Clank of chains. What will happen? thought Padre. And if the barrio is overrun? If Guardia go house to house and pull people out? Down in the street: a shuffle of feet. The women beat hard on their cooking ware. It sounded like a howl rose up across the earth.

—Avenida Central!

—Armored column! someone shouted.

Bells rang: chimes and a shrill laughter as some kids dangled on the ropes in San Sebastien belltower. Padre knew a thousand lives hung in the balance, but he felt irked at those kids taking advantage with their pranks. Suddenly it was a clangor of shots, bells, pots and pans, banged casseroles. And now the barrio elders, Alcaldes de Vara, began to beat their ceremonial drums and summon a few hundred Indians to come join in the dance of death. In his mind's eye Padre saw Guardia tank turrets swivel before erupting in flame, pulverizing the adobe facades.

—What a waste, he mumbled.

He heard the report of .22 rifles and hunting guns as insurgents crouched in doorways, behind a parked car. He heard footsteps on the Colegio roof, a fighter going on cat's paws; but an RPG whistled past the window where Padre Velasquez stood and forced him back. It was followed by a cry, a tinkle of glass. Staccato yells rose from the street below, as men fell wounded.

XIII

Later, when the shooting lulled, Alma Giner rose to one knee in the darkness. She put off the cover Padre had draped over her and shivered. Poor Padre: he had grown quiet, collapsed from exhaustion, and now snored fitfully with a flea-like sound. He lay oblivious to the murmurs, muffled footsteps, men sprinting past. She couldn't quite see but she looked toward him tenderly: even Padre's snore sounded sort of religious, like a responsory the children sang at Sunday mass.

She rose trembling, so afraid she couldn't think of anything, or know the risk she was about to take. Once in motion she felt relief from the guiltiness, like a stomach ache. Even Doña Faustina didn't have herbs against this sort of hurt: it was the one that got you where you prayed.

—Oh!

She stubbed her toe in the dark.

Through the afternoon she was jolted from dreams of Lorenzo by a wrenching sense of shame. And she thought: the eagle's claws. Where was her brother? At Sunday mass the Padre talked about «brother's keeper» and now she thought: I'm the nasty thing who is not my brother's keeper. Was he already captured by Guardia and taken away to prison? She shuddered, and it was all her fault they locked him behind bars and he was hungry and thirsty and the rats nibbled his toes. Miguelito must be scared: oh! she knew all about prison where there were no nice pictures or books, like the sea otter story he brought her, no cool drinks like remolacha (beet) to make the hot, boring afternoon pass quicker.

Look at her: she's a bad one, that Alma Nubia. She liked to call herself Nubia and put on airs when she was alone, but she couldn't even deliver a simple message Doñita got from the muchacho: that boy, already a man, whose face was like a crescent moon in August when the wheatfields in back of Faustina's swayed and rustled to a night breeze. Maybe the eagle's claws meant run away fast to Granada and avoid being taken. Ay! Her own brother and now he would never tickle her mercilessly: rough her up when he felt restless or read her nice stories. He would be in jail, and the idea stunned her so she didn't see the risk. Was it too late? Was there still time before they snatched him away?

During the day she heard, in her dreams, Miguel argue with Padre downstairs. Beyond that door there was fighting going on, with the devil in the middle: the devil oiled and tarred like Choncito for the yearly festival, the Tata Chombito. She heard heated words; and she had to go out and search for her brother because that was the only relief for the way she felt. Like a cat she slipped through the door into the corridor. The stairs creaked and seemed to tell on her so she swooped off her sandals in a fluid movement. They creaked! Padre might wake any minute from his sensitive sleep, not like Juan Ramón's loud gusts across the Calvario. Nubia took the stairs sitting gingerly, one by one, but they creaked. The Colegio was old.

In the front entry, in the dark, she worked with the big bolt until it opened. Poking her nose she heard shots maybe closer, she saw sparks over the low roofs of the square. Deeper in the barrio a cock crowed and glimpsed dawn in the sudden flashes, the pockmarks of light in the sky. There was a sudden uproar: the smoke of explosions fumed over the low homes. Where could she go? Where look for her brother in trouble?

Alma slid from the threshold of the Salesiano, like a swimmer into rough waters.

XIV

Late afternoons, Faustina moved through her garden and picked weeds from her plantains and few rows of tomatoes, toward a visit with Doñita. Oooh, here comes a comunista! thought Doñita as her neighbor, once a homegrown beauty, tall for a woman, emerged in the heat of the Calvario. She could have had any man, so she chose a humble one, Juan Ramón, who did housework unlike most machos, and only abandoned her one time to drink rum. Doñita's birthmark glowed scarlet when Faustina started to talk about sex: Doñita scandalized easily, though she craved gossip. Faustina's presence was like the sun burning mist off a cordillera.

—There's news of Alma.

—Ay! said Doñita, folding her hands: for two days she had been in a state.

—She was hurt. Chon Muñoz took her to the Colegio.

—She's alive.

—Overcome by teargas. Another, the boy Lorenzo of Pochotillo, got it worse.

—Alma is with Padre?

—See how the vampire sucks our blood for a few cordobas a quart?

Faustina erupted, laughing. Doñita frowned mightily since this vampire was her very own idea of a president. Didn't he pay the people who donated blood at his Plasmaferesis plant in Masaya?

—Look what is happening to us.

Through the barrio kids went house to house and raised money. They collected bits of tin and metal for the contact bombs. What a sight it was: Monimboseños in the streets in their traditional masks, more like a holiday if it wasn't for the horror. No sign of Guardia; but a red and black banner unfurled outside the church.

All Doñita could think of was Alma out there in the madness, lost, hurt, or worse.

—These bandidos, they'll get us all killed.

Yet Faustina was brimming with confidence since Macho Pedro had been driven from the barrio. How? With machetes rusted by the juice of a hundred harvests, with primitive pistols, rifles, the famous Masaya cannon that might break an eggshell if it ran over it.

Doñita heaved a big sigh. All she could say to the other's gush was:

—They should be ashamed, destroying property.

Her neighbor gave another peal of laughter.

—They burned down Salon Perla. What do you think of that?

For years Doñita Reyes had advocated just such an action. Salon Perla was a notorious whorehouse.

—It's for the authorities to do, not delinquents.

—Who do you think they found in there? A top Guardia officer came running out with Carmencita Verga's black lace panties round his neck.

—Dios primero!

Doñita caught her breath. Carmencita Verga was the most prodigious prostitute this side of Managua. Graduating classes went to her. She taught seminars up on Coyotepe, the Guardia fortress outside the city.

Faustina gave a cackle. She leaned forward, a finger to her lips.

—They say, you know—

—What?

—Anastasio Somoza likes to be tied to the bedpost with La Dinorah's garter.

—Madre mia!

—And then—

—Then what?

—She puts on his official Presidential Sash.

—Oh!

—In her high heels, and just the sash: naked, both of them.

Faustina pulled her blouse tight on her breasts.

—Ah!

—Bueno, she rose abruptly. I should go now, visitors.

—Wait! What happens next?

—No, you're already too excited.

—Tell me.

—Well, they make believe she's the Commander-in-Chief, and he's—

—He's what?

Faustina laughed merrily on her way through the door. But she called back in a low tone:

—A Sandinista!

XV

Dusk crept along the Calvario, reconnoitring, as the old woman rode out the hours in her wicker rocker. Through the brief early evening she sat on the front porch; she worried about her children and cursed Iván Giner for producing them. Why didn't Padre bring Alma to her? At least send word: was the girl in the hospital? A few times she rose shakily: go to the Colegio? She was a recluse who never ventured further than Chepe's store; besides, her ankles were so swollen she could hardly walk.

She didn't sleep. The morning brought news from a boy passing
by: the death of an old man she knew, Santiago Potosme, and of the
young poet Lorenzo from Pochotillo barrio. With this Doñita began
to lose hope for her daughter's safe return. But she thought quickly.
She gave the boy ten piasters to run to the Colegio; and he returned
saying Alma was no longer there. Nobody knew where she'd gone!

In early afternoon President Somoza came over the radio. Doñita, despite herself, imagined him in his birthday suit and tied to the bedpost,
being tickled with a feather. It seemed to deal her hopes a further blow.

—"With prudence and forbearance Government Forces have managed, so far, to avoid bloodshed. This despite the hostile actions of
outside agitators, subversives."

But she nodded to herself while Tacho addressed the nation. His calm
voice belied Faustina's slander, like a guarantee of Alma's safety. He said
in a stern yet confident tone, about the shelling of San Sebastien church:

—"This mission of inspection was requested by the priests."

The poor old woman tried not to think of Tacho Somoza pleading beneath the godless fleshpot, La Dinorah, who considered herself a latter-day Cleopatra. What was the bad thing she did to him,
which he dreaded and craved?

Later, Doñita's mood took a nosedive. More news arrived, as she
greeted passersby from her porch. Martial law had been declared in
Masaya. From hour to hour the situation was a slow fuse. Guardia reinforcements, elite EEBI units had arrived from the capital, and
Macho Pedro was planning a decisive counterattack for that night.
Also, something mysterious was in progress at Faustina's: a kid
went in with a wicker basket, which caused Doñita to stop rocking
and watch. The boy poked about the yucca patch with a stick: an
arms cache in Juan Ramón's garden? a box of homemade explosives?
Dios mio.

Last rays of sunlight shot over the low roofs of Monimbó, glinting
on leaves of an almond tree like a jewel. The shadows spread their
carpet on the parched ground. There was a scent of freshly cut jas-
mine, as evening took its positions through the beleaguered barrio.

XVI

The funeral cortege of Lorenzo Lopez moved toward Monimbó cemetery with Miguel Giner in the lead. At dusk a cock

crowed as the people went along, carrying the body of the teenage poet. They walked quietly down the unpaved lanes without a pause: an attack was impending as Macho Pedro's forces regrouped up on Coyotepe. Miguel led them the length of a dusty path bordered by nispero trees and thorny bromelias. He leaned to straighten the blue and white flag of Nicaragua draped on the boy's coffin. The march was greeted by a group digging trenches at key entry points into the barrio. Further on there were kids who smashed Milca and Fanta bottles; strewed the glass shards to hinder Guardia pursuit. They joined in, cavorting on the fringes with their wooden guns. Miguel gave a grim smile as old Carlita Garcia passed them by: she toted a frayed satchel full of something. Tortillas? Or contact bombs from Lazaro's pyrotechnical workshop? A number of men had rags to catch up the teargas canisters; while most carried lemon and salt in a wet handkerchief to suck against the fumes.

He urged the procession onward: up the hill toward Cementerio Central beside the Rinconadas. He looked back: the line had lengthened and beyond it, above the city, the long trails of smoke rose and dispersed on a red horizon. Salon Perla lay in ashes. Cine Guadalajara had been set on fire. The fighting had ignited La Estación, a strategic sector. Miguel gazed back at the panorama with its fiery streamers.

And then he saw, with a frown, little Alma on the outskirts of the spreading crowd. As in San Sebastien when he spoke from the altar: it was strange seeing her here. Had Doñita lost her mind sending Alma out in these hours? And why hadn't Padre transported her somewhere away from the Colegio, out of harm's way? Of all people she was least able to perform the simplest errand: you sent her for aspirin to Chepito's store on the Calvario and she came back with a few drops of cooking oil. She was *vaga*, propelled by her whims, dreaming her little dreams: as stable as a flock of swallows that skipped over the tall grass of savannahs to scare up a meal of insects.

Alma waved at him and smiled. Maybe she thought this was playtime?

—Hold the ropes, muchachos!

—Easy.

—Start the lowering?

The men, maneuvering Lorenzo's coffin, glanced at Miguel who paused amid the crowd of a few hundred.

—Wait. I'll give a eulogy.

More people poured across from the Rinconadas.

—Then hurry, compañero. We're exposed here.

XVII

Alma left the edge of this large gathering for her classmate who used to tease and poke her along the Colegio corridor. His insides had gushed in the dust, he was ready for lowering into the earth and she felt so sad, sad for Lorenzo, going to the place where God looks after all the dead people. Heaven was an orphanage run not by the cross Doñita but by God who must be kind, a friend of children. Surely you could feel right at home with la Juana, Miguelito's mama who died the same day he was born. Up there Maria became everybody's mother, and Maria hadn't made herself into a nervous wreck like Doñita from never setting foot outside the house. You could have a lot of fun: Lorenzo would poke her again, Juana would tell her the sad story about Don Justo and elopement and Las Salinas. Everything would be the way it was before.

—Someday I'll go too, thought Alma: so enthused by the idea of paradise she forgot the eagle's claws and the muchacho who came to Doñita's. She heard her brother delivering a speech over the open grave, but she didn't listen. —I can't wait to go, she thought; maybe if I pray hard . . .

But suddenly, just like it was inside church, she heard the roar and whirr of a helicopter beyond the treetops. This time the people understood at once and fanned out quickly; they tripped over gravestones as the huge chopper hovered closer. A few ran for cover behind a mausoleum. Others had guns and started shooting wildly at the sky. The Guardia dropped a grenade onto the panicked crowd, and then a great howl went up. It was stark terror as figures hurtled away and raced for the maze of the Rinconadas. Alma glanced up and saw a second helicopter coming; she felt stunned as it interrupted her wonderful daydream. At first the infectious panic swept her along, away from the grave.

For a moment Miguel used the bullhorn and tried to direct traffic. Then he took cover behind a gravestone; while on the far side Alma peered from a patch of tall grass. Only a few remained: those too badly wounded to move. One yelled for help but went unheard in the din of gunshots and swishing rotors. The two helicopters sidled in and opened fire on the headstones festooned with moss and mould. Lorenzo's coffin still wasn't lowered, poised by his grave in the upper cemetery.

Miguel hid out of sight behind one of the stones, while a Guardia door-gunner took potshots at Lorenzo's coffin ten meters away. The wood splintered, revealing the boy's bloated body dressed in a Sunday suit.

Then Alma remembered her message and nearly lost her mind with the sense of urgency. She imagined the terrifying things had come on purpose to arrest her brother. As always, it would be all her fault! She really was a bad one, as Doñita so often said during the lonesome day of staying at home, rocking nervously while she hoped for a visit from Faustina which would annoy her no end.

—Miguelit-i-i-i-to!

The shots, screams, groans sounded insane but a dread fear for her brother outweighed everything. So she stood up in full view of all, she cried out but her words went unnoticed in the exchange of gunfire.

She waded into the battle zone where wounded men and women lay squirming as the gravestones sparkled. She waved her spindly arms at the gunships like whales that could fly, that prodded their fore-heads in mid-air. But her voice was a gnat's; she felt puny and forlorn beneath the huge metallic force stomping, exploding from above.

—Get away! Get away from here!

Miguel stood up, like a cadaver restored to life. He gestured at her.

—The muchacho! The muchachito who came to Doñita!

Lost in the uproar she tried to tell him the whole story. Her words floated out like butterflies among the bullets which ricocheted. She screamed at him with a sense of relief since she had finally relayed her message.

—He wore a red and black neckerchief!

But one of the helicopters dipped down toward Miguel in a flurry of bullets. The return fire was all but silenced. Lorenzo's body had fallen halfway out of its coffin, his black suit smudged with dust and blood.

Miguel ran headlong, leapt like a dervish as he shouted:

—Over here, estúpidos! Try and catch me!

In seconds the helicopter had trapped him in a circle of machinegun fire, as Alma stood frozen fifty meters away. He tried to dart to one side, but the door-gunner was skillful and had him sighted and immobilized.

Down, down came the metal monster fanning the grass; it raised a whirlwind of gravel and dust. It whooshed and descended above the rows of tombs that chattered beneath the onslaught like teeth. Sud-

denly a rope ladder dropped forth alongside Miguel's head. Alma
watched in horror as a Guardia soldier climbed out, jiggled right and
left, and then jumped off. He popped his prisoner's skull with a hand
pistol; and a red blotch grew on Miguel's forehead.

—Stop that! she cried and ran forward. Stop that!

But the EEBI took him on one shoulder like a sack of corn and
back up the ladder, which zigzagged to and fro.

Alma ran about, flailed her arms, cried. Then she fell to one knee
gulping for breath. Her hands went limp by her side as the uncon-
scious body disappeared inside the fuselage.

And then she knew it was too late. She had caused the very thing
she was trying so hard to prevent.

XVIII

There was silence punctuated by groans. A soft breeze stirred the
sun-blanched grasses hiding one grave from the next. There was the
fiddle of a cicada, the call of some scavenger bird off beyond the treetops. The wounded groaned. From the city came sounds of combat,
rifle reports, the pop of explosives. Cautiously, first at one grave, then
another, faces reemerged. From all sides, the Indian features perched
on the gravestones to stare in silence. As if the dead had reawakened
in the thunder a moment before: here, there, they stared with the
transfigured gaze of their ancestors at the body, puffed up, riddled
now with bullets, of Lorenzo Lopez. His splintered coffin lay over-
turned by the open pit.

The hammock maker; the weaver of baskets from sisal hemp; the
pyrotechnic, Lazaro; the fashioner of wooden toys whose name was
Presencio; the mechanic Fasael, the shoemaker Ramiro:—all gazed in
silence, like ghosts outliving time. And then quietly, without ceremony, they moved forward to bury the first martyr of the February
uprising while others looked to the wounded.

XIX

In her house on the Calvario Doñita Reyes waited in a simmer of
panic for her daughter to come home. The first night had passed with
no sign of Alma or Miguel; though the latter was beyond hope by
now, after a childhood so filled with mischief and mishaps it made

her tired to remember. Miguel was an animal like his father, Iván Giner, but Alma was only a child and subject to a mother's, a foster mother's, authority. She hadn't been indoctrinated and spoiled by the subversives.

The creak of Doñita's rocker sounded like heartstrings, as she waited hour after hour for either of her two children to return. She stayed on her porch listening to the shots and havoc down in the Masaya streets. Another night passed sleeplessly for her, and then it was Sunday. Over the radio President Somoza announced a counter demonstration for those decent citizens who opposed violence and vandalism. Doñita approved of such a decision, but she would never have dreamed of going outside her house for any demonstration. Miguel, when he got fed up with her, used to call her some long word and shout:

—See a psychiatrist!

But his advice was hardly likely to change her ways. He was mad himself from all the books he read, his visions like a child in a fantasy world.

Later, that Sunday morning, she listened as the shots came closer, in the wheat field that bordered Faustina's property.

Suddenly she heard men's voices:

—Open up!

—Who's there?

—The Frente: let us in.

—Who?

—Viva Sandino!

—Viva—

Then more shots, deafening, just outside! Ay Dios! She crouched by her window, where sunlight poured through the casement. Please God, don't let them come over here. Please, not in my house . . . A group of barrio people had begun to arrive: they hurled taunts at a contingent of Guardia. Doñita listened to the commotion, the tension building until troops sprayed bullets randomly to protect their advance. Then a woman screamed her hysteria, tearing the air. Ah! How long since the last time Doñita risked a step off her small plot, intent on avoidance of a world given up to sin? And now life, the most brutal reality, now violence! It came like a flood tide toward her very own front porch.

Then, huddled by the window, she saw the crowd raise sticks and machetes, shout, gesture on the edge of the field behind Faustina's.

To her right a Guardia tank bucked over ruts of the Calle Calvario. A high voice, perhaps Choncito Muñoz called across:
—What about human rights?
A soldier barked:
—Macho Pedro's in charge here.
—Have pity! cried a peasant woman. Aren't you a mother's son?
Doñita knelt next to her window sill and peered into the glare toward her neighbor's. Ay, señor! The whole army with its arsenal was on hand, a tank on either side, the churning whirr of helicopters: dozens of Guardia Nacional converged around Faustina's patch of plantain.

XX

She watched as a Guardia went up and knocked on Faustina's door.
—Open! he shouted and pounded his gun barrel.
Doñita cried silently. The tears streaked her cheek where the birthmark looked on the verge of an explosion. She thought of Alma; she thought of her neighbors, where the bad thing had come to pay a visit. She raised herself, squinted out, sniffled. There was a cry from inside Faustina's:
—We're innocent!
Suddenly, the soldiers opened fire from close range.
There were screams of protest. Doñita ducked her head from the bleated agony, male and female, the pule of a few children.
Screams.

XXI

In a moment the rebel leaders, Camilo Ortega among them, lay perforated as irrigation sprinklers in the fields of Don Cornelio Ferrán's plantation.
There were others in the house: a family on their way back to Pacayo after buying rice and cooking oil at Chepito's store. It was their bad luck to seek a moment's refuge from the heat with Faustina, whom they knew, and not across the way.
Doñita watched in horror as a pregnant woman reeled forth bloodied and swore in the sunlight. Inside, they made people do

things. They ruined Faustina's husband, Juan Ramón. Later, two children were found in a back room with their hands cut off.

The soldiers raged and accused everyone of making contact bombs. They forced Faustina to go from room to room and list every item on a piece of paper. They made the survivors fetch dirt from her garden to strew on the pools of blood. And then they raped her, one and another: the collaborator Doña Faustina was raped by the Guardia Nacional. And then Juan Ramón, originally from Jinotepe, a day laborer and a father of four, took a bullet in the head as he lay semi-conscious, his eyes two slits, on the floor. It was done casually, as they left, marking a period to the orgy of death.

XXII

"Ferrán Plantation
Las Salinas

3 March 1978

Padre Antonio Velasquez
Colegio Salesiano
Masaya

Dear Padre Antonio:

Please receive my most cordial thanks. It is hard to avoid, during a lifetime, passing through troubled periods when cherished values are threatened with extinction. You, Padre, have exemplified your calling in word and in deed, during the lamentable events of these past two weeks.

Tacho, I know, is extraordinarily gratified by the demise of the criminal Camilo Ortega S. Fitting end to a most ignoble ambition. A potent insecticide must be applied to those pests of Ortega's breed, else the crop of democracy be blighted in our land. As for the recreant poet, Miguel Giner, we will put him in a cage where he may sing prettily. Ever ready to such tasks is a Macho Pedro.

You see: by cutting off the head the body falls. No further insurgency. Your concern with the schoolteacher, Asunción Muñoz, called Chon, is shared in higher circles. Also, the one whose pseudonym is Claudio, true name Hilario Sanchez, an Indian from León and a dangerous element. We have our eye on him and, of course, a few more.

Your contact, Morell, will let you know our intentions as these become applicable. Please believe that, as regards military excesses, I am not in favor. I do concede what the President puts forward: the need of a firm example. Our forces have been a target, you will recall, of the unholy «contact bomb».

One opposes violence. One submits to circumstances. The home of my secretary in Masaya, Velia Suazo: was it not arsoned? Yet it is my nature to abhor bloodshed.

Dear Padre: our nation is under attack by an international conspiracy whose center is Moscow. At stake are our sacred values, lives, loved ones, property we have striven a lifetime to acquire. Energetic measures are the order of the day. As in the past we rely on your faithful support; and believe fervently, as you do, in the supreme God who blesses our civilized way of life, our righteous cause.

In this respect please accept the enclosed check made out in the name of the institution you administer so capably.

Again, our warmest regards. Our nation has been purged of barbarism. Today, the banner of freedom is unfurled with pride over Masaya.

Yours truly,

Ferrán.”

PART THREE

I

In Tipitapa, in the prison, the fingers stretched like human feelers between the double grating. They prodded the place where painful emotions, of prisoners and their visitors, seemed to converge. Despite the exchanges a high, concerted chant could still be heard: the women, the wives and mothers who paraded their grief outside the prison gate. The guards on duty glanced around. They looked edgy, awaiting an order to end the visitation hour.

Miguel Giner beat his brow dully against the divider; as a tear, the first in a long time, streaked the grime of his unshaven cheek.

—Doñita, I'm sorry.

He clutched the wire with two hands; thudded his forehead on the screen.

—Stay back, said the guard, Robles.

The song of a hundred women, the angry chorus, seeped through the walls of the Carcel Modelo.

—Don't touch!

Miguel stared darkly at Doñita Reyes.

—Mama . . . When this is over, I'll bring my wife from Rivas. We'll live together, and take care of Almita.

It made Doñita nervous to see a macho weep. Her face lit up when he called her mama, and darkened, like a blustery sky, when he gave a sob. Since February he had been through Macho Pedro's hell, a week in Coyotepe; and then months of darkness, isolation, bouts of torture since his transfer here. Now he looked broken: as if his spirit were torn by the news of Juan Ramón.

She attempted a smile.

—Josefa is here. Out there with them.

—Oh.

He looked at her then, in such a way.

—I should have let her visit you.

—Never mind.

—She's the one you want to see. I couldn't help myself.

—I love you both.

—You're only allowed one visitor. I'm too selfish!

She lowered her gaze, and started to cry.

—No, you and I needed to be together this way.

—Did we?

She frowned. A tremor went over her features.

—But you have to be stronger. Keep up your spirits for Alma.

—I'll try.

—And remember, Doñita, what I said. No more visits, if it means filling out forms. They make up lists.

Now the tears flowed on her flabby cheeks as the fact sunk in: he had called her mama and said he loved her, which overrode all the rest. She wept for the boy she had brought up and admired, trying to smother him with love but he only laughed at her and abused her to defend himself from so much emotion. She stared across at him through glazed eyes.

—I can't help myself.

—I know, Mamita. When the war ends, when every house is filled with flowers and children playing happily, then we'll live together. If Iván is alive he will come home, and we'll all live in peace and tend a garden.

—Alright.

Abruptly the visiting hour ended. Robles banged his club on the metal grate and the fingers drew back.

—And please don't lose faith anymore. It dishonors Juan Ramón.

—Basta! barked the guard, Teniente Robles.

—I won't.

Miguel rose and said:

—Tell Josefa I love her, I kiss her—

—Time to go!

—What?

—And Chon Muñoz: tell Chon I—

—I can't hear you, son.

His last words were lost in the chorus of goodbyes. And then he disappeared: escorted away from the double grating and through a door.

Doñita stood up, shaky. But there was something almost girlish, a lilt in her bulky figure as she moved away. She had gotten what she came for. But she didn't realize until she was through the gate, and sounded out a woman about the questionnaires, that she forgot something. When, in the days following her foster son's arrest, she told Padre Velasquez about the muchacho and «the eagle's claws», the priest asked her to have Miguel clarify what it meant.

—How? Can you help me write him?

—No, go there.

—Coyotepe?

Padre smiled. It was too unlikely: Doñita trudging the steep and dangerous road up to Macho Pedro's stronghold.

—He's in Tipitapa. I'll make a call and arrange transportation. They'll let you in.

Sí, señor. The good Padre had asked her to be sure she cleared up the mystery of «the eagle's claws».

II

She forgot again, some weeks later, permitted inside the prison. Once more she upstaged Josefa; and, in the visitors room, she lied to him, and said his wife had returned to her life as village laundress in Las Salinas. Doñita Reyes knew it was a sin, but she couldn't help herself. The temptation to hear him call her mama was too great. Anyway, sinning didn't seem so bad when you did it yourself; and hadn't Josefa, who spent her days depressed, spoken of her return south to the small fieldworker community in the shadow of Ferrán's manor house? So it was only half a lie. And the form they obliged Doñita to complete was a brief one of no interest to anyone. There was a question on references: people to contact, in the event of this or that, so she penciled in the name of Chon Muñoz. She saw no need to mention this to Miguel. Rather, she entered the prison intent on relief from her anxiety over Alma, who acted more bizarre with each passing week. She told Miguel of Chon's help: how he would arrive, of a late afternoon, and talk to the poor girl, his former student at the Colegio . . .

Chon frowned at Faustina's place in a strange effect of sunlight and shadow. A speckled tiger-beetle scampered from man's passage along the stone fence. Plantains grew in an untended patch, and a tree rat scurried, fur ripply, amid a clump of piñuelas further in. A few stunted pines; a cypress motionless in the heat; an outhouse of gray planks, in back, tilted in the weeds which grew unchallenged. Faustina's had an air of death in life; but Chon paused to look at a scarlet and yellow orchid that flared between chinks of the low fence. All the loquatious life of the place had turned to silence and a flaming flower.

Across the way he knocked.

—Anyone home? said Choncito, ironic.

The paranoid Doñita couldn't open her front door without a view of things she had spent her life trying to avoid. She didn't go into Masaya meeting and greeting; but sat in here with her work. She eked out a meager living as a seamstress; and townspeople sent her jobs since she had skill with a needle: she made fancy brocade, revamped antique lace.

—Hola, she said, in her whiskered voice.

—Hola, how's the muchacha?

He stepped over the threshold and filled the small dark room. She knew his reputation as a troublemaker, but he was Miguel's best friend since childhood. He read Alma's behavior better than anyone, besides Padre, since she adored him. Chon sympathized with the crabbed spinster, and didn't tease her, like Miguel.

—Ay, that girl is acting up. I called back awhile ago: you come here! Minutes pass, maybe ten. Then she bursts in, jumps around my chair. Sticks out her tongue!

—It doesn't help the way you both sit in here and sulk.

—I know she's upset with me, but why? I tried to grab her and give her a good whack. But she's too fast: she got away and I fell off my rocker.

—Hm, said Chon, with a solemn nod. How was your visit to Tipitapa? Did they let you inside?

—Oh . . . , Doñita cast a guilty glance at her visitor. Padre Velasquez is helping us.

—Padre?

—He says monthly visits should be possible, if Miguel behaves.

The schoolteacher looked at her sternly for a moment.

—Hm.

—The boy stirs people up with his ideas. No doubt he means well, but what's the result? He only gets in trouble.

Chon glimpsed past Doñita toward the girl's cubbyhole in back. Nodding, he moved quietly past the old woman in the rocker.

III

There were nights when Almita woke up in tears after she pleaded in a dream for something she couldn't name or explain. Mornings she rose from bed feeling better and asked to go look for her little friends along the Calvario; but the lighter mood didn't last long. She seemed to wilt with the intense heat, in a same depression as she languished through siesta, and grew nervous at nightfall. This was hard on Doñita. Before February the girl tugged constantly on her apron; chirped like a caged bird to fly away outside. Then she was spirited and stubborn, like her brother; and the daily give-and-take enlivened Doñita Reyes in her loneliness, in her obsessions. For years the poor woman's thoughts had been stalked by disaster, a poignant unease, a fear of life on the planet. Miguel and Alma were bright and filled with life, before the uprising. Now it darkened Doñita's mood when the girl no longer resisted her overprotection, her compulsive control: when Almita gave up a struggle which her brother had won, two years before, by trapsing off to Managua where he joined a circus.

—Muchacha! she bawled. I've got toothache, I need my aspirin from Chepe's, oh-oh-oh!

Silence. Doñita wrapped her flaccid jaw in a handkerchief, knotted the ends and gave a groan. Ay! It was bad if she didn't even answer, not a sound.

—Do you hear me?

What could she be thinking about, all alone in there, hour after hour? Entire days by herself with hardly a murmur. She was like a little Doñita: nearly a week since she went out to play.

—Do you?

Silence. Nothing, for a full minute . . .

Then an eruption, right by her ear:

—Hijuelagranputa!!

Doñita jumped a foot from her rocker. That bad Miguel! Before going away he had trained the macaw to say curse words. Back then he would sit with a thick book beneath the tigüilote tree, through

the afternoon, and each time the gaudy thing uttered some horror
he would hand up a peanut.

IV

One afternoon Chon Muñoz dropped by with a copy of La Prensa,
the opposition newspaper in those days. The teacher looked weary.
His kind mestizo features, stolid, sly like the Monimboseños, seemed
to ooze fatigue.

—Buenos dias.

—Coffee? she asked.

A dog barked and sent its yawp along the Calvario as Chon handed
her the paper. She knew that mongrel, its bark like mangy flesh, but
she caught her breath reading Miguel's name across the literary page.
More blasphemy? "Portrait of God in a Beret" was the name of
Miguel's new poem about how Jesus ate monkey, and brambles
dripped blood instead of dew . . . when the Guardia passed by on patrol. It made her think of Iván Giner and the pagan life of the mountain guerrillas. She stared glumly at her visitor.

—Listen, he said. We need a messenger: someone like Alma, a girl
who's alert.

—You mean for the Frente?

—Bueno, Chon frowned. Not directly, and only because it might
help her snap out of—

—No, señor!—The old woman rocked at full speed, her chair mo-
torized with sighs, groans and comunistas. —She may be crazy but
she's no delinquent.

The teacher leaned and put his arm round her shoulder. He shook
her gently and said:

—What we're doing is . . . necessary.

—Jesus in a beret.

—With a star! Compañera, if we don't help ourselves, who will?

—Hmph.

—Na, Mamita. You know Miguel doesn't want the two of you to
mope. I'll go in and talk to her.

—Madre Maria, said Doñita, and glanced sidelong at the poem. It
wasn't Jesus who wore a star on his beret, it was Che Guevara who
did that: an atheist, a son of presumption, as Padre Velasquez called
such men. Then she cast a glimpse across the way. Not a peep for days

from Doña Faustina. Well, her loud mouth had brought down the wrath of God and the Guardia Nacional. Now all she could do was hide her wounds, and live her life in grief.

Doñita sighed deeply as Chon sipped his coffee.

—I'll go in and talk to Alma, he said.

—Are you a psychiatrist?

—I studied some psychology, but that isn't the main thing.

She nodded, then gave a start:

—Ay, Dios! I'm sitting here with a comunista, in my own house.

But if she didn't understand Choncito it wasn't because of politics and the Frente. There was something different about him, a mystery he carried around. You never knew what he was feeling . . . Because he was a teacher, an intellectual? Padre Velasquez was more a scholar than Chon, yet she didn't sense a distance in Padre's presence. No; the older man had fine manners, a smooth confessional tone: he knew how to ingratiate himself with the gentle sex. Chon Muñoz had a family: a wife named Filomena, several sons. But Chon seemed to keep his little secret all to himself; he brooded even while engaged in conversation. You could read Miguel's mind even if you didn't understand his words: he wore strong emotions in his dark luminous eyes. But Choncito was different. She remembered how the two friends had not been so inseparable in months prior to her son's departure for Managua. Maybe they hadn't seen quite as eye to eye as when they were boys busy with adventures, and the whole barrio loved and admired them? For a moment Doñita stopped rocking. She sat and thought: the wan look on his face sometimes, like someone out of place, a man unfulfilled. His sad, sensitive smile unlike the other machos, with a touch of the feminine in his steps, in a gesture. Doñita mused. She tried to pin down the mystery of Chon Muñoz.

V

In the midday heat the barrio grew placid. In the treetops the cicadas geared down with intervals of silence. On the branch of a cotton tree a broad throated iguana soaked up heat, its eyes two liquid globes. A motmot bird perched in a dusty acacia. Because of the fighting in February, its aftermath of putrefaction, there were chromelined cockroaches. Colonies of leaf-cutting ants ventured down new paths; they caravanned through the dwellings of the Calvario. The tangled lianas and other varieties of epiphytes had a stranglehold on the sunlight. And vultures flew in circles, coasting on shredded wings above the Lagoon.

At siesta a breeze sniffed the wildflowers about Doñita's house. A bottlefly shimmied on a wall. Little else stirred in the torrid heat. But in the low choza there were quiet voices with pauses. Choncito coaxed Alma, ever so gently, to remember. What happened that day in February, at the church? at the cemetery? He wanted her to tell him, and it felt worse, almost, than going through the events again. This was the third visit since they started to talk. At first he asked her simple things.

—How old are you, Alma?

—Twelve.

Her voice sounded strange.

—Where do you live?

—You know, here.

She hung her head. In those days of pain she had difficulty speaking even to Doñita. But Chon was so kind, like the father she always imagined. An answer to his questions was like drawing water at the well. So he made them easy at first.

—Are there horses in Masaya?

—Some. I saw a tick.

—Did you?

—It got on Doñita's leg, and she yelled, and I pinched it off.

—Do you like songs?

—When the men play mariachi at the market. Lorenzo had a guitar . . .

—And ice cream?

Her eyes lit up and faded.

—Yes, she said, very low.

—What flavor?

She did like it, a lot, all flavors. The few times she was able to have any. At Chepe's store they didn't have ice cream: there was no icebox, no electricity. Once, Miguelito ran all the way from San Sebastien with a strawberry cone, but it melted, stuck on his hands. Then he made her tickle his feet while he lay reading, reading. Just

now she felt sick: did Chon trick her? The thought of strawberry and
her brother only made things worse.

—I'll bring you some, okay?

Silence.

A lengthy, ruminant silence. In her stomach and chest there was a
mean feeling. She stared at her teacher, and his face seemed to distort. He didn't look so kind then. She glanced down quickly.

VI

Next afternoon he brought her a nice book with pictures: about a
boggy pond surrounded by savannah where a bunch of birds, fish
and small animals, even plants and trees went around acting like
grownups. Another afternoon he brought her a picture of Miguel
dressed up like a clown, clipped from a newspaper when he was in the
circus. Smiling, so handsome and intelligent he could get away with
anything. Then she thought of February, how they reeled him like a
fish into the helicopter, and it made her want to cry. Oh, she knew
about Macho Pedro because the boys at school talked about him: a
mean man who enjoyed hurting others, and now he would beat up
her brother. Day after day she lay in her little bed and the whole
thing, Macho Pedro, torture, mouldy prison food with cockroaches,
hurt her too.

Suddenly Chon said:

—Who put Miguel in prison?

—What?

His voice sounded brutal. She didn't want to look at him.

—Whose fault was it?

She worked her lips, unable to speak. Her face had a twitch.

—Whose, Alma?

This was his third visit. He had slipped away from his rounds, the
teeming activity under a calm surface. In the second session he
probed and sought a way to talk about February. Now he plunged in.

—Who caused the arrest?

Her throat felt blocked. The night before she awoke from a nightmare. Doñita had to sit with her.

—I did, she murmured, her features contorted.

—How?

Her lips tried to form an answer.

—Because . . . I didn't tell him.

—Tell him what?

—The eagle's claws, like the boy said.

—What boy?

—The boy who told Doñita, that morning.

—What morning?

Chon asked her rapid questions, and her breathing quickened. Like the Americano Infantíl when it came to Masaya each spring and the children, watching trapeze artists tumble and somersault high overhead, gasped.

—The day Padre . . . spoke in San Sebastien and he told the people be calm, God doesn't like it.

—The day Lorenzo . . . ?

—Yes, she said, low.

—Was that your fault?

She bowed, sort of rocked her head.

—N-no.

—And then Miguel was arrested.

—Yes.

—When, the same day?

—No, later.

—Were you there? said Chon.

—When?

—When he was taken.

—Yes!

—Where?

—In the cemetery.

—Hm. Was it only him, or did they catch others?

—Only him.

—And other times?

—They took Lorenzo. And at Doña Faustina's.

—Was there a message for the other muchachos? Did you have to warn them too?

—No, said Alma, thoughtful. Only Miguel.

Her head went a notch lower. Her lips quivered.

—Was it your fault for not telling them?

—No. Was it?

—If the helicopters hadn't come, and there was no attack, you would have told your brother, *correcto*?

—Yes.

—You would have given him the message?

—Yes.

—But once the uprising started you would have had to tell them all, Lorenzo and the others? Why just Miguel?

—I don't know.

—And even if you did that,—Chon thought a moment,—say you told the muchachos to run away to Granada, run from the fighting. And so a few, maybe Miguel, were left all alone. Would that be good?

—I don't think so.

—Why?

—Because they have to stay and fight him.

—Fight who?

—Macho Pedro.

—Why?

Alma sat wide-eyed on the edge of her bed. She blinked, breathing in little gulps.

—He hurts us, he laughs with his teeth. He spits!

—How does he hurt us?

—Children sick, no food sometimes!

—What else?

—They come—

—Who does?

She gave a big sigh, a sob. Tears burst in her eyes.

—The Guardia.

—And do what?

—Arrest people, shoot!

Silence. Chon stared in her eyes.

—Who arrests?

—*They* do, soldiers.

—Who did they arrest?

Alma paused a moment.

—Him!

—Who? Name him.

—Miguel, my brother.

—Why? Did he do something bad?

—He told the truth, he made a speech.

—Is that a crime, telling the truth?

—No.

Chon waited an instant.

—Then, Alma, please tell me this. Whose fault was it when Miguelito was arrested?

Now she sat poised, alert, on the edge of her bed. She seemed to face an approaching enemy; though in her lap she held the children's book which he brought her plus a doll with faded hair, a bit of rag on an ice-cream stick, Consuelo. She whispered:

—Theirs.

—Name them for me.

—Macho Pedro, Somoza puta, gringos!

She blurted it out and swallowed for breath. Her skinny breast shook.

Chon Muñoz held off a moment; nodded in silence. Then he grinned warmly. He smiled approval at her, and Almita thought: my father Iván. Chon rose from his chair and leaned to give her a hug.

—You have courage.

She murmured:

—Don't tell Doñita.

He stayed a few minutes to talk about a book he had seen in a shop on Avenida Central: not about a sea otter, but a long-horned beetle with a friendly face, who had adventures. Before he left they also discussed the various flavors of ice cream and how they would go for some soon, to La Estación.

The past couple days she had experienced angry spells in front of Doñita. But now she felt relieved, awfully relieved, like playing with Consuelo, or climbing out the window.

—Hola, estúpidos! cried the macaw from its perch in the tigüilote tree.

They heard Doñita swear back at it, and silence as she crossed herself.

VII

Chon was a stocky man with broad shoulders, a pensive air beneath the stolid, stubbly grin. His gait was determined, his gaze impassive as an Indian from Nandaime where his ancestors had lived by their hands, carpenters, shoemakers, among the best. Barrio folk didn't get so close to Choncito, but they respected and liked him, and their children at the Colegio loved him. Unlike Miguel he had tact: he left his militancy behind when he walked the Calle Calvario for a visit with the nervous seamstress, whose foster daughter was getting along better.

—Keep your spirits up, Doñita. Otherwise, you know, it's selfish.

A child whimpered in a nearby hut. A dog barked as the barrio came alive toward suppertime.

—Don't worry about us, she said.

Her chair creaked; it plodded nowhere. The mongrel yapped and competed with the thin bawl of the child.

—There might be a pension for you.

—Me?

—Because of Miguel's arrest: you being his mother.

—Pension from who?

She stopped rocking.

—The Frente.

—You mean comunistas.

She started to rock again, accelerating.

—Not a lot, but it would help.

—Gracias, no atheist money.

Chon smiled and shook his head. He had brought a newspaper with two more of Miguel's poems. These were smuggled out from prison to La Prensa literary page: proof the controversial poet was still alive and well enough to set his mind on writing. Doñita's gaze fell on bold headlines:

PARLIAMENT HELD HOSTAGE AS
NATIONAL PALACE RAIDED
MONIMBOSENOS SAID TO PARTICIPATE IN
FRENTE ACTION AS PROTEST SPREADS

—Dios primero, she mumbled, and crossed herself.

—Fuego! cried the macaw from its limb.

Chon backed into the sunlight and said:

—Think about Alma becoming a messenger.

—Shh! Not so loud: one subversive is plenty in this house.

She pointed a finger at the tigüilote tree.

VIII

In Monimbó, in Paises Bajos and Magdalena, the days and nights seemed to grow attentive beneath the sounds of men puttering in patios, kids squeezing in a moment of play before bedtime. The wild grasses, color of grasshopper sputum, swished slowly in the breeze beneath a cargo of insects. Cicadas screeched, dogs barked, birds chirped as always, but there was a new feeling in the air. A second revolt was on the way. The Mercado Central closed early with a kind of premonition.

Chon Muñoz hardly saw his family from day to day: so urgent were preparations for the events in store. As husband, father, teacher of children, he impressed everyone as a soft-spoken type. Yet he organized demonstrations. He spoke at street corner rallies, at indoor meetings. His personality was always of a softer cast as he played second fiddle to Miguel Giner who impressed people, provoked them and yet got his way. Chon worked overtime for a slightest advance; he had pulled himself up, thanks in good part to Padre Velasquez, from the plight of his artisan parents to become an educated man. It pained him to come in conflict with the Colegio director, his mentor and source of support while earning, with great difficulty, his degree and teacher's credentials. Chon sensed a hardness in the professional revolutionary called Claudio, who had no ties in Masaya and based his actions strictly on the situation with its demands. Claudio never appeared to tire or slacken the pace. Vanguard don't get tired. Claudio didn't seem subject to frustration, fatigue, momentary depression like a normal person.

But if Chon Muñoz felt inadequate, dwarfed when he thought of what was coming, then the reason, the cause of this anxiety lay elsewhere. Often he felt exhausted morally and physically; often he wondered, after a few hours of troubled sleep, how he would face another day. Masaya must be ready when its fatal hour came: when a general strike was called and the people summoned to the streets for a terrible test of force. The idea that violence would engulf the community again, his family, loved ones, friends, caused intense mental pain. But this too would have been surmountable if an awful secret hadn't tinged his experience, and his hope.

For others he emerged as a leader, a comandante; though it seemed to contrast with the quiet humanism of his style. At daybreak his mind roamed freely; and then an anguish worse than Somocistas paid a call on the intimacy of his dwelling. Then his life seemed unrealizable,—a prey to his secret like ripe fruit to a devourer worm. With a bitterness he thought of his death and doubted the possibility of survival. At dawn he revelled in self-pity since in these moments of inner communion, the loving Filomena, asleep beside him, seemed far, far away. How could she understand?

And yet, quietly, steadily, he went about putting things in place. By the side of Claudio, Ulises Tapia, Marta Navarro, he prepared the compañeros for the upcoming confrontation, and the real day.

IX

—Ready to do a job?

—Very ready.

Chon ushered Bulu into the safe house. Bulu's eyes almost popped out when he saw the quantity of rifles and submachineguns leaned against a wall. Hombre! Just arrived in stock. In peacetime a cab-driver, now he stood enraptured. But Choncito didn't look so good for some reason. No: he looked like he just put his nicest pair of boots in a cow pie.

—Everything fine, brother?

—Here's your gun, said Chon, looking away.

—Better give me a Garand, said Bulito. It's prettier.

They started cleaning the guns. Ulises and Marta were on hand, leaders. Bulu worked in a trance, dismantling, oiling, side by side with them. Chon Muñoz knew the combat order hung on a thread.

—Ready, muchachos? said Ulises. Let's do it for Lorenzo Lopez.

—Who knows the Institute? said Chon.

Bulu knew the Institute. His grandfather worked there as a sweeper. Bulu knew the Institute inside out, so he said:

—I know the Institute.

That morning a boy's body had been found along Ticuantepe Highway. It bore marks of torture. Now Masaya in the silence, in the vertical sunlight, waited through a tense siesta.

Later, they went out. They deployed combat units.

One group went to the highway. Another moved toward the Guardia outpost on Los Coquitos, renamed Lomas de Sandino since February. They took positions. A third had the task of opposing tank entry into the barrio: it formed two columns, stationed at the Colegio and also Avenida Real.

Chon went here, there, indefatiguable.

Bulu wore a white shirt with «M–A», the initials of his baseball team. But he took it off, preferring to fight without a shirt.

—It's prettier.

Choncito said to Bulu:

—Bulu, you're in charge of the zone. Get the people moving. Let them make barricades.

So Bulu rounded up kids, all the *chavalitos,* which was easy. He got a small army of them together, and started.

—Compañeros! he shouted at those barefoot kids. We've got to move! Uh. We've got to pile up Somoza's paving stones, and build trenches. It's time to finish off these Guardia dogs. Pues, vamonos. This is the insurrection, compañeros!

Bulito's speech. Before he could even smack his lips after that oration worthy of Caesar, all the barrio children were on their way. They made a big pile of junk and stones, and Bulu mused: compañero, what a moving sight. He noticed old Carlita among the crowd, and she cried out:

—Here come the muchachos. Here comes the Frente, aren't they handsome? Come on, my sons, come on!

But what was going on with Choncito? thought Bulu. And why the big sourpuss when Miguel Giner's name was spoken? Didn't he like him? Bulu used to see the two of them walk arm in arm through the barrio like they owned it, and he felt a surge of admiration.

Now everybody stood cheering the fighters. Bulu felt like a famous statesman, right on the spot. Many wore San Jerónimo masks, but not him, not Bulu.

The people shouted slogans emotionally.

X

Across Masaya a tremor shook the low adobe structures. Barrelling detonations of the long Guardia guns, a 50 mm. positioned before the Magdalena. Bells chiming, shouts, a flurry of contact bombs from a strategic street. And women's screams interspersed, like sirens. From San Sebastien the clamor carried the length of Calle Calvario, out to Doñita's house, where the booming roar, the frenzied whistle of combat burst in the windows of the recluse.

Alma had spent her day in her room, fretting about Miguel. She daydreamed of her father, Iván Giner. How many times the lonely Doñita had told her the story of Juana's elopement and embroidered the few known details until it seemed she had been there: herself dying in childbirth so Miguel might live. The tale of passion had filled Alma's mind with thoughts of death and all sorts of curious notions. She wondered who her own physical mother had been, but she knew better than to mention that to Doñita, after one or two attempts. It hurt the poor woman, Alma knew, who all her life had wanted more than anything to be a real mother, and felt sad and deprived. But the most painful was to remember the cemetery, and how they hit Miguel on the head and took him away to a bad prison: as if the bright plumaged macaw had its wings clipped and couldn't squawk and cut up anymore, away from the air, locked in a cage. What were they doing to her brother in prison? Could they clip his wings?

When the fighting erupted she sat up in bed and listened closely, alert. She thought of Chon Muñoz asking if she would like to be a messenger. Then it seemed impossible; but Choncito knew the secret of making her feel better, unlike Doñita who always wondered if she was «normal» or not, and said she should stay inside. Chon looked sad too. Why? Why was life so sad? Sometimes she went about the house doing her little chores. On good days she even attended school, when Padre opened the Colegio; and then he kept her afterward and asked her some funny questions. Too bad Padre didn't make her feel better like Choncito did: maybe he stayed alone too much, when he worked on Colegio accounts.

But then, during the anxious weeks of July and August, she rarely went to school. She lapsed into silence again and became withdrawn, staying in her room. It felt like she was suffering. Once, when Carlita came by and said four students and a worker had been machinegunned during a protest in Carazo, Alma wondered why everything on earth was all her fault, and too sad to endure. Of course, Chon had told her not to grieve all day in her little room. But such thoughts still hurt her, a lot.

XI

Alma emerged. She left her room and cast a glance out the front window at Faustina's, whose house seemed to huddle and play possum among the overhanging chagüite, plantains. The clapboard trembled with the impact from San Sebastien. The macaw had left its perch: no more curse words and nuts cracked fastidiously in its bill.

Doñita Reyes sat in her rocker: a somber mass, like an iceberg at twilight in Alma's storybook about a sea otter. Cre-e-eak . . . , said the rocker. Psst-blam! a terrific explosion in the distance. Squ-e-eak . . . , you see? you see the results? Doñita's rocking chair always agreed with her mood. The girl stood at the window silently. Then she turned, looking strange, her eyes wide, and announced:

—I'm going to help Chon now.

Doñita lowered her head, getting up steam.

—Do what?

—He needs me. Miguel does.

Cre-e-eak! . . .

—You'll do no such thing.

The minutes passed. Across the way a plank fell, the restless spirit of Juan Ramón.

Detonations, a mile distant. Sounds of fierce fighting.

—What would Iván Giner think, if I let you go out there?

Alma paused.

—He would think: don't wear your school clothes.

Doñita stopped rocking. She bowed her head as if bludgeoned, and there were tears in her eyes. The tears ran along the birthmark that covered half her cheek. Now a long, silent struggle was reaching an end. Miguel had wrested his freedom at about this age: at thirteen he would hardly obey her. He was the pride of the barrio, and she his menial servant, his slave. So she had been from the start, if truth were told.

—I'm going.

—No, muchacha.

But suddenly, unlike any time since February, the girl came alive, herself again. She moved about grabbing up a few things. —Sandals, she murmured. Doñita didn't answer. —In your room, chica. She answered herself and darted back there. Miguelito seemed present in those moments; he ordered her about with a snap of the fingers, he got her ready.

Doñita, defeated, sat weeping like a faucet.

—If I was faster on my feet I'd stop you. Ay, your poor . . .

Poor who? Alma danced about. Poor mother? Blushing, a smile burst over her features. She leaned over Doñita and hugged her neck.

—You're my mother.

She kissed her cheek quickly, not like Faustina who used to give gueyser hugs to the children. Just the kind Alma could never stand; but she submitted, quietly, her skinny arms dangled.

Explosions came in waves across the city. Doñita moaned.

Alma said:

—Miguel is in prison. Chon is out there with them, in the fight. Mamita, I'm going.

—You're only a child.

—I can do things, too.

—Your whole life is ahead of you.

—What life, if my brother is in jail?

Ay! Doñita gave her foster daughter a tragic look, and hung her head. Alma looked nimble, ready to move.

—Please try to come back.

—I'll come tonight and tell you.

The bombs, *boom! boom!,* the swooshing rockets slammed into the barrios with a crunch and cascade of debris. The girl jumped from Doñita's low door, askew on its hinges; she ran out into the stark sunset that flooded Calle Calvario through the trees. Sí, señor! In those minutes hell surged upward into the open air. She thought of poor Juan Ramón, she would never see him again. She thought of devils flinging sinners on their pitchforks. She thought of Macho Pedro torturing her brother up in Coyotepe: poor Miguel, who was spoiled!

Behind her, Doñita Reyes took a last look at Alma who trotted off as she had in February: when they tried to relay the message about eagle's claws, and the consequences were not long in coming.

—Come home soon! she called, but her voice broke.

XII

The whole barrio was in motion. Women cried out and gestured from their doorways. Boys ran, jumped between the lots; they carried wooden sticks instead of guns. On all sides the shots and contact bombs seemed to pierce her eardrums. Everywhere there were cries, orders shouted amid a general confusion; howling dogs; flashes of light in the growing darkness, as smoke rose up to obscure a first twinkle of stars.

Down the back alleys and garden paths of Monimbó the men moved stealthily. A neighbor's veranda or patch of plantain had become a strategic crossing, as they moved forward and kept low, guns and bombs in hand. They went toward a confrontation with fresh detachments of Guardia. The point of convergence was the GN outpost on Lomas de Sandino, called the Comandito, where the people once petitioned President Somoza for a marketplace. It was located across from Cailagua Furniture.

A few boys sped by. Alma ran too: she was caught up with the rest as a stiff wind whooshed toward the Lomas. But she paused and looked around, she glanced back and forth with wide eyes. A woman cried,—This way, muchacha! To the Comandito!—Was that one afraid? Alma scurried like everyone else toward the battle site. There was a dizziness and her feet touched the ground far below as she ran along. A wind like a hurricane pushed them onward. She needed to find Choncito: he would give her a message, an errand . . . Miguel would be proud.

She arrived at Cuatro Esquinas on the south side of the Comandito. Men dashed out profiled in the flickering light as they hurled contact bombs at the Guardia outpost. The police couldn't defend that side. She tugged someone's sleeve:

—Where's Chon?

—The maestro? Over there, inside Santana's.

Alma looked both ways and up at the sky before she sprinted to the cantina run by a man named Santana. Inside, she found Chon: he directed operations amid the confusion. Ulises and Marta had taken two units to the Guardia garrison in Parque Central; but here, in Monimbó, the schoolteacher stayed in charge. In the flashing darkness he stood surrounded by Monimboseños and men from other barrios, with new recruits every minute.

Suddenly, a BECAT zoomed into the sector. Tipped on two wheels: a half dozen men fired furiously into the shadows. The Guardia reacted at being denied access to their mates trapped inside the Comandito. On the corner diagonally across from Santana's a few soldiers knelt shooting behind a barrier of paving stones; they hindered movement on that side. In a hail of shots and contact bombs the jeep careened and crashed against a stone wall. Fighters pounced forward. There was a series of flashes with more shouts and groans.

—We need a mortar, said Chon Muñoz. The command post appeared impregnable, and combatants had been hit by return fire. Chon stared out the window of the Cantina. Alma, he said, calmly. Run to Lazaro's: tell him we need dynamite.

A boy Alma's age lunged inside. She knew him from the Colegio: such an idiot there, she never expected to find him here. He announced in triumph:

—I killed a Guardia in that BECAT. I dropped a bomb from a tree. Look!

He held up a polished Garand, like a trophy.

Arms were few in number compared to fighters. They had to be liberated. Chon frowned at the boy.

—Were you in one of the schools?

—Bueno . . . , he hesitated and cast a sidelong glance, afraid the gun would be taken away.

Chon said:

—You'll need to be shown.

Alma paused a moment but then slipped out the door toward Lazaro's with her first message.

XIII

Beyond the tall coconut palms there was a smear of purple. Stars peeped behind the fumes, as trails of smoke hung like funnels over Masaya. In the tumultuous streets the mood turned to anguish: the decisive attack drew near. Insects swarmed on the fading headlights of a stalled car. Gunpowder and burnt odors mingled with the dewy sweetness of gardens.

Chon Muñoz stared out the cantina window and waited. Across the street a dozen Guardia sweated out the minutes, poised over submachineguns in the chink of a window. They had stopped saturating the square: their ammunition must not be unlimited.

A messenger arrived:

—Central barracks still resisting. Can't you send arms?

—Resistance here too, compa.

The plan was thirty minutes: overrun the Comandito, send captured arms to Parque Central. But a half hour was passed. Alma hadn't returned and still no dynamite. By waiting out the Guardia some lives might be saved here and yet lost at the more critical fighting round the main garrison. For Chon it became a torture, weighing the factors: in the heat of action he felt relief, but this indecision . . . The messenger insisted:

—Ulises Tapia needs to know.

—Wait a few more minutes.

If he sent in his armed fighters without dynamite, it would mean a bloodbath of Monimboseños. Alma, he thought, dreading every sort of mishap: muchacha, a simple message, safe sector, what is keeping you?

—We're using up our supplies, said the envoy. They have a tank which limits mobility.

—A bit longer. I'll send Ulises his answer.

More people arrived. They came forth in brigades; they appeared on the threshold of battle after decades in the passive shadows of their hovels. Women brought pots of coffee, tortillas, rice and beans for the fighters. Muchachos turned up with .22 rifles, assorted light arms, antiquated pistols. After all the drunken Sundays, the endless succession of workdays for a few cordobas, with rising debt at Chepe's and the other shops; after how many family scuffles, hurting words and blows and shame the morning after, a lot of bruised women: now here they were reporting to Muñoz for orders inside Santana's. All in a rush to have it out at last; and yet the comandante with a hesitant look had to tell them: wait a little longer.

Alma skipped pertly through the low door and announced:

—Here comes Lazaro.

In an instant Chon's weariness seemed to vanish. He began to prepare the decisive attack. Lazaro arrived with two helpers from his workshop. He explained a few things, and then the first wave of fighters stood set to move out with explosives. For a moment the fighting lulled except random shots. The Guardia fired at its own fear from what no longer was a superabundance of ammunition.

—Free homeland! yelled one bearing dynamite.

Two others answered:

—Or death!

Alma hung off in one corner. She stared at them with the soft brown eyes of a foal. Free homeland, she mumbled to herself, thinking of Miguel, or death.

XIV

The night erupted in bright flashes, guttural screams amid the explosions. The impact slapped Alma on the cheek where she stood at the window. Her eyes glittered alertly by the popping light of contact bombs, the desperation fire, like sparklers, from Guardia submachineguns. A second crescendo of dynamite interrupted the flow of the attack. Return fire was more intense, a last effort to parry the wave on wave of insurgents joining the assault. The battle lasted twenty minutes before a high voice rose out of the clamor:

—Viva el Frente!

The dust was settling, and the blood was flowing. Inside the Comandito bodies lay tossed along the crumbled walls. Alma saw severed limbs. She watched as a spotlight touched the form of a soldier set into the wall by the blast. It seemed Lazaro knew his business, like the artisans who wove hammocks fit for the angels, and wickerwork that would last forever. A dead Guardia stared up through the torn roof—his arms flung wildly, he implored heaven. Was this how they treated Miguel? Would his jailors be very, very angry when they learned what had happened?

A mild shoemaker named Ramiro (Alma had never heard him raise his voice) kicked a wounded Somocista and insulted him. Others lay grovelling among the debris, but Chon ordered:

—No vengeance!

Monimboseños gave whoops of joy and chanted slogans while their enemy bled, dribbled saliva and blood in the dust, uttered low animal sounds, vomited. Alma stared at the scene of carnage while Chon directed traffic and tried to control the recuperation of weapons. All the while Alma wondered: what would Doñita think of this? What if she saw these dead people, and pools of blood, and men acting violent? Somehow this was the unspeakable thing, the true horror, what Doñita Reyes would think. Alma made the mistake of rubbing her eyes, which began to burn.

Chon Muñoz dispatched members of the Rufo Marín combat unit to Parque Central.

—Brothers! cried someone. It's a shame to see human beings lying in a pile.

—Did they love us?

There were Brownings, a number of Garands, crates full of shells.

—Here's an informer! declared a fighter, shoving an older man with a craven air. Everybody knew him for a longterm spy who reported to Velia Suazo.

—Let's judge him!

—Judge all of them, dogs.

—And the dead ones!

—God will do that.

—We should wait, said another. They need a regular trial.

—And who's the judge, Cornelio Ferrán?

—Bueno, we'll try Ferrán too.

—In Miami?

Claudio had appeared: the veteran leader. There was something grave, imperturbable about him.

—Build a bonfire. We'll hold a trial here in the intersection, before anyone else has to die or go to prison because of these Somocistas.

Quickly a fire crackled in front of the Comandito. Men and women gathered round the edge, backing off as the heat increased. Their sweaty faces flushed red and seemed to broil with passion. After a few minutes the Guardia corpses were hauled out and tossed on a seething pyre. Human flesh began to roast and sizzle; while Claudio, eyes aflame, stood enumerating the dictator's crimes: the death of young Lorenzo, and arrest of Miguel Giner; the people's long history of hard work and little pay. Some thought Claudio too gung-ho, ruthless, a political robot exempt from human emotions like gratitude, sadness, weariness. But the Indians of Monimbó stared with a glum ardor from the fringes of darkness, as Claudio spoke of past insurgents, Diriangén the cacique chieftain who fought against Spanish colonizers; Cleto Ordoñez and Francisco Morazán, leaders of rebellions in the 19th Century. Claudio's eyes glowed when he recounted the sins of the tyrant, whose elite units hated this barrio. Chon stared from a window of Santana's and felt envy of the leader's implacable calm.

Flames rose above the charred bodies of Guardia Nacional.

—Lord, said a woman, what will happen to us now?

Claudio capped his oration with slogans, and then the people's tribunal began. Women brought more food and water to the scene, while others tended to wounded combatants.

—That one, he never hurt us.

—Sí, hombre. Let him go!

It was a soldier whose gaze, staring penitently at the ground, seemed to say the world was nothing if not naughty.

—This one's from Diriamba. I know his parents.

—But if we let him go, then what?

The bonfire sent up clouds of cloying smoke. Orange flames licked the walls along Lomas de Sandino. As Alma trotted after Chon, back inside the cantina, the terra-cotta night was filled with gunshots from Parque Central. The Comandito was a skeletal structure in an aura of dust and smoke.

More arguments were presented, as Claudio presided. The one from Diriamba was allowed to leave; but this other soldier had come last month, after midnight, and taken away Presencio's uncle. A third, injured now and unable to stand, had abused the grandfather of Ramiro the shoemaker, who lived two doors down from the Rodriguez family.

XV

Inside the cantina Alma listened while they talked things over. She waited for another order from Chon, but they were discussing defense of the barrio. This had to be weighed against reinforcements for Ulises Tapia in the Parque Central. If they overran the Guardia garrison Masaya would be liberated. But if they proved unable, then the repression would fall harder than ever. So far the dictator had directed most of his firepower at Matagalpa and Estelí, cities of the North with insurrections also in full progress. The men said: your decision, Choncito. Send troops? Keep them here? Alma stood to one side. She felt sorry for her teacher because he looked so tired and everyone relied on him as the leader. Poor man, when would he get a rest? When would he see his wife, Filomena, and his sons? Not tonight.

From outside the voices of the people's court could be heard. A woman bleated forth her accusation, crying, while others tried to calm her down.

—Where's the messenger?

The men looked around, suddenly aware of the compañero's absence. Chon wanted to ask him something: where had he gone? Outside with the rest of them, listening to Claudio? In the amber darkness the teacher sought out Alma's eyes. He said to her:

—You remember the messenger?

—Sí.

—Go find him. Bring him here.

She skipped out the door into the smoke-filled air. Her pretty mestizo features took on a concentration as she strained to make out faces among the shadows weaving over the ground: dark banners above the Guardia funeral pyre. Intently, the girl popped up here and there among the crowd absorbed in solemn proceedings. She felt worried about her errand: where was he? Where was the one Chon wanted? In the cantina they waited impatiently, like when she went to fetch Lazaro. Nothing could go forward until she returned.

Alma tugged a man's shirttails:

—Have you seen Ulises Tapia's messenger?

—The muchacho? He was over there.

She ran to the edge of the crowd and found Presencio. He fashioned wooden toys in his workshop in the Rinconadas. She asked him:

—Have you seen Ulises' messenger?

But Presencio didn't know who it was. And neither did Fasael, the barrio mechanic, standing beside him. Now Alma started to fear. Maybe the fate of Masaya depended on her completing the task Chon gave her. Look what happened in February when she failed to run a simple errand. Presencio and Fasael watched her, so pretty with her dark eyes and the hint of blond in her hair. They liked to see Alma trot about and look businesslike, mature. But then their gaze was drawn back to the tribunal.

She scanned the crowd but couldn't find the one in question. Then another man, a stranger, took time to reflect and said:

—The one with the checkered kerchief?

—That's him!

—I saw him leave a few minutes ago, toward Parque Central.

She stood wondering what do to. The hot fire made everybody's face glow red. The wounded Guardia looked dizzy; they might faint, and fall. Alma thought of visions she had, in her sleep, of people in jail. Slaps, hateful laughter, cries of pain. Doñita came back depressed from visiting him because prison was horrible. It was rumored President Somoza tortured them himself sometimes, and this must be the worst of all. Some said they raped girls up on Tiscapa where the dictator had his headquarters. Raped, ay, she knew what that was. And in jail people ate food that made them sick, and there were no toilets, just buckets, and not enough water to drink. Rats; no window for the sun to come in . . . Alma thought about what to do.

XVI

The streets leading through Magdalena barrio to the park were dark and dangerous. She started to run along, glad she hadn't worn her white school blouse like in February. Then, at the first corner, she tripped and fell with a cry. As she jumped back up her palm began to burn and bleed; she felt the stickiness. In Magdalena there were no lights: the sky flashed up ahead in Parque Central. Doñita Reyes would have a fit if she knew about this; but Miguel would be surprised and proud. A mighty hand propelled Alma along as the ground shifted beneath her feet, and she knew a sudden elation, pleasing her older brother. Doñita, the coward, worried so much it was abnormal. But when somebody Almita loved was having a hard time, like Padre who suffered from hives, she sort of went through it too and had a tension in her stomach.

She ran along the street and nearly stumbled again, frowning up at flashes over the rooftops. The buildings jutted starkly and dissolved in darkness. There were no stars. A breeze had risen off the lake, and she heard a faint rustle of palm trees in the patios. But she had to run faster: the men waited on her and would grow angry. Chon Muñoz must be disappointed, shaking his head.

Suddenly, she heard a motor. Behind her? Did the muchachos control this sector approaching the park? Automatic fire echoed, ratatata, and then the engine again, beneath the roar. A jeep turned at the intersection behind her, a block away. The thing drew closer. Somocistas? A BECAT? Alma ran on wondering if she should try to hide in a doorway. The jeep came closer, without headlights. Nobody would open their doors to her at this hour: they were riding out the night of war in the anonymity of their homes.

The gears growled: right behind her! Three more blocks to Parque Central and Ulises Tapia's messenger. She whispered a prayer to the Virgin Mary, but the words garbled with her crying and jolt of her pace. She glanced around and saw a glint of shiny helmets. The jeep geared down: it pulled right beside her, cruised; men laughed as she sprinted in a panic and couldn't escape.

She turned the next corner, and they followed after, merry. Ay! A BECAT with four Guardia. One said an ugly thing, and she understood. Then another:

—Geev me one leetle kees'—

She sobbed and ran from them with all her force. The houses, the sky vaulted up and over: she had an awareness of losing control. Then her feet flew from under her. She fell, fell in a sickening blackness that spun round.

—Miguel! she cried out, but no one heard.

There was a helpless bumping, thumping another few steps. Poor Doñita: what would she say if she knew? There was a sense of abandonment and nauseous pain; and a sadness: as if it was happening to someone she loved.

XVII

Bulu was a taxi driver but scooting around on foot these days. So he went along with his people to Calle Real. He floated on air, blood and guts being Bulito's favorite food; and the first mad minutes of combat, as they neared the park, his hors-d'oeuvres.

Back at the Institute he had thought Ulises, Marta and the others must have finished with the Guardia dogs by this late date. But he also thought about Choncito's strangeness and turned it over in his mind like a problem to be resolved. Qué pasa, hombre?

But then it started. Just as they met up with Marta Navarro and moved on a Guardia position by Kikatex factory—

PRA! PRA! A volley of .30 fizzed right by his ear.

—Get down, compañeros!

Oh, man! thought Bulu, this shit is not a bargain! That Claudio has gone crazy, sending us here. A man could get himself killed!

There went la Marta rushing out toward the firefight; but the .30 kept after Bulu, it probed, and he thought:

—Grandioso! Already to die, Bulu boy? Without firing a shot?

He drew away and fell backward in a gutter. Then, trying to regain his poise, sprawled there, he remembered the teacher dressed in a traditional costume for the yearly Tata Chombito festival. That's it! Bulu filled in the missing piece to his puzzle, and opined: carajo!

But he mumbled:

—Pure mud around here . . . Where's Marta?

In a moment he stood up, shook himself off and glanced about for his people. Pfzzz!

Whoomph!

Hombre, this sector is hot!

Someone cried out:

—Over to the sugar factory!

But everybody had dispersed. He started off alone toward the marketplace, and sneaking along the southern side of Cecalsa he mused: good God, Choncito a marica? Shh! Bulu kid, don't slander the comandante. Where would we be without him? He recruited you. Ay! Bulu thought, anguished: I always sensed his softness, his mincing ways. But . . . can a maricón be married and raise one son after the next?

—Shh, not a word. Guardia doggies, where are you? Gone in hiding, Macho Pedro, now that Bulito hits the scene?

XVIII

Through the night Masaya garrison defended itself against the combat units of the insurrection. With more fighters arriving from the fallen Monimbó command post, Parque Central swarmed in the darkness. The Guardia station, a reinforced structure with a stubborn life of its own, hung on like an animal at bay. The muchachos hugged the walls. They darted forward and sought openings to toss in a bomb.

The city came alive with people at work on barricades and trenches. So many, during the midnight hours, that passage became difficult for combatants. The women brought coffee. In moments of lull the barrio kids zipped here and there on errands.

Chon Muñoz knew similar events were underway in León, Estelí, Matagalpa. The population had responded to the call of the Frente, whose leaders tried to coordinate the attack. The people caught a whiff of victory, thought Chon, and then arose and followed it out into the furious zones.

A rumor spread that the GN garrison had been overrun. Some danced in the streets even as shots rang out from the park. Except for that sector, where fighting still raged, the insurgents did control Masaya. Muñoz was kept informed by courriers, and toward dawn he went with a few others along the same route taken by Alma a few hours before.

For the moment he was worried about so many things, so many lives at stake, he couldn't focus on the girl's disappearance. He remembered sending her from the cantina, and with an effort he might have recalled why. But the burden was too much. When his best friend Miguel got arrested in February, it proved a heavy blow. And now Alma's failure to return, if he let it register, might bring on the full weight of his discouragement. There was so much to do at present: he couldn't dwell on negative things with the pressure of decision-making on his shoulders. The fate of the girl began gnawing at Chon Muñoz like a temptation to despair.

Toward dawn a cool breeze blew in off the lake. The trails of smoke drifted upward and deployed like flags above a grisly scene. The low dwellings took on form at the borders of Parque Central. With first signs of daylight the smoke clouds went a copper hue above the streets strewn with litter, and the fallen like congealed shadows.

On the south side of the park Chon found Ulises Tapia and Marta Navarro. At once he asked:

—Have you seen the girl, Alma?

—No sign, compa.

—Miguel Giner's little sister. I sent her on an errand.

But Ulises and the valiant Marta shook their heads, exchanging a glance. There were advance units along the Loco Bolaños, poised on the rooftops. A captured van mounted with a .50 mm. harassed the garrison, but it had to play cat-and-mouse with a Guardia tank that prowled in defense.

When Chon arrived on the scene, the tank was moving slowly past Teatro Masaya. Unmolested it roamed and hindered mobility in the sector.

With the two others Chon talked over the situation. Suddenly Ulises made an angry gesture:

—What's that compañero doing?

Someone had fired a shot at the tank, and now their position was revealed. The chance of ambush vanished. In the moments before daybreak the Guardia tank came prodding its way toward the three leaders. Its turret groped in the gray-blue shadows, like a feeler. It gave forth a burst at the roofs where fighters perched to return fire with carbines and M-1s.

Ulises said to Marta who had a fierce look, curly hair, a kerchief round her neck:

—Tell them go back. No reason to hold these positions.

Muchachos scurried along the eaves: feet pitter-pattered like rain. Half-crouched, rifle in hand, whistling signals, their white teeth glinted in the early light. After ten hours' battle they moved nimbly and fell in with Marta for the withdrawal. But the tank had already turned the corner, and it came on methodically, as they watched its form in the dim intersection.

—Move! said Ulises. Wait for me at the corner.

—By yourself? said Chon.

The tank rumbled over the ruts. Ulises paused, fitting an antitank grenade to his FAL.

—It only takes one.

After Monimbó the other barrios had been liberated: Magdalena, San Miguel, Pochotillo. But without the fall of Masaya garrison there would be no victory. And with every shot fired, with each passing hour the initiative might swing back to the Guardia: as Somoza deliberated where to respond next with his air power and elite EEBI.

For the moment this single tank proved an obstacle. And so Ulises went out in the street as the armored beast loomed larger. Chon waited to one side. Marta, along with Bulu from the Rufo Marín, had retreated round the corner.

Ulises Tapia went on one knee and took aim.

—Why doesn't he fire? said Chon.

The tank gave a burst, bucked; but Ulises held his ground. It came on, turret levelled, aware of the threat close by. He knelt and strained forward in the middle of the street, but his FAL would not function. Something had gone wrong with the grenade launcher.

Others began firing from the corner—ping! ping!

The .22 bullets flew off armor like gnats on a windshield. Ulises worked his gun and changed positions, scrambled, rolled on his elbows.

The tank let go a second blast, and he gave a lurch. He broke his fall sideways and slumped backwards as the tank advanced.

Chon Muñoz stood rooted; he tried to make out through the smoke what had happened. But Marta stepped from the doorway in full view of all and began to yell:

—Compañeros! Are we going to leave our brother in the street?

Ulises had fallen lengthwise and lay in the path of the oncoming tank. He made strange movements with one arm.

—In the chest, murmured Chon, and Marta glanced at him as she passed by.

For precious seconds Muñoz stayed glued to the spot, unable to respond. He looked stunned in the depths of his being. But Marta Navarro pounced out toward the fallen leader. And the indomitable Bulu had crept forward and lobbed a first grenade, then another. The tank stood motionless at thirty meters.

—Grab his FAL!

Bulu, naked to the waist, appeared to swim amid the smoke of explosions. At the same moment four Guardia emerged from behind the tank, creeping ahead on foot. Bulu took aim on one knee and nailed the foremost just beneath the helmet, which spun off.

Marta knelt, gesturing Chon to help drag Ulises backward by the legs. Ramiro, the Monimbó shoemaker, had grabbed up the wounded man's gun. He shook it.

—Jammed!

Round the corner the others retreated. They fired back with every few steps and shouted:

—Viva el Frente!

Again the Guardia tank came on—ping! ping!

Bulu was out of grenades, so he drew back also. Marta helped pull the body into a doorway. With dawn aglow over the rooftops Ulises Tapia left a glistening trail as they dragged him along. A fringe of billowy cloud took a pink hue out over Masaya Lagoon. The dust and gray mist of detonations had a tinge.

Chon Muñoz helped Marta bring in the dead weight of Ulises from the line of fire. But for a dazed Choncito, in those instants, it was going through the motions. His tough resourcefulness had abandoned him. From the shocked instant of the compañero's death he was merely following Marta's orders.

XIX

Caramba! When the leader Ulises Tapia fell, it was like a mule gave Bulito a swift kick in the cojones. His spirits began to plunge at once; in fact, the hero's first impulse was to stage a hasty retreat. But then la Marta whose own cojones were sizable, for a woman, cried out:

—Cowards, you run now and I'll shoot!

So at that point Bulu reflected, and said:

—Heu! Is this woman giving us lessons?

He turned and tiptoed toward the scene of carnage. But on the way he passed Chon Muñoz who stood stock still. He stared at Chon questioningly; their eyes met, and then Bulu looked down. Oh, señor! He moved past, wishing he hadn't traded a glance with Choncito, and thought: Correcto! He is, and I know he is, and he knows I know he *is*.

Marta made a cursory check and found out Comandante Ulises was stone dead, a martyr. The tank shell had sheared off a glob of arm before it exploded his chest.

—A goner, thought Bulu; and Choncito, too, a goner.

Bueno, Marta saw the man was dead. When she yelled at the compañeros she guessed he was only wounded; but now she told another compa to go for a coffin, if he could find one, because Ulises wasn't going to be left there rotting on the ground.

—None of you wants to stick around here, she said, so why should the compañero?

A little lesson in courage from la Marta.

Bulu and Elias went to find something to carry him. Then they laid him out on a strip of planking and sang the Frente hymn. But all the while a pensive Bulu scratched his head and cast glances at Chon Muñoz. He even took his «M–A» baseball shirt from his back pocket and put it on, since he felt kind of naked in the presence of a genuine marica and didn't want to give the compañero any ideas. But it seemed very puzzling to the astute Bulu because maricones were a breed apart, an all but extinct species in Masaya since most of them migrated to certain districts in Managua. He scratched some more and couldn't figure out what all that had to do precisely with Chon Muñoz, a comandante if there ever was one, a husband and father, leader of the February insurrection. Heu! Brother, life did play some pretty tricks if you didn't keep your wits about you. You have to be careful around here, thought Bulito.

XX

In the Colegio, Padre Velasquez heard the people's laughter fade to whispers as momentum swung the other way. Rebel forces must be running low on ammunition, and Padre knew it was a matter of time before law and order prevailed. At night the Guardia ventured out on forays. The lethal BECATs (Special Battalion Against Terrorist Attacks) had been beefed up under Macho Pedro's competent command. President Somoza stated over the radio his intention to make Masaya an example.

Two nights after the death of Ulises Tapia there came a rap, rap on the front door of the Colegio. Padre went downstairs and found a curious personage on the threshold. The man wore peasant dress with a leather packsaddle over his shoulder, a broad sombrero.

—What is it?

—Psst! said the campesino, peering beneath the wide brim. Don't recognize me, amigo?

Morell . . . Padre caught his breath. He seemed to confront one of Satan's lower echelon functionaries. Just as, on holidays, a farmer dons an inexpensive suit for his trip to town and looks jaunty, citified: so Morell appeared ludicrous in his proletarian costume. The trousers resembled burlap. The check shirt was a bit too bright even in the shadows.

Upstairs, Morell accepted a cup of tea and installed himself in an armchair.

—Señor Ferrán believes a critical moment is at hand. The delinquents are on the defensive and about to take a drubbing. But we need certain information. We must be careful in our dealings with them.

—Ah, said Padre, and moved to the window when he heard noise down below. Two little boys went past with rags and bottles.

He knew some of the women had come up with a «tortilla bomb» which they carried in wicker baskets, ignoring the danger. Kids tagged along after the bearded insurgents and asked: Did you come from the mountains? Do you know Iván Giner? Padre heard one muchacho say: Don't you recognize me? I know who *you* are.

Yes, Padre had watched the children squint up at such romantic figures. Chocho! says the kid, you're José from La Reforma, your mama sells mondongo in the market!

Morell finished sipping his tea and said:

—We need a list. Of all people, you, here at the Salesiano, should be able to furnish an accurate one.

—I'm not an expert in subversives.

—What we're after is the local leaders. Your help in the Faustina affair was crucial, and your country thanks you. Now we need names of Monimboseños who have participated.

XXI

Antonio Velasquez came from a wealthy Granada family: the eldest son of an industrialist. Endowed from childhood with a strong intellectual memory, and ever pliant to the regimen of his teachers, he graduated with distinction at every level. At university in Mexico City, in Catholic seminary where he excelled as few before him, he showed a wondrous grasp of Christian theology and what might be called, in his case, the mechanics of spirit. Honors abounded. The reality of sinful Man seemed to invite his soul to a life of pious action. His gaze lingered on the visionary masters of the past, Saint Augustine and Saint Thomas Aquinas, Saint Francis and Kierkegaard. And so, upon graduation he felt himself the possessor of a high calling, the vocation of a righteous pastorate. Down the line for Jesus Christ he would set his steps, his devout life in a love relationship with difficulty and pain as he sought to comfort others. He wanted to be a great disciple.

The first station on the way was an appointment in Río San Juan Province, where Iván Giner would take his petulant bride, la Juana, a few years later. The young padre plunged into the malarial life of San Carlos and the drenched scorched villages, Las Azucenas, El Castillo, as far as San Juan del Norte, called Greytown by the

English, where the river flows into the Caribbean. At first, for a number of months, his fervent determination did battle with the deplorable conditions, sickness and illiteracy, lack of communications: the backwardness of his parishioners. He brought them the most fortifying gift of all: the divine and self-sustaining Word applicable to every trial, and the sinner's eternal triumph over sin. They heard his sermons and humbly accepted his offering; he thought they would have preferred a loaf of bread, a lump of sugar, a box of powdered milk for the newborn child. At times the Gospels, their infinite significance, seemed a kind of gloss over problems so great, so all pervasive, in Río San Juan Province, and the young priest could only feel at a loss. Oh, they gathered to hear him of a Sunday, their spirits laved in his pure homiletics, the tender influence of the Scriptures like a waking dream. He spared them the retributive passages when Divine Mercy no longer seemed to apply, and a vengeful God set His hand to the winnower. Padre looked down from his pulpit and saw the malnourished children, the distracted adults with their cup full of troubles, and felt the distance between himself and this parish.

As the months went along he met them on the margin of muddy streets fissured in the sunlight. He called at their low chozas, and they invited him in, polite, ill at ease, offering of their paucity. Settled in to the Río San Juan life he felt stuck on square two of his progress toward great discipledom. Perhaps he was tempted by more worldly things since in this backwater far from a center of higher learning, or anything like a library, he began to grow impatient. Young, willful to make his way in the world, he saw himself stagnating in this alluvial region, with its misery. He dressed well for a shepherd; and this, too, separated. His flock came clad in necessity when he called, but many avoided mass for lack of a Sunday outfit.

One afternoon he visited a family living in a tent, in the most wretched poverty, on the outskirts of San Carlos. Greeting them he mistook a teenage daughter sick with hepatitis for the mother. In all the province there were two doctors, who served the merchants,

the administrative sector, those who could pay cash. Padre Velasquez lingered to visit the poor and dispense words of hope. He
invited them to pray with him even as, in the pit of his stomach, he
felt a sinking. Until this day he couldn't admit his inadequacy to
the task. Where, in what school, might a man prepare? How did
you speak to the morbid stare in a child's eyes? What sort of training in self-abnegation could lead you through the Via Crucis where
great disciples were made or fell by the wayside, like carcasses of
faith? All, not excluding this family in the last degree of destitution,
envied his nice rectory with its electric lights and creature comforts:
the unheard-of luxury of hot water, a shower bath, window screens,
a refrigerator, ice. Their laughter could be construed in other ways,
when they asked him of such amazing things. Their words, not his,
were the revelation of a truth known intellectually, for a long time,
but sentient now, in the place where the Word converted and became flesh.

Less than a month later he fell feverishly ill and boarded the
steamer, the Victoria making its stops on the wide lake, and returned home to Granada. Then, convalescing, he fought his fear
and kept a solemn resolve to resume the pastoral work. But talks
with his parents, a mother herself unwell, an entrepreneurial father
whose golden staircase did not ascend from fluviatile Río San Juan,
at length dissuaded. He sent for what books and possessions he had
left in San Carlos, and never went back. In his native city, the
leisurely Granada with its colonial architecture fronting the cathedral and tree shaded park, its high-ceiling'd offices fanned slowly in
the still afternoon, he met with success, respect, a social round ap-
preciative of his sensitive intelligence. In years following he rarely
mentioned Río San Juan and kept his recollections to himself. But
he thought of the river towns, their winding streets and stilted wa-
tersides, morning rains, and thorny matorrals; and the memory
seemed bathed in a tragic haze. Never mind: God's ways to great
discipleship were many, educator, civic leader, preacher, humanist
theologian, all of them wondrous.

It was only when Miguel Giner burst on the Colegio scene, over a
decade later, surprised by his own brilliant mind like a tropical flower
revealed overnight, that Padre Velasquez relived his early San Juan
experience. Then he felt it, poignantly, like a goad. As if, after all, the
heroism planted scripturally in his soul had come to blossom; but he
didn't know this, at the time, and never went beyond.

XXII

Morell waited calmly, hands folded: like a Colegio student being good. A list, thought Padre. Slowly, he turned back from the window and removed his horn-rimmed glasses. He rubbed his eyes, tired with poring over school accounts, clerical work. Padre's gray hair swept back at the temples; he should have been handsome, though angular at the jawline. His strong neck had a sort of inner whorl that conveyed movement to the ladino cast of his features. Now, replacing his glasses, he considered the visitor. Morell sat there, a discrepancy in the leger. A list . . . Former students. Certain teachers. The pyrotechnic, Lazaro. The artisan Presencio. Ramiro the shoemaker, whose pathetic sins Padre had absolved for a decade in the silence of confessional. They came to mass. They greeted him with a smile in the street. They sent him their children. Parishioners. Their heads had been turned by the subversives. Stubborn, individualistic, schooled in the ways of disobedience; they had lost touch with God. A list . . . Who else?

Chon Muñoz had betrayed his mentor's trust. He came forth, sensuous and perverse if the truth were known, to be a leader, and take his place to the fore in the godless ranks. Moreover, he had a moral authority, having taught their children well and always taken an interest. The man stepped forward and made his choice: the reprobate loathed his own redemption, and would not turn . . . In the evening quiet Padre Velasquez knit his brow, slowly shook his head: another effort gone awry for the great disciple. He had tried to raise up Chon Muñoz from the Lazarus couch of his poor background. But the laws of God were inscrutable and obeyed their own necessity. Who punished? Who redeemed?

Morell said:

—Well then?

—Wait.

A difficult moment for Antonio Velasquez. His heart went out to the longsuffering people who lived beneath his gaze: they sinned, but they loved, and trusted, considering their priest God's representative, unto them. Tacho Somoza could hardly be termed the wisest of presidents, but what was the alternative at this stage, if not communism, Moscow-inspired and -subsidized, atheist; at best a bureaucratic blind alley, at worst anarchy like the last few days, Armageddon in the barrio.

—Well?

Velasquez turned and stared at the spy. Now a few names burned as little flames at the tip of his tongue: others beside Choncito, a betrayer who never heard the cock crow. For an instant he imagined them stepping forward to hear their name pronounced: when the awful strokes began to toll, and all Man's history of conflict seemed a paltry thing alongside that roll call of doom and the tumult of prophesies fulfilled.

—I'm waiting, said Morell, and glimpsed his wristwatch. I have a meeting with Macho Pedro.

As yet Padre had never doubted. Always, he felt his faith could meet any test. It throbbed, in his ordained nerves, at this decisive minute. There remained an unwavering oneness with the will of his own superior: who, unlike Morell, unlike Macho Pedro, and Don Cornelio Ferrán, and even President Somoza, could never know the throes of indecision. He made no errors, when He drew up His sacred decrees, and compiled His lists.

XXIII

—Carlita? Psst!

Bulu found the old woman hunched in a pew of the Calvarito, at work on her rosary. Instead of dying she would just go up, some late afternoon, and take her place with Chuno and the saints by the altar.

—Bad boy! she hissed, with her tallowy smile.

Bulu was spooked. Marriages, funerals, churches made him nervous.

—Ready to do a job? he asked.

Carlita gave a grunt, glancing around.

—Ready.

From his satchel, carefully, he handed her Cafe Presto jars, one by one.

—Bombs?

Carlita raised her eyebrows. She looked conspiratorial and pleased.

—Sí, señora, cooed Bulu. These bombs were fabricated with shit.

—Don't say so!

—It's the famous shit-bomb.

—Ay, Maria.

—You take some feces and stuff 'em inside a jar, like this. Then put on the cover and wrap masking tape, and let it set a couple days.

—Then what happens?

Carlita looked like Saint Theresa in ecstasy, receiving her charge.

—Bueno, you know excrement contains gas. But the bomb is really made up of psychology; a psychological thing, see? Choncito explained the deal to me: you throw it, and whoof! The jar explodes. Shit sticks like melasses on that Somocista's body, with a strong smell.

—You stink for days.

—Weeks! Bulu whispered. We use it on elements suspected of spying. Snoops. Why go further? It could be one of us, someone we trusted, but no point in hurting their family.

—Dios primero, said Carlita and resumed her prayers.

—La bomba de mierda, said Bulu, solemn. When it explodes in your house you can't stay there anymore. It's a mental thing.

After a moment she took a newspaper from her bag; she showed him the headlines:

GUARDIA COUNTEROFFENSIVE
PRES. SOMOZA DECLARES MARTIAL LAW
TANK BATTALION WITH EEBI STORMS MASAYA

. . . .

SANDINISTAS AFTER 70 HOURS COMBAT
RETREAT INTO BARRIOS
NAT'L GUARD BEGINS MOP-UP OPERATION
MASAYA CENTRAL MARKET ABLAZE

Meanwhile the wooden mask of Jesucristo gazed down at the two conspirators from the main altar. God's mystery spoke in those features from beyond the grave to the septuagenarian, Carlita Garcia. The devout Bulu crossed himself and made a genuflexion, before he swaggered the few steps of the Calvarito's central aisle and went out in a blaze of midday light.

XXIV

Hundreds of people waited in the rooms of the Red Cross. They heard the thunder of Guardia guns reach one climax and another. As helicopters overflew the city there were tanks and armored cars moving down among the barrios. Rebel firepower had proven insufficient and now it was the army's turn. One task was to dislodge insurgents from the Ferrán mansion: thus fighting had ranged and reerupted in that sector through the fourth morning.

Many arrived at the Red Cross for sanctuary. Outside, the horror was on the march: just as in February when the soldiers went about shooting dogs and cats to get in practice. In one corner Comandante Chon sat elbows on knees. He looked like someone trying to solve a problem. But the leader Claudio had melted from view and hid out probably in the Rinconadas.

They waited in the airless rooms of the Red Cross building. The sun was a white-hot flame at shortly after one p.m. when a Guardia contingent arrived. Scowling, like a mass of olive drab shadows they regrouped by the front entry, while the Red Cross director went out to parley. Here and there sat leaders of the insurrection, like Chon dressed in civilian clothes. For a few minutes the administrator prevented GN entry, citing some international accord. But they shoved him aside and pointed at people with their submachineguns.

Chon Muñoz ran his fingers through the hair over his temples and stared straight ahead. He recognized Somoza's EEBI and expected to see the local leader, Macho Pedro, come walking through the door. Chon gazed at their somber faces streaked with sweat beneath the helmets. They seemed to bristle as if drugged up. Any slightest gesture would increase the suspicion and already unbearable tension. Chon shared a glimpse with Marta Navarro sitting cross-legged along the aisle. Marta, the full-fledged urban guerrilla, was dressed in a clean blouse and skirt: she looked like a pert schoolgirl. No one spoke. Would there be an informer in the gathering? Was one of Macho's toadies on hand?

The elite troops lingered in twos and threes, breath audible, gear clicking.

Suddenly, a voice rang out:

—Where are the delinquents?

Silence.

There was a bad odor in this room like a furnace. Near the Red Cross building two corpses lay, in the great heat, ready to burst. The fear, the quiet took on their smell.

Outside, from direction of La Reforma came a flurry of gunshots. Somoza's troops met pockets of popular resistance, and this outraged them.

Chon sat stiffly still. Everybody knew him. Knew he was the leader.

XXV

The soldiers moved about the wide treatment area. They pointed, on the basis of chafed elbows and knees, at certain of the males. Nobody spoke, but by the entry a two-way radio spluttered.

Chon watched as they led away Dejanira's husband. She sat in a mute, abeyant hysteria. Blear-eyed, she bit her lip and it bled. All in the room knew she had become a widow.

—Woman! shouted an EEBI. Who are the guerrillas?

Dejanira sat in shock. She stared unseeing. She gazed like a stunned animal at something beyond time and space.

More rose on order, led away.

A knot had formed in Choncito's stomach. A dozen times, in the past few days, he exposed his life boldly and with a will; although too busy to fight at the barricades. As a teacher in the Colegio he had the soft hands of a clerk, not a scratch on his elbows. He had led the insurrection from Santana's and later in the billiard parlor at Cuatro Esquinas, but he sat unruffled now and neatly dressed.

—Who are the leaders? cried the sharp voice. Give us the criminals!

More men rose, led away.

Dejanira sobbed. Nobody spoke.

—Tell us, and we'll let yours go free.

Everybody knew Choncito was the comandante.

—It's not too late!

As the knot grew tighter, and he wondered if it would make him vomit, Chon thought of Alma's disappearance. Raped? In all likelihood: a pretty girl like her; they liked the young ones. Chon cringed in his depths. And shot, or her throat slit? Probably; though so far nobody had turned up. He should have told her, if he hadn't been so busy with his own accursed problems he would have told her: come back if Ulises' messenger isn't here on the Lomas.

But he was in the heat of battle. He never thought of it.

The knot tightened. He remembered his best friend, Miguel, arrested in February and currently on hunger strike inside the Carcel Modelo according to La Prensa which had printed more of the inspired poems. Chon felt a deep love: a tragic, physical yearning for Miguel Giner; and then a shame, a guilt that compounded his sense of self-hatred at sitting here disguised in his effeminacy, his figure hardly that of a fighter.

More were led away.

Nobody spoke except a soldier pausing alongside:

—Marica, who might you be?

Chon felt an intimate jolt.

The EEBI man had an ugly smile, standing over him. He stared down at Muñoz with a chuckle.

—That's right, maricón, you.

—I'm a teacher.

—Name?

He poked Chon in the chest with his M-16. He laughed and gave him another nudge with his spit-shined boot before moving along. By now the knot in Choncito's stomach was an onset of rage, as he thought of the young poet Lorenzo; of the butchery at Faustina's back in February; also of his daily illicit daydreams and desires that made him forever at odds with himself, and wouldn't go away. Everybody loved and admired Chon Muñoz: above all now after he showed such courage and leadership. Nevertheless Bulu had looked him in the eye and read his diary. Bulu knew the truth plain as day. And that brutal soldier knew.

Across the aisle a second woman sobbed quietly, unable to control herself as more of the men were ushered away at gunpoint. Marta Navarro was passed over with a macho remark, request for a sexual favor.

Chon thought of Ulises Tapia going out against a tank, his chest torn open a few blocks away from this same Red Cross. Really the sum total was too much, and Comandante Chon flushed on the verge of giving himself away. He remembered how he froze up not from fear but because he was over his head in personal failure and humiliation, and he could hardly bear it anymore. Sitting here became a labor too much for Hercules. How many had been massacred in the barrios while he went overlooked because of his clean hands? Not a speck of dirt under the fingernails. A Managua manicurist couldn't have made them more artistic.

XXVI

A firing squad had formed up outside.

The first shots rang out, and the groans of the dying were brief.

A woman sighed and fainted, falling on her side.

Dejanira was a widow.

—The leaders! shouted a soldier.

Then he laughed, and moving back past the teacher gave a playful nudge with his boot. The insult was clear, and Chon hung on the verge: in moments, with his great strength, he could strangle at least one of them, that one. And then what? How many more would be slaughtered? We're innocent! the muchachos had yelled inside Faustina's. Then another leader would be gone: if he even budged or said a word in protest to this death squad. In his heart he wanted to die a dozen deaths and felt he deserved them. But any mistake meant a shadow over the future of people he loved. Filomena, their sons; Miguel for whom he yearned in the debacle of impassioned imaginings; Alma who was missing, dead or ruined; the Monimboseños; his country. Giving way to passion would do the enemy's work gratis. You might as well go over and become a provocateur.

More men were led away by the EEBI.

Everybody knew Choncito was the comandante.

The women sobbed, like a chorus.

No one spoke.

XXVII

Since Alma's disappearance there had been no sleep for Doñita Reyes. Her appetite was gone, and she actually began to look a bit less corpulent. She sat in her rocker listening to machinegun barrages which grumbled and echoed across the city. From the sound of distant screams and smell of smoke she thought it must be the apocalypse. The bright macaw had flown away for good: Miguel's parrot, taught to utter vulgarities and then snigger.

All day and through the evening the old woman rocked and moaned. She made a pilgrimage back to the cubbyhole where Almita slept, and the sight of her child's little possessions made her want to cry. A comb, a coquettish braid, a pen and pencil set she won two years before at the Colegio, still in its case, unused. A book of stories called *Historias de Loco*. She read them over and over till the pages grew yellow.

Saddened, Doñita was about to sit down on Alma's bed but caught herself just in time. Beneath her bulk it would have crumpled to bits.

That night there were bands of drunken Guardia who went about terrorizing the inhabitants. They appeared at the end of Calle Calvario and right away found the scent to Faustina's place, where a dozen of them converged. But the voluptuous housewife, whose loud mouth was shut up in February, had fled with her daughters and nobody knew where.

Finding no one home they crossed to Doñita's and banged their gun butts on the front door. The low wooden structure trembled. A red-eyed man growled on the threshold.

—Open up!

—Sí, señor, Doñita whined, fairly lunging the few steps from her rocker.

—Who lives here?

—Only me.

—Nobody else? he stared inside, pug-nosed, hilarious as his cock's eye sized up the old maid. And the subversive poet, no? It's his home.

—He's in prison, she said, looking down.

—Well . . . who lives over there?

—Doña Faustina.

—A luscious bitch! he slurred the words with drunken arrogance, unshaven, sweaty. He paused a moment, indecisive, by her door-jamb. Then said:

—This one's ugly. Pfui!

Next afternoon she felt waves of anxiety when a passerby told her a tremendous piece of news. Arturo Velasquez had been assassinated. Velasquez, Padre's first cousin, was leader of Masaya's Conservative Party: not always a loyal opponent of the President's National Liberals. Guardia on their rounds from house to house, conducting searches for any hint of sympathy with the insurgents, had arrived at Velasquez' house after midnight. When the politician expressed a frank criticism of Somocista policies, the soldiers took him seriously. They led him outside and shot him like a dog.

Velasquez lay in the street until dawn and died later that day in the hospital.

—Poor Padre, thought Doñita; her eyes ran over at the idea of his grief.

XXVIII

She dozed by the window. Hour after hour she heard the crackle of fires and torched huts in the barrio. Chon had warned her against sitting beside the window, but horrified as she was of violence Doñita was even more ensconced in her habits. She drifted on the periphery of sleep, reluctant to let herself go, a prey to anxious dreams. There was Alma curled up foetally in the flames . . . The chair gave a squeak amid the old woman's sonorous snore.

Awhile later something emerged along Calle Calvario. In her dream she listened as cicadas stopped their racket. A bird give its chirp in the turbid slumber of the forest. Only the night bugs kept up their buzz and flit of wings nose-diving in the starlight.

Fear hung in the air with an odor of rotten meat: the defeated Frente. And then a strange bark, the bawl of a puppy, almost human. Doñita Reyes sat upright in her chair.

In the night hushed with dread some sort of creature came along the Calvario; it croaked with pity. She held her breath. She hoped the thing would not come in her yard and start to poke around.

Not here, Lord. Let it go look elsewhere. But the sounds came on, and Doñita's first response was to bolt the front door. The feeble yelp drew closer. Dragging itself over the dust; and then it scratched, suddenly, her door, *hers*, with a rasp:

—Please.

Then she understood and lurched forward on her bloated ankles. She opened and saw Alma prone on the doorstep. The girl shook her head in the void, trying to knock some more. She lay tattered, dirty, a dead bird on the roadside. Her hair wild, matted with blood.

Doñita Reyes stared into the darkness. She knelt and took the girl in her arms; and found, to her horror, that Alma had no hands. Only a coagulated, filthy stump at the end of each arm.

Then Doñita lost control. Her big shoulders shook. She dropped Alma who lay in a ball at her feet. The girl moaned, in shock. The night, the Calvario, all was hushed as Almita's eyes rolled upward, from consciousness.

XXIX

The muchachos faded from view in Masaya. The barricades were bulldozed by the National Guard, and Somoza's *Novedades* reported that the insurgency was finished. For weeks the city had a moribund air. There were bad smells wafted up from the Lagoon, enveloping the sectors. The central market lay in ruins, its ancient gateway charred, spectral, a vestige of September. People went through the motions of everyday life, but Guardia were everywhere. Glaring helmets, scowling faces. The BECATS patrolled the streets.

One by one the Pacific Coast cities had been subdued, as the President softened them up with Push-Pull light bombers and then sent in troops to mop up. Where was Juan José? Where were Maria and Boanerges? And Presencio whose workshop in the Rinconadas had been set on fire?

A jeep lurched round a corner. Men in camouflage jumped to the sidewalk and dragged a passerby to the ground.

One morning in October there was a meeting of the Frente leaders: two doors down from the bakery where Miguel, Chon, Marta and others used to spend afternoons when they were adolescents, discussing philosophy, reading poems.

Now at noontime the sun cast its shadows like spikes driven into the white adobe. At this hour the bread was rising; it suffused the street with a rich oven smell. Claudio had reemerged for this meeting of leadership; also Marta, Chon; the gorgeous girl named Cecilia whose nom de guerre was Delia. Unknown to them two BECATs entered the barrio at breakneck speed, passing in front of the Colegio where Padre Velasquez had been able by this time to reinstate normal classes. They raced past the school toward Cuatro Esquinas.

—Here come fishermen! yelled a sentry posted outside the safe house.

—We'll make them eat milk curds, said Chon.

But Claudio, eyes wide, mesh of dark hair over his forehead, gave Chon a look.

From outside the watchman gave a holler:

—It's the *animales!*

Marta and Cecilia moved quickly toward the back. Big Claudio scrambled through the door with agile strides.

—Run, muchachos!

All but Chon Muñoz vanished down a back path, beyond a patch of plantain. The teacher stood frozen in his tracks. He didn't move. He felt a sudden release of long pent anguish. With a groundswell of exhilaration, from his depths, Chon steadied to meet the Guardia. He gazed out the window, into the sunlight, and wondered who let them know. Who was the informer? Poised, in the instants before the end he felt a serene strength, as a first and second jeep lurched to a halt and sent up dust. The misery of degrading desire; the beauty made ugly by the eyes of others: in a minute his life would flare up one final time and explode. Then he would be free to love, free to cherish in any way he pleased, for eternity. O Filomena: not even you knew the secret. O my sons, your father was a comandante, a hero who died for his people, and the inadmissible truth. O my beloved: dare I whisper your name? By night on my bed I sought him whom my soul loveth: I sought him, but I found him not . . . Only you knew; but certain others had gotten a glimmer; they suspected and fought the obstinate devil of their own homophobia for my sake, the kindly, intelligent teacher of their children. But sooner or later, the terrible truth . . . ah! better to die now in a blaze of glory, having carried the cross with dignity from station to station. Better to fall a martyr with one's life still intact, a reputation untarnished, in the love and respect of one's family, and forgiving community . . .

But suddenly Chon jolted and seemed to waken from a trance. Who told the Guardia? Who informed? Ah! ah! That same morning he had let slip a word to Padre Velasquez.

He leapt forward, stumbled, knocked over a chair.

He lunged for the back entry.

—Slime!

Four Guardia stormed in.

The street lay deserted. Not a face visible in the broiling noontide of Cuatro Esquinas. Only the sweet farinous odor of hot bread, and the snarl of Guardia Nacional.

—Comunista shit!

In the next instant he was sinking. He turned, head over heals, in a nightmarish chaos as they rained blows with their gun butts, kicks with their boots on his head, his body. Chon's senses disintegrated and fell away, dimly, in bits. His blood gushed, spattered their shiny boots, their fatigues. They grunted for breath, they paused and drew back. For a second they inspected their work and then trussed him rapidly, like experts, and dragged him out through the door.

They heaved him in the first jeep. His head bounced on the metal floor: he tried to mumble something, regaining consciousness, his voice a wheeze:

—Nazis.

One leaned and beat him on the groin.

—Shut it.

A blow to the head, and Chon's mind flew in pieces amid the extinguished stars, which smelled of sulphur.

XXX

Now the jeep made its way, jerky at first, gears clanking, its driver nervous.

The BECAT moved through the silent, sunbaked barrio. The Guardia carried away the leader of Monimboseños.

They had ripped off his shirt, and one of them tossed it back in the dusty wake.

A boy darted out to retrieve the bloodstained tricot. One person appeared in a doorway, then another. The jeep, with Chon Muñoz in back, moved past. It didn't linger.

—Adiós, Choncito!

Someone, unseen, let out a cry. The jeep speeded up while others started to call out farewells. Carlita Garcia cried from her window beside the square:

—Adiós, my son!

Then Chon's bloody head appeared for an instant.

Somehow he rose, elbowing up, and glanced fiercely from the jeep. He took a final look at the barrio where he was born and raised, and had spent his life. Where he played and romped as a boy with Miguel Giner; where he spent the fragrant afternoons of adolescence discovering ideas and culture with Miguel, Cecilia, Chiri Robles and the others, in the bakery of Filomena's parents. Where Padre Velasquez helped and pushed him to become a teacher, and then . . . then . . . adiós my wife, goodbye my sons! . . . O Miguelito whom I loved more than a brother, so much, much more . . . ! And never, he sobbed, through drowned eyes, never . . . adiós my people! and forgive me, all of you!

The sunlight poured down in a torrent. The world revolved in a blur. Like heat fumes over the parched summer fields, Chon's mind was a flicker of brilliance.

The BECAT passed down a side street on the way toward Parque Central.

But a high female voice rang out as it turned the first corner:

—Choncito!

And another;

—Ciao, hermano Chon, ciao!

—Y gracias!

Their cries went up, like shrill birds, above the wake of dust.

PART FOUR

I

On and on the women moved, three and four abreast, round the corner of the Modelo. By the prison entry the chants grew louder: they bleated their slogans at Guardia standing to attention behind the metal fence topped with coils of concertina wire. Hour after hour the chorus went on, a few hundred wives and mothers who swayed slightly with grief and fatigue. At twilight the line thinned: in shifts they went off in the shadowy fields, and their campfires gleamed in the countryside.

At dawn they regrouped, replacing those who had kept a vigil through the long night. With strong coffee they grew more vociferous by mid-morning. Their ranks swelled; and by midday, despite the sunlight, their numbers surpassed the day before.

As the day went on, into late afternoon, the protests had a fatalistic note which boded ill for someone.

The press arrived: a television crew from Mexico; a Dutch team with its van marked TV in taped letters, full of electronic gear.

The urbane Anastasio Somoza went drunk before the media, blustery as he denounced the Frente delinquents.

II

—Caramba! thought Teniente Robles, as the prisoner emerged from the squalid hole. It's incredible.

That morning in Managua Chiri Robles had thrashed an old man in the slum of Open-3 for saying Guardia were *putanería*, prostitutes.

—These politicals, he thought, all ready to die with a smile on their grimy faces.

One by one the Frente leaders emerged from their cells in solitary. Bent over, squinting at the light, joints rickety from lack of glucose, they could hardly walk. More like geriatrics cases than revolutionaries. Here they came: the famous Frente with their poet laureate, Giner. The hijueputas could hardly stand up, yet here they were going on the offensive. And the rant of a thousand females, flowing over that stark prison like a river, made the Guardia want to shit his immaculate khakis. Women who didn't know their place, namely the kitchen; or what was good for them, namely bed. What a sad thing, to be opposed by so many females at one time.

—Hola, he said, calmly.

The poet tried to look up, blinded by the glare. Into the twenty-sixth day of his second hunger strike. With the first, thirty-two days, he had gotten himself transferred from the old La Aviación facility out here, near his friends.

—Chiri.

Foul and grungy as monkey turd, he made to embrace his uniformed, clean-shaven childhood friend. But he laughed, a twinkle in his rheumy eye.

—Need a hand? said the Teniente.

—No, thanks.

III

Robles glanced ahead at the main office, and there stood Alesio who stared hard at the scene. The warden had an unforgettable look on his face, offended in his dignity, obliged to negotiate with *los yeicos*.

Slowly, the guards escorted five of them. One delinquent, not quite so bad off, took the poet's arm.

—No, Giner nodded, like a cadaver leading a charge.

Tortured by Macho Pedro. Interrogated with torture, for three days and nights, in the Oficina de Seguridad. Two extended hunger strikes. He went shakily, very slowly.

—Hola.

They greeted each other with a sort of tender mockery. Too weak to be demonstrative.

—Hola.

They went along the corridor, a parade of ghosts.

Prisoners stared from their cells.

—Viva el Frente, said Miguel, softly, recognizing a face.

His joints ached. The veins stood out on his forehead. He slept badly and hallucinated during the hunger strikes. A few times Alesio had made them offers, one by one, trying to split and weaken their resistance. No? Well, try a little of this instead . . . Now, because of the noise outside, and in the press, he staged a meeting. Here comes the glorious Frente, said his gaze, like a fashion show of bums.

Giner and the others kept on moving slow.

IV

In Alesio's office the meeting started.

The respected warden said gruffly:

—All requests granted. Weekly visits, right to sunlight. Just end this shit of hunger striking.

Two, three detainees sketched a smile. Not Giner, a regular maniac; and one other, beside him. Robles wondered: what do they do for an encore? Maybe administrate the place?

The poet argued with a headshake. Then a few words, like boulders hoisted from his mind onto his tongue; and from there rolled off, into the brink.

—Not yet.

The others, save one, stared at him.

The chant of the mothers went on: a tide on the rise, against the prison walls.

—Until when?

—Long as it takes.

—You want to die? said Alesio, with a macho leer.

—Release of all political detainees.

Not Giner, but the comandante, the leader of this hunger strike at the Modelo, began a litany of demands.

—Justice for peasant victims of Guardia repression in the North.

The others nodded. They looked too drained to argue or explain themselves much.

—We have thirty days. They make promises. Once we stop, the situation changes, and he knows that. We have the women, momentum. A few more days, a week, as long as it takes.

The poet nodded agreement.

—Bueno, said a third. You can say that. But what if we come out of this ruined physically?

The comandante said:

—Better to be ruined physically, than morally.

Robles thought: incredible.

Outside the Modelo, the women hollered and beat on pots and pans.

The times were tense and quite volatile. Robles knew negotiations had begun on several fronts, domestic and international. After September 21st, once the Guardia took back Estelí and the other Pacific Coast cities, talks started between President Somoza and various ambassadors under a U.S. aegis: all bent on saving the country from communism. Nearly everyone wanted Tacho Somoza to leave, so a plan could be implemented to salvage the status quo. Broaden the middle class perhaps: let more people in on the action. So the U.S. sent in their man, trying to mediate. A similar initiative was taken by the Organization of American States.

But Somoza refused to step down. And the Frente declined the honor of a deal with Tacho. They had their own internal difficulties, split into three tendencies; and many believed their sectarianism would finish them, surer than the regime. State Security had diabolical ways of fomenting discord.

Meanwhile the dictator beefed up his National Guard and began to buy weapons from abroad, a lot of weapons.

—No, said the poet. We're in charge.

—But we're dying.

Alesio watched them, because Alesio was no fool. He knew, and the Frente leaders knew, who had the last word when it came to hunger strikes. The rules of the game changed.

It became a gamble. They fasted until they lost consciousness and were hauled off to the military hospital where they either died or began to recuperate on intravenous feeding.

—We grant all your demands, said Alesio.

The five muchachos listened to the warden. They could hear the upsurge of female voices, the clatter and voluble protests. All felt the tension of the moment.

Later, Chiri heard over a thousand were outside, with more arriving each day to invoke the wrath of God on Somoza, and his lavish concubine, la Dinorah. Oh, compáy! He risked his good reputation and more as well, for the juicy thing.

The prisoners looked stunned. They gazed around slowly.

—No, said Giner, lips pursed.

And what did he do then? He smiled, rubbing it in. He grinned at the colleagues, and at Teniente Robles, his childhood friend; and at Alesio, as if to say: isn't it amazing.

The braggart, thought Chiri: hasn't changed since we were boys.

Robles escorted him back to his cell.

—How can you do this? he asked, before the poet crawled onto his pallet.

—It's fun.

—Are you joking?

—No.

—What's so much fun about it?

—I dream, he said, with a pathetic smile, of things to be, despite us all. Of things long past, which fortify.

V

He dragged the bulging yellow carp a last few steps; he seemed to reel it in from the darkness. The slimy fish, dead when he found it, had washed up on the edge of the Lagoon. Now it lay covered with dust, shredded at the soft underbelly, and stank.

—Cook it up, he ordered, manly.

He slung the drooling, stupid mouth at Doñita's feet: made her jump back.

—Go inside and wash, she said, a quiver in her voice.

In shanties set back among the trees, a few families burned a kerosene lamp for an hour. Voices came from the cabañas, with the hoo-hoo of an owl. Someone called between rooms over at Doña Faustina's: her husband, Juan Ramón.

Tomorrow was fiesta: the San Jerónimo.

—It's after ten, said Doñita.

—No, it's not.

She changed around the time: it was late, it was early, depending.

—After ten.

—Is not.

—Be eleven soon.

—Not!

—Shh, you'll wake the baby.

Another source of frustration: the tiny girl called Alma, and Doñita used her as a muzzle.

—Cook the fish.

—Watch it, I'll make you stay home in the morning.

Tomorrow was fiesta. They would dance the Tata Chombito through the streets.

Miguelito kicked the carp with his bare foot.

—Why couldn't I have a real mother?

Doñita hardly left the house anymore, and this made him angry with her. Sometimes he thought she was going crazy. He wanted to abuse her.

Along the Calle Calvario some men raised their voices, back late from Santana's. Drunken men. Miguel frowned; he stomped his foot and suddenly raised his hands toward her. Doñita's eyes went wide, but he started crying and fell to his knees. He beat on the carp with his two fists, and the fin rose and cut his finger. The men laughed disrespectfully along the Calvario. They spurred on the temper tantrum of the boy, and the thin voice of Alma, inside, who started to cry.

Tomorrow was fiesta.

Padre Velasquez, who loved to declaim, was reading from *Life Is a Dream* when he came to a passage on death in childbirth. The stilted language almost lulled Miguelito to sleep, along with his classmates who sat at their wooden desks day after day, uttering wooden responses.

—"*His mother, numberless times, in visions, saw a rude monster tear through her entrails.*"

In the semi-somnolent classroom draped with sunlight and shadows at siesta, Miguel sort of jolted forward. His ears perked up as Padre Velasquez continued:

—"*The heavens darkened; buildings shook; the clouds rained stones, rivers ran blood! And in that frenzy was Segismundo born, indicating his nature by killing his mother.*"

Miguel sat forward. The expression on his flushed face caused Padre to pause. No other student had a clue of the great Calderón, but Miguel hung on the words with a faroff look; his young breast heaved.

Sometimes he listened to his teacher, sometimes he daydreamed. What he liked about Lope de Vega, reading Lope's plays unassigned, was the playful passion of the characters.

> *Laurencia: But tell me, my beloved,*
> *Who killed the commander?*
> *Frondoso: Fuente Ovejuna, mi amor.*
> *Laurencia: So it wasn't just slander.*
> *Ay! you make me afraid—*
> *Frondoso: And how do I kill you, sweet maid?*
> *Laurencia: With a kiss, mi amor*
> *and with love, lots of love*
> *coming straight from the core!*

He felt sort of that way about a girl in class, Cecilia Asturia.

With Choncito, Elias, Chiri he sprinted whooping among the humble dwellings. They visited workshops where the men fashioned wobbly toy carts, coloring them red, green and yellow; and where the women wove palm mats, sombreros, cross-eyed dolls; or intricate butterflies made of wicker. There were hammocks of sisal hemp, fit for the siesta of gods. Some of the men like Presencio sculpted in wood, or worked in clay. They created statues of the saints, which their wives took to the central marketplace. Others made leather sandals and saddlery in the small workshops that were their homes.

They were glad to see Miguel and Chon Muñoz arrive.

—Muchachos, come inside. Take a little rest!

The wife of Presencio went in back for a tray of guayaba drinks, while the artisan told about the Indian general Zeledón: how he fought in 1912 and was killed, and paraded feet first on a mule through the streets of Masaya, naked, by the yanquis.

—Did he speak Nahuatl? asked Miguel.

—I think Spanish, said Presencio. He was a lawyer. But his forefathers were Indian, like ours.

—Did Sandino know about him?

—Sandino was a boy your age, said Presencio, and he watched, as they paraded Zeledón's body.

—Why? said Chiri.

The only light came from a narrow lane overhung with medlar trees.

—Why do you think? said the artisan, and placed his drink on a wood table.

—Well . . . , said Chon, pondering. Who did Zeledón know about?

—Lautaro, for one, an Indian who fought the Spanish.

—Did he speak their language?

—No, but he saw their bearded faces, appearing over the horizon. And he knew about them from the sound of their voices.

—Then what happened? said Chon.

—He beat them off, but more kept coming. And the invaders were armed. They lied; they made false treaties to gain an advantage.

—Who else? said Elias.

—Diriangén battled them, of the Dirianes. He threw himself in Casitas volcano, rather than be captured. His blood flows in our veins.

—Chocho! said the boys, putting down their cups.

Then they rose with a chorus of "Gracias, Presencio!" and ran outside to play in the hour before suppertime. Now their thoughts were on rebel chieftains, Cuauhtémoc who said:

*I found out
what it means to trust
your false promises
oh Malinche! (Cortes)
I knew from the instant
I failed to raise a hand
against my own life,—
seeing you enter my city
of Tenochtitlan,—
that you had reserved for me
such a destiny.* *

VI

The streets of Monimbó were narrow and unpaved, but a clean sand covered those nearer San Sebastien. There some were wide and shaded, with avocado and mazzard cherry trees, guanabanos and mandroños. Away from the central square, the low dwellings were constructed of reeds, bamboo and palm leaves, rattan. The earth of their ample patios was beaten smooth by the passing generations, and life didn't seem to change.

When Miguel, Chon, Chiri and the Rodriguez brothers reached mid-teenage, their interest faded in rugged games, racing about with a slingshot or toy rifle. Imperceptibly, at first, the mood grew more languorous: different words, and different intentions. They discussed girls and far places, beyond Managua: Mexico City with its university, the United States where money grew on trees, a land of glittery wonders, movie stars. While the sun went down, a saturated red behind the thatched huts, towering oaks and coconut palms, the teenagers made their way home from a bakery, La Calzada, where Choncito's sweetheart worked, and where they spent the late afternoon mulling over many things.

On Sunday there were girls from Monimbó, La Parroquia and Paises Bajos: they eyed the group of boys coyly and giggled beneath

---

*By Leonel Rugama, who also wrote: *Ahora vamos a vivir como los santos* the lemon trees in blossom. Miguel was tormented by shyness; he tried to think of a few big words which would impress them. He wanted to declaim a line or two from the adored poetry of Bècquer, but still he hung back, and his attempts at macho jokes weren't funny.

In every spare moment he read the *Quijote* on his own, or waded through Peréz Galdós, Spain's second novelist; he had begun to appreciate the Grupo Poetico of 1927, the difficult modern writers. By now Doñita Reyes thought there was something wrong with him.

—Don't you get tired of sitting alone?

—No.

He didn't look up.

—How can you read so much?

—With my eyes, with my eyes.

—I'm telling Padre not to loan you anymore books. It isn't normal.

She shook her head, removing a tortilla from the *comal* to fill it with rice and beans, a bit of pork, and Faustina's yucca alongside.

—Doesn't it confuse your brain?

He shrugged and gulped.

Now and again he played with Alma for an hour. He took a kind of pleasure in her pathetic little games, going to school, shopping in the market. A shepherd fell in love with a peasant girl; they met beneath a ceiba tree on the outskirts of the village, but her father didn't approve; and so they ran away . . . By this time Alma was a gentle girl who would do him a favor if he asked, and loved the trinkets he brought her from his jaunts each afternoon. She went about in her own dreamworld, third among the recluses; though she really liked to spend time across the way at Doña Faustina's. Almita almost never laughed, unless Miguel was on hand to tell her a story, or tickle her while Doñita hovered over and tried to make him stop.

Sometimes he read her a children's book but could not refrain from mockery of the characters. She began to cast sad glances when he did that: sad not for herself, but for the good fairies, donkeys who became princes, a sea otter involved in wonderful adventures. She saw them all as real beings when Miguel made use of his gift of mimickry.

But he often teased his little sister and made fun of her. Sometimes he carried on until she started to cry quietly. Other times he put such feeling into the magical story, she hardly remembered where she was, or who she was.

VII

At La Calzada Bakery they engaged in lofty discussions. Miguel read a new poem that described a road, a solitary tree in a field, a mountain; the sadness of slow-chiming bells; the midday heat expressed in the soliloquy of a sundew, an insect-catching plant. He would put the world into words. Among the La Calzada circle there was a strong urge to idealize. The Rodriguez brothers, Chiri, Marta on those rare occasions when she arrived: all were filled with an enthusiastic purity, often stated in religious terms. The girl named Cecilia Asturia had an air of seriousness: she was eighteen, tall, a barrio beauty; any boy would have wanted her for his sweetheart. Everyone knew Chiri Robles loved her; but it was Miguel who walked her home, some evenings, while the sun headed westward over the chilly Carazo plateaus and the small village where Iván Giner had spent his boyhood. Miguel told her of a hymn he had written to the worker in Masaya's home industries: it ended with an epiphany of human labor. And he had begun an epic about his hero, the national poet, Rubén Darío.

One day in the bakery he said:

—I want to travel far away, and then come back.

—Where to? said Chiri.

—I don't know. Managua, to start.

Chon said:

—Nicas are always leaving, *de viaje!* and they don't know where. It used to be Managua to get work, not a romantic voyage. Then in '72 the earthquake seemed to say: not here either.

Miguel stared at his friend with admiration but also a certain perplexity. Of late he had felt Choncito's need to cling to him and spend more time together; though Miguel was reading thick volumes as if he meant to emulate The Scholiast. Chon's attitude felt unnatural. Also Miguel, the foster child, had grown very independent; he could almost take people or leave them, whereas Chon Muñoz, a son of stolid peasant stock, had a deeply shy, proper, exclusive way of treating those he loved.

At times, lately, the two friends had spoken at cross purposes: the poet uneasy with his friend's persistent intimacy. He considered himself an artist, and apart; not better, but different; and he went so far as to ascribe special rights to himself. Sometimes he would posture, which his peers quietly resented. Was Chon jealous? Was that a virile emotion? Miguel sensed a certain queasiness in their relationship: suddenly he had to be careful about what he said. Things were no longer as simple as when they raced through the barrio in quest of adventure, and were received with smiles and treats wherever they decided to cross a threshold.

Filomena worked steadily in her white dough-stained apron. Bread baking in the deep oven was an ardent presence. She cast a glimpse at her fiancé engaged in intense discussion. Outside, some kids stared in at the poet, Elias and others who had become their idols: still boyish like themselves, in some ways, but respected like the men.

—No, I need to go away, said Miguel, where I can learn new things.

—What kind of things? said Chiri.

—Big-shot things, said Chon, laughing. But he'll be back. What's truly important he could find here.

VIII

That night he went home and wrote his sonnet, later published in La Prensa Literaria, about the 1972 earthquake. He was enthralled with language, bursting like a pomegranate with poetic fervor. Still a slave of words, he monumentalized the huge disaster of two years before, à la Calderón: "... *a primal rending/ a shudder of inner-terrestrial love/like a revelation of distance/and universal pang!*"

At two o'clock in the morning he woke up poor Doñita for a recital. She stared at him, half asleep, from her "dewlapped orbs." Next afternoon he tried the new poem on Alma, who clapped and asked him to read the sad story of the sea otter.

Along with Chon, Chiri, Cecilia and Elias he decided to start up a theater group, and began writing a play about Zeledón, the Indian general. They met in a café on Parque Central to speak self-consciously of beauty, love, poetry and art; the significance of the Gospels for social action; also relations between the sexes, as the elevated tone became a bit more personal. Miguel wrote an eclogue on the *juco*, a primitive instrument.

But the best of his early poems, perhaps, was one about the long-throated bird called guardabarranco, its song tinged with pathos.

Along sunlit glens and ravines of Monimbó, children chased after the lovely guardabarranco and its iridescent plumage. Boys ran about with their slings and arrows, climbing for fruit in the treetops where the warbler perched. During the afternoons populated with birds, the indigenous barrio went on with its hard work in the dignified tradition of the Dirianes, the Chorotegas, the Nahoa tribe. Across centuries the inhabitants of Monimbó heard the nervous song of the guardabarranco pursued by the children.

There was hemp drying in the solariums; while at night the sweet sound of marimbas danced with flutes. There was the stir of people settling in, like a guardabarranco rustling its plumage.

IX

One afternoon, in December of that year, 1974, they were together in the bakery. Chon's fiancée had taken a break from her work, when a boy ran by outside and yelled at the top of his lungs.

—What's this? said Chon.

Chiri Robles was on his feet and went to see. In a few moments he came back.

—There's a guerrilla action in Managua.

—What action?

—Some of Somoza's friends were having a Christmas party when the Frente overran the house.

—Somoza too? said Cecilia.

—He wasn't there, and the U.S. Ambassador had just left.

At Monges' there were a dozen people around the television. The Archbishop of Managua was shown as he entered the house of Tacho's crony in order to communicate with the Frente and hostages inside. The crony was killed the night before when he appeared from his bedroom gun in hand. Afterward the women were allowed to leave, and the house lay surrounded by Guardia Nacional. Several dignitaries remained captive.

The reporter on the scene gave way to a tinny voice, speaking by telephone:

—*"Where are the campesinos Santos and Genaro Díaz? Where are Pedro Hernández, María Castíl, Victor Flores, Juan Castíl . . . Felipe Aguilar and his papá?"*

Miguel sat alongside Choncito while the communiqué was read. Monge's wife brought in tea and cookies on a tray.

—"*Where is the Loza family except for the traitor Pedrito? The four children who were with César Flores, in a cave in Yaosca Central?*"

The sound of the distant voice sent a shudder down Miguel's spine. He thought of his father in the mountains, where guerrilla bands roamed and paid night visits on the campesinos, or attacked a Guardia outpost.

That night few people slept. Everyone gathered round radios and televisions, as in Managua the negotiations went on. Back home Miguel snapped at Doñita and told her she better shape up. He ignored Alma,—stared past her wildly as he went in his room.

—"*Where is Victoria Díaz? And the four who were assassinated in Rancho Grande? Also, the five campesino leaders captured in Chinandega when the lands were confiscated in Palo Alto? The dictatorship must answer to this.*"

Along the route to the airport there were thousands of Managuans. They waved and cheered.

Some blew whistles. Others held up their hands in a victory sign.

—Viva el Frente!

The people at Monges watched in silence. An hour later a plane carrying rebel leaders took off for Cuba from Las Mercedes Airport.

Somoza had met the minimum demands.

X

The streets of Masaya came alive with bright costumes, musical instruments, masks. A torrent of faces, gyrating limbs and painted shoulders rippled on the surface. There were hair-sieve masks and headdresses of flowers crowned with a soaring ostrich plume, while the dancers wore greaved boots with Indian motifs. From corner to corner they danced and gave a wild laughter to the beat of drums. Masaya was a swirling river in spate, as the yearly rites got underway.

The men ran in cadence, herky-jerky past the rows of people on each side. Many were masked, stripped to the waist and painted with black pigment like devils. A man-bull danced the Toro Venado: he mocked a Spanish courtier in love with an Indian girl, in colonial times.

Miguel moved through the dense crowd. Across the way Cecilia caught his eye: the blacksmith's daughter from San Juan barrio. She was very pretty; she might be his sweetheart if he crossed over to her, on this day of days, and took her hand. And then? For months he had thought of departure, striking out on his own, like Iván; but not to go hunt monkeys in the jungles of Zelaya North, or become a guerrilla fighter. No, he wanted a destiny in literature, like Rubén Darío; he would seek out educated men and women who knew Europe and got themselves published. Try his fortunes in the great world where poets sang full-throated, with love, joy and pain, compassion.

—The truly important things, Choncito told him, you could find here.

Chon had advocated a serious relationship with Cecilia Asturia.

In a few hours Lazaro's skyrockets would soar into the twilight as the regenerative ritual turned to an orgy of rum. Now the Monimboseños danced the Baile de las Inditas, and Miguel joined in the circle. In a poem that night he would catch the rhythms of the San Jerónimo. Now, after a year in his room reading, the call to life was irresistible.

Someone took his arm, drawing him from the dance. Chon Muñoz, in an embroidered toga-like outfit for the festivities, stood alongside his fiancée. His stout muscular limbs well oiled, sleek, he looked pleased with himself.

—Hola.

The crowd cavorted, with shouts. Kettledrums, voices drove on the aggressive rhythm. The line of dancers lunged in a sensuous abandon.

—I'm going away, said Miguel.

—Where?

—Managua, first.

—And do what there, amigo?

—The things we've talked about: live, learn to write.

Tenderly Choncito put an arm around his fiancée's shoulders.

—Hear that, Filomena? He's gotten too big for our little town.

But Miguel looked away. In his friend's eyes an old hurt, never to be shared or spoken, seemed to focus, for an instant, too frankly.

—When are you leaving?

—Tomorrow.

—So soon.

Filomena frowned and drew closer to her husband soon to be. Their marriage had been scheduled for the week of Purisima, feast of the Immaculate Conception.

The teacher said:

—You two wait here.

He skipped off in his sandals toward San Sebastien. He looked childishly lovable, and quite bizarre, in his toga. For a moment Miguel played one of his little tricks on Filomena. He could be mean in strange ways: he reduced Alma to tears with a story about the sea otter's funeral beneath the sea, or the macaw flying away forever.

—You'll tell your grandchildren about our afternoons in the bakery, the crazy questions we asked about life. That's over now, for us. Someday, maybe, we'll be together . . .

In a few minutes, when Filomena was sniffling at Miguel's sad words, Chon returned. He handed him an envelope:

—Take care of this. Put it in your pocket, and don't forget it tomorrow.

The two friends embraced. Such immensely important things in life, sometimes, which could never be expressed . . . That was sadder than all the rest.

Chon drew away.

—Come home when you need a break.

—Home.

Miguel frowned: he had made himself depressed with his stories. But Chon laughed, handsome in the late afternoon light.

—Do what you have to out there. Don't worry! In many different ways, we have to build our future.

When they shook hands, before parting, Filomena gazed with emotion in her fiancé's eyes.

Later, Miguel saw Cecilia talking with Chiri Robles, on the far side of an intersection where the dance had paused to form a circle, in its raucous course through the narrow streets.

XI

In the Colegio entry Padre Velasquez had an air of weariness.

He gestured:

—Why aren't you with the others?

—I'm going away tomorrow.

—Where?

At dusk, Masaya danced with a more convulsive rhythm in the distance. Every year it was the same, ending in drunkenness, until a sodden lassitude settled over the barrios. Marimbas, laughter and cries rose toward a strenuous finale.

—I'll go to Managua. I'll see what books I can find.

—Books! Padre stared at him. Boy, how will you live?

—Sweep trash if I have to.

—When will you study, and write?

With a stoical air Padre stared at him on the threshold. He loved the extraordinary student but resented his openness, independence, his willpower which wouldn't be deterred, perhaps, so easily. Padre remembered himself at that age: the aspirations to great discipledom, the sojourn in San Carlos, the sickness and eclipse of certain spiritual ambitions. Always he sensed a tinge of hybris in his prize student.

—Is this a good idea?

—Very good, Padre.

—Think of Doñita: her life is hard.

—I know.

—She needs you at home.

—Juan Ramón will keep an eye out. He'll help her.

—Sometime you should let her know you appreciate her.

—I do.

—But as a mother.

—She's not my mother.

Padre blinked. This was precisely what he disliked in Miguel: young, wildly talented, and ruthless. He might go far beyond what the Colegio could ever teach him, but there was a lack of humility, spiritual commitment, seriousness. For years this boy had inspired a keen ambivalence: almost a desire to write him off as a pagan, an aberration amid the fanatical religious fervor of the barrio. In this moment the educator felt a surge of resentment: the adolescent had been wayward, the young man would learn, one way or another, the fear of God.

—She loves you like one, and more than most.

—I know that, but I've got to leave.

—Well, Padre looked past him, I thought like you once. Idealism is a fine thing, but life proves . . . otherwise.

—And?

—The day came when I stopped trying to run away.

—From what?

—Myself . . . , he paused. From God.

—When spring comes, said Miguel, his mind still on Cecilia Asturia, you don't tell the buds not to bloom because a petal is such a risk. You can't be afraid of the wilting sunlight, or of men either. You have to go! It was you, Padre, who taught me the parable of the talents.

—I also tried to teach you humility.

—I've got a strong arm for sweeping market stalls. I've got a mind to learn my vocation: literature. Is that prideful?

—Literature! Padre sighed, gazed off and said: Ask God your questions.

—I did. You know what He told me? Never give up.

The priest frowned. A moment later he went to his bookshelf and took down two volumes: one a primer of the French language, the other *Don Quijote* in a leather bound edition. Miguel sniffed the pages, hearing marimbas and the beat of kettledrums in Parque Central as evening came on, and hundreds danced the Baile de los Diablitos. He said, offhand:

—Sandino read this book by his campfire in the Segovias.

—Hardly, said Padre, its major claim on our interest.

—Why?

—Sandino was a violent man.

—And Somoza, who killed him by trickery?

—Wrong also.

—And our violence, Padre?

—I don't harbor hatred. The only peace resides in the wounds of Christ.

—Fine, said Miguel. But a time is coming when abstractions will fly off to Miami, and the fancy boutiques.

A glimmer of anger played in the priest's eye.

—That's blasphemy.

Miguel was far from wanting to leave his mentor on a negative note. But the devil got into him sometimes, and he flared up at people's limits. How often, as an adolescent, he had maddened and provoked the barrio adults, who laughed a minute later and wrote him off.

—This is Nicaragua. Talk to the Guardia about Christ's wounds.

Padre had thought of penning a few letters for colleagues in the capital: it would facilitate things for Miguel. But then he considered, lips pursed: the fear of God! . . . Sunset spread its red aura over low rooftops bordering the square. Shadows gathered in the Salesiano entrance as Padre Velasquez watched his alumnus depart. Growing older, his soul no longer so vigorous as when he took Christ's message to the children of Río San Juan,—the softish cast of his features, and careful eyes, seemed to take on a tonality of evening.

It would be two years before he saw Miguel Giner again: late in '77, a week after Frente attacks in Masaya, Rivas and San Carlos had stunned the country. By that time Miguel would be married, and a poet whose star was on the rise. "Barrio Dance" would have appeared in La Prensa Literaria, recalling the afternoon when he came to bid him farewell, and they traded salvos over Christ's wounds. Ay! what a thing of beauty that poem was, with its classical turn, yet so enlivened. What prosodic mastery, what rhythms, what an apt disposition of images! The boy was a born poet, a prince of words and yet, most regrettably, a rebel to the core.

—Adiós, said the Padre turning, in his clerical robe, back into the unlit foyer.

XII

That night Miguel packed his few possessions in a knapsack. Too bad he didn't leave home every night: his mood was so much brighter than usual, tender to little Alma, and Doñita. At nightfall he visited across the way at Faustina's; and then, later, it seemed his foster mother's every glance was a sniffled plea not to leave, a silent reproach.

He let his sister sit in the room while he packed, teasing her gently. He read her the story of the sea otter and invited her to move into his room since he was going away. But this only made her cry.

Doñita appeared in the doorway and said:

—You're mad.

He gave the clear happy laughter that follows a difficult decision. He put Chon's envelope between the elegant pages of the *Quijote*: he hadn't opened it yet.

—Absolutamente loco! she cried from the kitchen.

—Will you write to us? Alma piped.

—Do you deserve it?

She paused a moment, and hung her head.

He threw down what he was packing, and took her pretty face in his hands. But he couldn't resist tickling until she hardly stood it anymore. He mimicked Doñita Reyes, the way she always scowled; and just then the whole ungainly mass of her appeared in the low doorway, with a tearful frown exactly the way he imitated. Alma watched him, and her features gave little hops of joy and sadness.

—Perdón! he said.

Doñita went back to cook some more: a banquet for him to take out on the highway: just as she had for Iván Giner, in the old days.

Past midnight Miguel lay in bed and composed a poem, his thoughts in a whirlwind. He went to the window and breathed in the dewy night air. Chon Muñoz perplexed him: what was it like? The hundred insects, an owl playing its oboe, the breeze rustling through the dark mass of trees: all nature paused, in a quiet jubilance before adventure. But Choncito . . . ? On first intimation of his friend's feeling a quizzical neutrality, a sense of inquiry had entered their relations. That seemed to give Chon pause; he drew back; though Miguel's exuberant nature took the thing in stride. It concerned his boyhood playmate, no one else. How fathomless nature was! The greatest poet stayed a prisoner in his own mind.

Outside, in the wide tropical night, there was a murmurous creep . . . creep. Spiders, scorpions prowled the deep humus of leaves, as centipedes and wood-lice scurried from their path. What were the dangers? What were the social implications for Chon Muñoz? The same owl gave its haunting call; a nightjar cried out harshly across the forest. None; because nobody would ever know. Chon loved his Filomena and would father children by her, faithful to the end, and uncomplaining. What could be more terrible? Taboo of love: exile from one's most vital forces. A bat flittered through the trees. A jaguar or tawny ocelot poised in the intricate darkness of the Calvario before its plunge. As long as poor Choncito strode the sun-baked streets and narrow twisting lanes of Masaya; accepted his share of joy and hardship; struggled, doubted, loved, hoping beyond all hope;—he would have the heavy thing in him.

—Isn't it wrong? thought Miguel.

In the early hours Monimbó lay quiet, exhausted by its festival no less than its secular toil. Now through the empty streets the lurching

Tata Chombito reechoed, but only the dreamy poet heard where he knelt by his window among the orchids and stars, the tangled lianas, and perching epiphytes, night perfumed by beds of wild cane beyond the Lagoon.

In the moments before dawn he went in Alma's room and hugged her.

—I'm going.

—Come back soon!

The girl, half asleep, started crying.

—I'll be back.

—Will you write us?

—Sure.

He paused on his haunches by her tiny cot.

—Your father was my father, he said. Our mothers were not the same, but our papi was Iván Giner, the wanderer.

—I know.

—Someday, when he comes home, we'll all be together, and happy.

She lay back on her beige pillow, with its bit of lace: the one Doña Faustina gave her last year for her birthday. In a minute the world would seem so deserted.

He found Doñita sitting in the kitchen. She looked spent and hadn't slept either. She muttered:

—Idiot . . . where's he going now, and who will wait on him, hand and foot?

He put down his knapsack and leaned to hug her.

—I don't need to be waited on.

Then he remembered what Padre said about calling her mother, but the word died on his lips. Juana was his mother, Juana the daughter of Don Justo, Ferrán's plantation manager. She must have felt this way: the day she eloped with a seasonal worker, and then there was more suffering than happiness.

Doñita cried quietly.

—Here, take your food. Try to stay alive.

Messy woman. The birthmark on her cheek crimson as the blush of sunrise.

—Don't worry about me, he said, on his way. And gracias, Mamita.

He went out in the dawn light and walked the Calle Calvario: past Faustina's place, past the little church of the Calvarito, and Chepe's store. Morning stars bounced to the rhythm of his steps. Iván made this trek, years before, after his visits.

Birds chirped. The sky was a ripe peach by the time he reached the highway. Then he opened Choncito's envelope and found seven 100-cordoba notes, a fortune, a year of his friend's savings.

On the dusty roadside he felt joy and a full heart. He was going out to meet the world and get a hold on reality. His heart raced, as he watched a first car along the road to Managua.

XIII

From day to day Chiri Robles spent a few minutes with his childhood friend. He went by the cell and asked a question or shared his thoughts on something said the day before. He was doing this on his own; though there could be a promotion in it, if he gleaned some detail missed by State Security in their own discussions with the key prisoner. Certain things had obvious interest, like names, but other bits of info might be worth a gold mine. A detainee, even an experienced revolutionary, rarely knew what he revealed. Yes, their boyhood friendship could prove a godsend.

Yet Robles didn't go by the cell simply on business. He began lingering from sheer fascination, without the warden's knowing. How did anyone, above all a poet, go through such misery and retain his sanity? And sense of humor! It was magnetic; he made your head spin. The *yeicos* drummed up their mystique; but couldn't Teniente

Robles, with his advanced training at the school for elite forces, see through any artifice?

One afternoon he said to Giner, trying to provoke him and find an opening:

—You're all dreamers. But prison is the place where you come down to earth. What makes you think the few dozen of you will overthrow Tacho Somoza?

The poet smiled. He smiled when you contradicted him. He liked to smile, when in pain.

—Hamlet. Ever heard of him?

—Who?

Chiri thought: this is interesting. Finally, a name; probably a pseudonym.

Miguel started talking about the compañero Hamlet. Whew! thought Chiri, nobody tells a story like this guy. He made you feel those people, better than TV!

—Hamlet's father was poisoned.

—That's bad.

Robles never heard of a case where State Security used poison on the parents of a comunista. But Tacho was inventive, a shrewd tactician. Maybe Dinorah suggested it, breasty witch.

—Hamlet loved his father, a just man.

Pretty soon the guard had to go. The round of duties called; though the conversation was just beginning. In the early '70s a scandal erupted when Frente prisoners subverted a corps of Guardia and involved them in study groups. The men were transferred to the Atlantic Coast.

Chiri Robles decided to wait before informing Alesio about this Hamletito character. What if it turned out to be a comandante? The poet let slip his whereabouts; and then, after Hamlet's capture, a promotion and a raise!

Next day the guard was back and paused outside Giner's cell.

—You were saying about, uh . . . ?

—Ah, Hamlet. Bueno, like I told you, his uncle married his mother soon after the funeral. Too soon.

—Typical Nicas.

—Seguro! But his uncle was not a just man, and Hamlet never loved him.

—Hombre, this Hamlet is too intense. If I had to spend my life thinking about who is just.

—Then Hamlet saw his father's ghost stalking midnight on the ramparts.

—Do what? Ramparts—?

—In the castle, you know, where they lived.

—Castles in Nicaragua?

—Sure: sort of like Coyotepe.

Chiri thought: some delinquent, living in a castle. They're just like everybody else.

XIV

He waited for Miguel to make a slip. He wanted worse than the devil to learn about this Hamlet, his description and modus operandi, his present whereabouts. So he phoned a contact in OSN for a list of castles. That should give me a clue at least, thought Chiri. Imagine Alesio green with envy when they offer me a banquet and distinguished service medal: *Teniente Robles showed truly brilliant skill in establishing rapport with the strategic prisoner, who, due to Robles' deft psychological maneuvering, revealed key Frente secrets* . . . Then Tacho kisses me on the cheek, like a brother, and offers me a million. And La Dinorah, ay! The shivers down my spine, as we dance, and her silken bust catches my tie-clasp, electric . . . Ay, doctor!

—Hamlet had a sense of honor. He couldn't digest the way his mother and uncle trotted down the aisle. Also the fact of the ghost, who told about foul play, poison in his ear.

—What did he do next?

—What would you have done?

—Bueno, let them alone I guess, if that's all they wanted. They had the power. They could wallow in sin as long as they liked. My turn will come.

—Hamlet was too upset. Frustrated, angry. He needed to take a decision, and act, but he couldn't.

Dark-eyed, emaciated, Miguel stared out at his childhood friend through the bars, and seemed to enjoy himself.

Chiri gave a start. There was a moment when he felt he might be gulled some way or other. Plus he had chores waiting.

By this time the Guardia officer had been around his share of comunistas. He found them slippery, and none too eager to play by the rules. Yet Frente detainees were respectful. They used sensitivity to get a hold on people's minds: lice-ridden, scratching themselves, they could charm you out of your wits. They were real. Of course they weren't above killing you, as they did Perez Vega, or Gonzalo Lacayo Murillo, Guardia brass. But, at the Modelo, they responded to the harshest words with courtesy; to beatings with a sort of pity, saying it was the system's fault, and a torturer was a victim. They didn't call you *bestia* in here. No, Miguel and the others looked for something to relate to, in their guards. Alesio had been warden at La Aviación that time a contingent of guards had to be rebilleted to the Atlantic Coast. So Alesio kept close tabs on his staff: no getting emotionally involved.

XV

—So what about this Hamlet fellow?

—What about him?

—He's interesting: tell me more. Is he comandante or sub-comandante?

Like a burrowing animal the prisoner squinted through his bit of barred window at the guard's well kempt hair and healthy, shaven features. He thought of sunlit afternoons when they moved together with Cecilia Asturia and Chon Muñoz amid the paths, the gardens and back lanes of the Rinconadas, visiting awhile with Presencio the artisan, Lazaro in his pyrotechnics workshop, Fasael the mechanic. Around Cecilia there was a scent of first love, a sweet fullness, the promise of adolescence.

—Does he rob banks and recuperate funds?

Chiri lent a touch of irony: you dignify your crimes with special terms, like a lawyer. He was on the other side, a Guardia lieutenant on his way up.

—Hamlet's the moody type, a thinker.

—Ah, even more dangerous. In the National Directorate no doubt.

—He gets depressed being so intelligent. Has a hard time deciding on a plan. Then circumstances go against him.

—Too much criticism and self-criticism? said the guard.

—He's hung up on words, words, words. Also, he has a sweetheart named Ophelia.

—The plot thickens, said Robles. Some of these women are hard-core subversives.

Miguel looked in his guard's eyes. He remembered Chiri as an eight year-old tagging after himself and Choncito: less independent, a trifle snot-nosed; always had to go home, his mama was a strict one.

—Hamlet is a comandante despite himself.

—Maybe the compañero needs a psychiatrist, said Chiri. And this Ophelia?

Another name: he made a mental note. Time to take the business to Alesio. And: my son will attend university in the States.

—Where does she live?

—Who? said Miguel, distracted, speaking with an effort.

—Ophelia.

—In history, señor.

—Ah . . . she died?

—Drowned, would you believe it? She couldn't swim.

—In Río Coco?

—Hamlet had so many problems in those days. Started talking to himself.

—Like a crazy prisoner.

—Too much time alone. But he saw his friend Horacio, and they discussed what to do about the family situation.

—See a counselor! Abide by the law. Work for democratic reforms.

Miguel paused. He gave his old friend a long, doleful look.

—I'm afraid thinking so much, being alone, has turned Hamlet into a coward.

—Comandante guerrillero, and a coward?

—He can't take the isolation, the mental aspect.

—Is he up in the mountains now? Maybe he has mountain leprosy.

—No, but sometimes he wants out. All he thinks of is Ophelia and trying his hand at poetry.

—Show me a Nica who doesn't write poems.

Chiri waited. He stared in at Giner oozing sweat and grime in the semi-darkness. He thought: my son, *my son* will have advantages I never . . . The guard spoke low:

—Would he make a deal? Trade certain information, you know, for . . . a ticket somewhere?

—In his heart,—Miguel's voice was languid,—now he just wants life, nature, his wife. But things have been happening too fast for him. He killed an old man by mistake.

—Ha! Comunista murders senior citizen in cold blood. Wasn't the case reported in Novedades?

—Same one.

—Who was the old man?

—An informer, a snooper. Like an adviser, all bloated up with propaganda. Before then, yes, Hamlet might have been willing to sell out.

—With honor, said Chiri.

—But the other side wasn't playing fair. So Hamlet ran him through.

—Bayoneted him?

—You could say. He had to come out of his solitude, and act. Shakespeare's men are actors.

—Shakespeare? The Comandante en Jefe?

Four names! This could definitely lead to a promotion. First a Mercedes for the wife; then university, in T-h-e S-t-a-t-e-s, for his son. To Alesio, right now, before he forgot the foreign sounding names.

What Miguel never knew, and the guard still remembered, was that Chiri had loved Cecilia Asturia with a fervor, and she rejected him. And then he felt a jealous rage, for the longest time, against Miguel Giner. It was assumed in the barrio that Miguelito and the blacksmith's daughter would make a couple. Chiri Robles, though a good enough kid, had been insignificant. It was the insightful Padre Velasquez who first suggested enlistment in the Guardia. Padre got him the initial interview up on Coyotepe. The priest felt pity for the boy who never amounted to more than filler in a Colegio classroom.

XVI

Robles stared in the cell with its bare floor, where the prisoner slept: no cot or pallet here, transferred to solitary. The stained walls showed the unpoetic lines of how many tragedies that made Hamlet look glamorous. The flaked paint was a geography of suffering, obscure struggles, defeats beneath a filth-gray bit of ceiling. A slop bucket drew flies, assorted roaches, spiders probably eaten like delicacies with the day's few rancid beans. Among the prison population there was a high degree of promiscuity, daily provocations erupting in fist fights. But Miguel Giner hardly lent himself to that. When not in solitary he mediated the disputes of other prisoners, who respected him more than Alesio.

As the days and nights went along, Robles felt him weakening. Giner grew so depressed you could see it through the bars. The guard stalked his silences, ruminated a plan and waited to hit him with the right question at the vulnerable moment. He told him the Frente would give its cadre a Mickey Mouse watch, with thanks for a ruined life. Alesio had given him carte blanche to tempt and undermine the morale of this prisoner, since the «especialistas» and torture teams with their electronic gear and gadgets had failed.

—Sometimes, Alesio said, with a grin, you can kill a subversive with kindness. A little attention spiced with flattery, and the hardrock is yours. But no books, no pen and paper! The man has a dangerous mind.

XVII

One night Robles passed by the poet's cell and heard him reciting a poem out loud. Words so beautiful, they made the macho prison guard want to sit down and have a little cry. He stood spellbound; he gazed at the wall and thought, suddenly, about Cecilia.

—You write that? he asked through the bars.

—No.

Giner didn't feel like talking, drunk with depression. For a moment Robles worried he might commit suicide: they didn't care about death very much, only their high-flown ideals.

—Who did?

—A man named Miguel Hernandez.

—One of Hamlet's friends?

—He fought the fascists in Spain.

—Ah, internacionalista. What happened to him?

—He died in a Franco prison. Never saw his own son.

Robles heard a sort of hiccup. He thought: promocioncito! Now's the time, if he starts sobbing in front of a guard.

—So his side lost?

—Yes.

—All for nothing, was it?

Silence. Unlike other nights, when he was raring to talk. No stories of Hamlet and the other compañeros. No astute theories as to why the world must be changed. In a gentle voice Robles said:

—Have you written any new poems?

—Without pen and paper? I dream them and can't remember.

By this time a few of his works were known throughout the country. Not always political, overtly at least. They seemed to burst on the scene just in those moments when they would touch something in people. No one knew how he managed it: he had a kind of knack for drama. Let there be a crisis, and there he was, caramba! On the front page of La Prensa Literaria with more inflammatory verse.

Robles nodded and turned away when he declined to talk anymore. But it seemed like a lost opportunity.

Next day he smuggled him pen and paper: broke a cardinal rule. Miguel gave the guard an unforgettable look. And Chiri thought, rubbing his hands as he walked away: Oh ho! Now you owe me one, Sandinista *de mierda!*

That night Miguel Giner wrote his poem: *Iván Confers with the Sacuanjoche Flower.*

As for Robles, he was already implementing a little «escape plan» he and Alesio had in mind. The game, between guard and detainee, became one of establishing trust.

A deadly game.

XVIII

Managua, 1975: the sprawling marketplace squalor of the Orientales. Eerie streets and weed-grown ruins of the center; a dilapidated Grand Hotel. From dawn until a scarlet exhaust-filled twilight there were kids scooting from corner to corner selling chiclets. Little girls dressed in tatters held up their tortilla platter at a bus stop. Rusty dinted cabs scavenged fares, while a limousine made its way, sleek and aloof, up toward Tiscapa and the Hotel Intercontinental.

Beyond the Cathedral lay Lake Managua merged with the azure mist of Momotombo volcano. A small railroad puff-puffed into the cordilleras far across, as a pair of white heron glided smoothly over the composite blue water. Rubén Darío profiled against the horizon: Rubén striding among the configuration of clouds hemmed with a gold lace of sunlight, on the first morning of Miguel Giner's residence in Managua.

Soon the small fortune contributed by Chon Muñoz was nearly gone.

—Bah! A modernist.

He went among the U.C.A. students smelling of market stalls. He heeded their quips, their flippant learning with a kind of respect. He would probably never know enough to become a serious poet.

—Professor! You're deceived by superficialities: Proust was a realist.

—Symbolist; a metaphysician, who practiced Kant.

—And Darwin.

—As you like, said the one called Jaime. But he read Kant because Kant was a web spinner like himself. Whereas the philosopher caught life-in-death in the web secreted by his own triple-synthesis spinnerets, the artist sucked death-in-life with his proboscis from a carcass social class. Artists are the proboscises of the race.

—There's no class struggle in Proust.

—Mon cher, said Jaime with a nasal accent, you think if workers aren't portrayed in freedom's final battle there's no class struggle. Proust didn't know it, but he did it.

Miguel stared at Jaime, who laughed at him and winked.

The poet didn't understand a word they were saying.

—Next you'll want your Proust in neat Marxian paradoxes.

—Was Marx a Marxist?

—Such mystical beings spring up like fungus on the unscrubbed places of reality.

—Always the pyrrhonist, Jaime.

—No, colleague. I don't want my Proust dressed up in Parnassian drag. Find me a copy of La Recherche in Nicaragua, and we'll hold a national debate.

Miguel blurted:

—You haven't read it?

—3134 dense pages, said another, a million words. Single sentences over a thousand.

—The long Proustian leap to quality, said Jaime, and looked away.

In the downtown ruins he found a tumbledown fragment of one-storey house, like the prow of an ancient galleon stuck in a reed bed, tilting sideways. He brought in a scrawny tomcat, pleased to share its ticks rather than have the rats get his *Quijote*. He draped a bit of canvas over the splintered floor and used strips of cardboard as a bed.

Mornings he went to the Mercado Oriental, saluting the pork peddlers, charcoal sellers sooty in their coarse apparel; hawkers of fresh vegetables, shellfish, sherbets; firewood, coal, coconut sweets, shoeshines, maize drinks fermented or otherwise. Miguel gave a

Hola! to chiclet vendors eating up their proceeds, as the market rushed, with a same masticated rhythm, toward noontime.

—Pork-pork-pork!

—La Preeen-sa-a!

—One-peso-one-peso-one-pesopeso!

A motorbike zipped by, farted exhaust.

The poet greeted the women selling tripe soup, who would provide his one meal. In the Orientales he passed vats of chicha (fermented maize), pozol (boiled barley) with milk, cacao and tamarind drinks, pitahaya (cactus) with lemon, jícara (calabash) seed, a hundred sapid refreshments. He saluted the army of vagrants scrounging a meal from scraps.

He gazed with sorrow at yesterday's tamales, at piles of gumdrops old as the pyramids. His stomach gurgled a slogan against hunger, whiffing rice and beans topped with sour cream.

Everywhere the cries of taxi drivers competed for a fare, whistled at some gringo's Bermuda shorts.

At nightfall he trudged back in the ruins to study by candlelight until dawn. But after an hour he lay felled with exhaustion while his hard earned candle guttered in an onslaught of moths.

Early one morning Jaime entered with a leather satchel. He gazed at Miguel Giner's lodgings.

—A bucolic setting, he said, dubious. You live here?

—For now.

—Well, I brought you a few books, but I'm not so sure. I hate to donate the only exemplar in Nicaragua to our needy rats.

—What books?

The poet rubbed his eyes and gazed at a makeshift sundial. The U.C.A. student, shaking his head, produced three expensive volumes.

—You may keep these for two weeks. In your life you won't have another chance.

Miguel tried to make out the title; but Jaime, possessive, stroked the gilt bindings, the Bible paper.

—I'm grateful.

—You must guard them with your person. You must keep the diluvial tide of Orientales garbage from the fine woven pages. Perhaps they will not be devoured at a gulp by Rattus Muridae.

—I'll rig a papoose.

—No dust! In God's universe, alas, but not in genius.

—Don't worry, said Miguel, laughing.

—Two weeks. 3134. No sleep.

—I'll take a sabbatical.

—Three of us have skimmed it cover to cover and made notes. Soon we'll have our debate. Is this gentleman in touch with reality? If you knew to whom these artifacts belong, you would appreciate the seriousness, hombre.

That night Miguel began to read the voluminous edition. A breeze stirred off the lake like a lover's fingers. A near full moon shimmered in the stubblefield of downtown Managua. The air was lush warm and creased with insects, as he read by candlelight until his eyes closed, and night's inhabitants scurried and nibbled beneath the splintered boards.

At moments he felt very lonely. He missed Doñita, Almita, Chon Muñoz and the Padre. He thought of Cecilia Asturia gazing across to him at the San Jerónimo; and seemed to hang onto the tortuous sentences, like a lifeline in rough waters.

He rose to one elbow and yawned. Preceded by Jaime, a man in a leisure suit stepped through the tall weeds. He wore dark glasses and had a distinguished air. The poet thought it must be Proust himself come to leave his card in the tropics.

—Hola.

The rare volumes rested on a cinder block beneath a bit of tent canvas, alongside his bed of boards.

—Meet Lisandro.

The man, a writer and critic, edited La Prensa Literaria. Lisandro gave a wry smile and gazed off at blue Momotombo, its volcanic spume cloud-high over the lake.

—His books?

—Yes.

—Please, take them. I'll finish sometime.

—What do you think? said the visitor, bespectacled, exuding Managua establishment.

He shared a glimpse with Jaime: a pleasant experience, Proust to a savage.

Miguel rubbed his eyes, yawned and ran his hands through his hair.

—Compare this with the ancients, he said, hefting the books, with "Achilles' wrath . . ." or Sophocles' Electra. They are inside life's drama, destiny, from the first word; whereas this writer takes a subordinate element, description, and elevates it to a compositional principle. There: a vital organism in life-determining action. Here: not the organism but the nerve endings and so, you might say, passive. I suppose his idea of literary vocation, recurrent if not consistent, is the main character: he can be great when he talks about the artist's experience, as man and artist, insofar as he cares about it, being so sex starved . . . And then,—Miguel paused to formulate,— his view always from above, on the aristocratic periphery: this prevents him from living and expressing the mainspring of life in his time. From this results the lack of proportion, the elephantiasis of analytic description. About art, great, sometimes; about society, one-sided and hopelessly subjective, brutal at moments, insensitive. Look how he makes every mistake of the young artist, discourse, didacticism, and in fact it's a young man's book. But we forgive his lack of art because he tends to leave his skin in these generalizations, and we learn. Oh, sophisticated Europe marvels at this extended adolescence: they clutch at anything, except the grapnel that has them by the seat of their pants, grapnel of history, which they deny! No doubt the Proust critics love and forgive him, making capital of that high fetishism (not high seriousness), the beautification of an alienation they share, in fact revel in—last train to posterity, publish or perish! And so they make a fetish of difficulty, obscurity, symbolist externals, looking for novelty since they have nothing better to do, and can't risk the truth. But there can be no maturity, full development, literary or otherwise, without a rich and difficult participation in society's central struggle. Oh no, not in our day. Lions of the literary establishment, I call your vocation missed! Immature, or . . . rancid on the vine, unfallen. Proust criticism must be as fulsome, all in all, as the Joyce criticism I've seen, fawning over footnotes. But it couldn't hide, from me, that the author is fixated, as a man, from lack of vital participation—fixated in love, with his crude determinism, like a broken record for . . . well, I've read almost two thousand pages, of the three. Fixated in art, a stagnant sensibility, turned in on itself, acrid, morbid. Look at the eternal subjectivism of the artist Elstir's moment by the river: this shows the historic nada of Proust. Instead of high seriousness we get refined conversation, intellectual shimmer, no depth, Kantian chimera. And since he has no hold on reality, all is relativized beginning with character: the same person a devil and saint on the same page. The servant Françoise's insensitivity (she's the people!) with her "perfect care" during sickness in Proust's family: there is no surprise in that surprise, counterbalance of opposed character traits in the same person, since that happens on every page, like a formula. But above all he lets history off the hook; so no wonder bourgeoisie, those classic-makers, love it. For him Dreyfus is history.

Lisandro, patiently, said:

—Proust, like the *Quijote,* is comedy, not tragedy. No need to preserve the unities.

—The *Quijote?* Miguel laughed. Look how he writes so impertinently, without sympathy I feel, without lyricism but only a disengaged analysis. Look how brutal he can be, in a casual remark, an anecdote, because he hungers so pitifully for the real. He writes behind people's backs.

—He shows us things.

—Safe things. Politically unthreatening.

—Homosexuality?

—Seen from above. He'll stay above that fray, while all the others come in for it: his psychosexual dissection. Except for his mother and grandmother whom he idealizes, and himself by and large, a gloss: all is bathwater, the human essence reduced to . . . to vulgarity.

—Proust vulgar? said Lisandro, flushing. He's so intelligent.

—Enormously, and misses the point. I know it's heretical . . . This aesthete memorialist, or miniaturist, not a novelist . . . might have seen our Nicaraguan struggle as a kind of curio. I don't think he would have understood us, we're not fashionable enough. I don't believe he would have helped: too much to lose. Oh, he wanted his Goncourt Prize so badly, and to be famous.

—Perhaps one needs to be European.

—I'm just a poor Nica, I have my own mondongo to worry about.—Miguel shook his head, thinking.—No; the deep down everyday mediocrity and discreditation he saves for others, from beginning to end. Nothing else survives.

—But you haven't finished.

—Here, take them. I will sometime.

—No, keep the set another week. Toward the end, when he returns from his stay in a sanatorium, a better idea emerges of what he was after.

—Think of the ancients, said Miguel. He never will get into it.

Lisandro smiled and shared another glance with Jaime. He said:

—Perhaps you've heard of Roque Dalton, Otto René-Castillo? The Circulo Literario Universitario?

Miguel shrugged:

—Tell me.

The discussion lasted all day. From the earthquake ruins to a fine restaurant in the shadow of the Intercontinental; and from there to the swimming pool of one of Lisandro's friends. Then a private screening of an old French movie. It was past midnight when they arrived, all drunk and chattering excitedly to uphold their opinions, in the downtown shambles.

—You really don't mind? I'll tell you a secret.

—What?

—I love reading the stuff.

—But you—

—There's so much life!

—Then by all means, finish it. Soon we'll begin our analysis in earnest. By the way, please give Señor Jaime a poem or two for me to look at.

A month later, three of Miguel's early poems appeared in La Prensa Literaria.

XIX

Chiri Robles began spending longer moments with his star prisoner. The warden had proven as interested as he in the delinquent Hamlet, Horacio, compañera Ophelia martyred for the cause.

—These are pseudonyms, said Alesio. Get me the real names, whereabouts, safe houses, I'll see you promoted.

But Chiri was after even bigger fish: the comandante Shakespeare who appeared to be Numero Uno. Slowly, his visits to the poet's cell were preparing the conditions. He wasn't ready to take Alesio fully into his confidence, since the risk of failure, a fiasco, loomed as real. His conscience was clear, inducing his childhood friend into a bogus escape plan. Cecilia Asturia was strangely on his mind, and he thought: all is fair in love and war. Besides, he brought the detainee some distraction and made his life in solitary a bit easier. Chiri felt he was owed the information.

One afternoon Miguel asked him:

—Robles, what do you do when you leave here?

—I go home.

—On the bus?

—I have a car.

The Modelo protocol forbid such exchanges. Tell a prisoner nothing. Lie. But he couldn't help himself, he wanted to impress.

—New car?

—Yes.

—Then what, when you get home?

—Play with my kids, watch TV. Eat dinner. You know.

Miguel grew thoughtful.

—You love your wife?

Chiri blinked, staring in past the bars. In that instant he had a vision of Cecilia, tall, svelte, her restless dark eyes. She was still his idea of beauty.

—Who doesn't?

—Never get lonely?

No good: when the other started asking the questions. Giner could talk rings around an oak tree, you never knew where he was heading. Week after week he stayed buried alive in the bare and reeking cell with only a drop of light from the hallway as he burned out his eyes over a poem. Yet he wasn't lonely, perhaps—alone, yes, unbelievably, and the cause was no substitute for touching his wife, strolling in sunlight. But it made Robles think: who's the lonely one?

The guard crouched by the cell in silence. He didn't think about such things much. If you stepped back a moment, the words echoed in your brain like lunacy. While you were there, his tone imparted a sense of closeness, understanding. Like that act of his in the Americano Infantíl: it was magnetic.

Robles said:

—Is Hamlet lonely?

—Anyone out of key, who puts off steps to a remedy, will feel lonely. But tell me really: do you love your wife?

—Sure, and my kids. What I do here, my job, it's for them.

—The future looks bright.

—Bueno, the benefits aren't bad. Once you're on board awhile, they offer you things.

—I have a wife, said Miguel, in an altered tone.

Did he have a wife! Chiri saw her once: he caught Josefa's act when she was dancing in the circus. That was in the Orientales, and the whole tent went berserk.

—Children, he nodded, in the darkness, a son is what I want most on earth. But . . . , his voice trailed off, thinking; if it has to be otherwise . . .

—You could make money, Chiri jumped in. You're known, you can write.

—What I want?

—You can't do things the way you want. A time comes to be realistic, grow up. This Hamlet fellow for instance: where will all his deep pondering get him?

—I'll never write to support a family.

—Not for her?

—No.

—That's selfish.

The world selfish gave him a little jolt, as if Josefa had used it.

—Things aren't always clear, he said. Some people find love, some loneliness, turning into their opposites.

As the days went on the guard grew impatient playing Horacio to this prisoner's Hamlet. Too many words, he wanted deeds! When Miguel mentioned castles with ramparts, ghosts who conversed with the living and spoke in verse to inform on murderers, Chiri drew back and scratched his head. He understood the poet's main love in life was himself, and no one else; his vanity knew no limits; all the mystique about his wife, the Frente, the power of ideas, beauty: it was no more than overblown self love. The guard took sparse pleasure in the visits, forcing himself to sit there. With Alesio's help he put the pressure on, 24-hour music piped in (classical: as if Bach, or Bax, were the warden's supreme torture); spiking his water with various substances to cause cramps. They held out, and withdrew, a visit from Josefa.

A normal convict who got close to a guard would probe for ways to capitalize. Robles hated his stubbornness. He hated the pet phrases and grandiosity, casting a dreary light on his material ambitions and career as a Guardia officer.

For a few days they served him special food, a plate heaped with rich morsels.

—Weaken his resolve, said Alesio. Our trump is his wife.

The haggard poet stared at that catered food, petits fours, a stuffed lobster tail from Los Gauchos, a flan caramelo.

Alesio felt betrayed when La Prensa Literaria served up four more brilliant seditious poems, causing a sensation.

—Shit or get off the pot, said the warden.

—He'll come around, said Robles. He's hinting.

—The sonuvabitch is a prima donna.

—Give it a week.

—Look, we'll dangle his wife, and hit him with our little scheme.

—He'll break, chief, I can feel it. He could hand us the Frente leadership.

XX

—*Right this way! Learn the secret of life and death! The unknown wonder of the world!*

The circus aura lit up the blue twilight of the Orientales. A carousel sent its whimsical strains over the vast boarded-up hive of stalls. There was childish pleasure in the bright tent lights; in the lilting music with a spirit of fairy-tale adventure. Miguel dreamt of distant cities, the unlit shanty towns, the red-tinged dusk of Dakar.

—*Our famous tightrope belly dancer, Voluptuosa!!*

—Hijos de puta!

The ticket taker bawled at a group of kids pestering the customers. He turned, with a ruffled charm, to a well dressed woman on her escort's arm.

When Lisandro paid Miguel a hundred cordobas for "Effects of Evil on the Dancer," he began sitting ringside night after night: to the chagrin of more affluent circus-goers, since the poet smelled like his day sweeping out offal. He had fallen in love with the divine Josefa, who danced in center ring for the Americano Infantíl. Now he understood Dante and Petrarch, the elegiac Keats and sickly Leopardi moaning over Sylvia, all whose universe was illumined by ineffable love.

The Americano pulled out of Managua for a swing through Pacific Coast cities. In León, Miguel hung around outside the big tent until a ring assistant came along whistling.

—Hola.

—Huh? said the circus worker.

—How long will you be here?

—Depends on the crowds.

—Sure is hot.

—Worse in Chinandega.

—The circus take on help?

—Sometimes. When one of us gets fed up . . . to here.

He gave the throat-slitting gesture, mysterious.

—What happened?

—Brother, there's a curse on this outfit. Of our two stars, one ran away to Costa Rica and his lover, the dancer, just tried to kill herself.

By daylight the Americano looked dirty and too sad for words in the oppressive heat. Flies swarmed round the animals. A child cried in one of the trailers. An emaciated dog sat in the shade of the big tent panting, its pink tongue out.

César was the circus master. He gave orders and brooked no discussion; he handed out fines. Rakish, preening himself, a key figure in any skit, he was captain of center ring.

The owner, warted and whiskered, spent her days on accounts in an air-conditioned trailer.

—Where's Josefa? Miguel asked the ring assistant.

—Forget it. Another stargazer.—The worker glanced around disgusted, as departure for Chinandega drew near.—She belongs to the other, he's come for her.

—Hans?

—The Rooster. Came back last night from Costa Rica.

—But he left her. He dropped her.

—You know a lot about women.

—She could have died.

A taxi pulled up. Two emerged in the sunlight: the strongman's wife whose lover was Rafi the Midget, and one of the animal trainers. A third, unsteady on her feet, needed to be supported.

—Board 'em! César yelled, deep-voiced.

The Americano moved out, on its trek north.

They played before packed houses the first nights in Chinandega. Soon Josefa was back on her feet and able to dance, thanks to the circus master's coaxing, and threats. César even devised a skit for the talented young woman: about suicide of course, and everyone agreed it improved her as an artiste. Miguel was so in love he became an object of laughter as he cleaned up after the animals.

—La! cried the strongman's wife. That one belongs in the circus.

She gazed fondly at Rafi, who swung his legs while he sat on her knee.

Josefa wrung out clothes on the yellow dust. One of her trailer mates winked slyly, while Miguel declaimed a new poem called "León Nights."

—Halt! cried César, fresh from a chat with the owner. That's it! The thing itself! We'll use this idiot in the new skit.

The packed crowd laughed as the ragamuffin, raking furiously, made snide remarks on César's less than genial abilities as a script writer. Josefa appeared in a pink tutu, a glittery diadem in her hair. Miguel frightened her and left everyone at a loss when he screamed:

> It is her, she comes, my life's idol!
> If only these pathetic lines weren't written
> by a bathetic donkey with bad grammar.

Applause; feet stomped. He bowed at a flushed César.

Here came The Rooster.

—Hola, slave.

Hans tipped his cap at the loser and eyed Josefa salaciously. Miguel was supposed to thump his heart and fall in a swoon. But not this time, not tonight in Estelí. He interrupted the oaf whose feet at least were of epic breadth.

Ooh! Look at me, and gloat.
I'm the amorous cock that crows
with multiple joys at midnight. I have fun
in my pocket, and you can ask
any gullible girl . . .

Hans cast a glance at the audience, creating a character finally, and turned toward the magisterial César. But the other, the young fool expressed adoration with a glimpse, a sigh. And then, sketching a caress, he recited:

In my beloved's eyes I see a vision:
two heron pink-winged over Lake Managua.
At sunset I watched them
intricately distended
fly homeward toward their young as, wings on fire
they seemed like sparks from the ignited clouds.
Then, toward the horizon, side by side
they soared above the stippled twilit water
homing toward ocean beaches, the Pacific.

He grabbed her hand and gave it a spasmodic kiss.

She looked at him wonderingly. Her stare, full lips parted, girlish and sensual, departed from the script as well.

César stepped forward, stentorian, flexing his great mind for the benefit of the audience:

—Never before seen in any circus, señores, true love!

But the following week, in Matagalpa, the circus master lost all patience. His nether lip protruding, his eyes like hellfire glimpsed through a mask, he gestured:

—Avast! Damned agitator, leave these precincts!

—Eee-aw!

Laughter, applause from the rickety stands where barrio kids plunged grimy fingers in a gob of cotton candy bought for them, and distributed with fanfare a few moments before, by the poet. The packed crowd hung on Miguelito's every gesture: now he stuck out his tongue at the pommaded gorilla who was his boss; it ignited a furor of whistles and catcalls. For the word had gotten out. Local newspapers wrote up the young poet of La Prensa Literaria whose antics, whose irruptions of love for a teenage dancer, whose inspired acting with the note of actual passion had entranced ever larger crowds. Matinee idol of the provinces! It was the greatest thing since Mother's Day, and gate receipts far surpassed anything previous. The mediocre Americano took on cachet, an aura of genius like gold mined deep in the people's needs, as the northern swing progressed. The Napoleonic circus master spent his free moments daydreaming a triumphal reentry into Managua.

But suddenly Miguel Giner threatened to go on strike if the Circo Americano Infantíl wasn't turned into a cooperative. A few weeks ago a nonentity, he would stir rebellion amongst the troupe.

—*Cooperativo!* he trumpeted, enlisting support during a performance.

And César, red-faced with rage, no longer the debonaire ringmaster:

—Be gone, pendejo! Quit this stage!

—*Co-ope-ra-tivo,* said the poet, with a wild laugh and a caper.

In those days he wrote his cycle of early love poems: the beloved as protean devotion, homeland, life-tilled idea, in her many forms. In dust swirled up from a campesino's cart as he hauls his produce over back roads; in the scent of wet hay above the October fields; in a chill misty rain rippling along the Río Escondido;—he loves her, and listens for her voice.

Patriarchal trees, hoary oaks dot the northern hills, the alluvial plateaus where a voyager wind tells her lover's yearning, the heart of the Americas.

In Segovian forests drenched with rain and morning sun the quetzal sings her free song untranscribable, invoking mystic union. (The quetzal, bird of freedom, cannot live 24 hours in a cage.)

In the South the swallows in sky-shoals quiver and veer, a cloud bursts in a thousand spangles out across the savannahs.

From a cafe the Rockanola sends its tinny rhythms into a Managua barrio, Open-Tres, where the kids play marbles and knucklebones around a smoothed-off circle of dust.

Outside a Carazo village, high on the coffee-growing ridges between Managua and the sea, the father flies an owl-kite, in the salt-
tinged Pacific breeze, beside his son.

The lovers sigh; they whine with deliberate pain; they mount,
groan, penetrate the deep midnight. The rending distress! Through
the hours they entwine, like a camoodi crushing its prey, with their
deep-gorged repetitive cries.

The women peddlers cry out in the early morning marketplace: *el
atol-l-l-l-l!*, they hawk their gruel of maize.

Through her he loves all things, the life-sustaining corn; the caules-
cent orchid with its scarlet and yellow blossoms, prized by ancestors;
the shimmery elytra of a carabidae beetle; and so life seems to unite.

He finds her in the curassow, the penelope guan, the wild mountain hen. In them he possesses her, translates their cry into living idea.

To the vast mahogany and india-rubber forests of the east; to the
remote grassy plains of the interior, with their sugar and indigo, and
pasturing herds; to the mountainous regions accessible, for the
prospector, by mulepack; to the fertile Eden land of the east, bathed
about with murmurous ocean,—he brings his beloved like a blessing
of beauty, of hope.

One evening in Jinotega the circus master juggled roles: it was
Josefa who cleaned up after the animals instead of Miguel. Then the
student poet came along, forlorn, with a lyricism to his gaze like the
moon on Corinto harbor. He recited his pastorals. By now César
hated the two of them, and with his venality looked to extend their
parts in degraded ways. He loathed their youth and talent, but they
made his reputation.

Oafish Hans came on scene with a swagger, a leer. Indubitably
suave, he doffed his sombrero like a ranchera crooner with brain
damage. Then, for the overflow audience, he raised a cuff showing
the knife strapped on his garter, and glared his macho jealousy.
Alright for me, señorita, to have my fun; but if you look at him or
any other fool I'll stick you (gesture) with this!

He manhandled her. They disappeared behind a hayrick. And then, with a change of décor, he was selling her on a Managua street. From the peasant girl so unsure of herself she quick-changed to a *zorra*, a fox in a provocative costume. One by one the circus workers, mechanic, ring assistants, Rafi the Midget, took their turn; while César's commentary attained a sublime pathos, and the clowns gamboled for fun.

The poet's mood, mooning while the worst occurred, went to a glum despair. But then he arrived in the city, blinked at the sights and sounds and did a dance that won him every heart. As night fell, amid bright lights and honking cars, the girl approached him and sniffed a fare in the boy's bewilderment. Someone in the audience laughed; and so, stepping boldly from his role into the spotlight beside her, Miguel pointed at César:

—Funny, compañero? What if this Somocista sold *your* dignity for a few dollars?

—You're fined! shrieked the circus master, his eyes operatic, in the impasto of makeup losing way to age. Don't listen to him! He's a nitwit who loves the girl in real life, but she sneers at him behind his back! In reality she's gone on this bumbling idiot! This hands-and-feet! This ox in white socks!

—Ha! Miguel cried. Listen to the liar, hypocritón. You could paint your house with the hair dye he consumes. He loves her himself, but he has so many wrinkles he only attracts face-lift salesmen.

—Driven mad with jealousy, señores, the dunce would say anything to get his way. Look, I don't have wrinkles, no wrinkles at all. Still in bloom at thirty-nine.

But Rafi the Midget had snuck up, with portentous gestures, from behind. In a wink he unsnipped César's suspenders and down fell the great man's pants, revealing striped crimson drawers.

—You're fined! You bum!

The virile Hans gave a broad chested guffaw, as César stumbled across center ring in pursuit of the gleeful Rafi.

Miguel slipped from the spotlight. With the tent in an uproar he took Josefa by the hand and led her outside into the night air of Jinotega.

A length of wall glimmered as they moved in the mountain evening. No streetlights, no cars or passersby: in those weeks, late

'76, the stories of Guardia reprisals were on everybody's lips. By his side she gave a shudder, but he put his arm around her and kissed her until they gasped for air. Beyond the last dwellings the lowlands and pastures lay before them.

There were misty emanations, odors of mown hay and pine trees dotting the ridges over the town. There were fields with a sense of steep ranges in the starglow. Josefa had been a slender fanciful girl when she caught César's eye in the street one day, in San Rafael del Norte. Now Miguel felt her opulent femininity by his side, and for life. In her the night took on body and soul; he knew their painful wait was about to end.

—I'm afraid, she said.

—No need.

—But it's dark.

He kissed her, and they went on their knees together in the tall grass. He held her head in one hand while caressing her breast as they lay on the earth. Scent of livestock on a nearby ranch; a fresh mountain breeze stirred the trees. Her breathing seemed to plead as she moaned beneath him and pushed up with her palm on the curly hair of his temple. Now she scratched at his nape: the keen edge of life incised her soul. A sudden release, a sweet gush and she took him to her, gentle and violent, with a soaring urge to prolong.

> *The quetzal's lovely song,*
> *the quetzal of misty forests*
> *high in the liquidambar tree*

—I'm afraid, she whispered.

—We're hidden by the grass. Are you cold?

—No.

—Do you want to go back?

—No.

> *Wild plantain and tree fern, liana and palm,*
> *royal bird of the Aztecs*
> *resplendent*

She blinked over his shoulder at the stars like gentians, the dark range of brooding hills, the far luminescence.

—Never go back?

—No.

—We'll stay out here then.

—Yes.

He held her to him with an ache of tenderness. In those moments he was inside his poor parents' lives: Juana who died in childbirth so he might live; Iván, the mountain guerrilla who roamed these forests and high wild-blossoming cerros, hungry and cold, if he hadn't been martyred already, so their country might live.

But she whispered fiercely, forcing him up.

XXI

In mid-January of '79 the warden, Alesio, met with the State Security head to discuss Miguel Giner's escape from the Carcel Modelo. The seduction was completed: the prison guard Chiri Robles, a childhood friend of the poet's, had him in his trust. Nothing could have been more timely, said Alesio, than the foster mother's visit with news of his best friend's death, and maimed little sister. He was plunged in despair; no more of the poems had appeared in La Prensa Literaria.

—We let the old woman in. We hoped for revelations on the criminals Hamleto, Horacio, Opheliacita who drowned. The one we really want is the bandido Shakespearrr', he's the leader.

The government official stared at Alesio. He knit his brow.

—Dios! Such an ungainly woman with a birthmark over half her face. "And when do you think it will end?" she says, lighting into him, "By that time we'll all be dead or ruined for life like Alma." "What?" On the monitor we heard him jolt forward. "Sí, señor: she went to help Chon Muñoz and came back with her hands cut off." Silence then. The old bag spoke in such a vengeful tone, I almost felt sorry for this comunista. "And Choncito is dead, you should know that too. Filomena buried him in Monimbó cemetery and went away with her children." We heard their silence, louder than the voices of visiting hour, the non-politicals. But I was cheerleading for her: now blab about Hamletito, now betray the whereabouts of Horaciocito, and the biggest bandolero of the bunch, Shakespearrrito! But she had gone too far: he got up and left her there, he motioned Robles to take him back to the hole where he would deal with grief. "Choncito is dead," she said to him, "Padre thinks he should've stuck to teaching school." But a chair scraped and then we had lost our chance.

The official, a member of President Somoza's inner circle, glanced at his wristwatch and nodded.

—So we've got him in solitary. I've given orders to listen for any wall tapping, whistles, voices. The moment this man opens his mouth, even in code, he's a treat to national security.

—Do we have a date for the operation?

—He's grown sickly, it should be soon. I've got Robles on the hustle; but, in such matters the details must be finessed.

Chiri turned his key.

—Compa?

He had spent so much time here, among their mannerisms and fake sympathy, he even talked like them; he called his wife «compañera» now and again. In the dark cell two eyes beyond the campfire of human life; a spasmodic cough, tubercular volcano: you heard coughs like that in Acahualinca, the poor barrios. He had brought the escape plan, a scheme so certain to end in disaster he felt pity for his boyhood friend. A short-lived pity since he wanted a promotion and had earned one. Moreover, he would fall from grace if he failed; and could imagine, in a land like Nicaragua, his son not at university, not headed for a well-paying profession but impoverished, neglected by society, wracked with a cough like that one. You couldn't help feeling affection for a man this patient in wretchedness, and dedicated. But hadn't they «smuggled» out his poetry for him? Hadn't *Cordillera* and *Ballad of Claudia* appeared in print already, their «chromatic threnody . . . consummate form» (said a critic) causing a sensation apart from the political message? In all sincerity he thought his guard had been infected by a misguided idea of justice, the revolutionary example. Or perhaps by a memory of childhood, an afternoon deep in the Rinconadas where they were the apple of Presencio's and Fasael's and the Monges' eye? Chiri remembered, with a pang, the tall daughter of Don Lazaro, la Cecilia, whom he had desired with the sorrow and spite of an unrequited first love; but she wanted Miguel instead. No, no—he had used them to get his poems published, now it was their turn.

—You have a heart attack. We take you out on emergency order.

—And then?

—Between here and the military hospital your comrades set a roadblock. You go free.

He yearned, how he yearned to see his wife and hold her in his arms. Since leaving Rivas, a few weeks before the arrest a year before, he had not seen her. They tortured him by letting Doñita in, with her terrible news, and keeping Josefa out.

—And you?

—Oh, Teniente Robles gave a low chuckle, I'll ride Ticabus into Costa Rica. I'll send for my family.

One look, so sick of his days in filth and misery, a hacking cough,— he knew they had him.

—Roadblock?

—I'll be in the car with you.

A silence. Then:

—You're crossing over?

The chess moves had been discussed at length with Alesio. Robles paused in turn.

—I'll need a contact. That's all. I'll give him alternate sites.

In the darkness, Miguel peered out at his old friend.

—Driver?

—I'll take care of it. We'll switch routes.

The silence, the tension was such between them, Robles had a fleeting doubt.

—I need to think.

—You said Hamleto thinks too much. He's hard on himself in the criticism and auto-criticism sessions, for indecisiveness.

It was late. Few cars moved through the nicer neighborhood where Chiri Robles lived. Nocturnal insects, wing flappings in the dewy air. A breeze off Lake Managua stirred palm trees in patios and courtyards. Some tropical bird sent its call over the rooftops.

—You're not asleep.

—It's okay.

—What's wrong?

—Nada. Go back to sleep.

What point in telling his wife now? Tell her when the time came: this was a war, a fight to the death. Distinguish oneself, feed one's family, live out of the barrio, in comfort. A war, Guardia and Frente.

—Do you want anything?

—No.

The plan might backfire. He could be shot out there, along the highway, as Guardia emerged suddenly around the ambulance. Or, if he survived they would single him out later for retribution, like Perez Vega and other officials. Frente vandals, stubborn to the end. But Miguel was a poet, not hardened cadre: he didn't look up to him as he had once, running and laughing through Monimbó with Choncito. Tomorrow Miguel would collapse, defeated, ruined morally not by Macho Pedro, but by kindness. If Cecilia could see them both now, which would she choose? Cecilia Asturia: where could she be? Frente? No, in Mexico or Miami, married to a gringo, with her looks. He would see her again someday: dressed in officer's khaki, if not an expensive suit, in an air-conditioned office suite. The stakes grew higher.

—Amor?

—Huh.

—What is it? Tell me.

—A headache.

—I'll get you an aspirin.

The rumorous dawn came in like a tide. Go out there, thought Chiri, do your job. Then come home from another day's work—as if nothing had happened, except a promotion.

—Hola.

Robles felt nervous, opening the cell door. His voice played tricks. The aroma was unpoetic; he resented the smell of human waste and blamed it on this prisoner who had something he wanted.

—Well?

Miguel broke down coughing. Besides being asthmatic he was probably consumptive, having suffered through two hunger strikes, long months in a pestilent prison cell. Now he was ready to go: dying, literally, to get out of the Modelo and he didn't care about the cost anymore, to himself or others. No regrets! He just wanted to go out in the sunlight and be with his wife. Wrenched by a cough he choked forth the word to his childhood friend.

—Gracias.

—All ready?

—I knew . . . when you brought me the first pen and paper, I knew you were a sincere person. And now you want to risk your life for us, for your country.

Caramba! How disgusted Chiri Robles was with all their deep talk, their Hamletos, and discourses in solitary confinement. How sick he was of the glorious Frente, and playing Sancho Panza to their idealist mierda. Man, sell yourself and let's be done with it, but spare me another lecture on humanity. The contact, he thought, the name and number: it would be a front person, not cadre; but from that small shoot, if cultivated with care . . .

—I've been thinking . . . not about whether I should leave the Modelo, that's clear, but . . . In all people there is integrity. Put them in different conditions, they change.

—Hombre, there isn't time for a speech. The escape plan: do you accept it?

—I need guarantees for the compañeros.

He was right there: anytime the Frente staged a «recuperation» of bank funds, execution of some circuit court judge, or prominent Somocista, the repression came down hard on detainees. For this reason Tacho Somoza kept them alive.

—You'll have me, said Robles, as your hostage.

—Correcto, Miguel smiled. And so we might ask: where does one's true interest lie? We might consider this in terms of the dialectics of self and others . . .

Lord, spare me. Another pompous lecture, starting up! The guard wished he had a cordoba for every time he heard a pedantic leftist use the word dialectics: he would go to his deathbed without a definition.

—We should decide.

—That, amigo, is the question, as Hamletito once said.

—Forget Hamletito. Save yourself.

The man was dying; he was doomed; yet all he could talk about was Hamletito. By now a knot had formed in Chiri's stomach, because the moments ticked away; and time seemed to run out for the two of them; and Alesio sat finger-drumming the wide desk in his office downstairs,—your results? And then Chiri remembered something, and the blood flowed hot into his neck, and he was glad for the darkness. Once, as a teenager, he had been caught in a lie about Cecilia, saying he felt her breasts in the back row of the Cine Lux. Word got back to her father, the blacksmith who came looking for him and reduced him to tears. But the worst was how nice she continued to be, though he had lost any chance.

—You want the name of a contact?

—Who is it?

—We have a code . . . Go to the library in Plaza España. At the reference desk, not too loud, ask for the number of Guillermo Shakespeare.

—And then?

—You'll be taken, by the contact, to a card catalogue.

—Card catalogue? This is complicated.

—In there you'll find a lot of names, Macbeth, Othello, Lear, with numbers.

—In Managua?

—They're here.

—Whew!—Robles, sweating at the hairline, shook his head and said:—What then?

—Give the number to the contact.

—What will she do?

—Get you a book.

—What book?

—Ask for Hamlet.

—Him again! . . . You mean this scu'—the muchacho keeps a diary, like Che Guevara?

The guard gave a small, strained laugh, pleased now with his prisoner. Finally! It wasn't easy dealing with subversives, slippery as snakes! But the plan would work.

—You can trust him, said Miguel, who leaned back with a sigh.

—How do I know that?

Closing his eyes the poet said:

—He'd rather die than lose his honor.

—Ah, we'll catch—we'll count on his honor.

—Some wind up comandantes no matter what.

The prisoner, a tear on his cheek in the dim light, turned his head to the wall. When the guard was gone he bestirred himself and felt about for a bit of crumpled paper. He began, slowly, to write, using a finger to space the letters: "*I am . . . therefore I struggle . . .*"

Chiri Robles had a brief meeting with the warden.

He jumped in his car and drove full speed to the library in Plaza España.

PART FIVE

I

Claudio, the leader in Masaya, paused a moment to dream of the Indian barrio where he was born. So much had happened there, births and deaths, friends getting married, since he joined the Frente. For a moment the emotion was strong: his childhood room in Subtiava, his little mother's wizened, kindly presence. Better think of the struggle: when would León rise up as Estelí had done? In Estelí a column of 200 fighters had stormed in and driven back the Guardia: they held the city a week before retreating through San Roque sector. Don't think now of marriage, children, a garden: better think of bloodbaths because one couldn't make people leave against their will, when the GN mopped up house to house.

Here came the girl. She flitted in, breathless, from the tense night outside.

—No movement.

—They're not mobilizing?

She stood before him, her short hair curly. Sweat streaked her cute face from running. She didn't smile or seek approval: she awaited the next order. She was a soldier after his own heart, who hardly spoke during her long, tireless day, who didn't spare herself but focussed on the smallest task with a grave determination. Strange, really: you couldn't imagine her in front of a mirror. He no longer noticed the horror at the end of her arms.

Alma hadn't been home for days: not since the Olla de Barro operation got underway. She stared in Commandante Claudio's eyes: next task? Her gaze was so fixed, he looked away.

—Tell me, he said.

—A few hanging around outside. Others stroll in the park across the street. They don't suspect.

—Before? Start with noontime.

Alma had spent her day with one of the juice vendors across from the garrison in Parque Central. Now she gave an account of Guardia movement down to particulars, and Claudio nodded. By the time GN mobilized and brought reinforcements to Catarina, Diriá, Niquinohomo, it would be too late.

The night was quiet with its sounds of suppertime, while commando units neared the appointed targets. Alma Giner waited in the twilit room in Santa Rosa. Like the others Claudio had taken a little time getting used to her, after she came back from the medical operation in Mexico City. As if she had something dirty at the end of her arms; or maybe she wanted pity, special treatment? Not at all: you could tell her anything and she would do it, quietly, the way you wanted. She volunteered for things nobody else touched; she stayed in one place for hours making a mental note of everything that happened. She ran errands behind guardia lines, or fetched a dozen kids in a matter of minutes and put them to work. But of her mutilated arms, of what occurred when she was a Guardia captive, she never spoke. The bad fact was enwound in her silence, like an oozing bandage.

—What now?

—Wait here, rest. It's about to start.

—I'm not tired.

Her arms hung at her side, ending in two prongs, like drumsticks. Her face was pleasant: so serious, with its direct gaze.

—Hungry?

—No.

Claudio had bread from La Calzada Bakery. It was still warm and very good to eat. He held out a piece:

—Supper.

She took it and chewed dutifully. She held the bread in her cleft forearms, which she had learned to use in a prehensile manner. In free moments she practiced with a pad and pencil she carried around, making crude letters, while the compañeros tended to glance at her sadly.

Returning from Mexico she was able to wash, dress and take care of herself to the extent that she resisted the fussy Doñita. Once, she looked at Claudio with contempt when he showed a sign of sympathy for her condition. She wanted no one's pity. She wanted her brother to be free, and rejoin Josefa, write his poems and walk in sunlight. Claudio watched her chew the fresh bread as she held it cleverly, in her forked antebrachia.

Salvo of static on the radio; a voice spoke in code. The combat units were in place: first the coordinated attacks, then an ambush at Olla de Barro, when a Guardia convoy arrived from Jinotepe. Other routes proved too muddy from the recent rains: they could only use that one.

II

The week before, during an assault on Catarina, the homemade bombs had not exploded. Chlorate obtained from an unreliable source turned out to be saltpeter, so fighters risked themselves in forward advance while explosives didn't perform. From a meeting that morning, here in Santa Rosa, the leaders came away confident but still imprecise as to details. Claudio, in charge of planning the ambush, needed a report on Masaya garrison. How quickly would they respond? Guardia might effect a pincer movement if they dispatched troops early. Almita completed her task and reported back, but this secondary aspect had gone overlooked. Hazy as to details! And this was the key.

He glanced at her and thought: it's critical, someone with a radio at Parque Central. Once the attack began, however, it would be delicate, Guardia all over. Touch and go, unwise perhaps: send her over there now, in the darkness? and after what already happened to her? But in these moments Claudio cared less about risk, the peril to one cadre, than gauging the initial Guardia response, reacting correctly. He valued her life, but he put that to one side and resolved his dilemma with the principle: and our people? I would go myself, but I am crucial here. She is the one.

—We need somebody at Parque Central.

—Why?

—To know their response. What will they send out, how many? Which route?

—Alright.

—Take this, he said, reaching for a walkie-talkie. Do you want a gun?

He hefted a .38 revolver in his broad palm. He held the gun toward her; but she smiled and received the two-way by its strap. She

looked at the comandante almost with pity: he wanted to win so
badly, he was becoming scatterbrained. He could overlook the bat-
like ugliness at the end of her arms.

III

She started on her way from Santa Rosa through the quiet barrios:
toward the Guardia barracks and command post in Parque Central.
At night there was no one in the streets, as the darkness drew over,
all but total. She remembered the previous September, during the insurrection: the night she started out from Santana's by order of
Choncito—find Ulises Tapia's messenger. She went along shudder-
ing at the memory, at thought of Guardia. Since her return she could
hardly look at a uniform, she couldn't think of a jeep, a soldier, of . . .
without feeling horrible. When a BECAT passed, when she caught a
glimpse of spitshined boots, sun glinting on a helmet, her pulse began to race and then she nosedived in depression. Chon Muñoz lay
in his grave. How would Filomena bring up their four sons? Miguel
sat in prison, dying daily since he went on hunger strikes and refused
to cooperate. Guardia Nacional swaggered about the streets and
abused the people.

When Alma came back from her operation Doñita insisted she go
take confession with Padre Velasquez.

—Prayer is a sacred art, he said. There is a hierarchy to prayer:
some are more advanced. I want you to begin.

Fear had been Doñita Reyes' response at sight of Almita's drumsticks. In such ways God revealed His anger at the godless insurgents.
But in Mexico City the doctors taught her what she might do with
the osseous prongs of her truncated arms if she practiced and showed
persistence. And so she began learning how to work. But in her foster mother's eyes the deformity seemed evil, like a punishment; and
so Alma must run to church at once and pray with Padre for the ab-
solution of her sins, of her grievous sins.

—Will God let Miguelito go from prison?

—It is vain to seek God's ways, and blasphemy to judge them.

—We have to do something,—her voice piped, birdlike,—we have
to get him out.

—Pray.

She stared in Padre's eyes, in the dim confessional, and thought: he doesn't have a brother in prison.

—I'm going to do something.

—What, Alma?

He glimpsed her forearms, laid on her lap.

—Help them.

—Who?

—Them, you know.

—No . . . what are their names?

—Cec' . . . Delia, Cony . . . Loco, El Muerto, you know.

Padre lowered his eyes. He considered the pseudonyms.

—Do you know their real names?

—N-no.

—Are they from here?

Subtly, Alma seemed to tense and sat forward. She was still the gentle, attentive girl he had taught at the Colegio, and she was different. She waited quietly to leave: no more girlish curtsies, the zany way she had of interpreting Doñita, Faustina and Juan Ramón, the adored brother who teased and tormented her, sometimes.

—No. That is, I don't know, they wear masks.

She had drawn some lesson from the gory nightmare, her hands hacked off by a machete so they would never carry a contact bomb.

It gave him pause. But he said softly:

—Outsiders then.

—Must be,—she gave a strange smile. —Don't worry, Padre . . .

Then she rose and went from him. She trotted off.

His look of concern turned to something else. For he believed that only a rebel victory could get the poet released.

IV

Now, moving along in the shadows, she thought of her last time with Choncito Muñoz. It was soon after she came back from her operation: only a few days before he died.

—What can I do? she said to him that afternoon, and held up the two white bandages.

—You'll do more than the rest of us, he said; but though he laughed easily, his eyes reflected the anguish in hers.

—How could I?

—There was a woman in North America, deaf and blind. She wrote books, she spoke out.

Chon paused. He grew silent; gazed across the way. He groped for a certain question; and she knew what it was, and felt afraid. Other visits, other silences: he had led her up to this; but she wasn't ready, she never talked about that thing, *that,* to anyone, not even Doñita, not even Consuelo, her doll. She never wanted to.

But, somehow, he was in it with her. Why? Did he blame himself? Since he gave her the order that night, and sent her after Ulises' messenger? She didn't like it, if he did. She would have to tell him, and help Choncito. But could she trust him? He was her teacher at the Colegio, with Padre.

Skipping along she glimpsed the Central Market set aflame in September. Charred, spectral, the macabre facade seemed to drip gray stone: a great dead thing spread out in the darkness. The streets were quiet in Masaya. People lived there she would never see again.

—Tell me, Alma, where were you going?

—When?

—That night.

—I can't remember. .

Did he want her to blame him? Why? Why was Choncito making her talk like this?

—Yes, you can. Where? What was the order?

—Take a message.

—Where?

—Parque Central.

—Why?

—You sent me. No, I decided—to go there.

Not Chon. Alma decided.

Her breath came faster.

—Where was the messenger?

—He left, he—

—Went away?

—Guardia garrison. The attack.

—So you . . . decided. You started out to go there.

—Yes.

—Alone?

—Alone easier . . . to pass.

—And then?

—I can't remember, she shook her head, I can't.

Just then a BECAT lunged round the corner, up ahead. She ducked back in a doorway. Since the uprising there was a curfew: only BECAT jeeps, and a few Frente commandos. Fitful, uneasy sleep in the barrios, families waited tensely for daylight. When would their son, or daughter, come home?

—Try to think.

—I can't remember!

—You went alone?

—Yes.

—Afraid?

—N-n'—I ran.

Chon, calm, confident, a teacher in front of his class. He led her down a path, and it was hard to stop anymore. Did he frighten her? He was there with her, to help. Strong now, he spoke softly:

—Then what happened?

—Then I—she caught her breath,—I ran faster.

—Were they close?

—Yes.

—Coming close?

—Yes.

—Who was?

—Guardia.

—Running? Behind you?

—In a jeep!

—Then what?

—They said something nasty.

—Then?

—I fell down.

Alma gasped. She winced as the pain shot through her hands. She clutched at her elbow; the two bandages collided, contorted her features.

—And then? said Chon to hold her gaze.

—They took me.

—Where?

There! Alma jumped back. Not ten meters from her, toward the corner, two Guardia on foot. She froze in her tracks, among the shadows, her heart raced wildly. Guardia patrols went cautiously on the edge of Parque Central. There were listening posts in the narrow streets off the park. Should she wait until the Olla de Barro

operation took effect? In a minute the night would flare up in Catarina, in Diriá, in San Juan de Oriente. Two more blocks to the garrison. She had to be there, in place when the attack began. But she was
having a nervous reaction to the two sinister figures, the glint of their
helmets, and soulless eyes. Afraid she might bend over and vomit and
give herself away. Now she needed Claudio's .38 revolver and the two
hands God had given her. She flitted from door to door, toward
them! She made no sound, but her heart was beating like the drum
in a gigantóna parade.

—They took me.

—Where? said Chon.

—In the back of the jeep. One sat on my chest because . . . because
he . . . They started to argue. The driver said better lower their voices
and head back to central command. The other shook his head, no,
no let's go have fun.

In her small voice she squeaked the words, breathed in starts.

—They took you?

—To a coffee field. They had a blanket and laid it on the ground.
It was cold. Wind.

Chon waited a few seconds. He said calmly:

—What did they do?

—They . . . they did that to me, you know.

She gave a sob. She stared at him like it was happening again.

—They hurt you?

—One, two . . . three . . . They had rum with a strong smell, and
laughed and lay on top of me, grunted . . . did the thing.

Alma squirmed in her chair. She concentrated her features.

Chon coaxed:

—What happened?

—I talked to Consuelo. I told her a story Miguel used to read me.

—And?

—One carried me on his shoulder; put me in the jeep. I should
have jumped out.

—Why didn't you?

—I couldn't walk.

—If it was now, he said, would you jump out?

—Yes!

—Why?

—Then they couldn't—they wouldn't—

—What?

—Call me a little prostitute, zorrita! Say I enjoyed it. All my fault.

—Why did they say that? Did you ask them to go to the field?

—No.

—Did you enjoy what they did to you?

—No! They were lying.

—Then why did they say that?

—Because it was their fault. They did it all.

—Is that when they cut off your hands?

—What?

She stared at him, stunned, as if he had slapped her.

—Is that when, Alma? Did they cut them off?

Suddenly, she writhed in her seat, and the tears ran down her cheeks. On the verge of hysteria, she couldn't speak; but he held her eyes. And Choncito himself was carried along, beyond turning back. He didn't ask: why make her do this? Will it help her? Or worsen her regression? Only instinct, his deep kindness, told him: free her.

—When did they do it? Tell me when it happened.

—Later, she said, breathless. Later they . . .

—They what?

—One . . . he said he saw me in Paises Bajos with a contact bomb. He made it up. He wanted . . . my fault.

—And?

She bucked her frail shoulders. She hiccuped between the words. At instants she caught a glimpse of the men: how they were, close; and then shook her head, tried to wipe the tears with her arm.

—They took me to a room. They did it.

—Did what?

—You know.

Alma looked down, heaved.

—How?

—With a machete.

—How? Show me.

With the two white bandages she made a sharp movement downward, and lurched violently, screaming. She fell from her chair; she crumbled forward, but Chon Muñoz was there, broad shouldered, strong: he caught her. He said at once, shaking her:

—Did they kill you?

—What?

—Are you dead?

—No.

—Did you live?

—Yes!

—Were they able to finish you?

—No! They left me! I got away—

—Who are you?

—Who?

—What's your name?

—Alma.

—Alma they couldn't kill?

—Couldn't!

—And whose fault was it?

—Theirs!

—Was it yours?

—Theirs! They did it, they did—

—What do you feel about them?

—I hate them!

—Why?

—I hate them for it! she shouted. They hurt Miguel, they put him in prison! Why? Why?

There was a pause, a silence.

Chon asked:

—Do you love anyone?

—Yes.

—Who? Tell me.

She hung limp in his arms, crying. She was bathed in sweat. One bandage had seeped through, grown red at the end. With a sigh Doñita would change it, when Choncito left.

—Who do you love?

—Miguel.

—Anyone else?

—Doñita.

—And?

—Choncito, teacher.

—What about your country?

—Yes, my country.

In silence, now, he held the girl and brushed back the light brown, curly hair matted on her forehead. She met Chon's weary exalted gaze with a look of surprise, and relief; a flicker of knowledge in her meek eyes.

—When this is over, he said, we'll find a school for you. But love is something you have to provide; it can't be requisitioned. Love you have to find in yourself.

V

She flinched and gave a shudder, about to fall. At close range, a pair of eyes looked in her own. Intent, hurried, a woman grabbed her arm toward the shoulder.

—This way.

She followed inside where it grew darker with scents like a mouldy pantry. The woman whispered:

—Muchacha, where to?

—GN command post.

The woman lit a candle on the interior without decoration besides a crucifix. Alma recognized her from the marketplace: one of those who sold clothing in the stalls. In the quiet Alma heard someone sleeping. The walls were like cardboard. She showed her through a first trap door and then another. Like a dream, she glimpsed seated figures in the shadows: a couple at a kitchen table stared fixedly, a man sipped tea on a wicker chair. There were curtains, more passageways, entries hacked in adjoining walls.

—It's Alma, the muchacha.

They went outside and crossed a dirt patio. Then a narrow passage, more rooms, an underground tunnel. They moved through the earthen maze with a sewage smell and then reemerged in the open air. Had the woman been in touch with Claudio? She didn't ask. To her right fifty meters away stood the garrison with its facade. The woman pressed her arm and said in a whisper:

—Patria Libre.

The night rose up in explosions. Alma clung to a tree in Parque Central across from the GN post, and the trunk shook. The Frente was attacking in Catarina. The muchachos were on the move in Diriá. The ground trembled as Almita crouched and waited: how would Masaya barracks react? Rapidly? With magnitude? Would they rush out toward the ambush at Olla de Barro?

Gnarled forms of tree trunks, a flash over the low rooftops. She stood alone: only her, as the dozens of Guardia started to stir and gather inside the station. One unit sped off in a jeep, on recon of surrounding streets. Three men appeared in front of the white building, sinister figures with their glimmer of helmets, bandoleros and fixed bayonets. A second BECAT slid off in the adjacent shadows, but Masaya clung to its hush as detonations continued, thud, thud with a whistle in the distance. Alma whispered code into the walkie-talkie. She held the plastic box in the crook of an elbow and pushed the button with her knob of a hand.

—Blue three, over.

She couldn't put up the antenna; they might see it like she saw their helmets. There was static; she turned the thing down at once. A foot patrol of four Guardia waded out into dark terrain by the garrison. They crossed the street in her direction.

Explosions continued. A dog barked in a nearby street. More Guardia stepped from the station: stared glumly into the night where violence lurked. They would probe the sector for signs of movement, surprise attack. Alma poised as the four drifted toward her. She tried to keep her teeth from chattering, her shoulders from shaking. Should she call Claudio and relay the info he needed, give away her position before they reached her? She would be detected: what happened afterward would go unreported. Besides there wasn't time. They approached in the treacherous dark, fearing traps, a contact bomb flung from a branch.

Her heart pounded as the first came close, a few steps from her. She could hear his breathing. She could have reached out and touched him if she had fingers. He peered around, and Alma smelled rum on his breath, like that night. She stood frozen with fear—if he caught her with the walkie-talkie it would be the end. She hung by the tree trunk to fuse with it as he moved past . . . ; a click of his gear, an inadvertent crunch of boot heel.

Another arrived. He prowled past her in the movemented shadows.

Rigid, too tensed up to breathe, she waited. But then, suddenly, a strange calm came over her limbs.

She held onto the two-way with her drumsticks that must serve as hands until the day she died. But again she thought of her last moments with Chon Muñoz, and something she never since then remembered . . . Later, it was, when he walked her along Calle Calvario, her first trip outside the house in weeks. Doñita sat moaning in her rocker since the headache was on her again, and she needed an aspirin from Chepito's. At the church of the Calvarito, Chon said:

—Let's go inside.

His face looked funny, but she always trusted him. She would do what he said and the Frente would win and her brother would be released from prison and live. She thought of cranky Doñita, who waited for relief and grumbled.

—To pray?

—Something like that, he said.

In the heat of siesta nobody was inside, not even old Carlita. Only Chuno hung up there, the figure of Jesucristo on his cross, like a piece of driftwood on the shores of eternity.

They took seats on a front pew, and Chon sat beside her in silence. Softly, he said:

—Never feel less than the next person, because of hands. That's what those Guardia wanted; and they sent you back to us so we could all have a look, and learn our lesson.

Over the primitive teakwood altar, like a stump, hung the lifeless hands of Christ with their carmine gashes.

—He didn't feel less, said Chon.

Alma thought her teacher wanted to sit there and tell her something. About hands? Then she realized he was in pain, a terrible pain, she felt; even worse than Doñita's, though it didn't make so much noise, and Chepe's aspirin wouldn't cure it. Choncito's pain hurt her as well, and made her tense, like when Padre had his hives.

—What they did to you first . . . in the jeep . . . they acted like devils, I don't know why. But when you do this with someone you love . . . then you love them more deeply, you love all people, and feel life's beauty.

She bowed.

—Sí.

—Men and women love one another in a pure way, and have children. They love them, raise them, see them into the world healthy and whole, to play their parts. Filomena and myself do this for our sons.

She knew these things. What was poor Choncito trying to tell her? Why was he suffering so? She wanted to help him and risked a glimpse in the shadowy light of the Calvarito. There was a tear on his stubbly cheek, and this must be serious for a grown man to start crying.

—I know, she said, just a peep, by his side.

—But I loved someone else . . . that way.

He couldn't help himself anymore. He sobbed and turned away from her. He put his arm beneath his head, on the back of the next pew, and wept.

She made to rub Chon's shoulder and comfort him. She almost forgot she would never rub anyone's shoulder again; or tickle Miguel's feet for an hour while he told her crazy things about Iván the mountain guerrilla, their father; and later he brought her an ice cream on his way back from the Lagoon, where he went to dream, but it was all melted, just the soggy sugarcone; and he held up his runny hands and laughed.

Beside her Chon Muñoz wept. His broad muscular shoulders shook. She stared up at the haggard face of Jesu who shed no tears, his body drooped with the sinewy wood, his gaze full of pity. She wanted to hug her former teacher at the Colegio and tell him everything would be alright. He had been so nice to her and made her feel better. She wanted so much for him to cheer up, but she sensed from the way he was acting that something had broken inside him, and it made her afraid. If Chon fell apart, and if Miguel gave up, in prison, grown men started to cry,—then where would she turn?

In the dusky Calvarito, assailed through a chink of window by the blaze of siesta, Alma sat quietly alongside her teacher. She waited until he raised his head: he wiped his eyelids with two fingers. Their shoulders touched. It was the last time she would be with him. Three days later the Guardia took Choncito Muñoz away, and he was gone.

VI

From week to week, by early 1979, the physical condition of Miguel Giner began to deteriorate. Certain literary figures including Lisandro, the influential critic at La Prensa, had made attempts to secure his release from the Modelo. They petitioned the highest echelons of the Somoza government, while Lisandro editorialized in his Sunday literary supplement for the church hierarchy to intercede.

Writers from many countries signed an open letter, in late February, calling for Giner's release. And the banners and slogans at demonstrations included a demand to "Let the Poet Go!", as if all Nicaragua, land of poets, felt imprisoned in the person of this supremely gifted descendant of Rubén Darío.

On the ground, militarily, the Frente tried to rebound from setbacks in September: the deaths of Ulises Tapia and Chon Muñoz in Masaya, plus a number of cadre elsewhere. On December 9th a Spanish priest become rebel commander died in a firefight with Guardia on the Southern Front. But in March the three Frente tendencies, having split after the death of their leader Carlos Fonseca in late 1976, signed an accord to reunite under one command. They staged attacks: in León and Granada; in Yalí, a mountain village north of Jinotega; in Chichigalpa. They hit the sugar refinery in San Antonio. On March 27th, eighty guerrillas of the Northern Front commanded by Germán Pomares occupied the town of El Jícaro. The situation was gearing up toward a decisive confrontation.

President Somoza, alarmed by FSLN reunification and dramatic attacks across the country, flew to Miami and lobbied the U.S. Congress for more military aid. He negotiated a loan of $66 million with the International Monetary Fund and agreed to devalue the cordoba to the tune of 40% less purchasing power for the average impoverished Nicaraguan. On April 11th, a column of muchachos moved into Estelí and took control of that major city. Barrio combatants, members of the Christian based movement, campesinos risen up from the dirt poor comarcas and outlying districts, with past experience at the barricades; old and young, women and children, civilians and militants, all pitched in behind the Frente. It became a crime to be young and go out in the streets; as Somoza's son, El Chigüin, arrived with a thousand elite EEBI to launch the Guardia counterattack. For five days, over Easter weekend, the helicopters and light bombers circled and dealt death from the sky above Estelí. Then, during the night, the Frente retreated on foot through the silent streets, where cadavers seemed to float on the surface of darkness. Ranks swelled by civilians who left their loved ones, homes, possessions,—one column filed out northeast across the Pan American Highway, while a second meandered toward the high range of Tomabú.

Frente communiqués, over Radio Sandino, began using the phrase: final insurrection.

VII

During those turbulent days three more of Miguel's poems appeared front and center in La Prensa Literaria. Ripe with the moment of crisis, vibrant as the cry of a chachalaca bird in a storm of wildflowers,—his verse burst on the consciousness of the barrios, the talleres and syndicates, the schools and open-air markets. It was a vintage violin played amid revolution, strung with courage, sorrow and rage, a bright and somber ecstasy. Josefa quivered in the arpeggio of his yearning to see her and grasp in his arms deliverance, a vividly sensual freedom. Beneath those flights the organ notes moaned, of his pain, of his fear and loneliness: like morbid vapors, the singe of death in the streets of Estelí. A dark fermentation bred the poetic forms, a beautiful contour, a sunlit burst from the site of decay; a dying man hallucinated his love.

He lay in his own filth dreaming of sunlight, the blue waters of the Pacific at Las Salinas: of the bronze shoulders and deep breasts of his wife, her fingertips on his misery. His death began to multiply and teem in the darkness of his solitary cell. Chiri Robles had been transferred. A guard came rarely to clean up and spray disinfectant. When the demonstrations grew in size, with a nationwide hue and cry for release of political prisoners; when the Frente attacked GN posts around the country including a major frontal combat in Nueva Guinea, in the South,—Miguel Giner received even harsher treatment and less food. The warden's patience had reached an end: once a week, for ten minutes, Alesio had him dragged outside where the sun tortured his eyes. He stood in the courtyard writhing from the waist upward, like a saint in tremors.

—Okeh, animalitos!

Jingle of keys. A guard yapped an order. Days and nights in a numb fear. It was life at the bottom of a well fouled by rotten meat. Explosions sounded far in the distance—Masaya? Thud, thud penetrated the prison walls, merged with his heartbeat in a stubborn hope. The

Modelo silence perked up, listened. In those times they held back his beans and neglected to bring him water.

He remembered the last time Chiri Robles came to his cell.

—I don't understand you.

—We all want to be rich and famous.

—No, that would be normal: something you're not.

—It isn't normal to love our children? If your son died of the bleeding measles, or some other curable disease, then you'd understand.

—If you love your children, go to work. And don't have so many. Stop playing dominoes all day long; don't spend money on rum.

—The economy is so skewed by Somoza and his clique, by outside owners, it can't sustain us. People under such pressure cannot hope to control their lives. Listen, compañero: my father was a seasonal worker, he slaved eighteen hours a day on Cornelio Ferrán's plantation. At night he crawled in a chest of drawers with the others, and slept on a hard board deeper in debt than when he started.

Robles gave a laugh.

—I know about Iván Giner. I thought of the day he came to the Colegio with you, when we were boys. Rumor is . . . he died at the slaughter recently in Nueva Guinea: the one they call El Viejo.

—What?

—So many corpses they haven't all been identified. The moment you show yourselves, we destroy you. How can you hope to win?

Miguel fell silent.

Robles gave a low devil's chuckle. The Hamlet scam had cost him a promotion; and now a transfer to Rama meant family problems, month-long separations, a lot of inconvenience unless they relocated to that river town en route to the Atlantic Coast.

—Adiós, he said. Have fun.

In the gloom Miguel didn't say goodbye. The Teniente's heels clicked along the corridor.

VIII

No guard arrived to walk him that Sunday. Or the next. He felt himself subside in a feverish lethargy. His mind given over to bitterness, he cursed the world of men from his fetid hole. Instead of rivalling his hero Rubén Darío and the European masters,—silence, obscurity, this abject end abandoned by everyone. Betrayed by his friends, by the Frente for whom his death would be a moral boost and get sympathy, attract attention to the plight of Nicaragua, he was a pawn in a game of political chess. Duped by their high ideals, his life sacrificed for others who didn't care about him, he broke down crying like a child and only dehydrated his body further.

But then he rallied. The new prison guard cleaned up his cell and brought him decent plates of food. He began to hammer away at his terza rima masterpiece: the lines of an elegy for Chon Muñoz. Over and over he sung them like a transfigured song. He threw all his rage of rebellion into breaking down the barrier between words, conventional prosody, symbol and myth, and a fully realized expression of love. How to voyage senses intact along those far-flung cañadas? Go where life went, and seek its meaning? where the future drank hope out of season? How to fortify and guide the fragile poet at such a task? Cut off from his joy, divorced from the moral of nature,—what aesthetic provisions? The best verses came in a warm revivified rush, all at once, perfect, from creation. His body might be sick, and recede: his nerves went madly atingle, Josefa in a gown of sunlight dazzling Tasso's cell.

One day Alesio himself came flanked by two guards.

—Carajo. These comrades stink!

Clank-clank, the door thrown wide. The prisoner, unable to straighten, squinted out like a snail.

—Time to go!

Along the Modelo corridor he tried not to fall.

From their cells, scorpion-eyed, the others watched.

—Adiós, poeta.

—Puta! There goes Miguel with Alesio.

The weeks and months of loneliness, torture, thirst, starvation dissolved like an ice tray in Momotombo. That was what he needed, that was the accolade: to be called poet. They sounded so happy for a glimpse of him.

—There he goes, but where?

They murmured and stirred echoes. Then one, and another, began to bang on the bars, flesh on metal, thud like the distant guns.

Bent over, his lice-infested hair a banner of revolt, he grumbled:
—Patria Libre.
One said quietly as they passed by:
—Comandante.

Glare of the office window. Bowed, Miguel put a hand to his slit-eyes caked with rheum.
The warden shared a glimpse with two other men, priests.
—You're leaving.
—No.
—Go on, get the hell out. Incredible!
In front stood a gray Mercedes. The youngish robed priests helped the prisoner in back, gingerly, due to the smell.
—I don't think he'll escape, said Alesio with a wave.
They drove to a house in Colonia Mantica, an affluent sector of Managua, and parked before the kind of suburban home you saw in gringo movies. An older distinguished man came forward to meet them: a Catholic bishop.
He shook Miguel's hand and said:
—We petitioned the government . . . Come in.
Inside, the poet paused, sick and none too steady, a savage in a salon. Bands of gold light sifted a profusion of lint, the dust of the rich, through fine Venetian blinds. Footsteps had their quietude, on the plush Persian carpet, and glister of parquet floor. A gray-blue Siamese cat appeared from behind a tufted velvet divan; emitted its plaintive meow, thing of comfort. Arching its refined rump, perusing the newcomer, it held an unhurried course toward the shins of the priest. In an alcove stood a piano that mirrored the play of afternoon light. Portraits lined the mantel: people who seemed to live in distant places; while a secretary-bookcase, in light pine, graced the inner wall. Miguel rubbed his eyes, glanced at the leather bound books and then a reproduction of Fragonard's *Girl Reading* in a gilt frame.
—What's going on? he said.
—Your room is this way, said the bishop. You can wash and rest awhile. Our doctor is expected before dinner.
—Why?

—You will find writing materials. Feel free to use my library. You might be inspired to compose . . . perhaps a comedia religiosa, or an auto-sacramental, modernizing Calderón. Our own presses in Mexico City might run a deluxe edition, and you would be remunerated. You see, we wanted you, of all people, to have freedom to write under favorable conditions.

—Does my wife know I've been transferred?

—Not yet, the bishop gave a concerned look. Dear boy, this is hardly a prison.

—Can she visit me here?

—All things in their time.

The church dignitary spoke with a demure sibilance. Long ago, he had trained for the priesthood in Spain: his speech, Miguel noted, affected Castilian touches. Meanwhile, the younger colleagues looked on intently. They nodded at their superior's words and blent in tastefully with the wainscotting.

IX

In the beginning he let himself be cajoled, since it felt like paradise. After Macho Pedro, and fourteen months of the Carcel Modelo, he shaved and took a hot shower—phenomenon he had experienced once, as a joke, at Lisandro's. The man of letters lived well; but this sumptuous décor with its indigestible meals, its servants and regimented comfort, a fragrant gentility, left the La Prensa critic's pretensions of good living far behind. After his morning coffee Miguel gazed out at the suburban neighborhood, where birds chirped amid manicured lawns and gardens perched high above the daily fray of the capital. There was a desk set worthy of Proust with stationery like the fine linen of a society woman. He yielded to temptation and sat down to commit his terza rima elegy to paper, elaborating and fine-tuning as the first days out of prison passed in a dream.

> *Weeping I want to be the gardener*
> *of the earth you occupy and fertilize*
> *so soon, my soul's companion . . .* *

---

*Miguel Hernandez G.: *Elegía*

He remembered Chon, their boyhood adventures on Masaya Lagoon: they raced through the barrio in the afternoon filled with games, and birds flocked over back patios in the venus-hair ferns. Death tinged his memories, all the past seemed an infinitude of pain and longing for Chon Muñoz,—like the wound, life-deep, in his side, where the first man's love was ripped into extension. Inattentive life and unforgivable death, nature and nothingness, nada in a word-storm of blind rays and strident stones and hunger and catastrophes issued forth from his hands. In La Calzada Bakery they talked of many things, so many things to speak of, compañero, yet, on the threshold of adulthood and struggle,—they would never be so close again, until this night. He marveled: Choncito stood lovingly before him, fully in his rights. The poet would grovel on the earth, dig it open again with his teeth for failure to love, for limits and miscomprehension. Torn in two with sadness, he would go up into Monimbó cemetery and kiss his compañero's noble skull. Choncito lay in a field of spuming almonds, his heart of withered velvet. But his beehive spirit buzzed in love with the flowers, his sweetheart sparkled her grief like a dew of universe in the winged soul of the roses. And the furrows spread away fertile with future and death-won freedom.

When, late the third night, his friend stood before him completed in death, fully realized, expressed, Miguel bowed his head and wept. He wept for grief and for joy: at the vision of someone who stepped forward and died (never saying he would die), who confronted destruction so that others might live, and step forward in turn. So it was. He cried late in the night for Chon Muñoz, and the greatness of life.

X

The next afternoon a specialist came to examine him and draw bloods: a man dressed fashionably, scented with strong cologne like Alesio; salt-and-pepper hairs festooned his nostrils. His face looked vaguely familiar as he emitted little orders and palpated solemnly. Ah! He had appeared on the front page of Novedades; he put his stethoscope with a professional air to La Dinorah's breast, a national treasure.

There were pictures hung on the wallpaper of Miguel's room: a sensuous Pietà by a Renaissance painter; a garlanded racehorse in the winner's circle at Hialeah; an old print of the San Carlos waterfront by some forgotten artist. The first days out of solitary he stared and stared at the smallest things: light, the beautiful green of the grass and trees; the rejuvenated blue of April sky; the porcelain glaze of sunsets and shades of night. He understood the Japanese connoisseur who knew ecstasy in front of jade. But he also yearned for people dancing to marimbas down in the barrios; a radio show he used to hear when he courted Josefa with the Americano Infantíl. "Our Daily Song," it was called.

In the late hours he heard sporadic fire from the Orientales, or further east, on the edge of the city.

He asked one of the priests:

—Can I see a newspaper?

—It isn't authorized.

—Any paper, Novedades.

—I'll ask the bishop.

—A radio?

—Unauthorized.

—This house is quiet . . .

—As prayer.

—Has my wife been told?

—I don't know.

—Can you find out?

The priest nodded and withdrew.

The grounds were guarded. This he sensed from hours by the window: vehicles reappeared, moving slow—Oficina de Seguridad? As the days passed, and his first week as prisoner of luxury became a second, he began to feel impatient. What was he doing here? Had the fact been publicized? If so, the Frente would contact him—and raid the house? He sat by the window and read, thought, watched. His physical state made escape unfeasible; but he slept long hours and ate the rich food. The bed and gorgeous interior, the writing desk, utensiles held his interest into a third week.

He conversed, of an evening, with his host whose wide culture and European intellectual formation made him engaging. The Catholic bishop mentioned writers and works Miguel had never heard of, with a sense of literary schools and periods that went beyond Lisandro's;

though his humanism seemed more epicurean, a study for its own
sake, retrenched from temporal concerns, than the critic's. Did the
two younger priests, always by his side during these discussions, serve
as bodyguards along with their other spiritual functions? They rarely
spoke: unless to nod amen at the invocation of St. Augustine, the
revered Aquinas, Origen or Duns Scotus. They listened as the eccle-
siast sought to win the rebel poet to a more amenable position. In a
fatherly tone, the accents of concern and mature leadership, he said:

—Your writing, for all its merits . . . and your people, for all
theirs . . . inspire hatred. You organise it, when you say all bourgeoisie is bad, all this, or all that. A true artist . . . actuates differently.

—Crush the infamous.

—Something like that,—the bishop laughed, wise with irony.

—We have no bourgeoisie. A few of the well-off have been helpful, yes, the group called Los Doce, business and intellectual leaders.
Exceptions. And they will help on a governmental level when we win
power. For the others: what would you have me do? Bless the Guardia
Nacional before they go into battle? Or the gringos who train, equip,
support Somoza militarily and ideologically? So much for bourgeois
democracy . . . To understand a dictator: is it to love him?

—To understand is to love, forgive. The sincere artist does that; his
art is revolutionary. You too will reap what you sow.

—To understand is to struggle. Across the earth, not only in
Nicaragua, the children die of malnutrition and related causes: and
the single most important factor in our day, not the only, is U.S.
global policy. Exploit us minerally, agriculturally; convert our population into cost-cheap labor, while the children die. And repress any
dissent: call it terrorist, communist, in your vast media apparatus.
But oh! the glorious United States could never terrorize anyone, not
in Vietnam or the Congo or Chile or a few dozen other small countries: no, those genocides, while the U.S. public sat idly by, ignorant,
uncaring, underwriting it all with their tax dollars, were in defense
of democracy.

—And what happens, my dear boy, when the communists take
over? Be it Stalin or Castro? You can say goodbye to classical art, in
any case. Give to Caesar what is Caesar's! Great art was never created
on a basis of political economy.

—Writers without it, in our day, are like children. Besides, Castro
isn't Stalin . . . And what are you saying? We should fold our hands
and do nothing for fear of becoming Stalin?

—I am saying art cannot thrive on those hate-organized generalities. Fine art must be life itself, as lived: sermons destroy it. The introduction of any didactic principle, such as I find in your poetry, I mean the immature aspects, the dross, will deny that vital third dimension, the surprise, the heart. Look at the most serious writer propagandists: Gorky understood this, and his response? Ten bad novels about philistines, preaching in reverse, after the great early stories.

—And one masterpiece about revolutionaries.

—That's saying a lot. A sermon.

—More! With its head up, undenying, sound; it points our way forward—worth all the Eliot and Thomas Mann, the classical masquerade, with a morbid odor of self beneath the word perfume.

—Look at Brecht, a dramatist despite his ideas. No, you have to choose: are you an artist forever, or a publicist of the moment, decked out in aesthetics?

—I'm with the material victims. Being one of them, I find it hard to amuse you.

—We, too, are with the victims—

—Here? Miguel gestured.

—It's the league I play in. And if you would play in the artist's league, the league of Dante, Shakespeare, Goethe—you must respect the rules. Art is sovereign; it accepts no passion beyond its own.

—And if you see these things through your own eyes? Greatness comes from the people. The dollar, more and more, has sincerity in an Antaeus stranglehold. All the dehumanizing vulgarity of television, U.S. culture, has broken the connection. They give us sentimental or brutal robots, as if all life were a childish "American." The writers put their true, infinitely rich development in hock for a few dollars, for fame. And make no mistake: you either participate or you don't: it's the big sell, or else obscurity. If it wasn't for the Frente, the real movement here, which you say I should abjure, I would be unknown.

—In the circus?

Miguel laughed.

—Known as a clown.

The bishop paused, in thought. Himself a past master polemicist, he reached out to the truth-tormented soul in a flock.

—Heine found a way. He beat the censor and became a classic with future significance.

—At what price?

—This we don't know. But . . . we do know that our modern writers and poets, yourself included, haven't found the key as he in his
way did. Jump into the fray and you'll be remembered, if you are, as
the writer of a day.

—Shall I be as detached and self-consciously classicizing as
Goethe, a metaphysician despite himself: Faust delves demonically,
that is ruthlessly, into life's secrets,—while people suffer and die all
around me? And the reasons are precisely economic? And by some
strange fate I have a chance, at this moment, to combat them?

—With your talent you should go to school with Goethe. Immerse
yourself in the classics, frequent art museums, attend concerts: you
might obtain a scholarship to study in Spain.

—Spain! . . . Listen, my Christ didn't run off to Spain. He didn't
spend his prime of life in a boulevard cafe, whining about cultural
priorities.

—He argued with the doctors . . . Great art, like human liberation, isn't built in a day.

—My Christ doesn't resemble that one up there,—he pointed at a
framed crucifixion in low relief, on the wall,—with pretty limbs fashioned by a goldsmith.

—Everyone has his Christ.

The bishop smiled.

—Yours then: did he hang around fancy homes like this one, and
soothe consciences?

—He is here, now.

—Really? He hardly lends himself to satire.

—Along the lines of Gogol's Inspector General?

Imperturbable, he laughed almost happily, and sipped his coffee
from a demitasse.

—If he's here, said Miguel, he is longing for the street, the workshops and markets where the people go out on strike. A new Christ,
not submissive and tender, like a 15 year-old girl; but finding himself in all of us, in the Monimbó artisan, in the proletarian worker,
just as eleven of his disciples were proletarian. A dark-skinned Christ
burned, his hair disheveled, by desert winds. Rough, delicate, pure
as a guaria orchid.

—Then show him to us. Write greatly. But I warn you, for the
sake of art: you must depict *our* Christ, I mean all of ours. Anything less, any limits on that vision, that activity, only does the

devil's work gratis. It separates. It organizes hate. Humanity will
not thank you.

—Bourgeois or non-bourgeois humanity?

—Both!

—You don't see the beam in your own eye.

—We've brought you a typewriter, said one of the priests, Padre
Timoteo.

They liked to spend a moment in his room and chat frankly about
many things. The two had shown early capacity, using the priesthood as a path out of poverty. They relished a good meal very much,
and didn't shy from a pleasant joke. They had both met Padre Velasquez in Masaya and spoke well of Miguel's former mentor; they
speculated that God in His infinite wisdom might put Padre in line
for a bishopric.

—I can't type, said Miguel.

—We'll teach you.

—Is there time?

In late afternoon they walked him a few blocks through the neighborhood. Slowly, he strolled between the two good-natured priests,
with a sense of State Security on the lookout in a random car, a quiet
residence. Were they using him as bait this way? Alesio's clever ploy
after the Shakespeare gambit had failed: Alesio intent on having the
last laugh?

XI

The prisoner regained some strength in those genteel surround-
ings, as the days went by. La Dinorah's physician never returned to
inform of the test results. Blood tinctured his urine, and he still
spiked fevers; but into the fourth week, despite 24-hour guards
around the house, he decided to escape. He felt politically degraded
by this lingering house arrest; and debilitated, morally, by the slum-
brous comfort of life with a Catholic bishop. Between spells of study,
plus a typescript of the *Elegía* to send, somehow, to Lisandro, he began his search for a way. All the bedroom windows had an iron grating, and Padre Timoteo alternated with his colleague outside the

door. But the bathroom, with its automatic fan when the light went on, had a small window above the shower. Too small: he measured the frame and himself. If he managed to pry off part of the sash without alerting anyone,—might he just squeeze through?

He began working at night: first to free the frame stuck fast with paint layers. Slowly, quietly, he chipped away paint with a nail file from the medicine cabinet, and the effort left him quickly exhausted. Dissolving the cream colored chips in hot water, he tried to disguise the damage from a housemaid who came in by day. A barrio woman, who brought her son to play outside as she busied herself in the rooms: maybe she hadn't noticed, maybe she had. The work went on.

Past midnight. He took his few things, a book they had given him, the fair copy of his new poems, a shirt and change of socks. A monogrammed pillowcase became his guerrilla's *mochila,* knapsack: he would have to return it. In the bathroom he opened the window; and then, poised in the darkness, he listened to the murmur of Managua off in the night. He hoisted himself into that aperture too narrow for a human to pass, and began to squirm through. No doubt a guard from State Security lurked in the shrubbery, attentive to any sound. Miguel wriggled, caught at the waist, like an insect in hard clay. Down the block a dog started barking, enemy of movement. With his hips he hung halfway from the bathroom window; he burrowed toward freedom as the dog yapped. The knapsack fell. He grasped backward with his hands, worked his rear through and his legs,—and then shoved off, flipped as he once did in the circus, onto the grass. Giddy with space, head bowed to the dewy lawn, he heard her voice in whispers of the dormant city. Josefa called him to her, like the ocean at night, its waves on the beach in Las Salinas. Could she be there? He rose and moved half-crouched toward confines of the yard, orienting himself. With his luck he would run into a spy; or tip off some kind of alarm.

In the hours before dawn he made his way down from the sidewalks and gardens of Colonia Mantica toward Carretera Masaya. Empty streets led out from the center. A moon like sweet plum meat rose low over the lake, as he walked, walked. Moonlight lit up the initials of an insurance company high on Motestepe hill outside the city. Who would insure the insurers when San Judas and Monseñor Lezcano and the militant Orientales raised up their barricades and expelled the hated dictator: erected another set of silver letters there? He meant to push himself until sunrise and then find a place to sleep and rest through the daylight hours. Safety lay in the arms of the Frente; moreover, duty called. But he had other arms in mind: he would not stop until he found her, and did not care about the danger. He went along in a pair of beige trousers with plaits, a white blouse and expensive shoes. The urbane bishop with his servants and gourmet chef, hot showers and cotton linens, liked to reenact Christ's temptations on a daily basis.

Suddenly, on his right a flurry of shots rang out. Half mile off? Semiautomatic weapons; pistol shots returned fire: an ambush. He lay face down in the dirt: so much for the fine clothes; and then rose to continue his way southward. Stars shone high in the predawn sky, like mantilla lace. Stars hopped to the rhythm of his pulse, his love on parade. He strode the thickets, slopes, underbrush a stone's toss from the main road; reluctant to show himself, ask a ride. Behind him the lights of the capital glittered toward daybreak, in a mood tense with decades of hatred.

Afternoon found him asleep in a field, his flesh crawling with insects. Very thirsty, his body sensed betrayal; he stood among rows of tasseled corn and wandered on, south, and south.

Who could blame him if he wanted to see his wife? If he drew back and dedicated himself to writing for a time? Good literature needed months and years of staid routine, a shameless comfort, bourgeois habits! Crazy to be out here on his own, in a strategic zone patrolled by Guardia. With any brains he would head straight for Monimbó and melt away among friends; the Frente might arrange for medical treatment in Havana, and yes, there he could write to his heart's desire. But Josefa? Where was she? Not with Doñita, he believed; but where he had left her, waiting for him to come home. In the village, near Rivas, where Iván the seasonal worker returned from San Carlos with his young wife, Don Justo's daughter, long ago; and then Juana died in childbirth so her son could live, and become a poet. She was there, and he would go to her.

Early afternoon. By now word had spread, an alert gone out. Picking burrs off his clothes, and bugs from his skin, he trekked in the kilometers south of Managua, headed toward Macho Pedro's domain. The Guardia captain awaited the prey, poised up in Coyotepe Fortress, with his BECATs; he would pounce on the prize delinquent, and then revel in torture sessions until not much remained to hand over to Managua . . . if he could!

Outside a thatched hut Miguel knelt by the pigs' trough, splashed himself.

From inside came a high voice:

—Mama! A señor who drinks with the animals.

A girl younger than Alma stood in the low doorway. Indian features, the respectful look of campesino children with rickets, her bare feet the color of beaten earth. She eyed him, her small hand in a mesh of black hair.

—Do you have clean water?

She went back in, and then came out with a full glass. Behind her, on the shadowy threshold, her mother held a baby on one arm. They watched him gulp and swallow.

—Looks like a doll, said the girl.

—Where's he going like this?

In back, a pig snorted among corn shucks. A third child appeared: a little boy waddled round the side, bowlegged, rachitic. Dumbly, he held a shuck to his mouth, squinting in a ray of sun.

The mother frowned.

—Who are you?

—Frente.

—Are they after you?

—Could be.

The woman nodded, looked down.

—I'll get you a meal.

The baby, the little boy, the girl: they stared at the stranger in his good clothes, as the woman served him two tortillas, a strip of cheese, a spoonful of milk curd, a mango. At sight of them he felt a tension: illiterate, painfully unsure, they gave what they had. He paused over the plate as if in prayer; he couldn't bring himself to take a bite. Miguel ran his fingers through his long, curly black hair; he stared in the woman's eyes, with a faroff look, so she lowered her head.

The girl whispered:

—Mama, the señor is sad.

His tears fell on the tortillas. He shook his head.

From his knapsack he took the copy of his *Elegía* plus a sheaf of short poems, "Love and Other Crimes," "Christ with Machete," "Eclipse of the Sun by a Streetlamp." Determined to eat the simple meal, he asked:

—Do you go into Managua?

—Our friend, Amadeo, said the woman, he goes.

The poems covered eight sides in neat, even columns of type. Outside, in the sunlight, a thrush chirped. Announcing the May rains, it frolicked amid a patch of stunted guineo, plantain. The woman gazed at him, pensive. The girl stared, with a sort of mistrust, at the white paper.

—A man named Lisandro, at La Prensa.

—Amadeo's going later.

Nothing to write with. He had left the pen set they gave him behind, from a sense of honor, and regretted it. Hopefully the woman, who couldn't have read her own name, would remember.

—La Prensa.

But suddenly her face lit up, in a smile proud of its few teeth.

—You're the poet in the circus.

—You saw it?

—In Masaya. How you loved the girl. I knew that.

—Lisandro . . .

—You're with the muchachos now.

—Sí.

She tapped the paper.

—Don't worry. Medi will take it for you, when he goes.

—Today?

If her mother smiled, the daughter beamed with delight.

Afterward, they made him wash with a bit of soap, and lay on their folding cot to rest. With her rough hands the woman applied some herbal mush to bites all over his back. Once the rains began, the countryside fell prey to dengue fever. She rubbed in the concoction while the girl grinned at him from the doorway. The late afternoon sunlight softened the campesina's features, and made her hair shine indigo. They invited him to stay, but after a few words with the neighbor, Amadeo, he was on his way.

XII

Buses rattled along the main road into Masaya, and some continued on as far as Rivas. In his pocket he had ten cordobas they had given him, so he could ride. But the roadblocks, and Guardia patrols? And then it was, as sunset lit up the sky beyond a lonely jícara tree, that he found a corpse with a red and black kerchief tied round its neck, and dusty boots. The dark eyes gazed from a gruesome texture of insects, eating the forehead and cheeks. Miguel stared at the fallen combatant, and thought of the Carcel Modelo, the stench. Somewhere a woman waited for the man to come home, and her heart still beat with love, a strong hope. But he lay out here beneath a tree; with ants in his nostrils, and flies straining for a grip as they sucked the jellied eyes. A spider with orangish pigment maneuvered on the bearded lips parted for a kiss. A single bullet had seared the material over the dead man's left breast.

Miguel stood alongside and debated a halt in Masaya, a visit to Doñita's. He looked about for a flat rock and then started to dig. Dirt soiled his plaited trousers. The scent of good living was gone from the sweat-streaked blouse. Then a button popped on the corpse's bloated belly, as he hefted him into the hole. Night had fallen by the time the mound stood strewn with branches, neatly, beneath the solitary jícara. There had been no papers. A human life vanished without a trace. He recited Chon's verse over the fallen compañero's grave, and sang the Frente hymn. Then murmured to himself: time to march. The stars came out in a darkness drifted about with eternity.

In early morning he walked across a meadow chest-high in the tall grass. He passed beds of wildflowers as the first sunlight cast its shadows like folds of a woman's skirt. During the night he had trod the back roads; he passed a shack here and there; backed off from a pair of fierce eyes, wolf or coyote lured in by scents of the war. Mongrels all ribcage and droopy jowl barked at his passage; but no one stirred inside the low huts among plots of quequisque and plantain. A distant flurry of shots, with a growl nearby in response; but no voices as he moved along. A cock crowed impatient for the sunrise or roused by headlights along the road into Masaya. In the early hours Miguel felt sick and went to his knees in a fit of nausea. He lay in a field dizzy and weak, his intestines in the grip of destiny as a tree rat came to sniff at his ear. He froze as a snake slithered past his calf. At dawn a pair of blackwinged sanate dipped and veered above the field; they greeted the new day with their clarinetted whistle. Thirst got him up, on his way again.

Then he ventured near the highway, lurking in a thicket where the road turns off for Ticuantepe. A hundred meters further a van sat parked on the shoulder. The driver stood alongside to stretch his limbs; he smoked a cigarette. He stared, up and down, at Miguel who emerged from the underbrush.

—Compa, I need a ride.

—Where?

—Mas'—no, Rivas.

—Bueno, you snuck on, I know nothing.

When the driver opened the back, a few feathers drifted up. A cautious stir, a few importuned clucks . . . a chicken coop filled with turds and feathers. Good for his asthma.

—Where in Rivas?

—Las Salinas.

—I'll leave you near the turnoff. If the Guardia stops us, don't sneeze.

Sneezing, he crawled in among the few dozen pullet hens, slurped their water amid a general consternation, and lay down lengthwise.

XIII

In the bright noontime Padre Velasquez picked his steps along the Calle Calvario. He rarely traipsed this way, and never in the heat of siesta; but a piece of important news had arrived that morning, and he needed a few words with the spinster Doñita Reyes. He hoped the girl would not be at home: alert, suspicious as the devil, she might try to keep the old woman tight-lipped. He supposed not: no secret could be made, for him, of Alma Giner's joining the Frente, and role as the leader Claudio's right hand. Only a child, yet a hard case. That's what they did . . . He came to the Calvarito squat on its mound: low medieval doorway and crooked cross, more like an outhouse than a place of worship. Inside for a bit of shade he found a figure in widow's garb among the primitive pews. Carlita Garcia, nicknamed The Gargoyle by Salesiano priests; a woman he could not endure.

—On a visit, Padre?

Her voice creaked, like a side gate to hell.

She scrutinized him as if she knew his secret (he knew hers in any case), while the peasant Jesus, mild, unjudging, gazed mutely.

—Say your rosary.

—Oh, don't worry, she said, with irony.

He had seen her confer in the station market with that madman Bulu, a delinquent with the Virgin Mary tatoo'd on his arm.

—Someone to confess?

He moved through the low doorway.

Faustina's place had run wild with weeds since the Sunday massacre a year before. Juan Ramón's widow rarely showed herself in Masaya because of the stares; but recently she testified before a human rights committee that Guardia Nacional soldiers had gang-raped her after killing her husband and cutting off his testicles. No chickens or pigs; no sign of her daughters at play in the patch of earthen patio. They had all gone away to wait for the war to end.

—Somoza puta!

Padre glanced around. Faustina was gone, but Miguel's macaw had returned to its tigüilote tree. Snide, with bright plumage and a curved beak, it cried:

—Fire!

Padre saw a firing squad in his mind's eye.

—Hola, he said to the bird, ruffled.

On Doñita's low porch he recalled the spy Morell's visit that morning to the Colegio. The military conjuncture was not the best. Although over a hundred insurgents died in the frontal combat in Nueva Guinea, they drew Guardia forces from key pressure points around the country. Thus events had escalated the past few days: a Frente column attacked the northern city of Jinotega; while on the international scene Mexico, suddenly, broke diplomatic relations with the Somoza government. Moreover, Miguel Giner had escaped from house arrest in Managua and, as his whereabouts remained unknown, the President called on Don Cornelio Ferrán to activate the intelligence network, local operatives on Ferrán's payroll, in Rivas.

—Hola, Padre.

Doñita Reyes came forward on her swollen ankles. She flushed at sight of Padre Velasquez and gave a sigh.

—Is Alma here?

—No, Doñita glanced down; she isn't.

—Not home? I have this form, about her matriculation at the Colegio.

—What form?

—She must attend when we are in session. She mustn't be absent.

Doñita said nothing, as he installed himself in a crude chair.

—How have you been? he said.

—A bit tired, Padre.

—And Almita?

She gave a gesture. Insensitive of him to ask again: the matter, an embarrassment, was out of her hands.

In her ungainliness Doñita Reyes looked haggard, saddened; she had lived a lifetime of sorrow in the past fifteen months. Her house gave off an odor of depression. After the last prison visit, and revelations about Alma and Chon meant to hurt her foster son who paid his family so little regard,—she had come away feeling helpless, crushed to earth by the force of circumstances. Let those women shout themselves hoarse and go on demonstrating, day after day: he didn't care about her despite his protests to the contrary; a comunista to the core! She was going home . . . And so she crawled back into her silence. For a week, and another week, only the birthmark across her cheek betrayed a sign of life. But then a man came to visit her—not an outlaw smelling of monkey forests, not a delinquent from a sweaty prison; but distinguished, well-dressed, the kind she admired. Lisandro, the literary critic.

—She should be careful, said Padre, where she plays.

—Ay,—the old woman filled his cup with coffee. She brushed at a wisp of hair, self-conscious about her baldness.

—You're alone too much, out here.

—I know.

—I haven't seen you in church.

—My gout, Padre. It's far for me.

He nodded. A bird sang in the quiet of the Calvario.

—I also wondered, he said, if you might know . . . You see, one of the bishops has offered to intercede . . . and get visiting privileges for Josefa.

—Oh?

Doñita glanced down. She's jealous, thought Velasquez, with a glimpse at the window.

—That is, for yourself and Josefa, on a regular basis.

—But—

—Hm?—The priest stared at Doñita, as if they sat in confessional. He waited, assured of his power over the seamstress in need of comfort, by herself now that Alma had joined the vandals.—Do you know where we can find Miguel's wife, at present?

Doñita hung on the verge of blurting what she knew. After all, the Padre had absolved her everyday sins for decades; she trusted him implicitly. Hadn't he taught her foster children at the Colegio? Hadn't he been Miguelito's mentor, like a second father?

Now he cleared his throat. He sipped the strong coffee and waited. Wouldn't she tell him what she could? But he didn't know of the surprise visit she received, the day before, from the La Prensa editor. In preparation for a series of three articles to feature *Miguel Giner: His Life and Times,* the critic had made his way on foot, like everyone else, out along the Calvario. "Do you know," he said in a tone unlike Padre's, "that your son has escaped?" "What?" "I learned this morning. We've kept it out of the paper; and Novedades won't print the story either, for their own reasons." "Will he come here?" she asked Lisandro. "Here, or to his wife . . ." "Ay!" Her rocker had creaked with a slow, uncertain rhythm; and it began to creak that way now in front of Padre. "Doñita," said Lisandro, "someone will come, I don't know who . . . but sent by State Security. And they will want to know: where is she?" "In Las Salinas!" she blurted, breathless. "Good, I'm glad you told me that. But if you value your son's life, if you want to see him again: don't tell anyone else."

The wan spinstress looked down at her knees. The silence strained her nerves as the good Padre kept his gaze full upon her. So he and his bishop didn't know of the escape; and he came here trying to help them, with Miguel's best interests in mind. Shouldn't she tell him? She breathed in starts, unable to hide her agitation. Who was this Lisandro? Ay, Madre Divina, a man she never saw but once; and here before her sat the teacher of her children, the confessor of her sins, kind Padre Velasquez whom she could never in her life deny.

—Well? he said, softly.

Didn't he have every right to ask her what he wanted? Mustn't she tell him, too? a just man, above all a Christian? They locked up Miguel like a jailbird for being in league with the comunistas, but Padre was persistent to help. But what if he knew? If he lied? If he came to her on a false pretext saying she and Josefa could visit when the poor boy wasn't there anymore? No, no, Padre Velasquez had a right to lie, a servant of God, a just man who meant well. In all likelihood he hadn't heard; moreover, in times like these Miguel would be better off in prison than with a band of godless rebels like his father, Iván the guerrilla, a soul lost to all hope. Doñita's mind raced. Didn't Padre have good cause, in the name of God, to help end the threat of atheism, anarchy, violence around the country? Think of the effects in past months on decent people, think of Almita, Chon, Faustina and Juan Ramón, all the horror of Masaya! The full force of reality came home to Doñita in her moment of decision: she must play a part in her own son's capture. And yet he had called her Mamita that day in the prison; and said he loved her precisely when she believed he would reject her forever. Sí, señor, they had found one another and shared an unforgettable moment, just when she thought they were lost. But now Padre arrived with an insistence that she betray him or else sin against her deepest beliefs, and forfeit her place in paradise.

—I'm waiting, said Padre, and put down his cup.

Strangely, in that instant, his features seemed to distort, like a face reflected in the bottom of a glass.

XIV

The truck jolted to a halt.

—Rivas!

Miguel staggered out. Grimly the driver surveyed his rider covered head to foot in feathers.

—Gracias. Las Salinas turnoff?

The sunlight poured down, as if to dissolve the thin strip of asphalt that led toward the border. On all sides tropical jungle, a glacier of green, with its devourer silence. No other vehicles in view. The van started up slowly, a fragile thing of man. Down the road a fist thrust out:

—Patria Libre!

On the lake side Miguel moved from view, in among the shadows: the leafage so dense, entangled, it quelled the violent light like an insect-catching plant. On a torn stump he saw a colony of white wood-boring grubs. The South, with its ponderous wingbeats in the summits; the shriek of a monkey from a moss-hung tree. Then the wide lake spread before him, its surface shimmered blue and gold in the mid-afternoon. Across the water clouds rose against an azure background. A white heron took flight, as Miguel walked on the edge dreaming of Rubén Darío returned to Nicaragua for a tropical intermezzo—Ruben spoke of Hafiz, of Sadi, of Baghdad and compared Masaya with its flowers to the fragrance of Persia. The feathers floated from Miguel's clothes as he walked toward the turnoff, and the lake waves splashed down the stretch of beach. He thought of Homer, once, treading a flinty strand beside the Aegean.

XV

After a three-hour bus ride over unpaved roads he walked on past the salt flats and communal well in the center of Las Salinas. Along this road Iván had passed twenty-four years ago, while Juana lay in childbirth. And then Don Justo, her father, had perished in the late 'Fifties beneath the machete of a seasonal worker hung from a tree the next day. And there was the Matamoros dwelling, a family who had helped Miguel and Josefa eighteen months before, when they fled the Americano Infantíl with hardly a piastre in their pockets.

He went along a dirt path and turned left for the ascent into the rain forest beside the ocean. From his shoulder dangled the Managua bishop's fine woven pillowcase. From his fancy blouse a feather flew upward.

And here was the hut they shared, those few weeks of happiness—this one.

—Anyone home?

No, not a soul. So he went to the next hut and peered in.

—Ah! The woman let out a cry.

—Where is she?

—At the river.

He took the path down to the estuary. At the confluence of a fresh-water stream the women of Las Salinas came to beat out loads of clothes upon the rocks. In the distance he heard the Pacific pound up and down the white sand, foaming over the reefs from point to point. Like a breath of universe, sweet and salty amid the profusion of un-dergrowth and trees, its roar enfolded the coastal village in a kind of hush. For a moment he almost felt safe,—weigh your human worries against the force of tides, seaspray up the side of cliffs, the white-capped immensity. But he knew one phone call and Macho Pedro or another could swoop in by helicopter and make a routine arrest.

Beyond the river lay marshlands. A seagull took flight with a sen-suous cry, calling its mate. A seabreeze rippled the surface past reeds along the edge. Las Lájas turned a deeper blue as dusk began to set-tle. His gaze moved down the riverbank for a sign of life: the breeze swept late afternoon shadows back up river, away from the sea. A woman appeared fifty meters upstream; it wasn't Josefa: she trudged in the shallows, bent over her bale of laundry. She had a girth to her waist, bosom, thighs. He stared at her, his face to the slant of rays over the gurgling stream.

The washerwoman drew her skirt up; she wiped her brow on a sleeve. But then a glance down the bank: she spotted the man watch-ing her and straightened, stepped barefoot from the water, unfurled her skirt. From her forehead she brushed a mesh of hair blond in the gold light. Miguel paused a moment, his heart sank: he had come for the lithe dancer of the Americano and found a laundress who arched back, a hand to her hip, in the posture of peasant women across the earth. He looked away and frowned; but she stared at him from the bank. And then she realized.

She took a first step in his direction and forgot the laundry. She moved nimbly now among the rocks; and he saw the woman he had left fifteen months before; after the Frente attacks in Masaya, Rivas and San Carlos; and a call went out for men and women to fight for their country. She approached him with a hurt look, she brushed the strand of hair.

—You?

She came outlined against the ripples and deepened blue of the river. A few feet from him she slipped to one knee; but he didn't reach forward, he stayed still with a look of wonder. She stood there before him, a tear on her cheek; her body started to tremble.

—You escaped?

He put his arms around her and closed his eyes. He felt her hair on his cheek, her strong grip dug in his arm, her full woman's breasts against his chest. For a long moment he held her, and the nerves calmed in his stubbled cheeks. Josefa cried, and laughed; fingered the fine collar of his blouse. But with a glance over her shoulder Miguel gasped:

—Your clothes!

A dress, a bed sheet unfolded out toward the current in the middle. She drew him with her over the rocks, into the cool water. Too late for the dress! It floated beyond their reach on a ghostly course toward the estuary. In a few moments the white garment would drown in the limitless ocean which whispered of love, birth and death, all the things beyond struggle, where it rumbled toward nightfall along Salinas strand.

XVI

A chicken feather flew up, and Josefa sneezed, as light on the river took a tinge of red. He kissed her, and ran his fingers through her hair loosened, darkened like the sky. She had grown bigger, sturdier; she left the graceful performer behind with Hans and César in the circus. Her features had lost their girlishness, with accents of worry, a touch of sadness.

—All day I wash, she said, now I'll wash you.

He kissed her soft hair, fallen on her shoulder. They went to their knees in a solemnity of prayer; and then lay side by side in the tall border grass. Las Lájas murmured on its way unsuspecting, at this late stage, of the roar and froth that waited just ahead. He kissed her neck, more sinewy, curved to her village burdens, with a ruddiness from life and work out of doors.

—I almost gave up, she said. Like the time, in the Americano . . . The pain was too much.

A frog croaked, driven at twilight to feed, and be fed to a snake or bird. A dog barked, back over the ridge: yowled for scraps at the door of a choza. The high grass rustled, the reeds bowed their heads toward the water, the marshland stirred with the breeze at evening. The air went a pellucid blue; but dappled, splashed with sunset, like a painter gone mad over red. He nestled down on her neck and burrowed his curly head in the depth of her breasts; and felt her beside him, alive, in the receptive flesh, after dreaming on this moment, at the Modelo, until his mind grew morbid. She bit his lips, she yanked him to her angrily, exasperated with desire, after the months of bitter absence.

Suddenly a spotlight shown down, in the twilight of the riverbank. Josefa reacted first, on her back—the powerful beam slid past, she thrust him to one side with a turn of her torso. The light lingered on a sandbank to examine the shallows.

—Guardia, Miguel hissed, come from Tola.

She cupped her hand over his mouth, glanced around.

They heard talk: two men, maybe a hundred meters up river, approached. They came as hunters, revolver in hand, with the strong light.

—Shh, in the water.

—You can't swim.

—I can, she whispered fiercely; we'll stay on the edge.

The men advanced, quiet now, stalkers. Only a police dog, and they had their prey in one pounce. The searchlight probed the grasses, the beds of peat along the banks.

She held his hand tightly as they slid together from the edge, jolted by the fear. Quickly up to their shoulders, the current ran more swiftly. The hostile beam lit here, darted there, right alongside. They could not venture deeper: suddenly she ducked his head, and held him, drew him beneath the greenish shimmer. They waited.

The men walked by, flashing the bright shaft over the water, further along. Miguel had watched them pass. They were Guardia, or else two of Ferrán's men sent looking for him already. Where could he and Josefa go when the wide world knew his face? Reemerged, he looked so tragic, like a mask, she held him to her with a long entwining kiss to hush his fears.

The voices faded back over the hill toward the cluster of huts huddled in their patch of coastal rain forest. So they had located Josefa's dwelling and would wait through the night for her return, while word was sent on to Rivas. Now there was no going home; and by morning escape would be impossible, with the countryside put on alert. She shivered, she held onto her man and glanced this way and that as if already trapped. She gave a low cry and grabbed at his hair where they crouched by the river's edge. She pulled him down, water swirling over their shoulders, and began to kiss his lips brutally. Let old Cornelio Ferrán come and Macho Pedro and all the other rapists, torturers, like the ones who cut off Alma's hands. She had paid for, and would have, her moment of ecstasy. She snapped at Miguel's cheeks and lips; she thrust her body toward him like a lascivious mermaid.

—Are you crazy? he murmured, and took her in his arms.

XVII

In Masaya, city of flowers and volcanos, the children's voices rose like a clear fountain across the resplendent green of the Salesiano playing fields. Masaya of melodies and witchery, wrote the poet, of nearby lagoons, and lush vegetation on the heights. Masaya of sunlit landscapes beneath a golden sky; the smiling grace of its women, the lyrical clamor of its violins, in the night—admirable violins, speaking of love, in a language of passion and fantasy. At noontime the Colegio recessed for lunch and the silent hours of siesta. For a moment the older students congregated in the small square before the school where so much had happened since a year ago February. Now all their talk was of Frente attacks, and battles erupting across the country toward a final insurrection. School only opened, in such times, on order from Managua to preserve appearances. As Frente ranks swelled with new militants, workers and campesinos, students, professionals, a large percentage of women, the U.S. Government maneuvered politically and sought diplomatic modalities to forestall a winner-take-all FSLN victory. Washington had supported the Somoza dictatorship for nearly fifty years and would do so until the end. Meanwhile, in the fresh shade, beneath the trees, Monimbó women sold their lunches, rice and beans, milk curds; drinks ladled from cool vats, tangy beet or pinolillo, fresco de tamarindo, cacao, ginger. Schoolgirls in blue skirts and prim white blouses passed by chattery toward the Magdalena or up into the

Rinconadas. Despite the nightly skirmishes in rural zones, a sense of all-out war impending, life went on in Masaya, city of flowers, vague nostalgias and romantic violins.

Into the pleasant scene strode a figure in dark glasses, who wore a bright shirt with natives in a jaunty dance. Morell stood back as a stream of schoolkids shot like a nozzle through the Salesiano entry. Briefcase in hand, he smiled without mirth and waited for them to pass. He had just descended by taxi from an interview with Macho Pedro up in Coyotepe Fortress: no mean trick to keep one's gaiety after an interview with that hero. The situation on the ground was problematic; and thus the Macho's tirades did not buoy up one's spirits. Morell entered as the last of the young scholars, enraptured with freedom, went past and clipped him in the ribs. Outside: trees, the hot sun, steep shadows on a pastel facade; inside: the studious halls, the quiet of a cloister. He took the stairs with his air of stealth, and touristic shirt from Miami gangland.

—Am I disturbing you?

Padre Velasquez sat bowed at his desk over Colegio accounts.

—No more than usual.

—We missed him.

—When?

—By nine p.m. we had two helicopters in Las Salinas. The lovebirds had flown the coop.

—Ah.

The Padre appeared distracted.

—Unless they drowned in the estuary.

—The Frente has them.

—Maybe; but where? We want you to visit with Doñita Reyes again, Morell reflected. Josefa's friends, something she said . . .

—He went to the Frente. Took his wife on the Southern Front.

—We don't think so. He's too sick for that kind of activity, as we know from the doctor's report. How he eluded our people in Managua, and made it south, defies the understanding. If he stopped in Masaya, we had him.

—Morell, I . . . I'm tired of pestering Doñita Reyes. The poor woman has her bitter cup.

The spy seemed to sniff the air.

—A foster mother of subversives . . . We've got our eye on the girl, we use her for tracking, one safe house to the next. We'll snatch her up when the time comes.

—I take my orders from the Archbishop.

—Of course! And he gets his from . . .

Morell gave a gesture.

After the functionary withdrew Velasquez fell into a kind of revery. He remembered Miguel Giner as a boy seated at his desk in one of the classrooms. Brilliant even then but uncaring, utterly free of pedantry and, it seemed, ambition, he memorized Garcilaso or Lorca at a glance, and recited with a natural feeling. Padre recalled Chon Muñoz, his protégé and gone now, taken away by Guardia and put to death. Choncito owed him more: who took the poor boy in hand, who prepared him for a career so he might establish himself and marry Filomena? Yet Chon betrayed his mentor, the Colegio, his religious principles. Subversive of the most dangerous, stirring the fickle people to rebellion, with never a word to his superior. How powerful and strange: this siren song of utopia. The young men tasted the fabled lotus fruit of justice, and went their way to ruin with a triumphant smile, comparing themselves to the early Christians. Look at Miguel: he had made himself into a creator, an inspired innovator of style. He might work a new poetic theme like a vein of the sublime, witness the *Elegía* for Chon Muñoz: it had appeared, a thing of stunning beauty, on the front page of La Prensa Literaria. Now Miguel Giner had become a national figure, who plunged along the mainstream rapids of great events. In his way he might even qualify as a «great disciple» . . . but of what master?

He lost track of time until the children began to return for a curtailed afternoon session. From the first-floor corridor their voices surged into his daydream on the nature of vocation. So he rose, wearily. With a cambric handkerchief he wiped the sweat from his forehead, and made his way to the stairs.

—Hola.

—Okay, Padrito.

—Pow! I'm a Sandinista!

The front entry blazed with sunlight each time it swung open. The Padre stared straight ahead and ignored the children; he looked almost transfigured as he went along.

And then, once again, he sat in tête-à-tête with the old woman out at the end of Calle Calvario. He posed his indirect questions and waited for her to respond. In her answers he heard an anguished note, and in the afternoon silence with its buzzes and chirps. What kind of madness could drive him from his study to betray a parishioner's trust and ask a woman to inform on her own son? He thought on apostasy. He had loved the precocious boy and admired his prize student's intelligence. He resented, deeply, the ruthless pretension of the man to set his poetry up as a court of justice. Unbowed, in a self-reliant pride, the son of Iván Giner knew the sin of arrogance.

—More coffee, Padre?

Doñita bit an unsteady lip. She gave him a stare like someone who has seen a snake. This second visit—he wondered how its motive could be disguised.

—I have important news, he said. Miguel escaped from house arrest in Managua.

—Ah.

She looked away with a nod. She seemed to know. The news had since been in bold headlines on the front page of La Prensa; someone had probably told her.

—He is very sick according to a physician's report. He needs immediate attention.

She turned sadly toward her kitchen.

—That's not all. In Las Salinas—

—What?

She had mentioned Las Salinas in their first visit; she could never hold anything back from her very own Padre . . . Then she justified herself: he could easily find Josefa's whereabouts: Miguel himself would tell him. In her heart of hearts she knew this wasn't true; the muchachos were careful to conceal such things; and for twenty-four hours she had been through a bout of depression.

—Someone saw him in Las Salinas, but—

—What, Padre?

—He . . . they slipped away. He resists our attempts to help him.

—Who is we? she said, with a side glance.

—The Church . . . But I'm afraid the Guardia might go looking for him, Doñita. And then we can't respond for what may happen. He could be killed.

—Ay.

She stared across at the priest, and blinked. Her big form seemed to hover on some threshold as the fear took over her features and lit up her prominent birthmark.

—Now we're wondering where Josefa has friends, someone who would help them in the vicinity of Rivas.

—I . . . I'm not sure.

—Maybe a girlfriend? a contact?

—Let me think.

—This is important, Doñita. It's for his own good, and we hope you can tell us. Who would give them refuge?

—She might have said something once . . . when we were in Tipitapa together, outside the prison.

—Who, Doñita? Who was it?

—I'm trying. Oh, if only I could remember that name.

—Tell me. So I can alert them.

—I'm trying!

—Believe me, their only chance lies in the protection of the church.

—Ay, ay.

She gave him a devastated look as if gazing on something unclean. Like the time Miguelito dragged home a carp from the Lagoon, a dead thing which stank to high heaven; and he knelt in the dust and pounded it in boyish frustration, cut his fingers on its raised fin . . . But then, between them, the silence seemed to reach a kind of climax. A crucial moment passed. And suddenly she stared down at Padre from her kitchen entry, and saw a man, and nothing more, or less—a man who told his stories and did his deeds and went his way toward the next encounter. Doñita brushed back a strand of corn-silk hair and gave a curious laugh; but her eyes told a tale that could amuse the gods, if not Antonio Velasquez.

—Well? he said, waiting for an answer; but it was too late for such answers.

Still he lingered: she might yet make a slip and divulge another precious detail. In an instant, like a microscopic lifetime, the nature of their trust had changed; and now he felt small before this poor, lonely, unlettered woman. Again she gave him the laugh and began to chatter like a magpie about some trivial matter. Ha! She would tell him, the bachelor, a few tips for preparing his yucca.

An hour after Padre rose to leave, Doñita Reyes made the first trip off her little bit of property, out there in Las Sabogales, for many months. She wanted to knock across the way at Faustina's, since she knew from long days at the window that Faustina had at last come home. But before that she hobbled her way down to the Calvarito and offered a prayer for her two subversive children, whom she loved in the depths of her soul.

XVIII

After their tense escape at the river Josefa knew they could not spend another hour in Las Salinas. With an unknown resourcefulness she took him first to a friend's house on the village outskirts; and the following day, by pack mule over trails known to the campesinos, carried him in a feverish condition to Rivas. From there they risked a collective taxi to La Virgen on the shore of the big lake. Security lay with the Frente, if at all, but he felt unable to rejoin the whirlwind of struggle; and, should the leadership opt to send him for treatment outside the country, he feared another separation from his wife. Josefa had a friend at La Virgen, named Miriam, who made way for them by moving with her children to a sister's in El Velero.

At first, in a state of physical prostration, he let himself be dressed and undressed, fed, caressed, all but played with like a doll. She brought water and washed him, levering with her strong shoulders. She combed his hair and kissed him while they brushed his teeth. They loved, petted, cooed with the ardor of a saint before an icon; and then, after lovemaking, she rose to pour a bowl of cereal pinol and pungent coffee for supper. Hardly the Archbishop's fare; but he felt gratified by life and didn't fear death, if he had this instant with her, with her.

—You've changed, he said, where he lay watching.

—I'm the same.

—No, life did its best to break you, Hans, César . . . then me.

—Don't say that.

—But it couldn't. I've never been happy like this: it pays and overpays for everything else. But I'm staring out at life from a sickroom.

—You'll get well.

—Life is beautiful, and tragic. Like this, I feel the pathos of Miriam, an unwed mother . . . Or the sensuality of those schoolgirls we saw in Rivas: oh, what do they care about sickness, swinging their hips?

—You'd better give poetry a rest, and eat.

She shoved a fold of tortilla between his lips.

He closed his eyes, with a sigh.

—I don't change, she said. But I am stronger, I know more.

She lay down beside him in the twilight; prodded him to eat, inserted a spoonful into his sad flow of words. He described the escape from Colonia Mantica. A tear bloomed in the crease of his eyelids for the dead combatant with ants in his mouth. Prison, the hunger strikes, Alesio. Doñita's visits. The boyhood friend, Chiri Robles, become a Guardia . . . How could you go through so much, thought Josefa, and still remain a child?

—The unimportant things are burned away in prison. Only the essential remains, the universals, injustice, hunger for life, hatred of oppression. The loneliness, the anger sear all the rest away. In solitary I thought: isn't it amazing? The Great Tradition seems to know so little of this, as if so-called Civilization were a gloss, if not a conspiracy; and so it's left to us, poor little Nicaragua, to teach the world. I didn't hate Alesio exactly, the brute; I will always hate the taboo he upholds, the choice and the silence, the human failure. Money, not Man. But prison is such a powerful thing: you wind up pitying the victim even in a torturer . . . Do you understand, my darling?

—And Tacho Somoza, do you pity him?

—I daydreamed I was the one who ended his misery.

—Ah, I thought you daydreamed about me . . . Mi amor, take this one bite.

—Like Rigoberto, justicer of the old Somoza; but I escaped and ran straight to you.

—Qué alegría!

—Kissing passionately, we fled down a back lane with a hundred Guardia on our trail.

—My hero . . . Will you sip this?

—They couldn't catch us. We were guided by love.

—Lots of love?

—Lots, like Homeric heroes protected by the goddess.

—What did we do then?

The spoon dropped on the plate as Josefa peered down in his eyes. With a look of frank desire she set all his sick insides atingle.

—They were hard . . . hard on our trail. (His words trailed into a kiss.) But we . . . we just couldn't wait . . . anymore. (Mingled with her breath.) And so . . . ripe to burst . . . (A boa constrictor kiss suspended the narrative.) We had to . . . we—

—What?

—Love.

—And those mean Guardia, my darling?

He bowed, kissed her breasts as his breathing came in starts, in flight from Guardia. He ran his fingers over her full hips, no longer the willowy figure of a dancer. In the reddish shadows she sought his eyes and pawed at his shoulders and provoked him.

He murmured:

—And you, love, what did you dream of while I was away?

She slid down beside him, her mouth against his, breath to breath.

—You free . . . our child.

She hypnotized him with her eyes. Singleminded, she bent him to her will as he muttered a few more poetic remarks. They lay together on the flimsy bed in Miriam's hut a stone's toss from Lake Nicaragua. A full moon shimmered on the dark water, and the young couple strained, thrusting upward, to set a new life in motion. She groaned; she no longer carried on like those days in the circus when everybody heard her and stared at her next morning from the trailers because she was so high-strung. Now she spurred him on with her hands and the mystery of her body. From the heights she cried out his name and heard it quiver in her depths. Her eyes drifted to one side, like stars at dawn, while he inundated her being with vital life. Off on her own, orbited, for an instant, in space, his name seemed to echo and fade.

XIX

At dawn a cock crowed. The first light gathered about the hut by the side of the big lake. They hadn't slept, as a ray of sun like a tickle touched the window sill. For a moment she laughed and bullied, rolled over him.

—I don't know how long I'll have you. We should contact the
Frente: every minute we delay, your life is in danger.

—Let's stay.

—You know they'll find you. You're too much for me, and this
life . . . But I want you stored up, inside me, so I can live.

She served him pineapple, a slice of cheese, bread. Later, Miriam
brought by two eggs, but Miguel asked:

—What about your children?

—Oh, they get plenty of eggs.

He laughed and handed one back.

When Miriam had left Josefa boiled coffee, sniffled a little, sang
to herself.

> *Mañanitas, mañanitas*
> *como que quiere llover*

The May sky kept its lakeside freshness with a hint of showers.
Mornings, early mornings, this mood of coming rain. Down the path
there were sounds of campesinos starting their day. The cock crowed
hoarsely against the hens' cluck-cluck, peck, assorted barks and birds
chirping, a rustic concerto. He lay on his back, eyes closed, in the
warmth of the sun. He felt tenderness for his wife, a love and gratitude for all life: from an ant on a corpse to the spirit of a people expressed in an epic poem. Think of the infinite intermediary forms:
the heroic struggles never heard of, the monstrous denials when no
cock crowed. He rose on one elbow and said:

—It doesn't matter.

—What?

—I fought the bad thing . . . I worked, loved.

—And?

—I'm ready.

—Selfish male!—She handed him more food, milk curds and a tortilla from Miriam.—Eat this and stop living your image.

A cloud covered the sun. Thunder rumbled out over the lake.
Josefa sang softly and watched him chew the good food.

> *Así eran las mañanas*
> *cuando te empecé a querer*

—Your slave, that it?

—That's it.

—«Better to die free than live like a slave.»

She leaned above him, kissed his curly hair. She moved to rub his nervous stomach while, dutifully, he chewed. A tear hung on her eyelashes, like sun and clouds in the unpredictable sky. Those were the early mornings, when my love for you began.

XX

The next day, and the day after, Josefa lived a plenitude of happiness. But she couldn't help meditating their prospects. She recalled the close escape in Las Salinas, and frowned. They both knew his safety lay not in her arms: only the clandestine network could hide a fugitive known, from newspaper photos, across the land. Soon he would rally physically; soon he would find the willpower to flee. And she would follow him into the jungle if necessary; or across the marshes and streams of Río San Juan.

With each passing hour she awaited a muchacho with a message: plans for a cure in Costa Rico; or Tica Bus to the border, with a plane fare to Mexico City; and then, too, they might be separated. Hardly able to stand upright, he could not be expected to pick up a gun and resume his duty. In a matter of months, he reassured her, perhaps weeks, the Frente could win; and they would be left alone to live in peace.

—Wait, he said. Any day, they will call for a general strike.

He began writing. Miriam brought them her oldest child's notebook and two pencils. In those tense days he composed two poem cycles among the classics of Latin America, with editions in seven countries and Spain. He lay on his side in the cot so unlike the Managua bishop's guest bedroom; and the verse ran and pranced like a spirited horse against the reins. He propped on one elbow and worked. He gazed at his wife where she sat knitting; and spoke the verse as it emerged in a meter no longer conventional but one with the emotion.

—I'm supposed to be alone in here.

He laughed.

—You can't fool a campesino about anything he can touch, see or feel.

—Great, we can expect the local authorities.

Her voice trembled. She had such a grimace that he got up, shakily, and went to her.

—We could go to Doñita's, he said, resigned, and expected her to jump at the offer.

She thought a moment.

—There's war in Masaya, the roads . . .

—So?

—We'll wait till it ends. Just . . . don't remind them.

At sunset Miriam knocked softly.

—Wait, I'll come out.

—It's okay, said Miguel with a smile. I've finished. Josefa's husband radiated happiness, like a choirboy.

But Miriam said:

—He should leave.

—Why?

—They know he's here, in the village.

Miguel looked unalarmed, smiling at the generous friend. He rubbed his eyes and glanced back down at his poems. While the two women stepped to the doorway he read over his work.

—Alright, Josefa said, low. We'll go to Masaya.

He raised a hand, his eyes still on the notebook. A first few raindrops fell on the high-pitched thatch of the choza.

—No.

—But you were the one—

—Do you know what happened yesterday?

—I don't,—her eyes went wide,—and how would you?

—While you were at the lake I walked in the village. Someone heard, over Radio Rumbos, that the Frente robbed every bank in Masaya: Banco Nicaragüense, Banco de America . . .

—You showed yourself to them, like that?

—I had to go out for a moment.

Lips pursed, with a stubborn look, Josefa said:

—We'll leave. You're ready.

—I'm too weak to go out on the roads. There's blood in my urine: wait a day or two.

Miriam looked at him in wonder: a comandante having his honeymoon while Managua and the Pacific Coast cities poised before all-out war. To her a little bloody urine wasn't the end of the world. In remote villages south of San Jorge the children caught hemorrhaging measles and bled to death, pore by pore. But no doctors, no dispensaries with affordable medicine; a doctor in Rivas made you pay three to four hundred cordobas, a year's earnings for a campesino. Meanwhile the dictatorship, the plantation owners like Don Cornelio Ferrán, the big fisheries such as Nicamar, Galipaxa, Caribia in San Juan del Sur, paid no attention. What was one undernourished child more or less, on this earth?

Josefa, her hands to her temples, stared out along the path to the village. In a shaken voice she said to her friend:

—Do you have a Frente contact here?

XXI

In Rivas center Morell slapped a dusty sombrero on his thigh. Take a room, he thought; wash up, after the afternoon bus ride from Las Salinas with its sweat and chickens and glum campesinos. Then a hot meal, red meat, served to the strains of mariachi music in the *Afrik' Ardiente* since Señor Ferrán had been so generous. Leave it to your grand gentlemen from the old school: they passed you a platter of *reales* once you got next to them. For nearly two years he had dealt with Velia Suazo, Ferrán's agent in Masaya, and the woman never showed him the inside of her house,—before the rioters burned it down,—much less her purse. Velia treated him with a haughty reserve; while Macho Pedro, up on Coyotepe, had contempt for such elements as Morell and underrated their services. To the magnificent Macho he was just so much scum in a summer suit; he reaped benefits while mindful of his manicure. Thus Macho, and thus Velia Suazo: no *reales*. But Don Cornelio epitomized liberality in the name of a good cause.

Shadows lengthened over the pleasant park in Rivas, where the Somocista sipped a fruit drink by one of the kiosks. In his hatband he had a scrap of paper with names of leads, one in San Juan del Sur, one in La Virgen by the lake: the wife's friends. Many were anti-Frente campesinos involved with U.S. missionaries, Protestant sects who came and sowed a few cordobas about the countryside; and they would talk to him.

Entering the *Afrik' Ardiente* he glanced around: still early for the serenaders who strummed their guitars from table to table, mariachi songs that stirred Morell in his romantic soul. A waiter came forward with a whisk broom and began to brush the dust from his clothes; he patted his shoulders with a smile. A famous maricón, thought Morell, and raised his arms as the waiter whisked. Without bestowing a tip he proceeded to a table and ordered absinthe.

A waitress in a bold miniskirt brought his drink on a tray. Her conical breasts jutted beneath a diaphanous blouse. You could say that for her: she didn't hide what she had. He gave a bristly smile, sat back and let the sweet ache accumulate in the place where he once loaned God a rib. Ah! woman; what a wonderful thing after a long, hot, sweaty day of doing a man's work.

—Care to order, Señor?

—No hurry, I hope.

So encouraged was his mood with the poet practically under wraps, and Tacho's gratitude assured, that he patted her derrière as she leaned to place a napkin beneath his glass.

—Don't touch.

—Please? he said.

He stared up with doleful eyes and sipped the bitter drink.

Things had gone well. He could count on tomorrow's arrest. But tonight he would play a little and spend some of Ferrán's money; he would get his sexual exercise and renew himself as befitted a man. Yes, life wore an inviting smile this balmy May evening in Rivas. He remembered a time when the Frente could not claim fifty cadre across the country; and in recent weeks they had lost an entire column, nearly 140 fighters crushed by vastly superior firepower in Nueva Guinea. Over a thousand Guardia diverted to the Southern Front with air support and artillery; and these tramps who had never held a real job, these nephews of Che Guevara thought themselves all set to assume state power? The moment they showed their faces in open terrain, presto! a slaughter. Among them a Frente leader, Iván Montenegro, had been «martyred» as reported by the evanescent Radio Sandino from the mountains. Could this be the father of Miguel Giner? the one known to military intelligence as Bocáy?

The 3-star restaurant began to stir with customers as the night drifted amid rustling trees in the park outside. A few well-dressed couples waited to be seated while Morell eyeballed the pert buttocks of the waitress. He recalled the seigneurial charm of Cornelio Ferrán, as the mariachi singers tuned their guitars to one side. When the girl came to serve his well-garnished *bistec* he reached up and touched her breasts, shivery as ice cubes, with the back of his finger.

—What are you—?

—Dessert menu.

She turned away; and the mariachi group launched into a song, luridly sentimental, with a promise of adventure. But he heard the words of Señor Ferrán, spoken that afternoon as they sat on the veranda of the manor house in Las Salinas.

—Honor, sir, and loyalty. The oldtime virtues binding man to man. I remember an era, strong, noble, when our forefathers knew the proper course of action and didn't pause to pursue it.

Across the sunbaked fields, dotted on the margins with peasant huts, stood a solitary ceiba tree. A monkey swinging in the summit could have seen the blue Pacific, the far horizon.

Seated side by side Morell and the comprador landowner sipped their drinks. The spy's features showed an eager receptivity.

—I understand, honor and loyalty.

—Now we need more honor, more patriotism!—Ferrán slapped the mint julep on a glasstop table so forcefully it might have cracked.—It is time, my son, you saw how the old school handled its affairs. Tacho is too tenderhearted for the tough measures of statecraft.

—Yes, sir.

—Nearsighted, individualist, he has isolated himself too much. You see it, moreover, in his dealings with the military: jittery, afraid of conspiracy, he insists on a dangerous centralism and keeps his friends at a distance.

—You mean the CIA?

—The plight of Diem, in Vietnam . . .

But the interview ended brusquely. Ferrán's secretary peeped through the screen to announce another visitor.

—Well, find the poetaster for us, Giner. This is what Tacho and I ask: find him.

Morell rose like an intelligent canine.

Ferrán went in. After a long illustrious career, his movements had such an aristocratic starch he wouldn't need embalming. But he turned and shook a finger.

—Oh, I know them, these poets. A quarter century ago his father caused a sorry scandal, down in my village there, running off with the daughter of my manager. The poor man, Don Justo his name was, never recovered. He cut that girl off and left her to die in childbirth. They say the wild ape, Iván Giner, came up here with a machete looking for me.

On his way out Morell met the secretary. The fellow's manner and accent resembled luxury imports; and he came forth with a tip so lavish, Morell might have rented a car in Rivas if he wished; or hired a biplane for the hop to San Jorge, his next port of call, on the shores of Lake Nicaragua.

XXII

At dusk the following day Miguel and Josefa walked hand in hand along the path from the village. A bit stronger, he grew restive in late afternoon and rose from his work. She spent her day pounding laundry with Miriam by the waterside; and when she returned, her heart sank to find the choza empty, with no hello but only the silence. And so she made her way to the cantina and entered the place, tears in her eyes: he was seated with village men at one of the tables.

—Will you come?

He stood, with a smile, and followed her outside.

—It is happening. Even they know it: the ones who haven't joined.

—You're careless.

He took Josefa's hand to slow her down.

—Many fell on the Southern Front, but they aroused sympathy. Each day some say goodbye to their families, and go off to fight.

She gestured back to the cantina:

—If only one is an informer—

—I think the dictatorship has more to do than track down a poet.

—You'll take that risk?

—For another day.

Nature settled toward evening. A bird warbled above the fields. A white egret took flight over the water, in the deepening light. There was war across the country: the peaceful mood seemed strange.

—Mexico has broken all ties with Somoza.

—More will die.

—So our people can be free.

Head down, leading him along the path, she thought a moment.

—It's my risk, too.

Another day passed. She lingered and feared to leave him alone for long. By now the Frente had been told;—had they taken steps to reintegrate him, amid the frenzy of training camps, night probes and maneuvering of forces, skirmishes on all fronts? But the moment came when Miriam appeared with laundry enough for two, and the friends went off to lakeside with their skirts brushed by the sedge grass. They talked in murmurs and scrubbed out laundry; and Miriam, abreast of the village rumors, said she wondered at the delay.

Yet a day went by, and a night. Miguel wrote his poems and took walks openly. He learned of fighting in nearby Rivas, a firefight the previous evening in a southern sector of the city as Guardia stormed in with tanks and .500 mm. machineguns forcing the muchachos to retreat through La Puebla barrio. Radio Sandino informed of an FSLN attack on Jinotega in the North.

It rained in early morning; or a downpour toward midnight left the air hushed, with the underbrush drip-dripping a restful rhythm. In the early hours they woke to a thud . . . thud . . . like a muffled drum, and they drew close and held one another. He got up to write by candlelight; while she had sudden starts, unable to give over to slumber. They stayed awake far into the night, and he counted out the vigorous meter of his verse along her spine. Or she woke up to find him in a transport, his gaze filled with future. Toward dawn they made love with a responsive tenderness, in a ritual dance that tapped the spiritual roots. And then thud . . . they clutched and loved as the fighting went on toward San Jorge, datdatda . . . thud . . . it came closer.

—Tomorrow at nightfall, she said, back from the lake the following day, we leave La Virgen. They're sending someone.

XXIII

They went outside and sniffed the dew, pure and pinkish at sunrise. The breeze brought a murmur from the pebbly lakeside. Josefa prepared breakfast and then, at shortly before eight, went off with Miriam to work a few hours.

It was May 24th. At mid-morning Miguel sat working over a longer poem: *In Love and War.* Papers covered with handwriting lay in a small pile; he bowed absorbed in the composition, lips pursed, with a faint smile. A small bird sang on a sunlit branch outside the window.

—Buenos dias!

A knock on the door. The muchacho come early? He sat back contented with his work for a moment, feeling better physically.

—Who?

He went to the door and found no compañero with a red and black neckerchief, but rather a man in civilian clothes. He glimpsed the seedy aspect, jaded eyes, the hint of eagerness,—and he knew.

—What is it?

—Miguel Giner?

The poet's look of well-being faded. This was no Frente contact, journalist, village acquaintance. At first he surmised a clerk sent by some circuit court judge, scourge of campesinos through the provinces. He wore an absurd gray homburg, like in gangster movies but rimmed with sweat in this climate. His inexpensive suit, rumpled in the heat of mid-morning, gave an air of a sinister clown. Miguel glanced down at the man's hands.

—I don't have time.

As he turned back inside, the other said:

—You're under arrest!

And this was the cue. Two Guardia, not Rivas garrison but elite troops, EEBI, jumped round the sides of the choza like wild beasts. Helmeted, frowning in the sunlight, they aimed submachineguns. Bandoleros, grenades hung on their olive-green uniforms.

—You're under arrest, said the functionary.

—I'll leave my wife a note.

—No notes.

Morell nodded at the soldiers. They stepped forward, somber in the glare.

—I need one or two things.

—Now! shouted the spy; his hand shook as he motioned.

A moment later they were gone. Silence. The bird chirped in the morning light. A breeze stirred like an afterthought, ruffling Miguel's papers on the small wooden table. They had left the door open. A slight gust rolled a stub of pencil from the top sheet, and off the edge.

XXIV

Siesta had ended by the time Josefa returned from her laundry. She felt nervous and excited about their departure into paths unknown, and went briefly through the village on last-minute errands. A woman kept her chatting on the threshold for a half hour.

—Miguelito?

She would sneak up on him from behind and tickle him the way he did her! Then he'd recite the lines she loved from Lope de Vega when the lovers exchange caresses: with love, lots of love, coming straight from the core. Afraid, exhilarated,—what kind of life would it be in the underground network? She also felt happy to end the anguish of staying exposed in one place, and wanted to prepare him a good meal before the journey. South to Costa Rica? Where would it be? Now she hurried along the path; she wanted to be with him since sometimes they quarreled over something trivial and didn't make love. And when he said: let's stop, she moved away: smooth things over so you can have my body . . . In a moment she would make it up to him—make it up ten times.

—Señor?

She went inside and found the silence. She picked up the stub of pencil, plus a sheet covered with his writing like a burst of wind. Papers, a few books, the table, the folding cot. She sensed his tender presence.

—Miguel?

Hands on hips, she looked around.

Off for another walk beside the lake? Or through the village in full view of everyone? After the long months in solitary confinement he had a passion for being with people. The slightest thing fascinated him.

The idea that he loved her exclusively, boundlessly, gave Josefa a thrill as she stood in the hut where they had spent three rapturous weeks together.

She turned and went outside.

She started down the path after him. There was a lilt to her walk, skipping a few steps: I have a piece of news for you, compañero, which will bring more joy than the lottery. It was too early to tell, but she could feel the new life just beginning to stir. The future took root, started to grow and unfold, inside her stomach. The fruit of their mingled lives, and all their love. The rest might be confusion, insecurity, dust; but the news in her stomach was true, clear, profound. Sí, compañero.

She looked in at the cantina.

One by one, the neighbors said they had not seen her husband. Miriam reacted with alarm; but at the moment she had to deal with her kids, while a stray dog chased a chicken out back.

Where was he?

—Not even a note? Not a few scribbled words to let me know?

Returning, she looked with her hands. Hadn't he left some sign? And then, as the bird gave its chirp outside the window, Josefa paused in wonder over the beauty of his poems. So much love he poured into them—lots of love! Alone there, unable to control her emotion, she felt the luxuriant earth, the men and women, the keen-spirited birds seem to vanish and leave her to a head-banging grief;—but then reemerge, and transform the pain. In these few weeks by her side he had written love songs to the campesinos and working people, those who produce life's richness but subsist on next to nothing; to a factory in production, a field in cultivation, a hammer or shovel, wildflowers and nightjars, a speckled tiger-beetle, and an angry peccary. In it all she sensed something of herself, their deep feeling for one another, their child-to-be's little fingers. Rain soaked the undulating barrio where the poor huddled beneath a leaky roof. They quarreled, they loved with an abandon behind the piñuela fences around their huts . . . Miguel had sung every instant of his time with her: the Indian with a sense of his greatness, the tragedy of his past, as he goes about preserving something of the ancient ways. The factory woman with a child strapped on her back; the illegal fisherman on the banks of an estuary; the leaser of a solitary mine far up toward the Honduran border. A mini-skirted prostitute steps high in Managua (her life like the vine once termed by Spaniards *vienparacá*, come here, with its entangling prickles). The teenage lovers play and caper on the edge of Masaya Lagoon; while Nindiri in the distance shoots up its sparks and ash, like a chthonic god clearing his throat.

For a moment Josefa stood there, head bowed, and read his poems. She waited for him to come home. The same bird chirped its hopeful song as the afternoon wore on.

XXV

Then she went to the door.

She stood on the low threshold and wrung her hands.

Almost dinnertime now, and still no sign.

She could feel his virile tenderness, his hundred ways of responding to her, laughter and pranks and abandon. She felt the sunlight in his smile and curly hair; and his absence turn into something hostile.

—Miguel?

She put a hand to her face: paced as she tried not to break down. Through the open door the sun went down in a stark orange light. She stared forth dully: the emptiness.

Silence. A stir of grasses, insects, murmurs at nightfall from peasant huts along the lake. Back inside she sat down, but then stood up in revolt against the cramps of despair. Her mind flashed back to the time in the Americano Infantíl when she wanted to destroy herself. She touched her stomach, with a pain like a mule kick on the fragile life she carried. She paused a moment, unsteadily, on the verge of a headlong fall beneath the weight of her loneliness; but then tore herself outside and made her way, arms swinging, down toward the lake. Was this some sort of terrible joke? Disappeared, without a trace. Did the Frente have him?

Josefa tripped on a root and fell forward; with a cry she jammed her wrist.

Night walked, its shoulders among the tall palms. The lake, deep blue and tinged with red, lapped at the gravelly shore. Night slogged the marshlands.

—Ay.

Head in her hands, hair disheveled, she rose to one knee.

No, he was back already. He had come—he lit a candle, thoughtful as he sat down to wait for the muchacho . . . Go back!

A white heron took flight, veered off across the water toward Omotepe.

A dog barked.

She pressed her fists to her midriff and doubled over.

Alone.

Nobody could help her now.

In Rivas, in Masaya, Estelí, Managua, they fought: men and women, killing. Barricades went up. Bursts of gunfire, homemade bombs, Guardia artillery sent a wind through the barrios. Jinotega had exploded, Miriam told her, with fierce combat across the city.

That was easy compared to this.

Josefa rocked. The tears flooded her eyes. She gave a soulful scream and the sound skipped over the dark surface.

In La Virgen they heard a hoarse shriek, the hysterical woman. What happened? Raped?

Suddenly, the night was punctuated with shots off toward San Jorge. A yell. Shots. Seconds of silence.

She stared at the purple smudge of the horizon. The world was a blur. Josefa crouched, whimpered, out there.

There were shots in the distance.

A world was dying. Nicaragua listened, on the eve.

XXVI

The meeting broke up after midnight, and the leader Claudio took his way with long strides toward a safe house on Lomas de Sandino. The walk felt good after his day filled with activity. Night air, pure stars made him think of other times, other places. For a moment, a lull in the frenzied preparations, he remembered leaving León for the countryside in the early 'Sixties. He had worked at construction sites and returned to his Indian barrio on weekends with a few cordobas for his mother. He began as a stonecutter and later became a mechanic on burling machines. Years filled with movement, events, life . . . Now, all at once, the mighty dictatorship tottered as the final insurrection approached: the day he could hardly hope to see in his lifetime.

Claudio went along in the starlight, but he heard soft steps behind him. Pausing, on a dirt path down from the Rinconadas, he listened to the nimble footfall.

—And Jinotega?

Alma whispered, by his side.

Moths flitted. Fireflies sparkled amid the herbage and low bushes. Hesitantly, a cicada fiddled, as a dog started to bark over by the Magdalena.

—We'll hear on the radio.

The Northern Front commander had led a column against Jinotega. A critical moment, thought Claudio: no weakness, no mistakes. Severely punish any personal departure: that was his credo. But the girl's conduct, her unswerving commitment and singlemindedness struck even him as extreme. She spent twenty-four hours at a clip on her feet. She did the work of three.

He glanced down at her:

—Not tired?

—No.

—Vanguard never gets tired?

—No.

—Or hungry?

—My brother ate nothing for thirty-six days.

It was strange when the girl with mutilated arms said such things in her bird's voice. The hardened comandante paused in his thoughts to marvel at Almita's discipline. Involved in all this for the poet's sake? From a sense of guilt? No matter, she was invaluable.

XXVII

He had toiled at a dozen menial jobs, mechanic's assistant, day laborer, brick hauler before joining the FSLN in 1972. In a fishery, in a pencil factory he earned his keep plus a few cordobas to send home. Once in the guerrilla he worked under Iván Montenegro and built demonstrations, organized strikes and land confiscations. He painted slogans in the cities; he helped recruit new members in the marginalized barrios. From Iván he learned to take on responsibility, and it weighed more than a pick or shovel. He was ten years old when he left for the countryside, halting his formal education; but when victory came, if he survived the final offensive, he would go back to school.

Lately, his quiet humor had begun to fade in the face of Guardia repression. Frente directives stressed that no comandante would launch an operation on his own or let himself be taken prisoner. Yet key cadre perished: the Spanish priest García Laviana; now Iván in Nueva Guinea. Compañeros gunned down in the barrios, or kept in prison where they broke down mentally: a few in fact chose suicide. Never prone to abstractions, ill equipped for ideological discussions, he went his way of pragmatic activity, he assessed the terrain and prepared Masaya for the uprising. He didn't laugh as often; but now the girl made him laugh, low.

—I'll get dinner.

—Cook mine rare.

—We don't have any steak, she said, fluty. The Doña left us beans and yucca.

In 1974 he attended an FSLN course in Chinandega. They sent him to El Crucero where he met Germán Pomares, military leader, and Eduardo Contreras political leader of the internationally reported hostage taking of Tacho's cronies at a Christmas party. Claudio participated. He flew to Cuba in the plane Somoza had to supply and remained outside the country until '76.

The work went on. Returning through Costa Rica, a veteran, he became second in command in Granada. With Camilo Ortega he coordinated attacks on Rivas and Masaya garrisons in October the following year. All the while he organized among the workers and campesinos, students, children, the dispossessed, vagrants: men who spent their prime of life combing the fields for an empty beer bottle to redeem, or a bit of rusted metal. But Camilo died in Las Sabogales, when Guardia overran the home of Doña Faustina during the February days.

XXVIII

In the safe house he leaned over the battered, retaped transistor and began to tune.

—Beans and yucca?

Martial law in effect. After dark a silence, across the city.

—Tortilla.

He nudged the tiny nob, soaring far into the night amid static: like the volcanic mist over Orosí where, he knew, the clandestine Radio Sandino had one of its three transmitters.

She brought the sparse plate of food.

—Eat well.

She took the transistor and, plying the drumsticks that served as her hands, tried to bring in the elusive signal.

—They'll tell us about Jinotega.

He ate the bit of food and leaned back.

—Take mine, she said.

—No, you.

Claudio closed his eyes and recalled a March '78 operation: he led the team that put a torturer, the CIA's man in Managua, to death. And then August, storming the Palacio Nacional, with the entire parliament hostage: he was there, masked: they gambled with death to gain support for the Frente. Key operations, but some died. Claudia Chamorro, from an aristocratic family in Granada—fallen shortly after Filemon Rivera in the North. Camilo. Ulises Tapia, one on one with a tank in the streets of Masaya. Chon Muñoz: Choncito who saved the day when Monimboseños mistook himself and Camilo for spies in February. Iván . . . Some died.

Alma bowed over the old cracked radio. In the darkness he felt her humble, girlish presence as she thumped on the plastic: a method all her own.

—Here . . . here it is.

He sat forward to hear. In effect she had picked up the signal. It pierced, honing in through the night of war.

Later, they heard the news: the death, in Jinotega, of Germán Pomares.

XXIX

—"*Nicaragüenses! The hour of decisive battle is at hand. On Tuesday, June 5th, 1979, the nation must stage a general revolutionary strike, and shutdown of all businesses . . .*"

In Masaya the three FSLN tendencies,—Proletarian, Prolonged Popular War, Insurrectional,—had come together under Claudio's command. He had hardly let the Frente split affect his non-theoretical activity from day to day. The pivotal action, once fullscale fighting began, would center on the Guardia garrison in Parque Central.

—Make a direct attack, said the very macho Bulu, ready for anything.

—Surround it first, said Marta Navarro. Lay siege before we pass to the offensive.

—Liberate a bus, said Bulito. Sharpshooters, bomb-throwers in front. All-out attack.

—We have the initiative, said the beautiful Cecilia Asturia, whose nom de guerre was Delia. We can't surprise them: we'll take unnecessary casualties.

Claudio nodded, thoughtful. Sudden attacks had proven success-
ful against all odds.

—Alma?

The girl stuck her head in the door ajar. Her eyes lit on Cecilia
who had shown her kindness like an older sister. As Almita peeped
in the candlelit room filled with muchachos, Cecilia caught her
eye with a wink of encouragement. But Claudio sent her off to
fetch the mechanic Fasael who knew how to jump-start buses
without a key.

Running along lightly as a fawn Alma thought of Miguel: the
news of his escape and then rearrest in La Virgen. Padre had told
Doñita and plunged the old woman in despair: "It's hopeless. I
spoke with the Archbishop of Managua who phoned State Security: there's no helping him." So in prison again: torture; and rancid beans with roaches when they remembered to bring him any;
and his asthma would flare up in the airless, fetid cell, and scare
him. For hours her foster mother rocked gloomily and grumbled
about comunistas and hurt herself with painful words. "Whose
fault? My fault I guess . . . a wild beast same as Iván . . . too selfish!" She bit her lip, pitiful, and the tears rolled down her flabby
cheeks. Alma felt sorry to see her that way; but not like she used
to with Padre's hives. She hugged the moanful Doñita, during a
brief visit, and stroked her bit of orangish hair like the silk on an
ear of Indian corn.

But Alma's thoughts wandered on the way toward Fasael's: she
couldn't stand to imagine her brother being tortured. Instead, she
pictured Cecilia's calm womanly smile; and the doll she used to play
with as a child, Consuelo. She thought about a boy she had seen, a
cute one with red hair: sort of like Lorenzo from Pochotillo, who
died in February. What if no boy ever wanted her because of her
hands? Scared of them. No muchacho to hold her close and show her
kindness, making that thing good again, like Choncito said? She
would risk it if he would. Once, she had been with Cecilia in a safe
house, in La Reforma, after Chon died. Cecilia couldn't show herself
anywhere; but sometimes she put on a lot of powder, rouge and mascara, and went out. In the safe house they talked about boys: why
they were so strange.

—You don't always know, at first.

— . . .

—You could fall in love with one, and not know it.

—Really?

—Suddenly, one day, the thought comes: it's him.

The tall well-built Delia looked sad then. But Alma glanced down at the maimed things she had to carry through life, and gave a gesture, almost obscene.

—No boy would have me.

—The right one.

—Easy for you to say. You could have any of them, even Bulu.

—Gracias.

—It's dirty, it is.

Her voice flew up. Her features contorted. But Cecilia moved beside her, and brushed a curly lock from Almita's forehead.

—It depends on what you feel.

They talked and comforted one another that afternoon, in the La Reforma safe house.

XXX

Carlita Garcia sat on a knobby pew inside the Calvarito. She couldn't pray, too nervous. The dictator had declared martial law in Masaya, so strict you couldn't visit your own outhouse. And since Holy Week such a level of tension, attacks, sniper fire; the populace said their evening prayers, or else adiós, south to Granada; or, the wealthy ones like Velia Suazo, Ferrán's secretary, up and away to Miami. And mornings, out along the highway, bodies. It was daily, the bodies that came. Young people, a crime to be young! When would Miguel Giner's sister show up that way, out there on the road shoulder by El Nido Motel? She took risks. Daily it was, horrible; but you couldn't tell who they were, eyes plucked out, brains like stuffing from a cushion. And everybody murmured about an informer, sí señor. Old Macho Pedro had his spy in the middle of Monimbó, like death pointing a finger. Then bring them home and pray over them: the barrio buzzed with songs of the novenas. Then burial up in the cemetery by the Rinconadas, alongside Lorenzo the poet, Ulises, Chon Muñoz, the hundred martyrs . . . She had her own idea: there was a certain priest who used his position of trust to ask a lot of questions, even in confessional, pfui! Better save your gossip for Chuno, up there on his cross with the saints. He could keep a secret. For the rest, citizens, prepare to attack. Boil up some water, thought the 78 year-old Carlita, and pour it down on their heads, beasts.

XXXI

June 2nd: heavy fighting as the Frente entered León. The Western Front attacked Chinandega. Combat engulfed Chichigalpa and the northeastern goldfields of Siuna, Bonanza, La Rosita.

June 4th: León fell. With the tide turning Catholic authorities led by the Archbishop of Managua drafted a document as to the «moral and juridical» legitimacy of the insurrection. A day ahead of schedule the country lay paralyzed by a general strike.

Not a soul in the streets of Masaya. No cars. A rare vehicle passed. Marta said:

—How can we surprise them?

—You're right, said Bulu, the macho grown adept at «critique and auto-critique».

—Study the siege, said Comandante Claudio. Get it ready.

A code knock on the door: Almita. She had been to Managua on a mission, through the network. She came in breathless:

—They've started. They raised barricades in San Judas. The Guardia made a dragnet of adolescents.

Wide-eyed she spoke to them. The capital up in arms.

June 5th: no shops open for business. The strike 99% effective in the Pacific Coast cities. The forces of the insurrection assumed their positions.

Claudio said:

—We take the GN station. Move in, overwhelm it. Then,—he pointed at a crumpled map,—we overrun the communications centers, zingo. Tipitapa Highway. Block these routes.

Claudio made a diagram.

—Two columns on the south side, led by Pancho and Marta. One from the north led by Domingo takes the Instituto. A fourth at my disposition: mobile combat unit, led by Delia. Roams the city in a van, with sandbags, MG-42, medium-caliber machinegun plus seven riflemen.

—Riflepersons, said the demachified Bulu.

The compañero made a great secret, except with his eyes, of his love for Cecilia Asturia.

—It reinforces the weak points . . .

Discussion on the role of popular militias. Function of the new barrio committees. Claudio nodded, moderated. All spoke tersely, wired to the electric circuit of the rebellion. He beckoned Alma:

—Go fetch tortillas from La Calzada.

She slipped out like a breeze in a bamboo curtain. Five minutes later she had tortillas, a tin dish of rice and beans, a plate of milk curds, thermos of coffee.

June 7th: martial law, curfew and state of siege.

XXXII

At noontime Bulu waited with a group of compañeros in the La Reforma safe house where Cecilia and Alma talked about boys one afternoon. He recalled the day they robbed all the banks: two combat units of fifteen each.

—So Pancho he's telling them: okeh! At ten in the a.m., militia members, hit the streets. Burn cars, raise barricades: make a racket, por favor! Cecilia, I mean Delia, and another compa enter the bank like clients. Chocho! If you'd seen her rouged and mascara'd, that kind of woman, a match for La Dinorah. We intended to recuperate four million cordobas, the coup of the millionaires. At ten they entered the bank: Reach for the skies, this is a stickup! Imagine the surprise: a gorgeous broad pulls not a perfumed hanky but a .45 revolver from her purse and starts directing traffic. In Banco de America the head teller, our collaborator, put on a big frown and rifled the till. Delia made a few gestures with the .45 and grabbed up handfuls. That lovely green cabbage filled up her plastic purse, but her bra was already too full to hold anymore, if you know what I mean. Just like a dame in the movies; and George Raft, the King of Havana, in the old days, would have been proud of her. Outside, the rumble was now in gear—puh! puh! That's me Bulu, giving it to the dicks. Shirt off, what a specimen! But the compañero supposed to back up Delia shitted himself and stayed away: you see our organization is made up of humans, even a militant Sandinista may be heard to say in such a moment: mamá! So Delia got a little nervous and made her exit. Bulu, says I, spotting her on the steps of Banco de America: cover that compañera . . . Later she told us: "I waited, waited. When he didn't come I thought: they'll trap me inside." She could have stayed and cleaned out the strongbox. Our collaborator shook his head seeing all that loot go to waste: two million cordobas plus a mess of green dollars and some jewels. When Delia met the compa Moises by the mill in Monimbó, she handed him a sweet but disappointing 128 G's.

Bulu paused, with a faroff look, and then went on:

—At Banco Nacional we hit a snag: no surprise factor. Sum total recuperated: nada. As Pancho later analyzed: "Bulu," he told me, "our economic objectives were not realized, but we dealt a severe blow to Guardia prestige, garnering a politico-military victory." Whew! If only you could have seen our own Delia on the steps of Banco de America, like a cross between Marilyn Monroe and Rosa Luxemburg. She's got something in her bra that's better than dollars, if you know what I mean.

In La Reforma a messenger arrived, as Bulu was finishing his story, and gave a counter-order.

—Stay here until 3 p.m.

The group had few weapons, scarce ammunition: a FAL, a carbine, one grenade, two .45 pistols, a .38 special.

Noon came and went.

They waited in silence, Bulu and the thirteen compañeros. After awhile Marta Navarro had to leave. And then, toward one o'clock, a compa named Roger went out.

Suddenly, in the torrid siesta, they heard the sound they didn't want to hear. A voice shouted in the loudspeaker so loud, you could hardly hear the words. They knew the voice, Macho Pedro. And they knew the meaning.

—You're surrounded!

Bulu thought: ay! who informed?

—We'll bring in a tank and mess you up, Frente animalitos!

El Machito was quite an orator.

But negotiations ended. Bullets whizzed like hail, fleeuuuw! phzzzzt! Bulu ducked. He rose up and sprayed the gate with sub-machinegun fire, screaming:

—Die, doggies!

A Guardia fell.

Inside, two compas limp at their posts.

Ammunition nearly spent. Why didn't we hold back?

—Give it up, clowns! Give it up!

Thus Macho Pedro, a diplomat.

—Your mother give up! cried Bulu.

Another Guardia fell. Almost no more ammo: may as well surrender. Who informed?

Ay!

In a garden behind the house they stood in a line. Ten muchachos. Guardia moved slow, like gorillas in the dazzling light, each with a Galil. They scowled beneath their green helmets. "Mierda," thought Bulu. "This is it."

—Into the street, bastardos!

Macho had a habit of fingering his manhood. His right hand lev-elled an M-16, his left hand strayed, sort of Napoleonic. A muscular hulk of a man, a torturer from the dungeons of Coyotepe: always touched himself. One by one, the muchachos moved from the garden.

TATATATA!

Felicito Franco went plunging head over heels. BANGUM! BA! BA! BA! Compa Carlos Montenegro, ciao Carlos! Compa Isaias Es-pinosa, dead forever. Bulu watched them fall, and sprawl. Compita Laura Espinosa, just that a.m. Bulu fantasized how lovely it would be . . . since Delia wasn't in his league . . . ay! Never with Laura ei-ther. Macho Pedro yelled:

—Give 'em a passport to Caiaphas!

Compañero Francisco Escobar—tatatata! Compañero César Navarette—pre-e-esente! Bulito still stood, wobbly. "Am I hit? I'm too young to get hypochondriacal . . ." All around him combatants on the ground, doubled over. Raoul Espinosa limped toward the far side with a compa called Cortes. Milton Navarro was still on his feet. First day of the final insurrection, like an Opening Day Parade. "The famous hero and martyr, Bulu Moratín, fell today . . ." POP! POP!

And then silence. And that was it: the massacre in La Reforma. A few muchachos made the tactical error of breathing and got duly finished off.

—Caramba! said Macho Pedro on the phone with Masaya garrison. I need a truck.

Bulu, where he lay wounded in the garden, risked a squint. He wanted to see if Macho fingered himself after a massacre. Puta! Sure enough: perked them up with his left thumb and index while he tried to requisition a van. So Bulu closed his eyes, with the fever on the march, and figured he would die with a laugh. He heard Macho say there was fighting all around Parque Central, and imagined the muchachos attacking head up, over there in the sunlight, and lost consciousness.

XXXIII

They applauded in a respectful way. No cheering; they clapped as the Frente column passed down the street toward the GN garrison. Carlita Garcia blew a kiss, enthused by the sight of so many fighters with their weapons. Grim, joyous, the people applauded. The soul of Monimbó, muddied with five hundred years of being trodden and trampled on, would clean itself in a great decisive battle.

Alma trotted alongside them. The whole barrio knew her; they knew what she had been through, and so the applause grew stronger when she joined ranks with the Rufo Marín combat unit, named for one of Sandino's soldiers. She glanced around and wished Miguel might be on hand, or at least Padre Velasquez who would be proud of her. But Doñita Reyes would raise a howl if you ever asked her to come out here. She would send Alma to Chepito's store for aspirin when it was time to go fight a revolution.

The girl slowed a moment, stepping in cadence. Stiffly by her side she carried the stumps of her arms. She didn't swing them rhythmically: they were no good for that. But so far she had mastered holding a taped pencil with her right forearm; and begun, laboriously, to write a few words.

At dusk the Frente column marched through Monimbó toward the Parque Central. Quietly, like a centipede through the crevices of a dead tree, they approached the combat zone where control of the city was contested.

XXXIV

That night the news of a massacre in La Reforma spread through Masaya. A dozen or more compañeros had fallen, an RPG been lost to the onslaught of Macho Pedro who overran a safe house after someone informed.

Who?

Across the city the people erected barricades, and sang "Guerrilla Priest" and songs about Sandino. Meanwhile the Guardia Nacional pulled in its head like a tortoise on a highway. The GN withdrew into its garrison and called Managua, teeth chattering though it wasn't cold, with urgent requests for air support, troop reinforcements, matériel. From hour to hour the insurgents increased the pressure and burned buildings adjacent to the GN post and hurled homemade bombs. Teatro Masaya went up in a billow of gray smoke, casting reddish shadows through the park.

Claudio, inside the command post on the Lomas, picked up Guardia communications with direct appeals to the dictator in his Tiscapa bunker atop the capital. In other cities the combat raged; and Somoza's son El Chigüin could only spread his elite

EEBI contingents more thinly. As night fell the government forces had responded with mortar barrages onto the barrios, while heavy machineguns stood emplaced to forestall a frontal attack. After dark nothing could dislodge the rebels from positions on all sides of the garrison. By midnight the sector reeked of teargas, but the fighters moved about holding bicarbonate and lemon water to their noses.

—Remember February! cried Marta Navarro.

A Guardia tank still roamed a 200-meter perimeter. Snipers took aim from the fortified tower of the garrison, where .30 and .50 millimeter guns erupted and returned fire.

—Reinforcements will arrive, said Marta. We have to do it now.

Claudio, with the mobile combat unit, would launch an assault from the rear. A «human machinegun» began forming at a command post three blocks from Parque Central with Alma Giner as coordinator. Fighters came forward in twos and threes, also children under twelve. Some held a contact bomb in each hand; and women emerged with wicker baskets of explosives, the stockpiles of months.

—Remember September!

Alma loaded, cocked and fired the human machinegun. While a muchacho named Jorge gave out the contact bombs, two for adults, one for the youth, she held people back and then sent them off at intervals. Pedrito and Mica ranged as marshalls up and down the line of attackers waiting tensely. They passed on instructions from Almita in touch with the compa Moises who ran operations via two-way from the park.

One after another arrived. Each stood poised before combat, as she marked time by a wristwatch looped on her bifurcated forearm.

—Okay, go.

Between the command post and garrison lay a stretch of sniper zone. She told them: not too fast, go steadily, stay in control.

During the meeting that morning Marta had said:

—No mercy if your enemy is on the ropes. He'll get up again and destroy you.

Those in line to reload looked exhilarated, and told stories in breathless, jerky accents while they waited. Jorge, experienced in handling homemade explosives, gave out one here, two there as Alma counted down the seconds. Two young boys sniffled and wiped their eyes to one side: she refused to let them join the chain. Three times they reappeared at the head of the line; but she knew their grade at the Colegio, and they couldn't go.

A bomb-thrower stepped forward with his face smeared in blood.

—Stop.

The compañero insisted:

—No girl tells me what to do.

He could hardly stand. She gestured toward Pedrito and sent Mica for the medical team. There was an aura about her as she stood giving orders, she commanded respect. They called her compañera and glimpsed her maimed forearms, and did what she said. February, Miguel's arrest, Choncito—these things showed, in the way she directed the human machinegun. She wanted Patria Libre so her father, the man she had never known, could come home. Iván, his feet covered with mountain leprosy, limped homeward from the Segovias. . . Iván in a beret, with a carbine raised over his head, emerged from the swamps of the Southern Front. Iván triumphant along the Calle de los Pueblos: greeted by children who jumped up to touch his beard. With one thought, with one desire in his heart—to embrace his son and weep for happiness: Patria Libre. Ah, and this is my daughter? She too fought with the Frente? And the tears trickled on his bearded cheeks like the bark of an ageless tree. So this was the tiny girl he sent to Doñita one night from the mountains, with a note: raise her like the other one. Her hands, you say? She lost them struggling for her country, and Patria Libre? How pretty she is . . . !

—Go.

She counted seconds. She wanted to win. And Miguel? Had he fallen in Macho Pedro's clutches again: in a torture chamber high on Coyotepe? How could he survive a second arrest? The dictator no longer cared about appearances; if the three fronts didn't converge on Managua in a few days, then her brother would starve to death in prison. There would be more massacres. Miguel, Choncito: they would be forgotten; not a school, not a park would be renamed in their memory. Peace of the cemetery.

—Go.

Alma watched for faces to reappear.

Some didn't return.

Now a hundred stood on the line eager. The thud of homemade explosives pounded the Guardia garrison a few blocks away. Claudio had assumed a combat role. Despite orders that no comandante should take part directly, he did, and he could be killed. Marta, Pancho, the leaders: they could all be killed. What if the Guardia proved invincible? Delia . . .

—Go.

Bueno, there was still Domingo. There was Anita. She passed their names in review. How could Claudio decide to risk himself that way? Why did Almita feel suddenly so alone? The pseudonyms mingled in her mind with the sound of contact bombs exploded up the line, in the glittery distance. If not them, there was still . . . Someone, walking past, pointed at her and said:

—That's Miguel Giner's sister.

XXXV

The line passed along Paises Bajos and debouched in back of the GN station. The attackers edged closer, ever closer and threw their bombs and raced back to ask for more. Off the people went into the night, hugging the walls. In the rear, at a command post by the Colegio alumnae club, a compañero dealt with all the homemade explosives brought in like hot cross buns. Two men broke up dynamite into chunks and covered it like the contact bombs in masking tape.

—I'm here! said Carlita Garcia.

She approached the poet's sister who laughed and said she couldn't go.

She looked her over: the girl turned a woman before her eyes, who assumed a leadership role, in fatigues like a soldier.

—Just give me one of those sacred bombs. I want my turn at that Somocista beast.

Carlita's voice grumbled like thunder.

—We need boiled water for the wounded . . .

She pointed at two little girls in sombreros, each with a packet ready to fling. The people had raised a protest saying children, more agile, should be let in the human machinegun.

—What a spectacle! said Carlita. It gives me goosebumps.

But a small form appeared: wobbled forward like a top winding down. It was a boy covered in blood and tatters, hiccupping for air, too badly off to cry. His body jerked, fell, convulsed as a medic went out to retrieve him. A group of five kids had opened a breach by Teatro Masaya; but one tripped and his bombs exploded,—set off the TNT in his pants pocket. Three died on the spot.

That was June 8th.

Through the next morning Alma stayed at her post and counted down the seconds to Nicaragua's liberation.

At 10 a.m. a Push-Pull light bomber began to attack Masaya. Till mid-afternoon it overflew supposed Frente positions and fired rockets. Many died outright, with many more wounded. Some went deaf from the din of explosions. Others went insane.

Seven combatants advanced with Molotov cocktails in a first attempt to set the GN garrison on fire: Operation Suicide. It failed. It resulted in 2nd and 3rd degree burns for several.

In late morning 50 EEBI arrived fresh from Managua, plus a Sherman tank. Aided by the fatigue of insurgent forces, they prevented the fall of the garrison.

Bayardo Lopez, Domingo, fell to the bullet of a Guardia sniper.

Once again, Frente columns withdrew into Monimbó. They slipped quietly down toward the Lagoon on Pacayo side.

Domingo's death dealt a blow to morale.

Two days later, Sunday, June 10th, Managua rose up against the dictator. This obliged the Guardia Nacional to withdraw reinforcements from Masaya.

June 12th: evacuation of U.S. citizens.

PART SIX

I

Nighttime: the dungeon darkness dotted with jungle orchids, phosphorescent. A long-horned beetle laughed at him from beneath a rock. The muchachos formed two lines; the couple passed under the tented rifles, shots filled the air; the guerrilla camp feasted the wedding: can of condensed milk, tin of sardines. Speak low: how long since you ate? O the taste of turtle eggs, as a boy, in Playa La Flor. Weeds grew in tufts on the floor of his cell. Parching thirst: catch a garrobo lizard and suck out the blood. He shivered: from a warm bed in La Virgen to this hell of stone with no chair, no slop basin, a cold slab and a specter of insanity. Strange scent in the air: what was it? Onions! Peel the layers from an onion, and you find—life. From the oubliette high in the hilltop fortress he imagined an embattled Masaya, like a lake of darkness dotted with fires.

—Where is central command?

—Luz y Sombra.

His dark eyes laughed at them: it was a brothel in Tola.

—Sonuvabitch . . . the Frente leadership.

They strapped him on a table.

—Last chance.

In the distance they heard nourished exchanges. More crackling reports, detonations in series: Masaya in an uproar. A woman screamed; someone shouted wildly: far off, beneath the furor of combat and Armageddon sounds. Carefully they attached the apparatus to his genitals: no needless brutality; these were specialists from Managua. Macho Pedro was out there. Be someone, he thought, who feels everything, thinks everything.

—Disposition on the Southern Front.

—Luz y Sombra.

The longicorn beetle took him on its horns, a fit of rage in a mist of sulphur;—and let him down unstrung, on a bed of nettles.

—Someone saw her there.

—Who?

—Speak low: Josefa, isn't that her name?

Cries, yelps in the night.

The Guardia captain emerged from the house with a grin. Some tail.

—She went mad, they say, when he never came back.

Along the row of dungeons a prisoner's voice broke:

—Something to drink! Please!

—See this little beauty? It removes fingernails.

—Courtesy . . . of your masters.

—Disposition of forces on the Southern Front: last chance.

—Thirteen, some piece. White slavery: you didn't grin the next day, with your ugly face all over the front page of La Prensa.

—Let's see, which is your writing hand? Contacts in Costa Rica, couriers, arms runners through Peñas Blancas, isn't it?

—Unnngghhh—hunnh!

—One down, nine to go.

—Luz—

—Be careful at night: the little beasties like to burrow in. They suck the bloody pulp. Rot arouses them.

— . . . y Sombra.

Scallions? In chinks and crevices of the heavy stone. The couple, in clean if mudstained fatigues, moved under the canopy of guns. The volley of shots rang out and echoed, wind-whipped, toward the river. Sorry, our room service was remiss: something to drink, cockroach? Fresh air tinged with gunpowder, there must be a window . . . He lay filthy into the second night, adrift with fever. Shots creased the air, curses, rant: the big fear eddied in, filling the dungeons chest high. Cries for water, groans. A window? Drink dew . . . O the turtle eggs, we were children on the white sand of San Juan del Sur, we ran in surf. Thank God there was a friend in the village, thank God for Miriam. In Masaya, far below, the battle rang out with a fierce clarity.

II

The second morning a guard came and gave the hostage a glass of water and plate of beans. A strip of sunlight pierced the slit of window. In the semi-darkness he gazed through the v-shaped wedge over an expanse of countryside. The fields beyond Nindiri to the horizon reminded him of childhood: a road of sadness, pressed against his father's chest. As the day wore on, a sporadic mortar fire sent tremors through the fortress. The Guardia sent down its calling card on the barrios.

In late afternoon two came to unlock the heavy grate with a clank.

—Your turn.

Dizzily, he rose from the stone slab.

—Feeling fit? said one: a mercenary, he could tell by the accent.

—Pure life.

—That's nice. In a minute you'll feel like pure shit.

In the room a bare bulb hung on a cord. Macho Pedro, a bristling bear of a man, waited. Back from his exploits, freshened up, he surveyed the juicy prisoner: he glared at the representative of a force grown so formidable as to attack major cities, and pose a threat to the dictatorship.

—Strip down, said Macho.

A case of cola, plus one of imported beer, a cooler. Various implements lay on the table, a box of surgical gloves, a lighter and carton of cigarettes.

Quietly, with no greeting, a man entered. Clean shaven, calmly intent; clad in the sort of beige leisure suit you could buy, for dollars, in a boutique at Las Mercedes Airport.

—Welcome, said Miguel, in English.

Overhead, reverberating in the underground chamber, the Guardia mortar kept up its bombardment.

—Strip.

The poet looked calmly at the adviser who gave his wristwatch, and the Guardia captain, a glimpse.

—Flight to catch?

Macho moved forward, and grabbed a fistful of hair.

—Communist.

—You're violating . . . the Geneva Code.

The two stared, eye to eye. Macho Pedro said low:

—Fuck the Code.

Nonchalantly, he reached back for his cigarette on the table edge, took a puff, and applied the lit tip, with a hiss, to the prisoner's cheek.

A shudder went over the poet's features, with a sigh like surprise. Though stunned, in the torturer's grip, he tried not to buckle. His eyes filled with tears, as he said:

—Code.

Macho Pedro reached around with the bent cigarette. The mercenary took the lighter and relit it. Another drag, the tip glowed orange. Macho said politely:

—Will you answer our questions?

Incredibly, a smile played on his victim's lips, only. The adviser glanced along the stone walls and frowned. Overhead, the mortar caused a tremor of dust round the bright bulb.

—I will ask you several questions. If you don't answer them by the time I smoke this . . . I will have them hold you down, and put out your eye with the butt.

—Milton was blind.

—Blind, said the adviser with his accent, but not dead.

—Why be a hero? said Macho. We'll say you died a coward.

—They'll know better.

—How?

— . . .

—Too bad. You could have played along, lived and kept your honor.

—That's not living.

The Guardia captain stepped back and began his examination. Same questions as the opening session: names, whereabouts of the National Direction, the Southern Front leaders. Strength and disposition of armed groups around Rivas. Where were the military camps? Who were Frente collaborators: in Los Mojones, Las Azucenas, Cardenas, Orosí, along the Rio Mena? The hint of a smile still played on the prisoner's lips. What priests? Who were the arms purveyors in Costa Rica? Who the couriers? Where was the Radio Sandino transmitter? The interrogator spoke in a perfunctory tone: he recited his lesson from the School of the Americas. As if aware that, for all his terrific force, he performed a futile exercise like the Coyotepe mortar hurling down projectiles on Masaya in the sunlight. He shared a glimpse with the adviser, who nodded slightly. From the table he took a spike-ended lancet, glinting in the stark light, and thumbed it.

—Your time is almost up.

Miguel, his face bathed in sweat, stood in a trance. He stared at space in the last moment of passionate life about to extinguish. Softly he said to the flicker of grace in his torturer, or to the light in himself bellowsed, a final time, by the great wind of death:

—Here we are.

Macho moved forward and nodded. With the two Guardia he took hold, grappled downward as the prisoner lashed out and resisted. It took a few minutes, with the spruce adviser lending a hand, before they had him immobilized on the floor—all resistance held to a spasm in the limbs; subdued, now, after the kicking and a blow that drew blood, the handcuffs perhaps, from Macho's nose.

—Last chance . . . , he said, more like a grunt between breaths. The Cessna plane, this famous Sandinista Air Force . . . Where does it land? Cooperate now, I'm telling you—

—Geneva . . .

He growled. With a quick jab he plunged the implement into the victim's eye socket, and blood gushed up and oozed like a spring in the sand. Drops trickled on the mercenary's hands, holding the head steady. Miguel groaned. His head bulged to burst. He gurgled in an effort to stay in focus:

— . . . Convention.

—You had your day, said the Guardia captain. You said things, in print, about your betters.

He maneuvered over the poet whose black hair matted in the blood on his cheek. He jerked at the head and poised the implement for a second thrust.

The adviser said:

—Strike one.

—Huh?

—Send him back, and let him think.

Macho Pedro drew away with a gruff purr, and said:

—Bring in the next. Good Christ, it stinks in here.

III

In the cell he faded from consciousness. For a long time his mind floated in a darkness peopled by sinister images. They came, he didn't know when, and bathed his body and made him sip water. He awoke. He heard a woman scream—her shrieks penetrated the stone walls amid the sounds of laughter, carousal. Later a man came, a doctor perhaps, who examined his eye, gave him shots and applied a bandage. A day passed, as the thin line of sunlight trickled across the wall. A day, a day. Someone brought him a hot meal, water to drink. The sight had gone from his left eye forever; but he managed to stand and take a few shaky steps.

More days passed: days and nights immersed in pain. One afternoon they marched him outside the fortress along with three others, political prisoners though unknown to him. This could be the end, a firing squad; but he did not mind going—anywhere, after the misery and loneliness. He stood upright, he walked slowly with a dire joy. The four prisoners approached a pickup truck swirling with flies. Four bodies lay sprawled in back. On a plot of rocky ground behind the fortress they were handed shovels and told:

—Dig. One big grave.

It was a windy day in June, blue and sunlit; a scent of scallions mingled with almond trees in blossom, the renewing rains. They stood in the shadow of Coyotepe Fortress and gazed down at Nindiri, a spiral of smoke above the volcano. Miguel paused before hauling down the fourth bloated body. He recognized her.

The flies flew about as the Frente prisoners dug a mass grave into the flinty ground. While they worked, shovelling in a slow cadence, the poet wept. Liquid oozed from his swollen eye socket, while tears fell from the other. He felt stirred in his depths with the inception of a poem, but it would never be written.

When they finished the digging, and the grave stood deep enough to contain the bodies, he looked down at the feminine form on the ground alongside. The young woman stared into space. A moment before, her life had been all before her, vibrant with an ideal. A moment before, she stood struggling for a just society and love on earth. A line on the bridge of her nose hinted the ferocity of that struggle. She seemed to say accounts had not been settled even in death; though she could no longer flick a fly from her forehead.

—Adiós.

When he had finished and laid his shovel to one side, Miguel knelt down by Marta Navarro, his classmate at the Colegio with Choncito, Cecilia, Chiri Robles, and took her head in his arms.

IV

In the early hours Coyotepe came alive. Shouts among the dungeons, with a clank of metal grating. There were groans, sounds of flesh on flesh, abusing the female prisoners? A pistol shot resonated along the cavernous stone. New troops entered? Reinforcements from Managua? Had the Frente overrun them and stormed the fortress? He stood up breathless with expectation; he wondered if liberation was at hand, if he should cry out for help. His heart beat wildly. Free . . . free in a few minutes! . . . But a Guardia barked orders. In that curse above the hubbub he heard the fury of a dictatorial state at bay. What was happening? Why the sudden frenzy of activity? He seemed to hear a rush of soldiers' footsteps: they came in, they went out.

Later, a howl went along the corridor, like a specter with streaming hair. The night passed slowly, startled by sounds of madness.

The next morning: a strange silence. The day felt like a Sunday, reminding him of all the Sundays, his boyhood, Choncito. He tried to raise up. He wanted to hoist himself from the stone slab but could not. Would they bring him water and food? He lay back shaken with fear, no longer able to stand. Would he die forgotten in this dungeon? He saw too late that his life had depended on finding the organization. They liked to call him comandante, but he was only a poet passive in his love for life, spellbound by a moment's happiness. One instant sublime with praise, a fanfare for justice, a voice that could make you feel first causes; the next a sentimentalist, nostalgiac and sensual, who loathed the egotism of politics and what it does to men. He turned to the line of sunlight so the tears of panic burning his cheeks would roll off on the stone.

But then, as morning touched his dark cell like a child's fingers, he heard another sound. He couldn't believe it. From somewhere in Masaya there came the strains of a marimba. Sundays as a boy in Monimbó, dreams of his father. Sundays by Josefa's side, their hours of happiness. Slowly, in stages, he rose from the slab and dragged himself to the loophole. He put his face to the opening and breathed in the gentle breeze. A bird chirped on the ledge. The marimba played like a dance. It sent a kiss high up from the sun drenched barrios of his childhood.

What happened during the night with its screams and moans of endurance? The Guardia fled Masaya? The garrison finally succumbed? In that case the local Somocistas had run to Coyotepe where they awaited evacuation by helicopter. If he could hold out one more day, maybe two . . . Without water? Soon, soon the Frente would triumph and drive the hated dictator from the land. Soon the guerrilla columns, with Iván Giner in the lead, would come marching down from the Segovias and up from the Southern Front to overwhelm all resistance.

Onions!

He sniffed the weeds rooted in mold beneath the stone. He could eat these, he would eat and drink onions. Miguel hung on by the window. He listened to the marimba wafted up from a park where the people had begun to celebrate.

V

The dark figures appeared to tread water in the play of shadows. They had been dancing in the adjacent streets. Now they looked on with a sense of awe. The Guardia station in Parque Central sizzled and crackled, a dark mass beneath flames. The life they had always known was going up in smoke.

Bulu Moratín came along jaunty, shirtless, his face smudged with ash, his shoulders sweaty. In La Reforma, wounded among the compañeros, he had hoisted himself up and taken his chance. He launched himself out of that garden stained red in the sunlight. The Guardia shot off bursts at the resurrected Bulito; he gave them a jolt, jumping up suddenly from a pile of dead people. He hopped along like a rabbit, he lost them in the tall plantains. That surprised Bulu, to survive La Reforma: if he'd died it wouldn't have surprised him at all. Macho Pedro was so busy fondling his own genitals . . . Then, shot of penicillin, take a little nap, he lit out behind a nurse's back for Parque Central.

The night before, under cover of darkness, the last Guardia moved out along Siete Esquinas and up the Calle San Jerónimo to Coyotepe. Well armed, they burst past a Frente unit; and that was when a number of compañeros fell, in a firefight at pointblank range.

Later, Claudio sent him with a few others to pour the fuel. They entered the GN garrison on tiptoes: the dead like dumped sacks here and there, covered with dust and flies. And then it happened: *pfffunt!* Someone made a mistake. Maybe there were live coals; maybe a container was mishandled. The thing went up.

Three fighters died.

Bulu took the nearest exit, a side window. No way, on the eve of victory, would he let himself be cooked well-done like a hamburger!

But he thought about Marta Navarro. They ambushed her. He brushed away a tear, him, Bulu, winner of first prize (a bottle of Flor de Caña rum) for machismo. Because she was brave, la Marta: remember when she went out against a tank for the body of Ulises Tapia? But now she would never see the Guardia station empty of dogs. She wouldn't watch it slump to the ground, in the first rays of sunlight, to the sweet sound of marimbas.

VI

Doñita Reyes stood squinting in the plaza as waves of fear and emotion flooded into her heart. In a minute she would swoon with the presence of so many people and the torrential afternoon sun. Her eyes grew blurry. By her side Alma spoke words of reassurance after insisting she hobble all the way over here. For three weeks she hadn't seen the shameless girl, and now what was going on? Alma patted Doñita's hand with those weird drumsticks; and the old woman wanted to sob with self-pity, she hardly knew why.

—Look, Mama! It's Moises, one of the leaders.

—An atheist.

Two thousand people filled the plaza.

—He will swear in members of the Junta. See them?

Doñita frowned. Yes, she saw them. She knew them personally, Mario, Elias, Constantino, a dumpy crew, and hardly her idea of civic leaders. When Tacho Somoza appeared on television, so dignified, dressed all in white with the presidential insignia over his chest, that was a government official. But to watch Mario, Elias and Constantino parade themselves this way in public, waving as the so-called leader Moises, who didn't even look Nicaraguan, announced them over a primitive sound system: what did they take her for, gullible?

—They've formed a new local government,—Alma touched her fatty arm.—It's just us, our friends.

Doñita looked up at the stage, and her gaze fell on Claudio. That one resembled an Indian, a stubborn mule of a man. The ceremony had been in progress nearly an hour, and Doñita, whose ankles bloated up beneath the girth of her hips, her sack-like calves, asked:

—Aren't they finished?

They weren't. And before long the shadows began to lengthen from the adobe church behind the platform. Mothers picked up their children. Muchachos lingered, wearing red and black kerchiefs, with that arrogant thing Doñita noticed in their posture. Many militia members were in the crowd side by side with girlfriends, Alma's classmates at the Colegio. Some carried guns. All stared at the platform and swearing-in ceremony. The Masayans applauded. Looking around Doñita thought: Constantino? . . . The least likely comunista she ever saw.

Between the plaza and Coyotepe stood the church, calculated to act as a screen. The park also offered protection, as one by one Mario Rodriguez, Santiago Palacios, Elias Lopez took the solemn oath to lead in reconstruction of the city.

Children played on the outskirts of the crowd, laughing in the background as Moises said a few more words. A boy whooped beneath the trees, followed by a dog.

But then they heard another sound, an ominous rumble. On the platform Moises gazed skyward, and said:

—Everybody disperse! Go to your homes!

Doñita Reyes wrung her hands and looked around for Alma. But the girl was a ways off; she beckoned people with the strange authority of her arms not to panic.

Doñita wondered where to turn as a helicopter appeared over the low roofs, its dark form tilted forward. Quickly the crowd fanned out; they burst past Doñita and swept her along. People ran in every direction: cries of fear beneath the trees! Arms, legs churned in the hysterical need to flee. The chopper hopped down from Coyotepe with its locust tail flung in the air.

The thunder grew louder, louder. Alma reappeared, grabbed the terrified Doñita's hand and moved her along, not too fast, toward the side streets.

—What's happening?

The engine roared just overhead; the rotor wash nudged their shoulders. The old woman went along confused, unable to breathe, but the girl prodded her onward.

Alma glanced back and saw a black object, like a garbage can, fall from the helicopter. It slanted down over the plaza.

—Cover your head!

Doñita Reyes heard screams and then buckled and collapsed with a thud. A whoosh made the trees bend and sway.

Roofs splintered, smoked. The ground shook, and the world went blank.

Ay! Her first foray past the confines of her place on Calle Calvario since visiting Miguel, and Doñita Reyes lay in the hot dust where the waves of fear had deposited her.

VII

From Coyotepe the Guardia bombed the city. They made helicopter runs, dropping barrels filled with napalm and gasoline, and 500-pound bombs. Luckily there was no electricity: who would have put out the fires?

—Apple 2! Apple 3!—The prisoners overheard the buzz and static of Guardia two-ways.—Drop that big tamale right on top of them! Drop it now!

And then an explosion down in the city: —PON—PONN—!

And Guardia laughter. Loud voices, late at night, echoed among the dungeons of ancient stone.

In Masaya there was no water to drink. The people drank rainwater, and for many it was touch and go getting something to eat.

Over Radio Equis and Radio Nacional came hourly reports the GN would reenter the city. The civilian sector should evacuate en masse, at once!

Guardia would soon raze every building.

Contingents of Guardia had penetrated by way of La Estación.

Guardia had already overrun some sectors.

Combat in those hours became constant, late into the night, with skirmishes as GN forces probed and tried to take back the strategic points.

VIII

During the final week of June a U.S. special envoy attempted, in the Costa Rican capital, to negotiate additional members for a Government Junta pending the plight of President Somoza. These would be figures who favored U.S. interests in the region, and opposed from within the influence of the Frente.

On July 2nd the city of Matagalpa was liberated, and the next day Sebaco fell. The FSLN had taken control of the northern half of Nicaragua.

From day to day tens of thousands fled their homes in Managua as Guardia artillery bombarded the eastern barrios.

Rivas stood partially in Frente hands, in the South.

On July 4th a mobile battalion stormed Jinotepe. Insurgent forces amassed in Masaya during a strategic retreat from Managua descended on the government stronghold, and by the morning of July 6th there was jubilation in the streets.

Guardia leadership flew eastward, including a general, Rafael Lola, known for repressive measures. Lola abandoned his men, but ranks of GN dressed as civilians wended their way out of town. In Jinotepe the streets filled: people danced to the rhythm of church bells.

Guardia supply lines to the South had been severed. The province of Carazo was declared free territory.

Estelí stood on the verge of capture.

U.S. helicopters staged a landing in Costa Rica, but were told to leave immediately.

President Somoza stated he was willing to resign if his party, the National Liberals, could be assured a role in the new government.

Two weeks before, when the Frente retreated from embattled Managua barrios, leaving only spent cartridges, traces of dried blood, the wind poking its nose among the dust and litter, Anastasio Somoza had proclaimed victory for all the world to hear.

But on July 10th the capital lay surrounded by the forces of the insurrection.

Tumultuous, filled with fervor, León fell.

IX

Coyotepe Fortress had become a scene of confusion and horror. Drunken Guardia swaggered about and cursed. Gun butts rapped on the metal doors. In a furor of liquor, cocaine, morbid fear, they burst in upon the prisoners and ushered them away to a torture session, a rape like chopping ice. Macho Pedro spoke by phone with military advisers to the dictator; though he knew no help could be provided, with governmental forces strained to the utmost on several fronts. During the day a hundred mirrors flashed up from Masaya at the fortress: the glare hindered the bombardment of Guardia artillery.

Macho greeted news of the Junta for Reconstruction with words that were his trademark:

—We'll give them a passport to Caiaphas!

At night Frente commandos attacked up the steep slopes. But Coyotepe, with its dominant position and stockpiled munitions, remained impregnable. A Guardia counteroffensive had been beaten back with help from the mobile unit under Claudio's command. Met frontally in San Carlos sector the GN troops proved unable to enter and entrench. They never passed the riverbed. But during the assault they managed to ambush and kill three combatants who advanced too quickly—among these the leader, Cecilia Asturia, known as Delia.

The poet lay on the stone slab with his eyes open, at times delirious. He heard them fighting, out there. He half heard the Guardia descend on the unlit dungeons to wreak havoc on moribund detainees. Drugged guards; slaps, groans, shrill pleas in the dark. He waited for his turn. Torture would come as an act of mercy, and then a peace that nothing could disturb. How many days since they brought him food and water? One afternoon he hung by the slit of window; he studied with his one eye the fields hemmed with verdure, bands of ochre and green to a treeline. A smoke cloud dispersed over the landscape. But he lay back, his temples throbbing. By this time he was so physically repulsive: the soldiers thought twice before a call on his cell.

He had spells of high fever that took him to the edge. He looked over and then drew slowly away. He waited each day for the rain, and then rose up to wet his fingers: licked with a parched tongue. He made a meal from the weeds, a scallion here, and there, in the chinks of the stone. He would devour any insect; but his reflexes had left him, so they devoured him instead. With the reek of death, feces, open wounds on this lower level, the spiders, rats, flies, roaches combed the cells and partook of a banquet.

He heard a woman scream.

—Masaya Libre! she cried, her laugh insane.

The screams rang out strong. Did she know? Had she just been captured?

—Hold on, compañeros! They're coming for us. Patria Libre!

Miguel's heart jumped in his throat. He shared a moment of the macabre joy.

Slaps. A drawn-out groan.

If he could withstand another day, two days, until the Guardia fled and the forces of liberation stormed up the hill . . . His mind drifted, summoned somewhere. His senses unmoored in the delirium as, from what seemed a distance, an explosion shook his slab. He wanted to live. He passed the hours trying to focus on life, and fix the image of Josefa.

Night fell. Far down the hill he heard the fighting intensify. A poem emerged like Venus fully formed, consummate. He lay in the dark and by his side God dictated. In love lay the secret, never satisfactorily explained, of human identity. Life determined itself each instant by ridiculous feelings of love. Iván Giner knelt by a stream in the Segovias and bathed away the loneliness of decades, with love. A tree stood alone on a plantation in the South; a breeze stirred its leaves with love.

In a vortex of fever he reawoke during the night of decisive battles. Such a sense of beauty tinged with loss, it would go unrecorded unless he made a quill of his toenail, and wrote in blood on the tablet of his flesh. For one instant a wondrous flower of spirit blossomed before his eyes. It transcended all the debates. It glowed with hope, the spontaneous mastery of a star. He wept with rage that the words would elude him forever,—but then he let it go, with a sense of self projected as universe, fully expressed.

Shots. Bombing. In a moment, the centuries of hatred would explode and gunshots go rhythmic, a celebration. Either this, or else silence over the face of a continent. The silence of dirge, after February, September, Chon's death, the death of a people, and the hatred had prevailed . . .

He made it through another night.

X

In the minutes before dawn President Somoza waited for a heli-copter on the wide patio of his Tiscapa bunker. He wore a blue-gray summer suit, an azure cravat with a gold tie-clasp. As the sky to the west lightened, a soldier wandered the narrow paved streets of the military complex. Disconcerted in his olive drab uniform, he looked numb with fatigue.

The President gazed off at the horizon. Birds chirped in expecta-tion of sunrise. Shots sounded intermittently across the city. Clearing his throat, he took a few steps toward the Hotel Intercontinental like a pyramid beside the bunker. To think the country's finest hotel had been a tropical pied-à-terre for Howard Hughes. But Central Amer-ica had little in common with Egypt of the pyramids: these small coun-tries would be long in discovering their greatness despite efforts by a few families worthy, perhaps, of the pharaohs. The kind of patriotism which produced sublime architecture was inconceivable here, in the lazy Sunday of Nicaragua with its aqua vitae and mock bullfights.

He glimpsed his watch: after six. The helicopter should have ar-rived. A passing soldier gave the head of state a salute and a rigid smile, though the latter barely responded. He mused on pyramids, and the woman his senses craved: the only vulture on earth so lovely and evil you yearned to stink with desire and be scavenged. A few days ago he had met the international press; and at Dinorah's bid-ding (something she told him as they lay drunk in bed between rounds of definitive sex), he announced:

—Señores, you know, I am a shit. A shit, as FDR once said, but *your* shit. Ha ha ha!

That was hours after a banquet of bodily delights to end all others. Numerous courses. His head still reeled when he made such a state-ment to the world. But those on hand seemed to take it the right way. The sheer magnificence of her made him drunker than any brandy.

On the far edge of the patio President Somoza's entourage had be-gun to assemble. Rener. Pallais. Valle-Olivares. They waited in the background, their grim features a homage to the historic moment.

Philosophically, the statesman thought of how all things must pass. The country was entering a more subtle phase; so his control of affairs, his power would probably be less direct in the short term. Wasn't the magnate Hughes long gone? he flapped out of Nicaragua on his fabulous wings toward some last adventure. It seemed a famous singer's dream of casinos to light up the Pacific Coast cities, with all that meant for development, tourist dollars, good wholesome fun, would be deferred yet awhile. At any hour, barring a fullscale intervention by the gringos (who had learned something in Vietnam, and might work more slowly), a modern Dark Ages would settle over Nicaragua and make it off limits for such impresarios and enlightened benefactors. Well, let the public have a taste of Soviet-style despotism, the godless hordes directed by faroff party bureaucrats. Welcome! The treasury was exhausted except for a paltry three million, non-liquid on such short notice. Long live free enterprise!

The grandeur of his family fortune comprised some 133 companies and major holdings of all descriptions—LANICA the national airline cars trucks coffee tobacco construction chemicals fertilizers machinery data processing magazines newspapers 63 cattle ranches dairy cinemas jewelry fishing shipping cotton aluminum warehouses boats 10 sugar mills ice blood television and radio stations rum banks slaughterhouses meat-packing real estate (organized smuggling; Tacho grinned: I *am* a shit) asbestos cement furniture lumber bananas buses rice oils savings finance S & L's ham insulation roofs Gran Hotel hotels in Costa Rica San Salvador Madrid laundry tractors farm machinery salt insurance soda cloth weaving pipe travel agencies and others.

With the Bank of America and BANIC Groups he controlled the economy for the prosperity of all. It was communist propaganda that 84% of the children suffered malnutrition and 20% died before age four,—illiteracy 74%, unemployment 36%, kids without school 80%, substandard housing 73%, overall malnutrition 60%,—all (U.N.) lies, lies. He felt himself, his millions mirrored in this unappreciative people. Who else could have brought in such a wealth of benevolent foreign investors,—American Cyanamid Shell Lloyd's Bank First National City Bank United Fruit Company Ralston-Purina Exxon Nabisco Inc. Sears General Mills British American Tobacco Westinghouse Hughes Tools Sheraton Hotels Monsanto Pennwalt G.T.&E. Mohawk Olin Corporation Mitsui Shinetsu RCA Victor U.S. Steel Borden Inc. Hoffman La Roche Colgate-Palmolive Abbot Laboratories Dresdner Bank Atlas Chemical Inc. H.B. Fuller Co. Quaker Oats Nestlé Evans Products Asarco Ward Foods Xerox United

Brands Winthrop Plywood Bank of America to name a few,—for the welfare and abundance of the country at large?

Alright. Not grateful? Not for us, philanthropists? Not one big Nicaraguan family after all? Then not for you either! Oh! We know how to respond to the tyranny of the majority.

If the comunista delinquents did arrive this far and overran what remained of the Guardia Nacional and frightened off his successor Dr. Urcuyo, that true Leonidas of the Americas; if the Cuban-backed bandidos arrived on Tiscapa they would find three cordobas he had left them, emblems of munificence, in a personal strongbox. Have a blast. Now let us see if ignorant boys can run a nation while the real leader goes to lobby awhile, and be among friends, in the United States of America.

—Cursed land! My father, my brother Luis gave you their lives, you ungrateful peasants. Washington made its promises in the days of the Rough Rider, and kept them faithfully until yesterday. Hearty friendship was guaranteed us just as any nation proceeding with «reasonable efficiency and decency in social and political matters . . . if it kept order, and paid its obligations.» I learned those fateful words by heart. For under such conditions prosperity is certain. And now?

Suddenly above the palm trees and cypresses outlined on a horizon like claret wine, a helicopter approached from Las Mercedes Airport.

Solemnly, Somoza drew back toward his followers. The rotor blades fanned the shrubbery along with his sparse but impeccably groomed hair.

He glanced at his watch: six-thirty. The dawn had come. He paused a moment to peer across at the longtime chauffeur of his limousine, whose wizened figure stood silhouetted against the white hotel. He gestured him to come nearer:

—I leave you with Dr. Urcuyo. Be his servant, as you were mine.

That was all. At six-forty on the morning of July 17th, 1979, the Señor Presidente walked gravely toward the boarding steps. He wore the same severe, haughty look as always, when in public. Silenced for

awhile, thought the chauffeur, were the naughty yelps in a sumptuous bed by the side of his concubine. Put on hold the childish delights, the bad boy being spanked for all his sins. Sí, señor: her sexual
favors tasted bitter on the palate of the defeated. Ended the long
bathroom comedy. Ended the forty-five year feast at the table of
state power.

It seemed to the faithful chauffeur that an aura of failure surrounded his master's departure. Rener, Pallais, Quintana, Valle-
Olivares, a few military advisers followed the dictator soberly into his
private helicopter.

It lifted off the patio. The big whoosh made the old chauffeur
squint and raise his hand, as if saluting.

And then he stood alone, perplexed, to await another order in the
dawn silence of the Tiscapa bunker.

That was all. Thirty years, serving them: the father Anastasio who
had danced so charmingly with the gringo ambassador's wife; who
put an end to the «Calvary of the Segovias» by having the rebel
Sandino assassinated. And then he too was shot to death while at dinner in a León restaurant. And the son Luis succeeded Anastasio Senior, and some said he was almost human, a mistake. For the death
of Luis had never been fully explained. And finally this one, the most
arbitrary, iron-fisted, violently avaricious of the lot; unless it was his
own son, the one they called El Chigüin, who led the elite EEBI. The
Somoza litter, dark legend in the annals of a tormented continent.
«Washington's sonuvabitch» for half a century.

And his chauffeur? Thirty years a faithful servant, and now what
was left to him? A liberal tip in appreciation? A few dollars from those
monstrous billions? A cordial word of thanks?

—I leave you with Dr. Urcuyo. Be his servant as you were mine.

He waited. For a moment his gaze had followed after; it soared in
the path of the helicopter, and rising sun.

Now without moving a step he waited five, ten minutes. Alone, in
a sort of daze. The new day brightened swiftly above the palm trees,
the cypresses, the odors from down in the city.

Birds sang, the sparrow and thrush, a zenzontle in a nearby shrub. The old servant waited. Amazed, he stood outside the abandoned bunker.

And then, far out across the urban sprawl with its mist of dust and exhaust, he saw a plane take off from Las Mercedes. He watched it veer slowly away from the capital, gaining altitude, and then curve with fiery wings northeastward. High above Momotombo and off toward the Segovian hills, toward Río Coco and Zelaya Norte and the northern border.

He watched. It seemed his decades of service dissolved like the trail of vapor in the morning sky over Nicaragua. Sky color of azure, of wide lakes whose depths had yet to be tested, and blue-misted pyramidal volcanoes. He saw his master depart on the first step of a journey, perhaps never to return, into exile. He lingered there, with a tear in his clear blue wrinkled eyes, the hue of El Hombre's elegant cravat.

XI

The news spread across the country.

In Monimbó people came out in the streets to embrace one another.

—The animal is gone!

—Na, my sons! cried a woman in mourning. If only you could see this!

The women who in normal times sold fresh juice, in the park across from San Sebastien, appeared with vats of strong coffee. Others brought tortillas. They went along with tears on their cheeks and smiles of hesitant joy. At the Magdalena they poured out drinks and called to one another and sniffled. Carlita Garcia said in a twangy voice:

—Bring out all the saints!

But another recalled the premature dancing in September and stepped forward:

—Too early for fiestas.

The Guardia Nacional stood intact, with Urcuyo in the wings ready to assume the presidency. The U.S. kept up an eleventh hour diplomatic activity to forestall a total victory for the Sandinistas.

A crowd gathered at the command post on Lomas de Sandino. Children jumped up and down in the street littered with wrappers, expended shells, torn-up paving stones. Alma Giner appeared and some people broke into applause:

—Patria Libre!

—We're free!

They cried out at new arrivals. But all the while the Coyotepe mortar maintained its listless rhythm: bangam! . . . bang! . . . every few minutes.

It had gone on for days until they were tempted not to notice anymore. Alma gazed up at the sky with its clouds like a caravan. She seemed to measure by their height the distance to the fortress. Tragic in the morning sun the medieval structure sat on its hill overlooking Masaya. She knew there were Frente prisoners who languished and could die of thirst, inside the stone walls. She thought of Cecilia who would never know of the tyrant's flight: never experience the blessed moments, this soaring sense.

Bells chimed. Bells rang out across the city: crazy kids swung on the ropes high in the belfry. Alma listened to the bells peal forth a victory palpable even while in the balance.

More people came out. They carried torches in their hands; the fumes seemed to liquefy at mid-morning. She frowned in the doorway of the command post. She raised on tiptoes to peer, vigilant and tense, over the heads of the crowd.

A muchacho sprinted toward them from direction of San Sebastien. He approached waving a submachinegun; cried out:

—Don't be overconfident: this could be a trap! Don't stay in a group this way!

But nobody listened.

From inside Faustino appeared by Alma's side.

—Viva el Frente!

Up and down the street rose a chorus of cheers, and the people began to dance. The Coyotepe mortar kept up its sullen bombardment. Like a beast it pawed the air and showed its ability to kill, but refrained from the open attack that would hasten its end.

Almita looked on quietly. She knew the struggle wasn't over. Claudio had been injured, and a number of new duties had fallen on her slender shoulders. It happened on the 13th: with GN raining mortar fire down on Barrio Loco where the muchachos had a command post. Claudio took shrapnel in the hand and leg as he darted round a corner.

At first she wondered what would happen without the leader. He was in charge of operations for the city. He knew the art of uniting forces and coordinating an offensive. But he gave way to temptation and went out on the front lines.

And then he lay wounded: transported to the hospital in Jinotepe. Faustino had taken his place, in full command of Masaya operations.

More battles followed: in the INCA and La Hielera sector where a «dog-catcher» column comprised fighters who had retreated from Managua. Firefights raged for control of the big INCA factory. And now Alma heard shots from that direction, not celebratory, but the arhythmic rant of confrontation.

She watched the early fiesta on Lomas de Sandino.

XII

A cock crowed on a nearby farm. Outside the slit of window a single bird twitted.

He opened his one eye, and watched a faint light play with the contours of the dungeon. He knew the end was near. It had rained the night before, when the earth held out a friendly hand which he was too weak to stand up and take.

The sun came out. Later, as it angled sideways, the line snuffed from his cell at midday, he heard a voice cry down the corridor:

—Somoza's gone!

A cheer, like a chorus of death rattles, went up from the live prisoners.

He lay afraid of drifting into unconsciousness.

So the beast had left with its jaws dripping lucre. At the news he felt pride. Though never a good comrade, never a Choncito, a

Pomares, he had done what he could and tried not to discourage the others with his moods.

He might not live to walk the streets of Nicaragua Libre. But others would. Josefa would, and the child he hoped she was carrying, his son or daughter. Alma and Doñita, the Monimboseños, they would. He saw them intent in meetings, in new markets, smiling at one another in the sunlight. They organized their own lives, enjoyed abundance, danced. Their heads were high. The children no longer had rickets, and polio was abolished, and malaria. Nobody malnourished. Everyone could read.

With a long involved effort he managed to sit upright. He felt panic at the idea of dying. There was a woman he loved. Maybe a holy infant on the way. There were poems to write, books to study and live with, classics; songs to sing together, hands to hold. He saw the blue surf at Poneloya; he tasted beer and shellfish, the salt on Josefa's beautiful neck; her smile was a convulsion of joy . . . The tender hands of the children; wildflowers and birds; the fields beneath the gentle rains.

His feet touched the stone floor. He tottered over heights, and tried to stand. He would wait for the daily rain. If he could just hold on another day.

Miguel felt his way along the wall. He slid his fingers through the wedge.

—Patria Libre, he croaked, like last words.

He felt about for a hint of moisture.

Dust.

He rubbed the dry dust with his fingertips. He brought them to his mouth, and sucked.

In a moment he would fall, and that would be it. Sliding his hand through the crack, he turned his wrist, nearly losing his balance. Now he could hang there by his arm and wait for the rain, or the muchachos.

After awhile he hung limp against the wall. A line of light touched the matted locks of his hair, and the bulbous slime which had been his right eye. He waited, listened for distant thunder, the maternal pitter-patter of the rain.

None came. He put his lips to the cool granite. He imagined a fresh well, a blue lake, a rain forest in Río San Juan. He thought of his mother, Juana. She was there with him.

Late afternoon.

And then it was dark already. There were explosions.

Still later he heard a chiming of bells in Masaya. Was it a dream?

He remembered the San Jerónimos of his childhood, the love he carried around for his father, Iván the Guerrillero, through his days in the Colegio.

He wished Padre Velasquez well, and hoped he felt saved, since that was what he wanted.

He hoped his father, finally, would be able to come home.

It all came back to Miguel—the sense of an infinite yearning, a tragic absence. He listened to the pealing of churchbells, in a distance aquiver with human will, voices, hope, joy.

XIII

On July 18th the muchachos began pouring in from Granada. The order came to move against Managua the next day, but first attack Coyotepe. Somoza had said he would send five thousand troops against Masaya, but Alma knew no fresh Guardia had arrived. She was engaged in a steady activity with Faustino to organize the dawn assault.

Word arrived that a GN mortar attack had killed combatants en route from Granada.

—Where? she asked.

—Motel Las Flores.

—Bad luck.

—No, they had on headlights.

That evening the sempiternal bombardment continued, pum, pum, on past midnight. Then, in the small hours there was a crescendo, as Guardia seemed to lose their composure and expend ordnance in desperation.

It stopped. A sudden silence settled over Masaya, like an air hammer turned off after days of noise. The muchachos spoke in low voices and readied themselves mentally. In other places, in other cities, the Guardia Nacional had disintegrated and scurried north toward Honduras in civilian clothes. Nevertheless, Dr. Urcuyo announced his intention to stay on as president until 1981.

At 4 a.m. the first Frente units waded off in the darkness. Alma watched, as the column moved to the approach points. She saw them disappear in the night, submachinegun in hand. No words. No unessential gear.

She wanted to join them, but Faustino needed her on the Lomas. She could tap and receive code as quickly as she could read, but to fire a gun was beyond her means.

The last of them moved past without a sound. The muchachos, nimble as deer.

She waited. Slowly the window lightened. Now, now was the time.

A woman came in the room and announced herself as Alma's replacement. But the latter had no intention of leaving.

—Tired?

—Not at all.

—You look tired.

—I'll sleep later.

The other nodded. They waited. Still there were no shots.

XIV

In the predawn mist they heard a cry. Like a cry of pain, but not close-by: in the distance.

—What's that?

But then it wasn't one voice. It was a chorus. The sound of voices flooded into the big silence.

Alma went to the door.

—Cheering.

She listened.

—Cheers from Coyotepe, said the other.

The jubilant shouts grew unmistakable. The Guardia must have fled the fortress after a binge of expending ammunition. Alma glanced back:

—I'll go.

But she reached around with her arms, and the other compañera had the same idea. For a moment the two women embraced.

She left the command post and trotted off, as the replacement watched her lithe, brave figure turn a first corner in the light of daybreak.

Alma broke into a run, thinking of times when she had sprinted for her life in the darkness. She passed the white structure, charred and gutted, of the garrison in Parque Central where she had spied on them the night of Olla de Barro. She turned another corner; and there, high on its hill, sat the fortress. A pink sunlight flushed the turrets, perched above the city still in shadow.

She ran briskly, though an hour before she felt exhausted.

Hung by the entrance was a red and black banner; it waved in the breeze. The compañero on guard looked at her.

—Where to, compita?

—Inside.

—The dogs are gone, he said, with a glimpse of her arms.

She moved past. It was dark inside with a smell of granite and a bad odor. That smell was prevalent for days down in the city, but not so concentrated.

Further ahead a flashlight beamed along the vaulting. A fighter asked her:

—How's Claudio?

—Better.

—Too bad he's not here.

In the first rooms there were crates of supplies, food, weapons, ammunition. In another cigarette butts everywhere, playing cards, empty liquor bottles and beer cans. She followed the muchacho into a third room, and gasped. Others mulled about inspecting the torture chamber: pools of dried blood, and such a stink. Implements lay scattered about, surgical gloves, nasty things tossed on the floor.

—What are these? said Alma.

The men stared at her.

—Condoms, said one.

—Hitler's nephews, said a fighter from the Mobile Battalion.

Another burst in:

—Listen! The puppet Urcuyo has fled to Guatemala.

—See that? Didn't even stay until 1981.

A few laughed despite the smell. They stood in silence another moment.

A morning breeze hummed through chinks in the stone, like a song from underground.

XV

A group had formed outside one of the dungeons. She heard someone whistle low, and the stench down here made her want to breathe through her nose.

A combatant from Managua said:

—Who let the girl in?

—What? she moved past them. She put a drumstick to his face, like a lesson.

Inside the cell a scene of horror presented itself. The sunrise seeped through the narrow opening. A curly headed figure hung in a twisted posture at the window.

Someone said:

—Is he alive?

—Wants to get out, said the Mobile Squadron leader.

—Skinny enough.

They paused a moment. Apart from its tang the place had a kind of hush; a sanctity enjoined the cocky fighters to silence. The prisoner's forehead nestled in an angle of stone casement. His hair stirred slightly in the breeze.

—Is he breathing?

They moved forward.

—Eh, compa! War's over.

Alma edged closer.

—Patria Libre, said another.

They tried to dislodge him; at first without success, since his fist, wedged, seemed to clutch.

—I'll help, said the leader; but after a moment he stepped back.

—Stubborn.

—Look at his eye.

One side of the face was bloated horribly, purplish, gray.

Someone put a hand on Alma's shoulder, but she shook it off and drew nearer. His black hair, the curly nape. She stood alongside as two tried gently to pry him loose. Then she too saw the eye: a mass of gristle wriggled with tiny white worms, maggots. And the pupil, off on its own, gauzy, stared at heaven through a veil. She felt a movement in the pit of her stomach, on the verge of nausea.

—Do we have to cut the hand off?

She gave a whimper, unnoticed.

—Died of thirst?

—Or gangrene.

—Could've made it if they fed him.

The sky gave a sparkle in the narrow opening above the hand. Day peeked in, flooding the horizon with gold. With an effort, two muchachos managed to dislodge the body; it fell sideways into their grasp.

The face had a willful air. Half looked incredibly handsome, like Che, like Jesus. Half mutilated: rotten meat.

—But it's—

—The poet. He's dead.

—No, said Alma, her forehead wrinkled. Some dead people don't die.

She stood alongside determined to control herself while they laid her brother on the stone slab, and straightened out his body. She stared at him through glazed eyes. She didn't collapse or begin to cry. She leaned and with her forearm brushed away an insect from his good cheek.

How would she ever tell Doñita Reyes?

As she went out the fighters stood back and sang the Frente hymn.

XVI

Groups of combatants arrived from the Southern Front. They streamed through the streets of Masaya. They headed for Plaza de la Republica, now Plaza de la Revolución, in Managua where a huge celebration had already begun. Bearded guerrilleros wept with happiness and kissed every woman who would let them as they emerged, after years of hardship, from clandestinity. The enthusiasm overwhelmed everyone. Many jumped on trunks and fenders of vehicles and joined the procession to greet the nation's new leaders, muchachos like themselves. It was July 19th.

Bulu Moratín felt a manly sadness and decided not to go. With a group of Monimboseños he went around paying respect to friends who had died. From the first martyrs in October '77, the attack on Masaya barracks, to the last who had fallen the day before.

—Vamonos, compañeros! cried Bulu.

They started at eight in the morning and went straight to the compañero Chon up in Monimbó cemetery with his red and black cross. Then Max who died in the October attack and the Rodriguez brothers, compañero Ulises Tapia, then Domingo. All the while Bulito grew sadder and sadder, thinking: Delia . . . so lovely the day we robbed the banks. And Marta Navarro who taught the machos a lesson in courage, when the tank killed Ulises. We'll never know where she is buried: never put flowers on la Martita's grave. Standing by each tombstone the combatants said a few words and placed some token of remembrance. After awhile a woman appeared with wreaths for the fallen compañeros. They visited Juan Ramón's grave, Faustina's husband; and Lorenzo Lopez's plot with its small cross: the young poet who died in the February uprising, when it all started.

XVII

The guns were stilled. Marimbas played. Marimbas, and kettledrums. In couples, in family groups the people stepped over their thresholds and took a look around. They squinted. Then they made their way together as if filing into church. They joined the human river on its way across the barrios, up the steep hill toward Coyotepe. The streets had a strange aspect. There was something different in the children's play. Faces appeared which hadn't been seen in months and became part of the flow.

Alongside the fortress, like a dead beast that glared at all this intrusion of life, there was a detachment of fighters. Alma Giner came out looking unwell, hardly in control of herself. She seemed to float past the others: so frail and delicate she was caught up by a breeze not of this world.

She paused a moment to stare down at the people who wended their way. She saw arm-waving, a woman whose movements seemed urgent. She heard laughter. Did someone call her name? Alma rubbed a forearm on her soiled blouse: sensed a sort of tickle from the insect she brushed off her brother's face. He was back in there, behind her. He was gone. The muchachos would take care of him.

Not a year ago February, and not today: she had never been able to deliver Doñita's message, the eagle's claws. Never saw him again. It was always too late.

A bird chirped. Alma saw Miguel beneath the tigüilote tree reading with the macaw.

—Somoza assassin!

Shots rang out. Isolated shots on the far side of the city. The dictator was gone. So was Miguel.

A fighter called out behind her:

—The Southern Front has arrived! They're coming through toward Managua!

Rhythmic shots.

Alma started to walk down the hill in the sunlight. She reached the first of those headed up. A man cried:

—Victory!

She flinched. It seemed like an endless line. A group began to chant as she passed; called her name. It was Alma, along with Marta, Chon, Claudio, Cecilia, who was most associated with the struggle in Masaya. She moved on and hoped she could make it to Calle Calvario.

Doñita Reyes was waiting for her.

The Frente would arrange the funeral.

—Ah!

She gasped and nearly fell. A man reached out and caught her before she went headlong. The people moved in a steady stream and made remarks about the Guardia; they gestured and laughed and cried. They also huffed and puffed because it was a steep way up.

Alma stood dazed by the roadside and wondered if she could continue. She stared at them blankly. Some others broke into slogans.

—Long live Bolívar!

—Long live Zeledón!

The man who offered Alma a supportive hand stared at her forearm which he had touched. Like an insect, she thought. There was a bad thing in her stomach, working its way into her throat so she might need to double over in front of them. But she couldn't. For a minute she went to her knees and bent to cough amid the tall weeds.

People passed by her. One, two others stepped from the line to help, but she waved them off. And they stood back and gazed at the forearm.

She got up, held her stomach and moved with an unsure gait toward the city. Birds sang. The Southern Front had begun to arrive on the far side of Masaya, and Alma could hear the commotion, shots and cries as she moved along in a daze.

XVIII

In front of San Sebastien a crowd had gathered to talk and comfort one another. They hugged and wept. A woman sat wiping her eyes by the church entry, and the shadow of the Romanesque portal draped her form.

Alma came on the scene: stumbled into the square. She stayed apart from the others, but there was a hush among people who noticed her walking shakily, with a lost look.

One of the Colegio teachers approached her, a young man whose students liked to call him by his first name.

—Almita?

—I'm sick, she said.

She looked so frail and alone, the priest embraced her while others drew around. She never studied in his class. The girls had a way of teasing him to make him say funny things.

—Poor girl, he smiled. We're free now, and what are we going to do?

From the crowd a bearded man emerged, one of the village elders. He stared at her with a look of pride, while the widow glanced up from the shadowy steps. Two little kids came along with dirty faces: one scratched his head fascinated by the girl with no hands.

Onlookers had formed a circle and expected the elder to launch into a speech. He said in a deep voice:

—Alma, you love the Monimboseños. How many times you tried to give your life for us. But God said you have more work to do. You're a leader.

A woman burst out in the high voice she used to sell drinks down at La Estación:

—Viva Almita!

—Alma! Alma! cried the others.

The young priest embraced her again and said:

—Gracias.

One of the muchachos gave her a paternalistic pat on the back.

Tears rolled down her cheeks. One by one they kissed her, the grisly chin of a guerrilla, the bewhiskered old woman Carlita, more dirty faced kids who had dug trenches, and carried messages, and thrown contact bombs when she let them in the human machinegun. She hugged a grandpa with a naughty twinkle. She kissed a vagrant who spent his days sponging cups of rum, his nights down by the Lagoon. Alma hugged them with her forearms like soft claws. They called someone else's name:

—Look at this one, a hero!

He stood jauntily, one of the first arrivals of the Southern Front. No new recruit, with his frayed red and black neckerchief. The muchacho gave everyone a victory hug, going one to the next self-importantly. Slender, he wore grayish faded bluejeans, tattered boots.

The tears fell from Almita's eyes onto her cheeks, her lips, hands.

XIX

The Southern Front poured through Masaya on its way toward the great victory celebration in Plaza of the Revolution. Trucks, vans, cars overflowed with fighters as they bucked over narrow streets like the San Jerónimo. Cheers, shrieks of jubilation propelled them along. Each gun barrel had a bouquet of wildflowers, each shaggy face an inspired smile. People sat down on the curb and cried. A thousand hands, like a flock of migrating birds, waved and haled the muchachos.

The war fronts went converging on the capital city, and the saints bounced up and down in the streets filled with tumult and color.

A fighter climbed down from a lorry when the procession stalled and began to kiss every woman the length of the street.

Someone shouted:

—They've got Macho Pedro in Monimbó!

The saints bobbed up and down over the dense crowd with enlarged photos of the heroes and martyrs.

—Commander in Chief Carlos Fonseca!

—Pre-e-esente!

—Comandante Germán Pomares!

Among the throng stood women who emerged from the months, years of worry.

—Have you seen Jorge Lopez?

—Who's he, Mamita?

She gazed from one fighter to the next with a rapt attention. Scraggly beards, rain runneled cheeks, the hard eyes of veterans. She looked for her son.

—Jorge Lopez!

—Mamí, was he Chico, or 101, or El Muerto?

—Ay Dios! cried the mother, and clutched her breast.

The muchacho gave a laugh:

—Go wait for him at home!

—What if he doesn't come? What if Jorge doesn't come back?

She trotted behind the van.

—Then be proud! From your belly came a New Nicaragua!

There were traffic jams with more impassioned kisses. There were portraits of Sandino that hopped to the rhythm of the drumbeats. A foreign journalist, expensive gear dangling, ran alongside one of the trucks:

—At this moment the battleship Saipan cruises off the Pacific Coast, he yelled. Do you think you're finished with Washington?

Blond, Dutch perhaps, he followed with comical strides and called up questions while finding a voice level on his recorder. One guerrilla struck a pose. He shouted a response unheard amid the commotion. A woman cried:

—They're judging Macho Pedro in Monimbó!

—Give him a passport to Caiaphas! Ha ha ha!

XX

That night nobody slept. It took a long time for the clouds of Nicaraguan confetti, namely dust, to settle.

—Be careful, muchachos! shouted Bulu Moratín in his taxicab. Some disbanded Guardia still have their M-16s, snipers!

Bulu knew a shortcut out to Kilometer 13 where people greeted the contingents of Frente. He had a strange feeling, happy and sad, and called out to friends, waved his arm. He felt buoyed by the people's energy, with an unforgettable feeling: what's it all about? what is happening to us? what now? Among those in line along the highway were women, wives, mothers. They hoped against hope their menfolk might surface after years of absence and clandestinity. Now was the time, today, tomorrow maybe.

—Hola! Hé, Bulu!—He couldn't believe his eyes. Doñita Reyes, the recluse, waited out there with them.—Buli-i-ito! Where are you coming from?

Didn't she know yet about Miguel?

—Masaya only, Doña.

Didn't she know the Frente was at her house this instant? all ready to make a big thing out of Miguelito, Alma and herself as well?

—You haven't seen—? she cried across the highway, but he couldn't hear in the honk, honk, honk.

—Haven't you—Iván—?

—Maybe in one of the trucks, Doñita?

—Ay!

He heard her voice call. He caught a glimpse of her in the rearview mirror, wobbly on bloated ankles, biting a strand of gray hair. She stood there, big, ungainly in the row of women. Some wore black. He craned his neck and yelled at her:

—We're all your sons!

Then Bulu made his decision. Carajo! He felt a surge of crazy joy, open spaces, where the excitement was! Two hours later he sped from one side of Managua to the other, out to Las Mercedes Airport, back in to the Plaza, his taxi filled with muchachos. Vamonos! Oh, the Plaza was mad with people! More bulging with life than Delia's—ah, she was gone. Big currents of it swept across like surf on the weed grown, roofless Cathedral. The massive crowd whistled and cried out. A Frente leader shook his fist at the sky:

—The people, united, will never be defeated!

Bulu couldn't believe his eyes because liquor had no part in it, no enticements, no «volunteer demonstrators» as in the old presidential campaigns. Oh, amigos! The new leaders, members of the Junta, had arrived. They sat perched on a fire truck. Bulito stood on top of his cab; he strained on tiptoes for a look at the Plaza gone wild. Slogans, sobbed chants, uproar. The kind of moment that made you think about your grandchildren.

XXI

The roof of the National Palace was almost empty. Up there the literary critic, Lisandro, saw a girl seated by the low parapet on the edge, staring down. She had a bandage on her throat.

She was dressed in civilian clothes: white blouse, black saya or dress skirt. A small boy walked across to request water for his sister. Lisandro had a canteen, and took it to her.

She looked at him and blinked, with beautiful sad eyes. Then she kissed him without saying a word, while he asked her where she lived, what was her name. The whole time she just stared in silence.

Then the little boy explained that she was a combatant, and her neck had been wounded in a military operation. A doctor gave her a tracheotomy. He saved her life, but she lost her voice.

This same afternoon she left the hospital and came to the National Palace where she could watch the people celebrate. Lisandro told her not to worry about anything, not to cry. He would write an article about her, and she would get her voice back. But the little brother opened his eyes wide, in effect telling him no, his sister's vocal cords were lost forever.

Lisandro kissed her on the cheek.

They embraced, and down in the Plaza you could hear the multitude of voices begin a song. It was the national anthem, as thousands upon thousands paused to sing sweetly after shouting themselves hoarse. For a moment the whole country had become a choir in church.

XXII

To Carlita fell the task of escorting Alma out along the Calvario. She was headed there anyway to say her prayers, and thank God after he gave the muchachos so much strength. Since all the others seemed distracted, she volunteered to see the bewildered girl home.

Midday had passed. Behind them the noise seemed to fade away and leave a kind of expectation. Turning a corner the two women came on a curious figure. Carlita didn't know him, but she had seen him. It was an individual she glimpsed one day outside the Colegio

Salesiano. She only noticed him then because he looked at her furtively, and tried to hide behind his own shadow.

Now his clothes were tattered. He appeared on the run, very much afraid as if he had undergone a jolt. His sorry person limped toward them from a block away.

And then Carlita noticed, not Alma who was too far gone, the smell. She gave a wry grin and thought: this fellow has been hit by a shit bomb. It could hurt his chances with the ladies.

Morell crossed to the other side as he skulked past. And Carlita thought of Padre Velasquez who had been on her mind. She hadn't seen him since Masaya garrison fell.

The two women continued on. The old one spindly and withered, the young one deformed, with a heavy burden on her frail shoulders.

They passed by Chepito's Grocery at the entry to the Calvario: Closed Until Further Notice, read a sign on the door. Good for him, thought Carlita, people's justice. How many times he gouged us for an aspirin when in need, a few drops of cooking oil. They went on past the clay colored Calvarito hunched on its mound, with the rusted cross askew, more like a weather vane.

—Hm! said Carlita as the girl leaned against her. I'll see you, Chuno, in a little while. Today is our day, and I could just kiss you.

They went along.

Standing in her doorway Doñita Reyes frowned, almost divested of flab after weeks of anxiety. To be so poor and yet so fat, thought the rail-like Carlita, how did she do that?

Doñita watched as the two drew nearer. The girl looked stunned, a ghost of herself. Doñita Reyes had come out on her doorstep to greet the worst: Iván Giner, where are you, man? She was in love with Iván and always had been, ever since they were children in the same Carazo village. And he knew it and took advantage; he gave her two children to rear. Miguel, my son, time to come home now.

Neither Iván nor Miguel had appeared. Only the girl ready to fall where she clung to old Carlita.

—They're gone from us, said Doñita.

Alma hung like a wilted blossom by the doorway.

Just then, across the way, a gray shutter drew back and Faustina called from inside:

—Going to pray?

Here and there the sounds of celebration still carried from San Sebastien and out along the highway. With a nod Carlita said:

—Hmph.

The blue sky hurt her eyes. The high spurt of clouds waved like handkerchiefs over Masaya. Faustina came out wearing a scarf and beckoned toward Carlita with a smile. Then she cast a glimpse off beyond the treetops.

For a moment the four women stood in silence at the end of Calle Calvario.

PART SEVEN

Mornings, at break of day
with a mood of coming rain,
those were the early mornings
when my love for you began.

I

Two years later, in June, Alma made a trip by bus down the Pan American Highway to Rivas. By this time she worked as a coordinator in the Frente Youth, and her days were filled with organizing for the Second Anniversary of the Triumph to be celebrated in Masaya. She still lived with Doñita Reyes, but she visited different cities and towns as part of the preparations. She had been sent to the Atlantic Coast for a week in April and, on her return, began to study English.

Members of the local chapter met her in Rivas. There followed two full days of meetings and planning sessions. Alma always kept up a steady pace, overly serious at times. She stayed intent on making things clear so proper decisions could be taken. But there were moments when undigested ideas intruded on the discussion, effects of recent studies, ideology. It wasn't until late the first afternoon when she laughed at a joke despite herself that the work started to flow smoother, and an overall picture of the festivities emerged.

At nightfall they went for a walk and drank refreshments in the park. So much political experience they wanted to share; plus there were other subjects, and one in particular, on their minds.

The morning of departure Alma looked worried. At breakfast one of her new friends asked:

—Anything wrong?

—I wonder . . . are there buses to Las Salinas?

—We'll take you. Paco has a car.

—No, she said. It's only a personal thing.

By mid-morning she went bumping along in a bus packed with campesinos and their children, with bags of provisions from Rivas marketplace; also a number of young men and women in olive drab. She stared out the window. The road lay unpaved, filled with ruts that shook the crowded contents of the old bus in unison. Here as everywhere she had expected to find signs of construction, people hard at work even in the rain forests. The entire country had awakened: the mass organizations, women's, youth, educational, health, all functioned at full tilt, and life seemed on the march. The literacy campaign had been a success and won international awards. Health programs had begun to eradicate infectious and curable diseases. Suddenly far fewer children died at birth or suffered malnourishment.

But she looked for proof of progress with every glance along this dirt highway back into the past: never paved by Don Cornelio Ferrán (now in exile in Miami), and still ridden mostly by pack mule and horseback. It was over this road, many years before, that Iván Giner carried Miguelito in a papoose after his wife died in childbirth.

People's heads bobbed with the ruts. Several boys hung out from the sides, while legs and muddy boots dangled from the top of the bus. Other small children kept up a singsong on their mother's laps. Almost every woman seemed pregnant; and this was a positive sign, thought Alma, «demo-graphi-cally» . . . It showed hope.

II

In Las Salinas she went in a small grocery and asked where Josefa Giner lived. The woman looked Alma over: Juventud Sandinista uniform (bluejeans and white blouse), knapsack with a few political patches; then the strange cleft forearms.

—Back that way.

—Down the path?

—I guess so.

The woman stared another instant at the girl's infirmity. Not in favor, that one, you could tell.

It was shortly after midday and quiet in the village of Las Salinas. A woman in black carried a pail across the shimmering salt flats to the communal well. Alma walked further along the dirt path as it made an incline up toward a cluster of trees.

Again she asked directions. This time a peasant woman escorted her.

—Do you have shortages?

—Yes. The People's Store doesn't receive some things.

—And the grocery?

—Forget it. She wants you to buy everything from her, or nothing. The woman marveled as Alma took a pamphlet from her knapsack.

—Can you read?

—My man and I, she nodded hesitantly, we went through the campaign. So far I'm on Lesson Six. There's so much to do.

There were twenty-three lessons.

—Did you pass the test?

—Well, Félix did. But me not yet. Still no Free Territory for Literacy sign over our door.

She laughed.

—This pamphlet, said Alma, it tells about economics. What those who don't like us can do to make things hard.

They arrived at a narrow path turning off beneath the trees.

—In there, Josefa lives the one, two . . . third hut down.

—Thank you, sister.

The woman smiled and brushed back a tress from her forehead. Wide hips, like a second pair of shoulders for the daily burdens; a sunken chest that had suckled her children. She moved back the way they came, pamphlet in hand.

Alma knocked and waited. She didn't recognize the person who appeared in the doorway.

—Yes?

The smell of a child's diaper mingled with sunny trees, fields in production, ripe wheat. And the ocean so close by: Alma heard its surf and felt the salty Pacific breath on her neck.

This was Josefa, but changed. Heavier, different somehow.

—Who are you?

For a moment they stood there, on the threshold in shadow. They hadn't met since July of '79, in days after the triumph when the Frente staged a big funeral for Miguel. Josefa spent a week in Masaya then. Add that to the week she passed with him at Doñita's, in late 1977, after departure from the Americano Infantíl. That time she had the ethereal air of a ballet dancer, and this was how Alma still thought of her. She seemed so high-strung back then, apt to brood over things and stay apart by herself.

Now Josefa had filled out, almost matronly. It struck Alma in a negative way; she gave a momentary frown, but held out her forearm and said:

—Don't remember me?

Josefa's eyes went wide and tears flowed into them.

—You?

—I was in Rivas a couple days, and . . .

—No excuses!

She came forward. The two embraced and kissed. Josefa spoke almost like the local people. Her face was still pretty, but hale and
broader of feature. Standing there, on the doorstep of the primitive
dwelling, her smock reflected the canopy of trees. She gave a hearty
laugh and took her visitor inside.

III

While she made lunch they talked about life in the countryside and
Las Salinas. Alma looked down; she wanted to speak of other things
but didn't know how to get started. They discussed the subject on
everybody's lips here as elsewhere: the Revolution.

Josefa, in her throaty voice, said all was not roses in the district. In
El Astillero, in Tola and Rivas wages were down. Hunger still existed.
Infants died in birth, and the first years of life remained a tenuous af-
fair; though less so in many instances.

Alma told of how the Contras, the counterrevolution, had begun
to form up in Honduras. How in the U.S. a new president vilified
Nicaragua and obtained millions of dollars to wage his war. Once an
ancient settlement called Numantia, in Spain, declared itself free of
Rome; and so the empire sent an expeditionary force and laid siege
to the people's aspirations and crushed them. What did the great big
United States care about how many Nicaraguans had to die, so long
as it took their mineral and agricultural resources as in the past, and
stymied the bad example to other small impoverished countries? The
U.S. would make the price too high.

—So everything gets harder, said Alma.

Josefa fell silent as the two picked at their plates. She hadn't mentioned Miguel. Amazed, she watched the girl eat with her makeshift
hands, roll the pieces of tortilla and break her cheeze.

For a moment Alma propped her cheek on one of the forearms. And
then it was her turn to sniffle and feel tears well up behind her eyes.

—You know . . .

—What?

—Sometimes. . .There were moments when he used to treat me
badly, I think.

It was an abrupt turn in the conversation, but Josefa knew perfectly
well who «he» was: as if «he» were sitting there with them. She gave
a brusque nod and took another bite of tortilla.

—How so?

—Oh, at Doñita's. When he spent his year reading, before he went off to Managua. It was,—Alma blew her nose, annoyed with herself,—like I wasn't his sister at all. Only some poor thing you could kick around. He might tease me, you know, tickle, but sometimes it was meant to hurt.

Since the day of her brother's funeral, in Monimbó cemetery, Alma had spells when she fought back her tears.

—That was him, said Josefa.

And she whispered his name almost as if afraid to hear it. Yet, with the recent two-volume edition of his collected works Miguel's name seemed on everyone's lips.

For two years Alma had been studying in a way never imagined while at Colegio Salesiano. She read the books of her people on sale in bookstores: Nicaragua's poets, Rubén Darío, Carlos Martínez Rivas, Leonel Rugama and others. She attended a study group to read the classics of socialism, and great Latin American writers such as José Martí, Recabarren, Che Guevara.

—Miguel was an imp, said Josefa, pensive. Oh, he could play with your feelings, and hurt you. Maybe he meant it. But it was also because of . . . because he had his mind on other things, goading him along, problems giving him no rest. Things would have been easier if he argued with you and called you a bad name, even hit you maybe. But he never did that. He only crushed your ego with some literary remark; or roughed you up, played a little too hard, tickled, as you say.

Alma frowned. She sat surprised by her sudden emotion, and couldn't control her voice to say a word.

IV

Josefa continued:

—I'll tell you a story. It wasn't long before Christmas, late '77. Maybe six weeks after we said goodbye to the circus. In those days he seemed to seethe, never calm, unless he wrote and studied. So one day, I remember he was in the grocery run by that sour woman, you met her. There were other men on hand: this was before the señora's husband died, and the machos liked to congregate and talk, on crates. They could go on about sports for hours. Miguel as well this time, he listened. He tossed in a word or chuckled with them, but there was something else on his mind. Maybe he observed them for one of his poems, I don't know. Matamoros was there, the head of our Defense Committee, a good man. But most of them could act pretty foolish at times, and they still can.

So they bantered with one another in that superb male tone of theirs, when one of the wives comes in. "Laundry done?" says her husband. "No, I—" "Why not?" he says, showing off: the same old story. Look at me, what a Hercules I am, and if you don't think my wife is under complete control, I'll smash your face for you.

So the poor woman turns to the counter, in the process of buying something, and she really wants no problem. But by this time all eyes are on her: the macho gauntlet has been thrown down. And he says, as if to a child: "What did I just tell you? Are you a donkey?" Well, you know the way. You can imagine. Please be a little careful, Almita, when you select a man.

His wife tries to inform him of something, and purchase what she needs, maybe food for the baby? But he gets rude, like a performance he'll put on, and makes his little threat. Finish the laundry or know the reason why.

Meanwhile, Miguel watches. You know how he could sit in silence and stare right through the walls.

"Get the hell out of here!"

The husband grumbles and pushes her toward the screen door. She goes out humiliated. But what seemed sadder, though it made the men burst into laughter, was a little boy there on an errand for his mother, who cried out in his high voice:

"Get the hell out of here!"

It echoed on the woman's heels. And Miguel observed . . . What did she need to buy? Some formula for their baby, back in the hut screaming? Bueno. The husband, contented with himself now, buys beers all around. But then the grocer brought a box of laundry detergent and looked toward the door.

"Where'd she go?"

V

—People still remember his father, Iván Giner. They could tell you the whole story of love and tragedy. Especially with the life Miguel came to lead: it entered into the lore and legend of these parts. At the time Miguelito went out to work in the fields like the others, all day, so we could have food on the table. People didn't quite know how to take him, he was so unpredictable. Once, Cornelio Ferrán tried to give him a commendation, 500 cordobas. It was a message to the other seasonal workers, a way of undermining the poet's prestige. They always liked to hear my husband's opinions and go to him for advice. Of course, to my chagrin since we were dirt poor, he declined the honor.

Me, on the other hand, the villagers didn't like and particularly the women. I was pretty conceited I guess, though stunned by the poverty we had known since quitting the Americano. I could act like the most refined little thing this side of Paris, France. And I didn't always get my work done, the basic chores, laundry, meals.

Well, Miguel never spoiled me. He wasn't into that like some men. Rather, he went about distracted. When he came back from the fields, all he wanted was to wash up, make himself a pot of coffee, and then read by candlelight for three hours. Unless he started to write and scratched away like a night bug. Then it could go on past midnight. You see the willpower he had, and the ego. There weren't enough hours in the day for him. If I could cook up something and slip it between his lips while he sat there, I considered my duty done. And then I waited. I lay in bed, wanting him more than I can describe; and that was my destiny, to yearn and pine for Miguel Giner.

But sometimes I lost pieces of laundry downstream, and the other women stood hands on hips and laughed. Or I brought it home muddy. When I burned our dinner you could smell it in the village, even the flies couldn't tolerate my cuisine. Once or twice a week Miguel brought home fish from the estuary and prepared it himself, he wouldn't let me near it. Food cost too much to make mistakes.

Long day in the fields; cook dinner; try to study and not let his intellectual ambition lie fallow . . . Meanwhile I made my silent demands, and from week to week the frustration built up in him: the demon murmured in his ear, the one that causes husbands to leave their wives.

He didn't write much. To write creatively you need leisure time, a kind of contentment filled with all sorts of unusual things. Miguel's spirit could hardly breathe during that difficult period. Another man would have become angry, even violent. But I know he really loved me. Yes, your brother did, Alma. And so he stored it all up in silence.

VI

—Well, to continue . . . Along the path, across the salt flats to the well, or down at the river: not many women would even say buenos dias when they saw me. So this is how it was, the day Miguel sat on a crate listening to all that seemed arrogant in that woman's husband. Probably Matamoros felt the same thing, but you know he's a quiet sort, he never says much.

Miguel stood up and left; the men resumed their chatter about sports and so forth.

Now, I was back in our hut at rest. Your brother came in and asked, with a stern look:

"Where's the laundry?"

"I did it yesterday."

"Alright, give me some clean."

He hauled out our few pieces of linen, underclothes, towels. He got together a bundle of laundry, stuffed it angrily in a pillowcase. I thought I had done something else wrong; maybe he meant to yell at me in front of the whole village. So I was on the verge of tears when I looked in his eyes, and saw the craziest expression. It confused me when he leaned over, took my head in his free arm, like the bundle he held in the other, and whispered:

"I love you a lot!"

Then he was out the door. He headed back down the path to the grocer's with our laundry slung on his shoulder. He went inside. Of course, the same men were there: they gabbed, made jokes, male gossip. Up to that moment they didn't suspect a thing. My husband entered. He went up to the counter and said, in a loud voice:

"How much for laundry detergent? I'll have that box, that one."

And he tossed down ten cordobas.

"I think," said Miguel clearly, "I'll go to the river and do our wash today. My wife isn't feeling well since I mistreated her, brute that I am." He looked at the wife tamer. "You see, I'm an ignorant boor, all puffed up with double standards, when it comes to women!"

VII

—You could have heard a pin drop in the store. The others showed a kind of mulish disapproval which comes over them anytime they disagree. But nobody had time to get angry.

Miguel went outside with his bundle and the box of soap. Never in his life had he done a real wash, more than the few survival items of a bachelor. Always waited on hand and foot by Doñita, and me. As he moved down the path a few kids tagged along, and soon it was a regular procession. I was on hand by now. Those men were there, they cast glances at me: as if I was the source of their troubles.

You know, Alma, your brother could be a terrific show-off. So vain! You wouldn't believe the things he did in the Americano Infantíl. That was how he won my heart. That was how he touched people despite everything, though they despised him, and sometimes rightly. He blind-sided us with his antics because he hated complacency, stupidity.

So he went down to the river's edge, and began to slap the rocks with our intimate clothing. Maybe he's the only man who ever washed out his clean laundry in public. But he made a show of it. And the machos stood by, and murmured: thinks he's better than us maybe? Some kind of hero? A first-class maricón is what he is. Most of the women gave a blank look, unsure what was happening; or they giggled like schoolgirls.

"Someday!" Miguel declaimed with a glimpse down river at a blouse that got away: a white sensuous one and just about his favorite: "Someday the men of this country will walk side by side with their women. Then we will live in an atmosphere of respect!"

He slapped some more, but I was embarrassed when he wrung out my lace panties, and some fool women tittered and looked at me. The blouse had become a dot down river: soon a whitecap out there in the Pacific.

He held up the panties, shaking them at the men:

"And the children will grow up in a spirit of joyous participation, and emulate their parents. They won't need to bluff and brag about their exploits. I'm talking about the new men and women of Nicaragua!"

He went on for awhile in this vein, he didn't blame anybody but made a political thing out of it. By the time he finished his speech there were brassieres, stockings scattered all around, a lot of people unsure whether to laugh or cry. A pillowcase floated away in hot pursuit of my blouse, which meant Miguel's asthma would suffer from the feathers.

That day the village of Las Salinas came out and watched its poet put on a show. In those days we didn't have much entertainment, no electricity this side of Ferrán's manor house, and his manager's. The kids sensed the excitement, they hopped along the riverbank like kingfishers.

He came trudging out of the stream with our clean clothes all streaked, smudged. He took my hand, bowed and kissed it in front of everyone. That was for the women who avoided me from the start. That was for the men who looked scandalized, the guilty ones.

There we went, side by side. When something dropped behind us, on the fish heads and clamshells, the children grabbed it up and followed their Pied Piper. Of course he hadn't known enough to wring out the clothes. But everybody stood watching us silently.

That night, Alma, I cooked your brother a fine supper. Didn't even burn it. Later, after he sat down to write something, I lay ready for him, I loved him in the quiet darkness, with only his forehead alit over one of the proud processional poems. Toward morning he made love to me in the most tender way. —

VIII

Afternoon passed amid fresh shadows, a golden sunlight in the thicket where Josefa's dwelling huddled with a dozen others. The leaves of an almond tree seemed on fire. Alongside the hut a cochineal fig tree drew certain insects from which a red dye was made. There were jalap plants whose root lent a medicinal drug; also a cluster of balm-gentle, the digestive aid.

—Let's walk to the estuary.

Outside, the first of the men, sweaty beneath wide sombreros, arrived home from their day in the fields. Alma felt tempted to stop and talk with them about the cooperative formed from rich acreage of the old Ferrán plantation. She smiled into their sunburnt faces.

There were kids playing after school; they ran from tree to tree.

—Pastora the traitor!

—No, you!

—They're in those bushes!

—The Contras!

—Bam . . . bambam.

—Tatatatata.

—Well fall down if you're dead!

—But I'm not the contra.

—Shut up. Who gives the orders here? I'm the comandante.

—You! What kind of comandante are you! A moment ago you
were a Contra, and now you want to be comandante?

The two women moved down the path. A balding man with a
thick beard snuck up behind them and tapped Josefa on the shoulder. He looked in his forties with a bit of incipient belly beneath the
army uniform. His shoulders were broad, like his smile; and perched
on one of them, quite contented, sat a boy child alert though he still
wore a diaper.

—José, said Josefa. You loafer.

His teeth gleamed. He was handsome, healthy, with an easy expression, Ulysses home.

—José, meet Alma, Miguel's sister.

—I'm honored, he smiled; extended his free hand. He pressed her
forearm as if he knew all about it.

—And this is Tito.—Josefa took the child's hand with a grumble
as she kissed the fingertips. —Miguel's son.

José nodded. He held the baby soddered on his shoulder with
affection.

—I'll wash up, he said. See you at home.

—Want me to take him?

—No need.

He moved back up the path between the tall grasses. Josefa gazed
after him, serious. Alma saw her touch his arm as he left.

In silence they made their way toward the estuary. The sun had
turned a deeper hue, it sparkled on the ripples. To their right lay the
white line of Salinas strand, and the last sandbanks before the ocean,
which Almita had never seen. An egret gave its call from the trees on
the far side.

IX

—José fought on the Southern Front. He knew Iván Giner. He
was in Nueva Guinea when so many died with Iván in early '79. But
he survived. We leave Tito with one of the village women for a couple hours each afternoon, so I can have a rest.

—Is he your . . . ?

—He loves me. And . . . it's touching to watch him, the way he
loves. He spent eleven years in the guerrilla, waist deep in swamps;

he fought, slogged. And now he wants his woman and patch of garden. He's still a captain in the army and takes an active part in local administration; sits in meetings for the new cooperative. José works so hard for the sake of others. But he wants his reward. And this too is correct. Sure, he'll go fight any day they tell him, if it gets hot in Río San Juan, and the Contra makes deeper incursions.

Alma frowned in the warm light. With time, and insistent current, the low rocks had come to resemble the women who came down to scrub out clothes, bowing to work as they did to pray.

She looked offended somehow. She paused, unable to say something.

—It's sad.

Josefa nodded, and said softly:

—It can be. But good, too . . . Alma, I loved Miguel. I could never love anyone else that way, like life itself. And he loved me. But he loved something else even more. As if . . . between heroic acts, the effort of grand poems, he needed me to be there, wife, mother, sister.

We were young. Loving for us was like the school where nobody gets their diploma, but can only give it, maybe, to others. And then, we spent all our youth, illusions, in that brief time together.

You wouldn't believe what it was to be Dulcinea in the flesh. The second time he got arrested, when Guardia came for him, you can't imagine what that did to me, already so tired and fed up with my role. Don't you see? The loneliness was worse than war itself, worse than the dictator. Let Somoza do what he wants, but give me back my husband. I could hardly forgive life, the muchachos, myself for the fact of his capture.

As long as he was alive I could endure it, somehow. As long as there was breath left in his body, hope, and no matter how horribly they disfigured him, that too. But he died, Alma. Miguel died so he could live. And the war ended. Life goes on, still wretched much of the time, despite our attempts. But not so wretched, not so unredeemable. And this because of the way he and the others lived, because of how they died for us. —

Wavelets gurgled along the marshy banks. A late afternoon breeze bent the heavy-headed reeds that contemplated the current. The egret called its mate in descending tones from an unseen spot across the estuary as, in the distance, the riverine waves could be heard dying to infinite life.

—It's sad, Alma nodded.

—Sometimes. But you said our people have awakened. They read, they write, they fight the age-old diseases. Form cooperatives. So life goes on, it has to! And better than ever because of people like you, Alma, workers and leaders. You don't know how I admire you. You don't know how the people love you. But I . . . I'm not that way at all. I'm meant for a wife and mother with her little toils and pleasures; not too pretty after awhile, but trying to please one man with all her heart, her insecurity, her devotion. Do you know I tried to commit suicide once? Do you know Miguel saved me? He showed me the way to womanhood, whether I wanted to, almost, or not.

But now I just need to live simply, and raise Tito the way Miguel would have wanted, and have my moments of happiness. Don't begrudge them, Alma. I care so much what you think of me: try to understand. Someday you'll love a man; then you'll see what I mean. —

The girl strained not to hang her head. She gazed at the water, her eyes blurry.

—What man would love me?

She raised her forearms.

—Listen, said Josefa. I'll tell you a secret about men. When they love, when they really love, no force on earth could stop it from happening. When they do that it's because they admire you. Sometimes . . . please don't repeat this: sometimes I think José loves me the way he does because . . . I was the wife of Miguel Giner.

—I'm ugly, said Alma. You're wrong about me, you don't know the way I feel.

—No, that's what you say. Others find your arms beautiful because of what you've been able to do with them. For us.

Alma bowed her head, crying.

—Even the mosquitoes know I'm a cripple. They take advantage.

—Well, Josefa laughed, find yourself a man with fast hands, and a light touch!

—They still drink rum.

—Many. But maybe less, because life is getting better.

—They get drunk on Sunday.

—If it were only Sunday!—Josefa took Alma by the arms. —Listen, how could anything about you be ugly? How could these be ugly when they got this way making us free?

—I am.

—No. If you think so it makes you prettier. I admire you.

—If you knew the way I feel sometimes, you wouldn't. I'm too selfish!

—You? Josefa laughed clearly, happily, above the gurgling water.

X

Returning, they heard José's voice mingle with the astounded laughter of Tito, who paused after each outburst to wait for more. It sounded like the two of them, the veteran combatant and the infant boy, enjoyed themselves on the same level.

—If we make any noise he'll stop. These men don't like us to see them being so human.

—Hola! José appeared in the side window. So you like to spy on us. Well, we don't mind, do we, Tito?

Inside, the child stared at Almita's forearms. He grabbed one of the knobs and inspected, licked, tried to gnaw it. With his little fingers he examined.

Later, they ate dinner together, talking about many things. That night Alma attended a meeting at the Casa Comunal where she was invited to speak. Others drifted in and by the time she finished answering questions most of the village people were on hand, along the sides and in back.

Afterward they held a rally outside. A tire was burned; its flames purled along the main road. Alma led a chorus of slogans and spoke again on the problem of shortages. Matamoros, the local coordinator, also spoke for a few minutes.

They walked home in silence. José carried a sleeping Tito on his shoulder. Josefa, in her own thoughts, had wandered to a place where no one could follow. Cicadas fiddled their nocturnal rhythms. There were rustlings in the underbrush as the three passed by. In the magic night a kind of sea mist seemed to hover. In the distance the ocean murmured, like Tito's talk, and Miguel's best poetry, a syntax of universe.

XI

In the morning they had eggs plus a sliver of red meat. Josefa looked a bit languid with her burden of stirred memories. Alma glimpsed in her, for a moment, the high-strung dancer of the circus.

Then it was time to walk Aunt Alma back down the dirt path where the old bus waited, rattling as it idled.

When they got there Josefa looked at her wistfully.

—Will you visit us again?

—Yes. But Doñita and I are expecting you in Masaya.

At this Josefa nodded and glanced at the passengers, crates, live poultry, kids, militia members, all in a cloud of dust and exhaust.

Alma embraced her sister-in-law:

—I'll visit you next year. —She shared a smile with José. —Very nice to meet you, compañero. And Tito too!

The driver called everybody on board.

In the bus two women squeezed to give Alma a seat. The old gears clanked. She waved at Josefa, José and Tito standing together in the morning sunlight beside the road. It was easy to see he loved them. There was room on his broad shoulder for all that life and more, lots of love. A gun as well, if there was no other choice.

The bus bumped on past wide expanses of what used to be Ferrán plantation, and was now cooperative. Alma glimpsed clusters of low huts set back beneath the trees, surrounded by gardens, uneven fences. She wondered which of those huts, if it still existed, had been Miguel's birthplace, the scene of Juana's death, and Iván's despair, on that night long ago.

The rickety bus jolted down the road among the fields. Caoba trees, yew trees, wild jacaranda and rose bushes, wild blackberries. A monkey screeched from a treetop. A tall ceiba stood in the middle of a sunbaked field. Alma thought of her brother and felt a loneliness which seem invincible.

A child in the seat behind her sang a toneless, lolling tune. They passed through Tola, and she thought of the Spanish priest turned Sandinista who was buried in the church cemetery. Suddenly, she felt overcome with a boundless pity for all the people she knew, and wanted to do something for them, and be kind. She thought: I must work harder, work and learn.

The woman beside her looked on: Alma, adroit as the next person, blew her nose.

The rusty bus clattered its way through the southern countryside, past fields dotted with campesinos against the low horizon. It went along stretches of muddy road. It wended its way past another village that seemed stuck there in the swampland forever.

The bus lurched and groaned over ruts toward Rivas. The child kept up its humdrum little song. In her breast Almita felt a hope as huge as the ocean resounding across the salt flats of Las Salinas.

XII

Doñita Reyes placed a demitasse of strong Nicaraguan coffee before her guest, the literary critic Lisandro, and said:

—Hold on a moment. Something just fell back there. The kid's into mischief again: I don't see how anybody, even a boy, can cause so much trouble all by himself.

Where he came from? Wait, I'll tell you how it was . . . Alma had come into her own. In '79 she was swept up in the war, you know, and didn't sleep here for a few months. After it ended she lived with me nearly three years, but then the Frente transferred her to Managua. She's a leader in their youth group now. One afternoon a soldier came for a visit and brought me up to date. "She's going with one of the compañeros," he said, "Mauricio." I sort of grunted: see how they move away and don't tell you anything? "Doñita," he said, with a smile, kind of funny. "You don't recognize me?"

"No, I don't."

"I came here once with a message for Miguel."

Gazing in his eyes I remembered him. Become a man now.

"The eagle's claws!"

"That's me."

He gave a chuckle reminding me of that very day, February 1978 when he showed up on my doorstep.

"And what did it mean, son? What was the message?"

"Eagle's claws meant the more militant approach. Miguel had two speeches ready for San Sebastien that day, after Padre Velasquez finished. The Frente decided now was the time, let's stir the people to action."

"You mean he wasn't supposed to escape to Granada?"

"What? He had to stay!"

"But how did he know, since Alma never. . .The church was too crowded, she couldn't get up the aisle."

My visitor shrugged his shoulders.

"Maybe he saw her from the pulpit. Anyway he got the message."

"But she always blamed herself!"

Well, Almita was a changed person after Miguel's death and all she had been through. I knew beneath the surface she still needed to laugh, and feel pretty. There was the same age-old curiosity about boys. But she no longer clung to me like before. And you couldn't keep her in this house ten minutes unless she was back in Miguel's room (excuse me, Rafael's room, that's the kid's name) studying like her brother used to for hours on end.

XIII

—It wasn't long after the big funeral they gave him, when so many people arrived from around the country, that I finally realized he was gone. And that I was all alone. You see, I always had the idea he would provide a cure for my loneliness, Miguel of all people! But parents have a way of thinking the strangest things.

Then I thought Almita might calm down and attend the Colegio here like before. But the morning after Miguel's funeral she was off to a meeting.

Then I thought: maybe Josefa will come live with me. She had told me she was pregnant when we sat together on stage in Monimbó cemetery. But no, Josefa wanted to live in Las Salinas, I don't know why. And then . . . hold on a minute, did you hear that?

Rafael, if you can't play right . . . Jesucristo!

Then I heard she had taken up with someone else.

So you see I was pretty lonely, I felt sorry for myself. Iván wasn't coming home . . . (Doñita paused to stare off a moment.) And after all the changes life still didn't seem much easier. Doña Faustina would come over and visit awhile; also that decrepit Carlita, the devil's own sister. But Padre Velasquez stopped visiting for some reason. I don't know why unless it's his hives, or the trouble he's had with the new government about military conscription in Masaya. Padre hardly sets foot outside the Colegio anymore.

Bueno. Some of them made a fuss over me; said I was mother of a hero and martyr. But I didn't really want to join their committee. I'm not much of a joiner.

So one day I'm coming back from the new market: see how I get around? My legs are better with those doctors that came. Anyway here's this kid dressed in a rag: he appears out of nowhere and starts to yank my purse. What a nerve! The bandidos get started early around here.

There we are in the middle of the street playing tug-of-war with my handbag. It was no big deal for me by the way, not since that 500-pound bomb almost fell on my head. But in no time my groceries lay scattered all over, good food trampled in the dust. And so, despite my age I caught that boy up and gave him a lesson on his bare bottom. Sí, señor. Then I paused a moment. Cart him off to the authorities?

"What's your name?" I said.

"No name!"

"What is it, you urchin? Tell me or else!"

"Hungry."

"What kind of name is that?" I held him tight by the hair. He frowned and stared at a squashed tomato here, a handful of dusty beans there. "Pick up my vegetables. Where do you live? Who's your father?"

But I still held him. He started bawling so I took him by the arm, runty thing, and yanked him just like he'd done my bag. Maybe a bit rougher than need be, you know. He looked scared to death when he saw the birthmark on my face. See it? Pretty, no? I can tell you God doesn't love me for my charms.

I brought him back here and gave him soup. I washed him and got out one of Miguelito's toys from the wooden chest. It gave me a jolt because there were things I had forgotten completely. A sort of doll Alma once played with, she called her Consuelo. In following days Rafael hauled out the rest as well; they seemed to break and fritter away in his hands. For awhile he sat all by himself, getting into the spirit of my house, you know. Then he asked for food. He played some more. And he slept.

Miguel's macaw had returned to its perch in the tigüilote tree. Would you believe it? Every now and again it cried out as if the war was still on:

"Fire, hijueputas!"

That made my heart skip a beat. It seemed something of my son had taken refuge in the bird's breast, its hooked bill cracking a nut.

A few weeks after my first encounter with Rafael I had him over in the marketplace again. Somebody approached us and said:

"I know this boy." Then softer, a whisper. "I knew the parents."

The woman was an old acquaintance, but I looked at her sideways. Rafael had his hands in something a few steps away: on the brink of disaster as usual.

"Knew?" I said.

"Working people. Lived over in Reparto Caldera. One night, after the garrison fell, a mortar hit square on their hut and killed the five of them. Or so we thought, but here's Dani."

"Dani?" I frowned.

The woman pointed at the kid and said what I suppose was his real name again. Out loud this time, gesturing toward him. Well, he had a piece of fruit in his little fist, a mamey. He sauntered up to me, and I couldn't believe my ears when he said, very clear, for the other to hear:

"Rafael wants this."

Maybe he had amnesia. Maybe he knew his real name perfectly well. But I had given him the other one, Rafael, for certain reasons I'll tell you. And I was giving him the mamey.

You think I should have changed it back again? I could have given the fruit to Dani just as well as Rafael. But I had my little reason.

XIV

—You see, there was a girl who worked in San Antonio Hospital, a nurse. But also a union member, so they said, who took pleasure in work with the Frente. If somebody got hurt making a bomb, got burned or wounded, they would call on her right away, and she knew the thing to do. She could clean a wound so it wouldn't get infected. She could sew it up with dental floss, and like that. She organized first aid courses and put her heart and soul into the things she did. You know the kind.

In the second week of June '79, a month before the change of government, there were Guardia in our barrio. They rolled in like a hurricane, three tanks, a hundred men trotting behind them, heavy weapons, what have you. They entered the sector.

At the same time this girl . . . she happened along with some medical instruments, a syringe, this and that. On her way somewhere to give an injection. You had to see her to understand: such a beautiful one with long dark hair, and the beads she liked to wear. The old people adored her, always so helpful and patient. Especially the doddering ones like Carlita, you know, on the lookout for a little attention. In the street it was always hello and a bright smile, not like most of them.

So the Guardia entered Monimbó. And the young nurse came down the street with her medical things. Of course she saw them and ducked in a house on the corner by the Colegio. Inside, a wounded man was receiving blood plasma. But three Guardia saw the girl enter and followed right after, they didn't concern themselves with him. Another tried to escape; and so they went after that one, two did, in back of the house, and shot him down in the garden.

There it was. The sharks smelled blood. They caught the girl like they did Alma that time, but I guess Almita was lucky after all. By now it was a group of Guardia, and they took the young nurse across the way to the Colegio. Maybe the surgical equipment caught their attention, but probably it was the pretty young face, so pure. Or they knew from someone about her political activity.

Because they took her . . . They dragged her inside the Colegio Salesiano and started doing atrocities on her. In a classroom. Where was Padre Velasquez that day? It's a well-known story, anyone in Masaya knows it. Some muchachos were worried she would falter under torture and betray them by giving names, the location of safe houses. Any weakness could lead to the doorstep of ten, maybe a hundred others.

But the worried ones are still around today. They lived to talk about it.

What those Guardias did then . . . I don't like to mention. You know I always gave them the benefit of the doubt against the comunistas. But what they did to that young nurse . . . really, I . . .

Sorry. It makes me upset to talk about this. But I want to anyway.

They cut off her tongue, señor. They commenced to raping her, over and over, but she couldn't cry out for help.

When two barrio men took the risk to go for her, and bury her, they found her sprawled naked on the floor with a classroom pointer stuck way up between her legs. That's right, and the face was hardly recognizable, burned all over with cigarettes, perforated here, there, with an eye popped out like they did to Miguel.

Why am I telling you this story? Ah, so you'll know how I chose the little boy's new name for him. Why I wanted to call him not Dani but Rafael.

She was a brave girl, and very kind. Ten times better than I ever was, I can tell you that! She gave her life for our sake. And we renamed our hospital, here in Masaya, after her.

The Rafaela Padilla Hospital.

XV

—I never liked crowds. But I could hardly avoid being present at the funeral they held for Miguel. They put me alongside Alma and Josefa up on stage in front of those thousands. I felt like such a creature that day.

The cemetery swarmed as far as you could see, up there by the Rinconadas where Choncito has his cross as well. For two days I had waited, waited for Iván Giner to return. For two days I hadn't slept. I think every mother's child came out to bury Miguel, and there were red and black flags everywhere.

And marimbas. And in the distance, church bells. And comandantes making long speeches, a fist in the air.

I sat on stage glumly, dead tired and beaten down by the grief. Alma stared at one spot and thought of the day Miguel was arrested, by the helicopter, in this place. Josefa leaned and whispered in my ear:

"Doñita, I'm pregnant. I know it now."

But I glanced up at the sky, and over my shoulder, and recalled the 500-pound bomb in the plaza that day.

"Don't worry" said Alma. "They're gone now."

She said it kind of quiet, in her girlish voice. And that's when the whole thing hit me, I guess. All the fine words of the Frente leaders in praise of Miguelito, they sort of passed over my head. But I looked out at the sea of people, and they stared as one person at us on the stage.

I realized why we were here, and what it meant, more or less. The speaker gestured toward me like some kind of madman—politics, you know, are for madmen—and said we must honor my son. My son! That selfish scamp I brought up, that angelic monster, always finagling? We were honoring him because he "created literary classics in a national spirit . . ." and because in his life "a more vivid expression was given to our experience . . .", sort of deep talk. Hm, I thought, here I am with a mess of subversives. My own son was one.

So I sat there holding Almita's hand—or her arm, you know. She rested her head on my shoulder and started to cry. On the other side Josefa, my daughter-in-law, put an arm around me, crying also. And spread far out before us, that sea of Monimboseños and others in the warm sunlight, sang one of their favorite tunes called The Internationale. Dios primero!

But at least no more helicopters, or bombs, for awhile.

When the song ends there's a solemn applause before another co-mandante shouts into the microphone:

"Viva el poeta!"

Huge roar. Loud enough to make all the dead in our cemetery rise up and stand at attention.

"Viva Alma and Josefa! Viva Doñita Reyes!"

Well, this was really too much, so I broke down and sniffled with the rest of them. There we were, as if the Three Fates decided to hold one another arm in arm and have themselves a good cry, after they wasted so much yarn. Weep their fill over poor, struggling humanity.

We sat awhile longer after the speeches ended. Everybody on hand seemed rather happy and relaxed, even though it was a funeral. The younger ones danced to marimbas over the gravestones of their ancestors.

Then, for some reason, I felt clean in myself, not so tired anymore. A job well done type of feeling, you know the kind.

Rafael! Hey!

Hear him? Good God, you call that play?

He's hungry.

I've chatted away too long, but it was a pleasure visiting with you, Mister Lisandro. Care to stay for dinner? Nothing fancy . . . Ah, you haven't time.

Well, please say hello to Alma for me if you see her in Managua. She's something, isn't she? A regular young woman. And so busy these days!

A year ago she made a speech here, in front of San Sebastien. That was fine, the way she stood up there and spoke to us. It was a nice day, the women were selling cool drinks. Monimboseños, we are, most of us—Indians.

Sunlight, people. Nicaragua Libre. I don't know, maybe it was the drink I sipped, or the fact that Iván came to visit me the night before, snuck into my dreams, that's right, and we acted like two children.

(Sigh.) All of a sudden my old bones, not quite so fat anymore you'll notice, they sort of filled up and overflowed with good feeling.

"Gracias, Almita!"

The cacao drink, in the afternoon breeze, after siesta. Sunlight in her hair, up there talking to us, the way Miguel had done . . . I guess it was a little too much for me, señor.

Ay, life is too full sometimes. All the love in it can hurt you, if you're not careful.—

Managua—New York City
1983–1989